Two Sisters

Young Adult Novels by Mary Hogan
Available from HarperTeen

The Serious Kiss
Perfect Girl
Pretty Face

Two Sisters

Mary Hogan

WILLIAM MORROW
An Imprint of HarperCollins*Publishers*

HarperCollins books may be purchased for educational, business, or sales promotional use. For information please e-mail the Special Markets Department at SPsales@harpercollins.com.

FIRST EDITION

Designed by Diahann Sturge

Library of Congress Cataloging-in-Publication Data has been applied for.

ISBN 978-0-06-227993-4

14 15 16 17 18 OV/RRD 10 9 8 7 6 5 4 3 2 1

To Diane Barbera Coté
1953–2010

Acknowledgments

I USED TO think writing was a solitary profession. It is. *Publishing*, however, is not. To the creative, caring, brilliant people who made this book better than it ever would have been without them, my deepest gratitude. First, limitless thanks to my agent, Laura Langlie, who is invaluable from beginning to end. To an extraordinary editor, Carrie Feron—smart, sensitive, slyly funny, and possessing just the right touch. Her assistant, Nicole Fischer, is a professional, cheerful delight. And I am over the moon with Emin Mancheril's haunting cover design.

For her help with Polish spelling and usage, thank you, Martyna Sowa. For letting me tap into her infinite reservoir of creativity, love to the late Liane Revzin. And to the goddess and author Adriana Trigiani—an amazing alpha female—thank you for inspiring and advising this lone wolf.

Finally, there are two people who merit more than thanks. First—and always—my husband, Bob, who fills my heart with joy and my life with uninterrupted hours to work. Second, my late sister, Diane, who inspired some of the character of Pia. Wherever you are in the Universe, Diane, I know you would be pleased to see how many times I used the word "perfect" to describe Pia.

That which ye have spoken in the ear in closets shall be proclaimed upon the housetops.
—LUKE 12:3

Part I

Solitary Confinement

Chapter 1

MURIEL UNFOLDED THE old bath towel and flung it open with a snap of her wrists. Gently, it floated over her duvet like a jellyfish, the frayed ends dangling in a tentacled kind of way. Each time she washed that towel the ends unraveled more, ensnaring socks and underwear in a knotted mangle. The dryer load was a mass of hapless intimates. Yet she loved the way the nubby rectangle looked so rugged and outdoorsy. So very make-do. It was the most absorbent towel in her apartment, perfect for the task at hand.

Guy Fieri was shoving an obscene amount of food into his mouth. Its contents dribbled down the back of his hand and clung to the hieroglyphic stubble around his chin. Both eyelids fluttered as he moaned, "Seriously, man, off the *hook*." Jalapeño, he said, added the perfect kick, while raw red cabbage cut the fattiness with its spicy crunch.

Barefoot, Muriel scurried into her kitchen. The soles of

her feet slapped across the parquet floor onto the faded linoleum. A huge tin of Garrett's popcorn—half CheeseCorn, half CaramelCrisp—sat on the kitchen counter like a grain silo. Still in her pajama shorts and cotton cami she cursed her late start. The *Diners, Drive-ins, and Dives* marathon had begun nearly half an hour ago. She'd forgotten to program the DVR. Guy's vintage red convertible had already motored into the drowsy town. The local chef had plopped ingredients into a vat of spitting oil. Brined pork butt had already practically shredded itself. Guy had taken a second sloppy bite and offered his official stamp of approval: a fist bump and man hug that he pulled into his keg-shaped chest.

Muriel hated when a perfect Sunday got off to an imperfect start. Grabbing the popcorn tin, she dashed back to her bed and popped the lid with a metallic *bwang*. She slid beneath the covers. Two pillows and a sham propped up her back. Atop the raggedy bath towel she balanced the open tin between her thighs and plucked one plump kernel of cheesy popcorn between two fingers. She inhaled the cheddary smell, let her eyelids flutter. Then she placed the popped kernel between her lips and sucked lightly, feeling the explosion of flavor excite the taste buds along the length of her tongue. "Seriously off the hook," she said out loud, feeling the day realign. Like a carp on bait she gulped the kernel to a back molar and bit down, hearing the satisfying crack of the truly well popped.

Sunday was Muriel's favorite day of the week. She used to prefer Saturdays with her mother/daughter excursions downtown, but that was a long time ago. Before everything went awry.

Now, while New Yorkers strolled with children and walked dogs and met for brunch and read the real estate section of the *Times,* Muriel swaddled herself in bed inside her apartment on a vicarious road trip through middle America with a stringy towel spread over her comforter to keep the neon orange cheese oil from staining the bedding she'd bought on clearance at T.J.Maxx.

The phone rang. Muriel ignored it. Who would be foolish enough to call during a Triple D marathon? Moaning luxuriantly, she nestled into the soft crater of her mattress and awaited Guy's next segment with a fistful of Garrett's nirvana. After two more rings, the caller gave up. *Robocall,* she decided, searching her palm for the next bite. With each crack of a popcorn kernel, a memory floated into Muriel's mind: scampering across a crew-cut lawn, executing a flawless cartwheel, selling pink lemonade from a rickety folding table ("Ice cold! Only twenty-five cents!"), shooing away a pillow-footed puppy energetically licking cookie crumbs off the hem of her sleeveless white dress. None were her memories, of course. They were a cinematographer's version of childhood, Vaseline lensed and shot in the tangerine light of sunset. Muriel preferred manufactured memories to her own. Unfettered by the recriminations of real life, fantasy flashbacks comforted her.

The phone rang again. Now she was sure it was Joanie. Only Joanie Frankel, her boss and best friend, would know exactly what she was doing. She was probably watching the same show and knew it was a commercial break. Wiping her hands on the ratty towel, Muriel fished around the bedding for her cell. "Talk to me," she said, her mouth full of popcorn. "Porkapalooza is next."

"You're home."

Her heart went flaccid. It wasn't Joanie. Oh, why hadn't she looked at the caller ID?

"I was thinking I might drop by after mass."

"Might?" Muriel tried to swallow but her mouth had become the Gobi Desert. Guy Fieri was back on the air introducing a Georgia pit master and his barbecue. Andouille sausage from scratch. *Dude!*

"Just a minute." Muriel put the phone down and hoisted herself out of bed, duck-walking into the bathroom to spit the half-chewed popcorn into the toilet. She swished tap water around her mouth and spit again. She washed her hands with soap. Splashing cold water on her face, she dabbed it dry with a hand towel the way they do in moisturizer commercials. By the time she got back to the phone, she hoped her sister had hung up.

"I'm relieved you're home," Pia said in a clipped sort of way. Muriel sat on her bed and watched the popcorn tin wobble.

"Is everybody okay?"

"Fine, yes."

"Good." She swiveled her neck left and right and evaluated her surroundings. Then she sighed a silent sigh. Muriel wasn't nearly prepared for a visitor. Certainly not her impeccable older sister, Pia. The limes in her fridge were green rocks and the club soda was flat. A brownish ring encircled the inside of the bathtub. Her fingernails needed filing and were truck driverish with their grubby edges. She'd been meaning to manicure them, do a whole evening of beauty maintenance and repair. But it was all so dreary and futile. Leg hair regrew instantly, teeth yellowed with the first cup of coffee, a décolletage crease formed whenever she slept on her side, and nose pores darkened overnight like freckles after a day at the beach. Nature was clearly out to get her. It began its annoying downward pressure after she turned twenty. Twenty! Didn't normal women start their disintegration a full decade or two later?

"You'll be home in a couple of hours, won't you?" Pia asked.

Muriel didn't want to answer. Not once had Pia failed to exhale an accusatory puff of air through her perfectly narrow nostrils when she saw her younger sister. Never had she forgotten to notice Muriel's untidy life, the way her rent-stabilized studio on New York's Upper West Side was a weaver finch nest— elaborately woven from found objects: a three-legged bedside table, a squat hand-painted pine dresser with brown, black, beige, and latte-colored coffee rings, two splotchy framed mirrors, and a spindled corner bathroom shelf missing half of one spindle.

Alone within her own four walls Muriel felt peaceful. By herself she could ignore how life had sort of *fallen* on her, the way raindrops splatted the bare heads of careless pedestrians. They should have planned better, tucked a collapsible umbrella in their handbags at the very least. Had they paid attention to the darkening sky, or believed the dire weather reports, they would have worn impervious gear and left the suede shoes at home. They wouldn't plod through life with strands of dripping hair.

"Well?" The impatience in Pia's voice was as sharp as a hangnail. This time, Muriel's sigh was audible.

Eight years older, Pia was not the kind of woman who needed days of notice before her life could be viewed. She lived in an endless house in Connecticut with her thicket-haired husband, Will, and their reedy tween daughter, Emma. Root Beer, Emma's Labradoodle, had custom dog beds built into cabinetry throughout their home. Days, Pia bopped about their white-washed village wearing Ferragamo flats and ironed cotton shirts tucked into True Religion jeans. Nights, she made family salads with organic micro greens and herbs from her garden. She took "me" time to pray and do yoga. Recently, she'd announced that Jesus Christ was her personal savior. The Bible, she said, taught her everything she needed to know.

Good God, thought Muriel, asking, "A lion never ate a lamb on Noah's Ark? How could you possibly believe that?" Then she rolled her eyes to heaven.

"*Faith*," Pia replied, without further bothersome thought. With Pia, life was uncomplicated and pristine. An easy smile was pasted on her lips. Shop owners knew her by her first name: "Put the cashmere in the Pia pile, will you, DeeDee?" In every imaginable way Pia was a custom-tailored sort while Muriel was hopelessly off the rack.

With the phone cradled between her shoulder and ear, Muriel said the only thing she could think of on the spur of the moment. "Um."

Walking over to the window, she hooked her index finger around the sheer curtain and looked out. Four stories below, spring was still holding its breath. The sky was baby blanket blue. Her beautiful brownstoned block was lined with trees, their branches resembling stalks of Brussels sprouts: tightly packed buds all poised to pop. One more week and the whole city would stretch awake after its long gray nap, squinting like a newborn in morning sunlight. Soon New Yorkers would stash their folded winter personalities somewhere out of sight, the same way they stored cable-knit pullovers, ski socks, and flannel sheets.

Pia groaned into the phone. She'd always been impatient with her sister's inability to think fast on her feet. At that moment, the only other thought Muriel could muster was how much she wished Verizon would accidentally drop the call to give her a few extra seconds to plot a way out of her sister's visit. Once, she'd tried to fake a dropped call, but Pia only shamed her by calling right back, saying, "That was beneath even *you*."

"Muriel." A sharp blast of air pierced Muriel's eardrum.

"Yes?"

"Well?"

Muriel loved the way spring looked through the window of her walk-up. Unlike most people, she didn't need to be outside to enjoy it. Sun gave you skin cancer, air conditioners fell from high-rise windows, cabs jumped curbs, strangers coughed directly in your face, dog owners left poop on the sidewalk, schizophrenics heard atmospheric messages from the CIA, planes flew into buildings, and manhole covers exploded straight up. Bad things happened outside. Muriel preferred sateen sheets—when she was lucky enough to unearth them in a clearance pile—a remote with fresh batteries, and sunshine filtered through gauzy curtains.

Two Chihuahuas were off leash down on the sidewalk. What if they darted into the street?

"Muriel?"

Of course Muriel would be home. When she wasn't at work or

at the theater for work or in line at Tasti D-Lite, she was always home. And when she wasn't, she wanted to be. Attempting an air of breeziness, she said, "I'll be in and out." Pia, they both knew, didn't even slightly believe her. Muriel reached up to smooth the spaghetti tangle of her hair.

"We need to talk," Pia said with a period.

There it was. Muriel's chin hit her chest. Her head dangled off the end of her neck. They'd "talked" many times before. Rather, Muriel had listened with eyelids hanging like velvet drapes. Dispatched by their mother, Lidia, Pia had nattered on about slimming down, toning up, getting a better job, moving into an elevator building, living a holier existence, highlighting her hair. ("Men really do prefer blondes, Muriel. It's a proven fact.") The female Sullivants couldn't comprehend a person functioning in a kitchen the size of a powder room or disfunctioning in a life that was perpetually blinking, on hold, as if at any moment a purpose might pick up. The Sullivant men—Muriel's father, Owen, and brother, Logan—seemed to do what most men did around her: they regarded her as if she were a window.

"Why don't we talk right now?" Muriel said to her sister over the phone. "You know, like we already are."

Pia got quiet before she said, "I need to see your face."

Her face? It had been months since her last facial. And three times as long since her last haircut. Dear God.

"How's noon?" asked Pia. Muriel replied, "Hmm." Noon was a tough hour to reject. Not early enough to say that she was in the middle of reading the book review, not late enough to claim it would affect her fake evening plans. Plus noon meant lunch and preparing a meal for her perfect sister with her perfectly high-lighted hair and perfectly toned body and perfectly arched eye-brows would totally ruin Muriel's perfect Sunday.

"Noon, noon," she said, as if flipping through an appointment book. "Let's see here."

"Noon it is," Pia said, not waiting for a final okay.

"Well, all righty then." Muriel tried to sound chipper.

"I'm taking the train in."

"Can't wait." Lying, as well as lying around on Sundays, was a Muriel Sullivant specialty. God forgive her. Honesty required explanations and justifications; both wore on her like a vinyl shoe, always rubbing the same spot raw. It was much less stressful telling everyone what they wanted to hear.

"Love you," Pia said in the same breezy tone she used with the Korean woman who did her nails.

"You, too," Muriel replied automatically. Then she pressed the off button on her phone and for a full five minutes didn't move at all. Her shoulders melted into two parentheses. Her bare feet felt the imprint of the perfectly good remnant of sisal someone had willy-nilly thrown away. Unmade and billowy, her bed called to her, the remote looking like a Hershey bar against the white sheets. A grunt formed deep in her stomach and made its way up her windpipe. Finally, she lifted her chin and put the lid back on the popcorn tin. She pulled the cheese-oil towel off the duvet, shook the cheddar dust into the tub, folded the towel, and put it away. After making her bed in a manner that would impress a hotel's management and shoving her strewn-about laundry in a suitcase at the back of her closet, Muriel buttoned herself into outside clothes and descended four flights of stairs to the sidewalk below where she cursed herself for forgetting her sunglasses. Head down, scanning for dog poop and fallen gingko berries— which were aromatically *exactly* the same—she marched to the end of the block to buy limes, club soda, and something lunch worthy, bracing herself for the storm that was about to blow into her cozy nonlife out of the clear blue.

Chapter 2

THEY MET IN a movie line.

"Warren Beatty could convert me to communism."

That's the first thing Owen Sullivant heard Lidia Czerwinski say. Though she didn't say it to him. Or maybe she did. It was hard to know with Lidia. She was a woman of ulterior motives.

"Or any other *ism*." She giggled like a girl.

Flushed and fluttery, Lidia huddled with her two married girlfriends outside Pawtucket's only cinema, their Rhode Island winter edging into town. She stamped her feet and rubbed her palms together, anxious to get inside so she could sit in the dark warmth and swoon over the Clavius moon crater in Warren Beatty's chin. It didn't matter that he was old enough to be her father. All three women agreed. For two hours, they would surrender to his rakish hair and tumescent lower lip and forget that their own husbands drank beer from a can and let their toenails grow until they poked through their socks. Or, that they had no husband at all.

"*He* likes blood and guts." Owen's date, Madalyn, inserted herself into the conversation with a flick of her thumb at Owen's sweater-vested chest. United by some secret chromosomal code, the women acknowledged her with a knowing nod and pinched lips. Owen wanted to accidentally kick Madalyn's shin.

"True?" Lidia asked, her neck lolling backward to drink in Owen's full height. *No Warren Beatty this one*, she thought, running her fingers lightly down her throat. Nonetheless, he had a full head of hair—dull brown though it was—and pleasant enough features. A woman could do worse. With a quick flick of her eyes, she glanced at his left ring finger. The reflex of a single woman over twenty-five. Madalyn spotted it instantly and reached for Owen's hand.

"Guess so," he said, positioning his unwieldy body in what he hoped was a casual pose. His feet hurt in his hard Sunday shoes. His arms seemed overly long and he was cold without the new Members Only jacket he'd bought but left at home. That damn weatherman had said fifty-five degrees. It was forty-eight at *best*. Madalyn's hand felt like a claw hammer. Her pouffy hairdo looked ridiculous. Touching it later would feel like reaching behind a steamer trunk in the farthest corner of a spooky attic. His pillowcase would smell like hairspray all week. What he wouldn't give to be in Providence, alone, at *Death Wish II*.

"Hah." Madalyn rolled her eyes. "Last week he dragged me to an old Hitchcock."

Owen Sullivant stared, blank faced. Why did Madalyn have

to say *anything*? They'd been standing quietly, companionably, minding their own business. She dove into a stranger's conversation like a humpback on a herring. And the way she spat out, *Hitchcock*. What the hell did that mean? The man was a genius. She had clung to his arm when the birds flew out of the fireplace, buried her head in his chest as Tippi Hedren ran for her life in that sexy narrow skirt. Afterward, she'd relived every scary moment over tequila sunrises and salted peanuts in the town's best cocktail lounge. What more did the woman want?

In baby steps, the line shuffled forward. Annoyed, Owen leaned out to see what was going on. Was someone paying in *pennies*? Pretending to cough, he retrieved his hand.

The plain fact was this: Owen Sullivant's desires were simple. He wanted *order*. Each morning at precisely seven o'clock he awoke without prodding from an alarm clock. He fixed himself one perfect cup of black coffee and a medium-size bowl of steel-cut oatmeal. Reusing a paper sack until it dissolved, he packed a turkey breast sandwich on wheat bread—light on the mayo—and a navel orange for lunch. In the fall, when eastern apples were at their peak, he swapped out the orange for a McIntosh, preferring the tart crispness of a Mac to the mealy sweetness of a Red Delicious. On Sundays he drove into Providence because the church there had a real organ. On weekdays, in his morning shower, Owen ran through the particulars of the day ahead comforted by the fact that one day rarely looked different from the rest. The only reason he'd bought a trendy new jacket when his brown suede blazer was still perfectly wearable was because Madalyn had accused him of resembling his father.

"We *are* closely related genetically," he'd replied, sarcasm surging past his teeth even as he tried to use his tongue as a sandbag.

"A man in his thirties shouldn't look like a man in his fifties."

"Thank you, Madalyn, for telling me how I should look."

"You're welcome," she said, as obtuse as ever.

The awful truth was, Owen had intended to break it off with Madalyn weeks ago but was still searching for the right words. It pained him to crush a woman's expectations. And he was certain Madalyn would respond overdramatically. Why, a few months ago, she'd been *apoplectic* when Edith Head passed away.

"Edith who?" Owen had asked, handing her several fresh tissues.

"My God! Audrey Hepburn, Bette Davis, Grace Kelly, Gloria Swanson, Ginger Rogers—she designed costumes for all the greats!"

"Was she an aunt? A relative of some sort?"

"Don't you *think* I would have mentioned by *now* if I was *related* to the great Edith *Head*?" Her eyes practically bulged out of her own head.

Owen had quietly sighed. Breaking up with Madalyn was fraught with peril at every turn. The great Edith Head, he found out when he looked her up, lived into her eighties. Had Madalyn thought she was immortal?

So every Saturday night as they made tepid love in the wake of a lackluster date, Owen examined his exit strategies. His mind flashed platitudes like a flip-book. *Everything happens for a reason. Time heals all wounds. If we were meant to be* . . . blah, blah, blah. None of it sounded even slightly manly, especially not while he was on top of her. And Owen's current ploy of indifference wasn't working at all. He had hoped Madalyn would notice what a cad he'd become, storm out on her own, and be done with the whole messy business. But, honestly, the woman was as thick as the goo she sprayed on her cobwebbed hair.

There in Pawtucket, in the chilly snail-paced movie line, he cast about his brain for something personable to say to the narrow-waisted blonde in the leotard, stretchy skirt, short leather jacket, and sparkly crucifix necklace who suddenly seemed to be standing with them. All he could think of was, "Do we know you?" but he was reluctant to use the word "we" since Madalyn took things so literally.

"The great Edith Head was Hitchcock's favorite costume designer," Owen said instead, cocking one caddish eyebrow in Madalyn's direction. Remembering this tidbit of information at that particular moment warmed his whole body. "She did the clothes for many of his classic films, including his best, *The Birds*."

Jaw dangling, Madalyn shot him a nasty look.

"*Rear Window* made me buy curtains," Lidia said, smiling up at Owen, her cheeks as dark pink as her lips. He shifted his weight to the other leg and moved forward another six inches in line. His tongue felt like a soggy loaf of bread. How do you respond to a statement like that? Of course she should have curtains, or at the very least a pull-down shade, whether Alfred Hitchcock made a movie or not.

"Probably a good idea," he said, flatly. To which Madalyn rolled her eyes for the umpteenth time and Lidia erupted in high-pitched laughter so loud nobody knew where to look.

"You're a riot," she said to Owen. Another statement that stumped him. Owen Sullivant was many things: a graduate of New England Tech; a mechanical engineer who designed cooling systems for large manufacturing plants; a native and resident of Central Falls, Rhode Island; an only child; a single man with no particular desire to marry; a gentle soul; and a wearer of white shirts and white socks. A laugh riot he was not.

"I'm Lidia Czerwinski," she said to him. Unsure how better to respond, he simply said, "Owen."

"Do you have a last name, Owen?"

"Sullivant."

"Nice Catholic boy?" she asked. Not knowing what else to do, Owen chuckled self-consciously and nodded. He was far from a boy, but this girl had a way about her that made his mind misfire.

The movie line finally surged forward. After Lidia bought her ticket, she gave Owen Sullivant such a lingering look that Madalyn snuggled up to his arm, making it nearly impossible to get his wallet out.

Chapter 3

DRESSED IN DARK-WASH Levi's and a black tee, Muriel pulled open the glass door to the corner market at the Broadway end of her block. She lifted a green shopping basket out of the stack and hung it on her arm, maneuvering in a zigzag fashion through the narrow aisles of the small gourmet store. To be on the safe side, she chose a *liter* of club soda and enough limes to flavor a pitcher of margaritas. Pears, too, though they were ridiculously expensive, plus heirloom cherry tomatoes, asparagus spears, a baguette, and spiced almonds. All items she'd once read about in a magazine article on effortless, yet elegant, entertaining. "Crud," she muttered to herself. Why hadn't she ripped out that page so she'd know what to do with the classy ingredients once she got them home? Does one serve mini tomatoes raw on a plate next to uncooked asparagus? Wouldn't that look too much like an exclamation point to be considered "elegant" in any way? And surely there must be some sort of *dip* involved. In the checkout line, she considered asking the girl at the register, but the unruly state of her ponytail dissuaded her.

On impulse, Muriel made one more stop before making her way home. The sturgeon shop next door sold delicious smoked salmon and homemade scallion cream cheese. Pia probably wouldn't want them, certainly not atop the carb load of a bagel, but it would be a nice treat after she left. Perhaps she'd have a smoked salmon baguette sandwich for dinner, with Garrett's CaramelCrisp for dessert? How long was Pia planning to stay, anyway? *Good lord,* Muriel thought with a jolt, *was she thinking of spending the night?*

As Muriel walked home with the plastic grocery bags choking off the blood to her fingertips, she was struck for the millionth time by the curious reality that her sister didn't know her at all, a woman she'd known all her life. By the time Muriel was born Pia was eight years old. Grown up enough to quickly tire of her sister-doll and wonder when she was leaving.

"Can't we get a *real* dog, Mama?" she once said with toddler Muriel galumphing behind her.

In truth, Pia had never been kind to her younger sister. Not that kindness had been encouraged. Theirs was a family unit that surfaced occasionally: an even blend turned odd. A girl was born to please the mother, a boy for the father. Then several miles down the bonding road, when relationships were already well cured, a fifth being arrived after an alcohol-soaked attempt to revive a comatose marriage. From the start, Muriel upset the mathematically tidy Sullivant square. Love, it turns out, isn't as accommodating as the movies would have one believe.

After Muriel was born, Owen morphed into a 1950s sort of father—silent, awkward around estrogen, spending much of his time at the office or tinkering in the basement with his son. Lidia made an effort at first. Then she grew exhausted by the sheer effort of it. Pretending Pia wasn't her favorite child felt like lying and Lidia was a good Catholic. Lying was a sin.

"MAMA, CAN I go in the waves?"

It was a sweaty morning at the end of July. The Sullivant family had rented a two-bedroom vacation cottage near Salty Brine Beach on Block Island Sound. Pia had already claimed the orange sunroom with the canopy bed. Lidia had unpacked her trunk in the front bedroom with the window-seat view of the foamy surf. Owen and Logan were "roughing it" a few miles down the road—camping at Fisherman's Park near Rhode Island's southern tip. Muriel was assigned the alcove off the cottage living room with the sleeper sofa. "Keep it neat," Lidia had commanded. "It's also where we watch TV."

"Mama, can I go swimming in the waves?"

That morning the Sullivant females had staked out a spot on the shore down beach from their little bungalow. Lidia wore a jet black swimsuit with a plunging neckline that occasionally revealed where her tan stopped and her breasts began. Her toenails were the color of a classroom chalkboard. Shaded by an umbrella, she reclined against a folding canvas chair behind Jackie O sunglasses, sipping cosmos she'd brought from the cottage in a shiny silver thermos.

"I feel a nap descending," she replied with an exaggerated yawn.

Pia was fifteen, slim legged and utterly fluid in her pastel pink bikini. Muriel was a roly-poly seven-year-old perpetually tugging at the bottom ruffle on her one-piece. Even then she hated the beach. All that sunlight made her feel accused, as if caught in the light of the open refrigerator at midnight.

"Please, Mama, it's hot."

Directly overhead, the sun was white. Pia lay flat on a towel, tanning. The three triangles of her bikini covered just enough. In a sliver of umbrella shade, Muriel pushed her sweaty bangs off her forehead. She sprinkled sand on the tops of her bare feet, like sugar.

"Ten minutes. I'll count."

Lidia said nothing. Beneath her fly-eye glasses, she pretended to be already asleep.

"I'm getting sunburned, Mama."

Languidly, Lidia roused herself enough to reach for her straw tote. She unzipped the inside pocket and pulled out a ten-dollar bill. "Take Muriel in the water," she said to Pia, waving the bill enticingly in the air.

"No way." Pia didn't even open her eyes.

Though her blond hair was layered, Pia had gathered it high on her head and contained it in a messy knot. Wisps radiated out like sunbeams. Her tanned arms glistened with golden down as if a rabble of monarch butterflies had just done a flyby. As with her mother, Pia had thighs that didn't touch at the top. Bathing suits didn't feel like nakedness. They didn't bunch up and make red marks.

"Half hour max," Lidia said, flapping the bill harder. "So I can get some shut-eye."

"What about *my* shut-eye?" Pia said.

"Don't be fresh."

As the sun shifted, Muriel scooted closer to her mother and the circle of shade. She asked, "Is it possible to get sunburned underwater?"

Lidia sighed. "Pia. Please?" She reached into her tote for another ten.

"Why do *I* always have to babysit her?" Pia asked.

"Who else?"

"Logan. Dad."

Beneath her dark glasses Lidia rolled her eyes. Her husband and son were useless, miles away gathering driftwood for their campfire that night or examining the intricacies of beach detritus or some such nonsense. She poured more fruity liquid from the thermos. Ice cubes hit the bottom of her plastic cup with a dull *clunk*.

"I'm hot, Mama."

"Pia?"

"God, Muriel." Growling, Pia opened her eyes and lifted her head off the beach towel. Only then did she see the incentive Lidia was still waving in the air.

"Don't use the Lord's name in vain," Lidia said.

Said Pia, "Twenty-five."

Setting her drink on the towel and pushing her sunglasses on top of her head, Lidia joked, "Muriel, call that cute lifeguard over. I'm being robbed by a greedy, ungrateful child."

Muriel made a face. What, she was supposed to walk all that way alone on the hot sand? Suddenly, Pia was on her feet applying lip gloss. To her mother she said, "Ha-ha." Plucking the two tens from Lidia's outstretched fingers, she added, "You owe me five bucks."

"Take your time," Lidia said, taking a final swig and rolling a dry beach towel into a pillow for her neck. Then she leaned back and let her head fall sideways.

"Get up, Muriel. I have a life." Pia tugged at her sister's wrist. Before Muriel had a chance to pull the back of her swimsuit in place, Pia was yanking her up the beach.

"The water is *that* way."

"I need to do something first."

"Like what?"

"Like mind your own beeswax." Pia let Muriel's arm drop.

With her toes clawing into the hot sand, Muriel hurried to keep up with her sister. Her skin was damp, the soft blobs of fat at the tops of her legs rubbed against each other in sticky friction. Ahead of her, sugary sand stuck to Pia's reddish brown calves. Her bare heels were pink.

"Wait here," she said when they reached the parking lot in front of the Snack Shack.

"Where?"

"Here. Right at this corner."

"Outside?"

"It's the beach, you ignoramus. You're supposed to be outside."
Softening, she said, "I'll run in and get us some Cokes, okay?"

"Then you'll take me swimming?"

"Yes."

"Mama said."

"I will."

"She *said*."

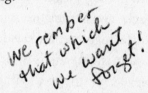

Pia shot her sister an exasperated look. Then she flitted off around the back of the cinder-block building, kicking up sand in her wake. "Don't move one inch, Muriel. I mean it."

Muriel didn't move one inch. Smoke from grilling hot dogs billowed around her. Her stomach growled. The soles of her feet were hot, hot, hot. She lifted them off the asphalt, first one, then the other. The sun seemed to aim its rays straight on her. A magnifying glass on an ant. It felt like an eternity before Pia's lean form reappeared around the corner. Muriel exhaled relief. "You'll take me swimming now?"

Said Pia, "Follow me." Of course that's exactly what Muriel did, not even mentioning the promised Cokes that were nowhere in sight. Instead, she asked her older sister, "Do you think jellyfish float on *top* of the bay or swim underneath?"

Typically Pia, she didn't respond. She made it clear that pudgy Muriel was little more than a barnacle on her life. She was blind to Muriel's adoring gaze, the way she memorized the dimples in her sister's lower back, her head-up walk, the lazy lowering of her eyelids when she lost herself in music, the way she flicked her hair out of her face in a quick upward *Z* motion. Muriel even took to biting her hangnails the way Pia did, spitting them into the air with a *pffft*.

With her long-legged gait, Pia hiked to the farthest edge of the beach, away from the summer crowds. Scrabbling behind her, Muriel tugged at the elastic edges of her swimsuit repeating, "The water is *that* way." In her bored, up-to-here kind of way, Pia clucked her tongue. Without turning around she marched toward a high pile of black breaker rocks at the very end of the beach, leaving her sister to only imagine how cool the water might feel on her hot skin. The way its sea foam would tickle her toes. How the mist would taste salty and the bay would swirl around her ankles in little loop-de-loops. The water would feel too cold at first, but her skin would get used to it. Jellyfish would swim away the moment they saw her feet.

"Hey wait," she asked suddenly. "Do jellyfish even *have* eyes?"

Pia of course said nothing. When Muriel slowed down, her sister circled back to snatch up her wrist and pull her through the sand. "I don't have all day," she said, sounding exactly like their mother.

"Where are we going?"

Silence.

"The water is *that* way."

Nothing.

"Owww."

Pia plowed on ahead.

"*Piiiia.*"

Pia whirled around and yanked hard on Muriel's arm. "One

more peep and I'm telling Mom. You think I *want* to spend time with you?"

Muriel shut her mouth. Not sure what she'd done wrong, she nonetheless knew she'd get it trouble for it. Pia was always tattling on her for something or other.

In pouty silence Muriel followed her sister to the end of the public beach, so far from the Snack Shack and the parking lot that no one else was around. Large shiny boulders were stacked up on top of one another and curved around a sandy nook. By now Muriel's shoulders were pink hot. The center part in her limp hair was singed. Her nose felt as if it had been scraped by sandpaper. At least it was cool in the shade of the boulders.

"Tada," Pia said, standing triumphantly. "I have a surprise for you."

"Mama said you'd take me swimming." A headache was beginning to form behind her eyes.

"I will. After."

"After what?"

"I want to take your picture. Help me dig a hole."

Pia dropped to her knees and began to grab handfuls of dirt. Muriel stood there and blinked. "Just stand there, Muriel. God."

"Don't use the Lord's name in vain."

From out of nowhere, a straw-haired boy in Hawaiian swim trunks and a loose T-shirt appeared atop the boulder pile. "Sweet," he said, flying off the rocks like Batman and diving to the ground to help Pia dig the hole. They looked like two Great Danes after a bone, all legs and spewing sand. Both teens glanced at each other, but said nothing. Their foreheads were shiny. The boy lifted his shirt off over his head and Pia looked directly at his smooth brown chest. They smelled like beach: suntan oil and fresh sweat. Timidly, Muriel knelt down to help. She disliked the feel of sand beneath her fingernails.

"Use your whole arm," the boy said, slightly breathless. "It's faster."

Soon enough, there was a hole in the damp sand nearly a yard deep and two feet wide. A human shoe box. Wiping her hair out of her eyes with the back of her hand, Pia caught her breath long enough to say, "Hop in."

Muriel scrambled to her feet. "*You* hop in."

"We dug it for you, Muriel. It's pint size."

She liked the sound of that. *Pint size.* Still, with one foot jutted out in defiance, Muriel gripped her elbows and didn't move one inch. Her cheeks were the color of cherries. Her hair hung in ropes. The waves sounded like faint cymbal crashes behind her. "Mama said you'd take me in the waves."

Pia groaned and Muriel set her jaw. The boy looked at her sister and she looked back at him. Shrugging, Pia sat on her heels and nonchalantly brushed sand off her bare hands. "No biggie," she said. "I thought it would be a cool photo. If you want to be a baby and go in the waves, fine. Seems to me it would be more fun to take a picture of my sister that we could keep and remember forever."

Muriel felt her lower lip quiver.

"Fine with me. Be a baby."

Muriel blinked back a rising tear.

"Waah, waah, waah. Muriel is a big, fat baby."

She hopped down into the hole. Thigh deep inside the earth, the wet sand felt blessedly cool on Muriel's hot legs. Its molasses color looked like brown sugar. "Kneel," Pia commanded. Muriel hesitated until Pia glared at her for so long she relented and dropped to her knees. Cold grit pressed into her skin and compressed her bare legs. It felt good against her sunburned shoulders. Her head was level with the ground.

"A perfect fit," said the straw-haired boy, who seemed in no hurry to go wherever it was he was headed when he first showed up. Muriel noticed a thin stripe of white skin just above the elastic band of his swim trunks. Fine dark hairs clustered around his belly button.

"Hey, Pia, look!" Muriel squealed, hoping to improve Pia's darkened mood. "Can you see my toes? Can you? They're all dug into the dirt."

Pia smiled and Muriel beamed. The two teens then bulldozed the sand back into the hole with both hands and forearms. As wet dirt plopped onto the backs of her calves, Muriel giggled. "It tickles."

The boxy hole filled up fast, up to Muriel's waist in less than a minute. Sphinxlike, she rested her elbows on the sand shelf while Pia and the boy filled in the rest. The damp sand embraced her whole body in a chilled hug. It smelled almost like cookie dough, earthy chocolate and vanilla. It felt good. "This sure will be a funny picture."

"Careful," Pia said, "don't get sand in her eyes."

"Careful," Muriel parroted back, "don't get sand in my eyes."

In minutes, Muriel was no more than a head sitting directly on the sand. The straw-haired boy gently patted the earth beneath her chin. Muriel gazed up at him and he smiled at her, his white teeth ridged along the edges, his tanned fingers pink along the cuticle line. Sealing the sand around her neck, he tapped his fingers all the way around. Pia smoothed the rest with the bottom of her bare foot. Chuckling, the boy said, "She looks like a soccer ball." Muriel laughed, cracking the sand slightly. The straw-haired boy brought a handful of wet sand from the base of the rocks to repair it. He sprinkled it like salt, then tamped it down with his suntanned hands. Muriel felt special, literally the center of Pia's attention as well as the boy's. *This is going to be the best picture ever,* she said to herself. Only then did she notice that no one had a camera. Must be somewhere behind the rocks, she thought. Must be.

With the cool sand hugging her body, the hot sun no longer burned. Muriel felt safe and cozy, as if she were a fragile gift packed in Styrofoam. Pia pulled a tiny comb out of her bikini top and gently untangled her sister's fine brown hair, fanning it out the back like an Elizabethan collar.

"You look beautiful," she said and Muriel nearly burst into tears.

"I'm going to get the camera."

Ah. So there was a camera after all.

"I'll go with you." Smirking, the boy circled to the front of Muriel's line of sight and quipped, "Don't go anywhere."

"No way," she said, laughing so hard the sand cracked again. This time, no one repaired it.

Behind her head Muriel heard the *swish, swish* of her sister's footsteps in the sand and mini grunts as she climbed up the rocks with the boy. Her neck couldn't swivel enough to see them go. *Was the camera all the way back at the cottage?*

At sand level, the beach looked like the nubby blanket on Logan's bed. Little hills rose up like folds of fabric. Some grains of sand were white, some black. From that vantage point the beach looked like a mix of salt and pepper. If the air hadn't smelled faintly of fish, she might have taken a lick. With each breath, Muriel saw grains of sand hop away from her nose. When she pursed her lips and blew, she felt like the wind itself, capable of stirring up a mini hurricane. But she didn't dare disturb the sand much. Muriel breathed evenly, in and out, careful not to cause another crack. She wanted everything perfect for Pia when she returned to take the picture they would keep and remember forever.

In the distance, the rhythmic sound of waves swelling and breaking made her sleepy. When she closed her eyes, Muriel imagined foamy white bubbles surging forward. Try as they might to grip the sand, the ocean would always suck them back. Silver-dollar shells would be deposited on the shore, their starfish patterns intact. Spidery sand crabs would suddenly find themselves homeless, scrambling for shelter after a wave dissolved their sandy caves. *How close was the water?* It was hard to see from her flattened vantage point. Really, she should have thought to look while she was standing up. She knew it was far down the beach, but how far *exactly*? And were the louder waves bigger than the softer ones? Could a really big one reach her soccer-ball head? Suddenly she remembered a sand igloo she'd built last year when their family came to this very same beach. She'd been sure it was far enough back, but a wave reclaimed it nonetheless.

Deep within her sand vault, Muriel felt her heart pump. A few hard beats at first, the rhythmic sound of a bass drum. Then the thumping grew louder, until her heart seemed to pump in her ears. She tried to listen for extra-loud waves, but the sounds inside her body were as loud as the ocean. Soon it seemed like waves were crashing one after the other, closer and closer.

"Pia?" Trying not to mess up the perfect arc of her combed hair, Muriel slowly swiveled her neck as far as it would go. "Pia? Do you have the camera yet?"

Wasn't the cottage all the way at the other end of the beach? Why hadn't she brought the camera with her? Who was that boy anyway? Do sand crabs ever scamper up to the rocks? Were big crabs hiding in the rocks right now, waiting to come out and crawl on her head?

"Pia?"

Like gathering debris in a funnel cloud, Muriel's panic started with loose bits of untethered worry then built up speed until a knotted, swirling mass of terror sucked her into its vortex. She imagined all manner of clacking sea creatures crawling over her head, pinching her earlobes with their spiky claws. Plucking her eyelashes out one by one. A starfish would wrap its five points around her face, suffocating her. A loose jellyfish tentacle would rope around her neck. One giant wave—only one—could drown her completely.

No longer concerned about her perfectly fanned-out hair,

Muriel frantically twisted her neck left and right, struggling to free herself. Grains of sand scattered beneath her nose like skittering ants. Her chest burned. She strained to move any body part—a big toe, a pinky, *anything*—but only the slightest motion was possible. Not nearly enough to free herself. The wet sand had cemented her in the hole.

"Pia!"

Knowing her big sister would call her a baby if she cried, Muriel clamped her teeth shut each time a whimper escaped. She tried to sound brave. "Pia? Could you please come back?" But it was no use. Tears rolled down her cheeks in thick drops. Guttural sobs boiled up from her intestines. Snot coated her upper lip. Before she could stop it, Muriel howled like a wild animal, caught in an ambush trap. "Out! Out! Get me out!"

Behind her, Muriel suddenly heard a sound on the rocks. "Pia?" Through trembling, snot-shiny lips, she quickly tried to blow the sand smooth. She faced front. Her sister would be mad when she saw so many cracks. "Please, Pia, could you let me out? I want to get out now please."

Silence.

"Pia?"

The sound wasn't Pia after all. Perhaps it was a sea breeze dislodging a pebble, or a trickle of water from an ocean pool in the rocks. Maybe it really was a full-size crab snapping its claws on its way down to Muriel's soccer-ball head. She never knew for sure. The moment she realized her savior wasn't there, the only discernible noise was Muriel's full-throttle, white-eyed screaming. *Help! Help! Helllp!*

At last, ruddy and dusty, Pia and the straw-haired boy flew down from the rocks and dropped to the ground digging like two street dogs at the dump. Sand flew everywhere. Muriel never stopped screaming.

"Help me! Help me! Help me!"

"Shhh," Pia said. "Shhh. Shhh." But Muriel was unable to stop. She didn't even understand what Pia was talking about. Her feral screaming belonged to someone else. She had no control over it whatsoever. Even after she was lifted out of the hole—damp, dirty, hunched, and shaking—with Pia's hand cupped over her mouth, she could hear the hoarse shrieking in her head. *Help! Help! Help me please.*

"It's okay now," Pia cooed, hugging her little sister's trembling body. "I'm here. It's okay."

The boy gave Pia a wide-eyed look; she returned it and added a little nod. He grabbed his shirt and scrambled back up the rocks to disappear in the same manner he'd arrived. Gently Pia said to her sister, "We're going in the waves now. Wanna go in the waves?"

Muriel shook her head. "I want to go home."

"Okay." Taking her sister's hand, Pia silently walked the full length of the beach back to their mother's umbrella. Neither uttered a single sentence the whole way. Muriel's head hung on her neck. She softly whimpered with each exhale, sniffed sand into her nose. Before they reached the towel island where Lidia lay asleep, Pia stopped and kneeled on the sand in front of her little sister, holding both her arms firmly.

"You're a big girl, right?"

Muriel's head felt like a bowling ball dangling on the end of her neck.

"Muriel?"

She nodded.

"Good. Big girls can keep secrets. That's what makes them grown up. And you're a big girl now, right?"

Muriel nodded again.

"So not a *word* about this to Mama. Promise?"

"Okay."

"Say it."

"I promise."

"That's the second rule about being a big girl. You *never* break your promise. No matter what. Promise?"

"I promise."

"Good."

Muriel, being Muriel, kept her promise. She never told anyone. Not a word, not a soul. Not ever.

Chapter 4

A HALLOWEEN PARTY in Pawtucket? At the home of a woman he'd met in a movie line? Owen Sullivant had every intention of tossing the invitation in the trash. It was absurd. He didn't even know the woman. How had she found him anyway? They'd never spoken again that night, though they had exchanged weighted glances in the murky light of the movie theater and again in the lobby on the way out. While Madalyn prattled on about Warren Beatty ("Does the man even *own* a comb?"), Owen felt heat radiate across the side of his face. Turning, he saw Lidia by the drinking fountain. Her dark eyes were bark beetles boring into his skull. Their intensity startled him. Excited him, too, frankly. He felt a stirring that had long been iced. Her waist was so tiny he could probably wrap both hands around it. Easily, he could lift her on top of him, feel her blond hair spill onto his face. It probably smelled like raspberries or vanilla or one of those expensive shampoos he saw at the drugstore next to the tar-infused one he bought for his dandruff.

That night on Madalyn's pull-out sofa, Owen made love so energetically Madalyn remarked, "Goodness! I should have worn this perfume *last* Saturday night." God forgave him for sex before marriage, Owen had long ago decided. Surely He could absolve him of having sex with one woman while imagining another? And for the little white lie he told Madalyn about fumigating his apartment for ants. How could he conjure up Lidia's fruity shampoo with Madalyn's hair spray smell all over his pillow?

The day the Halloween party invitation arrived in the office mail, Owen nearly tossed it right away. A fleeting fantasy was one thing, reality was quite another, replete as it was with effort and misunderstanding. Best to leave it be. It was the prudent choice. Surprised he was, then, to find himself tucking Lidia's invitation in his shirt pocket, pulling it out several times a day to read it from beginning to end. Once he even held the card up to his nose and inhaled, as if he might smell the scent of her fingerprints.

Never, not once, did he intend to go to the party. The very idea was ludicrous. On Halloween night, in fact, having told Madalyn he was visiting his parents, Owen planned a quiet evening alone in his apartment. He'd even bought a bag of mini Snickers on the off chance that neighborhood kids holding open pillowcases might ring his bell. There he sat on his couch, listlessly thumbing through *TV Guide*, perfectly satisfied with his decision to stay home. He mulled over supper choices: Pan-frying the strip steak he had in the fridge? A giant bowl of popcorn with parmesan cheese? Suddenly feeling a tad frowzy, he shelved the dinner decision until after he showered and shaved for the second time that day. Briefly, he considered putting his work clothes back on, but there was a freshly laundered shirt in his closet—still draped in plastic—next to tan slacks he'd bought the week before at Sears. The thought of trousers that had never been worn by anyone else pleased him. There was nothing like a factory press. The way the reverse pleats lay so flat against the pockets. Almost robotically, he donned clean underwear and socks and stepped into his new slacks. The zipper tugged slightly, but it would loosen with use. And when he tore open the plastic covering encasing his ironed white shirt, the steamy smell of the Chinese laundry made him feel faintly superior.

"There," he said, combed and dressed. As if his tidy appearance was a job well done. Even his toes felt satisfied nestled into their Sunday socks.

Owen padded over to the front window of his second-story apartment. He looked right and left as far as he could without opening the window to the October chill. Not a soul was on the street. No youngster in a skeleton suit or teen with a fake ax protruding from his skull. As with previous years, the neighborhood kids knew they could score more candy on another street, one with fewer darkened apartment windows. *Oh well*, Owen told himself, no one could accuse him of not being prepared.

Turning away from the window, Owen walked to the far end of his apartment, next to the still-steamy bathroom, and opened his linen cupboard. Ferreting through a stack of clean sheets, he pulled out a white pillowcase and carried it to the kitchen table.

There, he smoothed it flat and used the desk scissors to cut a long arch into one side. He then positioned the cut pillowcase on his head in a flaccid attempt to approximate Lawrence of Arabia. Careful he was to depress the top and secure the forehead with an old tie so as not to resemble a Klan member in any way.

Still content with his decision to stay home, Owen left his apartment and got into his car and drove the mile and a half into Pawtucket, just to see. A nice bottle of red wine rolled back and forth on the passenger seat. It was easy to spot the Czerwinski home. Their front maple trees were draped in cottony fake cobwebs. *They'll regret that tomorrow morning,* Owen thought. Lit carved pumpkins with maniacal expressions lined the brick walkway leading to the front door. He found himself impressed with the knife work. Did an artist live on the premises? A butcher, perhaps? At the door, Owen tapped his middle knuckle against the shiny black wood. Then he shook his pillowcase-covered head and scoffed. The music inside was so loud, no one would ever hear him.

"Hello?" Wine bottle in hand, he stepped into the foyer and stated, "I have an invitation."

Nobody paid the slightest attention. The dimly lit living room off to the right was a pulsating mass of flesh and flashy costumes—more than one Boy George, he noted, and several Madonnas. The even darker dining room to the left seemed full of legs and laps. At the exact moment Owen muttered under his breath, "What the hell am I doing here?" Lidia appeared from out of nowhere, pink cheeked and grinning.

"Evan!"

"It's Owen," he said, surprised by how happy he was to see her. Had she had such deep dimples at the movie theater?

"Forgive me, Owen," she said, not the slightest bit repentant, "I've had a beer or three." Lidia snatched the wine bottle from beneath Owen's arm, set it on a table, and dragged him into the shadowy living room where an old disco number was reverberating off the walls. In a throaty voice, Donna Summer sang "I Feel Love" over and over and over. Owen blushed.

"I've been waiting for you all night," Lidia boozily whispered into the pillowcase over Owen's ear.

"What?" he said. But she didn't repeat it. Languidly she draped both wrists around his neck and swayed her hips back and forth, letting her eyelids meander shut. Owen nervously glanced around the room, but everyone else had their eyes closed, too. Figuring *Why not?* he tested his fantasy and encircled Lidia's tiny waist to see if his fingertips touched. They didn't, of course, but he nonetheless convinced himself he could lift her with barely a flex. The mere thought of it quickened his breath.

Never an accomplished dancer, Owen shifted from foot to foot like the Tin Man creaking down the yellow brick road. Not that Lidia noticed. She seemed to be dancing by herself, lost in a techno beat Owen couldn't quite locate.

I feel love, I feel love, I feel love, I feel love, I feeeeeel love.

Lidia's closed eyes gave Owen an opportunity to study her face. The nose was a bit meaty at the tip and her cheeks were full for someone so petite. Still, even in the silly orange wig she wore, she looked unbelievably sexy. Not beautiful, but nowhere near ugly. The purple satin of her Jane Jetson costume suited her. He appreciated her whimsical guise, as he hoped she appreciated his. Anybody could dress like *Boy George*. And the juxtaposition of the dainty silver cross that nestled in the hollow of her neck with those thigh-high fake boots, well, Owen felt another flutter.

"Want a tour?" Lidia asked when the song faded to a close and her eyes shot open.

"Tour?" What the hell did that mean? Not that it mattered. Lidia hadn't waited for an answer. Taking Owen's hand, she bumped him into her friends as she led him through her childhood home. "Kitchen, powder room, guest bedroom." Upstairs, her index finger pointed: "Bedroom, bedroom, bathroom, bedroom."

"You still live with your parents?" he asked, stating the obvious.

"Not for long." Lowering her voice she added, "You know how it is. Irene and Rita will be *buried* on this block. Not me."

They passed a couple dressed like John and Yoko leaning against the hallway wall. Owen adjusted the tie across his forehead and wished he'd chosen a less flimsy pillowcase. John and Yoko both rolled their eyes at him behind their dark round glasses. At least he thought they did; it was impossible to tell for sure. Utterly unaware of anyone else, Lidia chattered on as if she'd known Owen all her life. "*Anchorage* is bigger than our entire state, for God's sake. Can you imagine never seeing Alaska or California or New York City?"

Owen thought for a moment. *Who were Irene and Rita? The other girls in the movie line?*

"I may even move to Texas," Lidia stated, petting her flared satin collar. "From smallest to biggest. Why not?"

"Alaska," Owen said.

"Or Alaska. Why not?"

He'd meant to correct her. In land size, Alaska was the largest state. Texas wasn't even the most populous. New York had that distinction. But Lidia had already dragged him back downstairs into the living room where a song called "Every Little Thing She Does Is Magic" seemed to be playing his thoughts. When she danced around him, the hem of her minidress rose higher than he thought appropriate. He tried not to look, but how could he not? He'd never met anyone like Lidia before. When he was with her, he, too, felt like someone he barely knew.

Chapter 5

FOR THE THIRD time that morning, Muriel's phone rang. She felt her cell vibrate in the front pocket of her jeans as she waited for traffic to clear at the corner of West End Avenue, her elbows throbbing from the weight of her groceries. *Buzzt. Buzzt.* She lowered her bags to the sidewalk, and they settled into pools of plastic. This time she looked at the caller ID.

"Pia is visiting," she said into the phone.

"Good God."

Muriel laughed as Joanie asked, "What, you wearing the wrong shoes for the Rapture?" Eccentric, atheist, foul mouthed, and a chain-smoking casting director who self-medicated stress with Hershey's Kisses, Joanie Frankel had no filter between thought and word. She was unapologetically herself at all times, caring not one whit what anyone else thought of her. Her bedspring hair was prematurely gray and the shape of her XL body was indistinguishable beneath layers of gauzy fabric. Joanie believed the world was big enough for everyone. "Don't like me? Move over."

Of course Muriel adored her. (Even as Joanie's nicotine-laced exhalations made their office smell like a bowling alley bar and did God knows *what* to her lungs.) In the two years she'd been Joanie's casting assistant, they'd been best friends for a year and a half. A fact that concerned Lidia deeply.

"She seems so lesbianish," Lidia had said, pinch faced, after meeting Joanie the first time.

"I suppose that's because she's gay," Muriel had replied.

Lidia gasped. "Dear Lord. You two alone in that tiny office all day?"

"Homosexuality isn't contagious, Mother."

"Isn't it?"

Though Lidia labeled herself open minded, she proudly snapped it shut on the subject of sexuality between sexes of the same sex. "If God wanted men to be with men and women to be with women, He never would have created a sperm and an egg."

"Is that why there are fifteen hundred species of animals who exhibit homosexual behavior?" Muriel asked, wide eyed.

"That absurd statistic came from your lesbian boss, I'm sure."

On that pre-spring morning in New York City, Joanie asked Muriel, "What brings Miss Priss to Gomorrah?"

"No idea."

"Need a wingman?"

"Wing woman?"

"Potato po*tah*to."

Pressing her phone to her ear with her shoulder, Muriel squatted down to gather her shopping bags and scuttle across the street before the light turned red again. "I should be able to handle one lunch with my sister, right? What's the matter with me?"

"Jesus, she wants *lunch*?"

For the second time in as many minutes, Muriel released a laugh. Joanie was familiar with the Sullivant family history. Most of it, anyway. She knew how Muriel's perfect sister made her feel like a Yeti. She knew how Lidia had lost her breath the first time Pia opened her eyes.

"Those eyelashes! Lips like a rosebud! How could fingernails be so tiny and pink? God bless you for my miracle!" For hours Lidia gazed at her firstborn. The spit bubbles baby Pia made with the tip of her magenta-colored tongue were works of art. The way her toes fanned out like the hood on a frill-necked lizard, couldn't you just die? Pia's creamy white skin was satin soft. Lidia couldn't stop caressing her. She felt a physical ache when they were separated during nap time; she wished Owen would vacate their marital bed so Pia could sleep beside her, cushioned in pillows, their heartbeats in sync. Instantly and permanently, Lidia Sullivant had fallen in love with the gift God had given her. She had a daughter and a legitimate Catholic husband. What more could a woman want?

"My beautiful *kochanie*," Lidia once said to a grown Pia at the family dinner table, petting her silky hand as if it were a rabbit's foot. "The only pain you ever caused me was your grand entrance into the world."

"Was I grand, too, Mama?" young Muriel had asked. "Was I? Was I?"

"Nine months of indigestion."

Reaching her sausage fingers across the table, Muriel tore off another chunk of babka.

"I'm here if you need me or ice cream," Joanie told her friend into the phone. Muriel smiled. To her, Joanie Frankel was eider-down. A soft place to land. It didn't matter that she was ten years older. Or perhaps that was the one thing that *did* matter. In a motherly way Joanie engulfed Muriel in warm squishy embraces; never once did she expect her to be anyone other than her flawed self. Joanie would never ask Muriel to keep ugly secrets or pre-tend she didn't know something that she absolutely did.

THAT HALLOWEEN NIGHT, well, Lidia had been nothing short of mesmerizing. While they slow-danced on the pale pink carpet-ing in her parents' living room, Owen wanted to ask her, "Do you think I'm somebody else?" He seemed so far out of her league. What would a girl like her want with a guy like him? Not that he was entirely inexperienced. Madalyn had offered herself quite willingly. And she was certainly not his first, in spite of God's disapproval. He was a college grad, after all. Engineering stu-dents seem more buttoned up than they actually are. Especially at quad parties with kegs. But sex with Madalyn was not unlike a grocery list. *Lips?* Check. *Neck?* Check. *Breasts?* Check. *Penetra-tion?* Exclamation point. That ought to suffice until next Satur-day night.

With Lidia, sex seemed to ooze from her pores. When she danced, her hips moved in a rhythmic figure eight. Eyes closed, lips apart. Oblivious to the electrical current that raced to Owen's loins whenever her pointed breasts brushed his shirt, she grazed him time and again. And when she walked him out to the car at the end of the night and pressed her body against his and stood on her tippy-toes and whispered, "Kiss me," he felt positively hyperthermic. The very taste of her was exotic. Beery, of course, but something waxy and fruity, too. Lipstick, perhaps? His own lips felt softer after they kissed.

"See ya," she said, waving her fingers seductively behind her as she swayed those figure-eight hips back up the driveway lined with all those carved pumpkins. Unable to turn away and find his car, Owen simply stared, limp armed, until he saw the shiny black door to Lidia Czerwinski's home shut with a definitive *whump*.

The following week at work, he couldn't stop thinking about her. Even on date night with Madalyn (who playfully accused him of taking virility supplements), he envisioned Lidia's swiveling hips and strained to recall the feathery feel of her warm breath on his ear. *Kiss me.* Lord Almighty give him strength.

Chapter 6

IT WAS AN altogether ordinary day early in November. Owen pulled his wrinkled lunch sack from the bottom drawer of his desk. Suddenly he felt a presence behind him. Without even looking, he knew she was there. Lidia Czerwinski appeared at his cubicle holding a picnic basket in both hands and seductively twisting that elfin waist of hers.

"Come with me," she said in a slightly commanding way.

Dumbfounded, Owen sputtered, "Outside?"

"I brought a blanket. Wool."

To Owen, each word seemed infused with sexual innuendo. The word "wool" itself made him blush as red as the McIntosh apple in his tired brown lunch bag. Conrad, one of the idiot engineers in Owen's department, hung his ape arms over the tweedy partition and said in a clearly suggestive manner, "Don't forget your jacket, O-Man."

Leaping up, Owen grabbed his coat and hurried Lidia out of the office before the other engineers had a chance to gather like hyenas at a freshly killed carcass. "Bye," Lidia said to Conrad, wiggling her fingers over her shoulder. It was the second time Owen had seen her do that. Obviously the behavior of a woman who knew she was watched from behind.

Cogswell Tower in Jenks Park was the focal point of Central Falls. Such as it was. High on Dexter's Ledge, the old stone clock tower was Rhode Island's own Big Ben, on a much smaller scale, of course. Lidia suggested they eat lunch there, which struck Owen as patently reckless. Not only was it cold out, they would most certainly be alone. Or worse, *not*. What if a band of hoodlums waited on the far side of the tower? Was he expected to fight them off? He was wearing leather-soled loafers! The only scuffle he'd ever been in was years earlier when the class bully purposely hit him in the face with the tetherball at recess. His bloodied nose had camouflaged the tears streaming down his cheeks. The massive amount of red on his face scared everyone. The bully ran, screeching, "Hemophiliac!" For the rest of the school year, Owen was mentally tortured with the nickname "Hemo."

Pasting an optimistic smile on his face—and surreptitiously pushing his wallet to the very bottom of his front pocket with the heel of his hand—Owen gamely carried the picnic basket along the rambling walkways into Jenks Park, careful not to huff and puff up the hill. Always slim, he'd never been one to work out, believing he'd achieve more success in life if he exercised his *brain*. If nothing else, the tetherball incident had taught him as much. At that moment, however, what with the multiple stressors, even his brain was flabby, unable to conjure up a single intelligent thing to say.

"Nippy," he blurted out, twice, turning away from Lidia and wincing.

As she had at the Halloween party, Lidia seemed unfazed by Owen's social feebleness. She chattered on about crispy leaves and chubby squirrels and the way residents walked right past the beautiful tower every day without looking up. "The way New Yorkers who live on Staten Island blithely pass the Statue of Liberty on the ferry every morning without so much as a glance. Know what I'm saying?"

He didn't. An engineer, Owen constantly looked up at Cogswell Tower, marveling at the brick barrel-vault support, the clock faces on all four sides, the almost-feminine ironwork of the surrounding pergola.

"Or San Franciscans who pay no attention whatsoever to the Golden Gate Bridge. It's almost a crime."

Owen nodded and attempted to arrange his features in a thoughtful way. Lidia was as opposite Madalyn as a woman could be. She was a runaway train, wholly unconcerned about who might be on the tracks. And she used words like "blithely" absolutely, well, *blithely*. From the start, she mowed him under. He was petrified of her. But he had never desired a woman more.

"How's this?"

In a protected nook at the back of the tower on Dexter's Ledge, where Owen would never *dream* of sitting, much less eating (no doubt kids smoked marijuana and did God knows *what* in that very spot), Lidia didn't wait for an answer. She spread out the thick wool blanket that she'd packed along with lunch and opened the picnic basket with her slender expert fingers. Quickly, Owen darted around the perimeter of the tower to make sure they were indeed alone. They were. A fact that both relieved and unnerved him. Upon his return, Lidia—settled on the ground with her legs tucked petitely beneath her coat—handed Owen a corkscrew and a bottle of Polish wine. "You like red, right? It's what you brought to my party."

So flattered that she'd noticed he hadn't arrived at her home empty-handed, Owen missed the natural window of opportunity to tell her he never drank at lunch. Wine made him sleepy and he had a meeting that very afternoon with a new client who didn't fully trust his competence yet. The cork let go with a *pop* and he shakily poured two glasses.

"*Na zdrowie!*" Lidia said, raising one arm in a "Hail, Caesar!" kind of way. Owen stared, blank faced. "It's Polish for "Cheers," she said.

"You're Polish?"

Admittedly, it came out wrong. Too much emphasis on the latter word, as if there was something distasteful about it. He'd meant to marvel at his own stupidity for wondering where the name Czerwinski came from when she'd introduced herself in the movie line. At the time he thought she said, "Zerwinky," and it seemed some sort of circus moniker.

With her lovely lips curled in only the slightest hint of a sneer, Lidia said, "My family is American, of course."

"Of course. I'm sorry. Oh geez. I didn't mean—"

"Babka?"

Holding a braided loaf of golden brown bread in the air like it was the infant son of Christ, Lidia said, "Fair warning. It's addictive."

Just like that, she was back to her seductive self.

They drank and ate and fell into conversation. An oniony aroma of homemade meat loaf rose into the chilly air and intertwined with the yeasty smell of fresh bread. "My family owns the bakery in Pawtucket," Lidia said. Owen took the mouthful Lidia handed him. Amazingly, the bread was still warm. Almost as sweet and fluffy as cotton candy. He took another bite and felt it travel through his chest. When they clinked glasses he said, "Here's mud in your eye," desperate to avoid a repeat of the "Cheers" incident. To himself he thought, *What an oaf.* When Lidia fluttered her eyelashes and replied, "I'd hate to see mud in those gorgeous green eyes of *yours*," Owen nearly burst into tears he was so thankful.

Really, he never stood a chance. Lidia Czerwinski was not the kind of woman a man like Owen Sullivant could refuse. Certainly not when she so clearly had him eating out of her hand.

Chapter 7

OWEN HAD BEEN the perfect gentleman. That first date in November, when he returned to work with Polish cabernet on his breath, he stoically endured Conrad's chiding.

"What'd you have for *dessert*, O-ween?"

All he said was, "Has the temp put on a fresh pot of coffee?"

The following week, flushed and wrinkled from another alfresco lunch, Conrad demanded details. Owen simply said, "Get lost."

"Lost in her *hair*," said Conrad, the moron that he was. With a hint of condescension Owen wondered if perhaps Conrad never did attend keg parties in the quad. Quite possibly he was a virgin and would be thus until the day he died. Certainly a woman of quality would find fault with those horsey teeth. Owen took to patting Conrad's shoulder sympathetically when they passed each other near the water cooler.

Of course, Owen had a larger problem than his idiot co-worker. *Madalyn.* As his relationship with Lidia deepened, his weekly date night with big-haired Madalyn freighted him with guilt. Not that she noticed. As thick as a two-by-four, Madalyn mistook Owen's sexual invigoration as a step closer to the wedding she'd been planning since third grade. Good heavens, just last weekend she'd hinted at a joint vacation in Florida after Rhode Island's winter settled in. *Joint,* as in one bathroom and one bed in one hotel room. Three meals a day together. Chitchat from soup to nuts. He had to break it off soon. Wasn't it a known fact that whomever you kissed at midnight on New Year's Eve would be the person to whom you were bound all year?

Owen groaned. If he didn't act fast, that woman would find *some* way to latch her lips onto his as the clock struck twelve. He knew it as certainly as he knew he would die if Lidia Czerwinski was not wrapped in his arms as they entered a new year.

"Madalyn?" He made the call from work. "You free Saturday night?"

"Of course I'm free. You think I'd make plans on our only night together?"

"Yes, right. Well, about that . . . um, I've made a dinner reservation at Le Chez."

"That fancy place in Providence?"

"It's quiet there. We can talk."

"Ooh. Talk about what?"

The hopeful tone of her voice made his heart sink. "Nothing important," he said, quickly. "Just, you know, stuff."

"Like what *kind* of stuff?"

"You know. Stuff."

Madalyn squealed. "I *do* know. And it *is* important, silly. I knew something was up. Why, after last weekend, I can barely walk!" She giggled girlishly as she whispered, "I'll wear that backless dress you like."

Owen pressed his fingers to his temple. "Please wear something warmer, Madalyn. It's winter."

"Whatever you say, sweetheart."

Sweetheart? Owen wanted to retract the entire phone conversation. He'd badly miscalculated. Apparently, breaking up with a woman in the town's best restaurant *wasn't* the gentlemanly thing to do. He should have scheduled a meeting instead of a date. In stark daylight. One quick jab to the heart, not a three-course prix fixe with charcuterie! She would expect wine, too, maybe even champagne, she was so deluded.

"I'll pick you up at seven," he said, a knot of anxiety already forming in his gut. Madalyn replied with a sigh. "I'll be counting the minutes."

Dear God.

When the dreadful night arrived, Owen's stomach muscles were so tight he could barely swallow his own spit. Mother Nature mocked him by releasing the season's first snow. On the drive up to the Summit section of Providence, Madalyn strained in her seat belt to drape her hand over his on the steering wheel. Dreamily she said, "We'll remember this magical night forever." He couldn't help but notice she'd had a fresh manicure. The gold pinky ring she normally wore on her left hand was gone. A blank canvas awaiting the ultimate decoration. He considered pulling over then and there and blurting out, "It's over." Wasn't that the *kind* thing to do? Why ruin the woman's dinner? But there was a bit of traffic. If he pulled over on the main drag he'd get a ticket for sure.

While Owen searched for the ideal place to stop, kill the engine, then douse Madalyn's dreams of their future together, Le Chez came into view. People were laughing inside, bathed in the flattering light of disposable income. Across the street from the restaurant were several open parking spots. He pulled his car into the nearest one, stepped out, and galloped around the back of the car to help Madalyn out through the passenger-side door.

"My, my," she said all singsongy, holding her hand up the way a princess would. "Such a gentleman."

Owen considered taking her hand and *not* lifting her up. In a dignified tone he'd calmly announce that he had no engagement ring for her professionally manicured finger and never would. But not to worry. They could still have dinner as *friends*. He would pay the entire bill, wine included. But Madalyn's face looked so damned expectant! Telling her right then felt unduly mean. The least he could do was soften the blow with alcohol. Besides, she would tell everyone in Pawtucket that he dumped her in a snowy parking lot. Word might get back to Lidia and alter their steamy encounters behind Cogswell Tower.

"Milady," he said, attempting to be a sport. Madalyn, of course, took it all wrong and beamed as Owen guided her out of the car and placed his hand on her elbow to escort her across the slippery street to the front door of Le Chez. On the way he noticed they were on *Hope* Street. Was there no end to his punishment for falling in love? And he had. Fallen in love with *Lidia*, that is. Though, hand to God, he'd been a perfect gentleman.

Number one, though Lidia seemed to prefer "their spot" behind Cogswell Tower to his warm apartment with a double bed and shower, he said nothing about feeling chilly. Who was he to pass judgment if fresh air made her frisky? Number two, he said not a word when Lidia burrowed under his heavy coat and rested her hand in his lap. Sure, he *thought* it, but he never uttered, "What are you doing?" That would have been rude. He let her massage him if that's what she wanted to do. God knows, he wasn't going to force himself on her no matter how much she excited him. Why, he'd given her *ample* opportunity to refuse him. Never once did she say, "Stop," when he so clearly responded to her touch. Quite the contrary. Lidia had pulled him toward her, kissed him urgently, and warmed his cold hands by slipping them underneath her cashmere sweater. It was *his* suggestion that they slow down. Didn't he offer to run down the hill to buy protection?

"I'm ready," she'd moaned, somehow removing her own bra when his hands were a trembling mass of icy thumbs.

What did God expect? He wasn't a *saint*.

Inside Le Chez, Madalyn removed her coat to reveal the backless black dress Owen had once found so sexy. He bit his lip, looked away. Following the maître d' to their table, Madalyn sashayed through the dining room the way Lidia had seductively swiveled her hips along the walkway to her front door on Halloween night. But few patrons looked up from their menus.

Owen looked down at his feet. He felt embarrassed for his date, as if she only owned one cocktail dress and wore it no matter what the weatherman said. At the table, he stretched his lips across his teeth in the approximation of a smile.

"Shall we order champagne?" Madalyn chirped before they even had a chance to properly settle into their seats. Owen glanced up at the maître d' and asked, "Do you sell champagne by the glass?"

Scoffing, Madalyn said, "He's joking. We'll have a bottle of your best. And please tell our waiter we'd like a few minutes alone. I'm not ready to order just yet."

It was exactly that sort of pushiness that shoved that Owen into the arms of another woman. At least that's what he told himself.

The moment the maître d' retreated, Madalyn reached her bare left hand across the table and leaned so far over that Owen noted her bralessness. The powdery aroma of her perfume slapped him in the face. Suddenly she looked grotesque with that heavy eyeliner and magenta goo on her lips. It was all he could do to keep from excusing himself and running back to the car.

"I'm all ears," she said in a kittenish whisper.

"Oh. Well. Yes, then." Owen cleared his throat. "I have news."

"News? As in an *announcement*. As in a certain section of the Sunday paper?" In Madalyn's Cheshire cat grin, Owen saw a lipstick smear on her two front teeth.

"I'm seeing someone," he said. Then he held his breath.

"Someone?"

"Actually, I've fallen in love."

"Yes. I'm aware of that, silly."

"With someone *else*."

He pressed his lips together and watched the news sink in. Slowly it covered Madalyn like a thundercloud, sucking the air out of her body. She seemed to contract right there in front of him, looking like one of those shrink-wrapped turkey legs they sold at PriceRite.

"What are you saying?" she asked, blinking.

"It's over. I'm sorry."

"But—" She struggled to find the right words. "What's all this?" Her bare arms spread open to include the restaurant.

"The last supper?"

As if materializing from the darkness that had descended upon their table, a waiter appeared and presented a chilled champagne bottle draped in a white linen napkin. "Duval-Leroy, vintage nineteen seventy, brut."

Owen nodded glumly. Madalyn pushed back her chair and ran to the ladies' room just as the cork went *pop*.

Chapter 8

"I CAN SKIP the gym today."

That's the first thing Pia said when she arrived at her sister's door, coughing and breathless from the four-story climb. Muriel quashed the urge to cluck her tongue. By now, she'd heard every version of that. After years in a walk-up, no one simply said hello.

"You must have great thighs."

"I guess you're used to this by now."

"My day's calories are officially burned!"

"If I lived here, I'd never go out unless I absolutely *had* to."

None was true, except the last one.

"Club soda?" Muriel asked her sister. "With lime?"

"Lovely." Kiss-kissing Muriel's cheeks, Pia coughed again on her way into the apartment, setting her fussy buckled handbag on the café chair in Muriel's microscopic kitchen. She looked pale even after four flights of pumping ventricles, but Pia had always been fair skinned and slender. The river of light between the length of her boyish legs had always been a marvel to Muriel. How could it possibly feel to have thighs that didn't collide in a fleshy pucker?

"Spiced almonds? A pear?"

Without answering, Pia smoothed the tan linen slacks she wore and ran her hands down her perfectly styled blond hair—shoulder length, razor side part, slight flip at the collarbone. She looked around, frowned, and exhaled disapproval. As she always did. Then she untied the flowery silk scarf she had expertly looped around her milky neck, lifted it off her shoulders, and said, "Isn't this pretty? I bought it in a boutique in Paris that sells *only* scarves. Can you imagine? It's like standing in a Matisse."

Muriel turned away to slice a lime. Shopping in a Parisian boutique that sold only scarves was not something she would *ever* do. The very thought of it made her squirm—the saleswoman's noticeably lifted brow when she walked through the door dressed in black outlet, her poseur smile.

"I also have popcorn if you're feeling adventurous," Muriel said over her shoulder. "Cheese or CaramelCr—" Suddenly, Muriel felt the warmth of her sister's body press against her back. Pia rested her chin on Muriel's clavicle and seemed to breathe in the scent of her hair. Stiffening, Muriel asked, "What's going on?"

"Here."

Still warm from her body, Pia draped the silk scarf around the back of her younger sister's neck. "I want you to have this," she said, turning Muriel around to face her. Poofing and twisting, she arranged the scarf exactly the way she liked it. Muriel didn't move. Sticky with lime juice, her hands dangled in midair. She held her breath until her chest burned. Muriel disliked people this near, close enough to smell her, feel the heat in her cheeks. Especially Pia, whose grooming seemed to go on forever.

"Voilà." Pia finally stepped back and looked pleased. Muriel exhaled hard, wiped her hands on her jeans, and walked over to the mirror she'd hung in her kitchen to make it appear twice as big. "Oh my," she said.

The billow of silk felt too tight on her neck. It created jowls. Her chin seemed to sit directly on her chest, the scarf spilling over her breasts like a melted Creamsicle. Swallowing was nearly impossible with the restriction on her Adam's apple. She hated it, couldn't wait for Pia to settle into her makeshift living room so she could slip into the bathroom and rip it off her neck.

"Bee-hee-yoo-tee-ful!" she said, sounding ridiculous. "Thank you."

"Now that you're properly accessorized—on your top half at least—I'm taking you to lunch."

Muriel blurted out, "Why?" Then she softened it with, "I have food other than popcorn. That was just one suggestion."

In her feline way, Pia smiled patiently and changed the subject. "Emma has always loved your little apartment," she said, wandering over to the window that Muriel had opened a crack. "So very recycled." With that, she perched elegantly on the secondhand love seat beside Muriel's bed and stared out the window with the same half smile on her lips. "Logan would kill for this light."

Fizzing glasses of club soda in her hands and a silk noose

around her neck, Muriel followed her sister into the living area and stood before her.

"Baguette? Asparagus spear?"

No question, Owen had maintained his composure at Le Chez. When Madalyn returned to their table all puffy eyed and purple faced, he calmly asked her to sit down so he could tell her the truth. She deserved as much.

"I never planned this," he said, starting from the first moment he met Lidia in the movie line. "As you may recall, I wanted to see *Death Wish II*."

"Man-stealing bitch!" Madalyn screeched. A restaurant full of heads swiveled their way. But Owen kept his cool. He endured the glares and let Madalyn rant. He knew how high strung she could be. Not once did he mention the fact that Lidia gave him a full erection merely by sucking his earlobe; that would be cruel. Quite deliberately, he chose not to let slip that he'd been unable to get Lidia out of his mind since the night they met. Madalyn would surely remind him of how easily he forgot her birthday and their six-month anniversary. Why pour salt in the wound? Owen wasn't that kind of guy. In full control of his dignity, he filled Madalyn's glass with bubbly and ordered the pâté appetizer for two. He did *not* point out the obvious: had nosy Madalyn kept her mouth shut that evening in the movie line, they might have continued to make lukewarm love every Saturday night. Owen said nothing of the sort. He was not the venomous type.

After drinking champagne and eating pâté in choked silence,

Owen offered to continue the meal, but Madalyn wanted to go home. On the way out of the restaurant, he held his head high in spite of the embarrassing bareness of her dress. He tried not to notice the imprint of the chair back. When she sat shivering in the passenger seat of his car, waiting for the heater to rev up, he resisted the urge to remind her that he'd specifically suggested she wear something warmer.

"Isn't the snow lovely?" he said instead, but Madalyn only snorted. He turned on the radio to camouflage the silent drive. At her front door, he leaned over to end their relationship with a proper good-bye peck on the cheek but she slapped him in the face. Slapped him! He couldn't believe it. Never would he act so rudely.

"I wish you only the best," he said to her slammed door.

A *gentleman* in all matters, that was Owen Sullivant's creed. On the way home, he couldn't stop smiling.

With visions of a new sexually charged life flashing through his head, Owen slept like a puppy that night. He called Lidia the next morning to say, "The warmth of the rising sun reminded me of you."

"Aw," she said. "How sweet."

Owen *felt* sweet and sappy and Gumby limbed. He made his way to work on Monday without a clue as to how he got there. Midday, he found himself lazily twirling in his desk chair. Life had taken such a lovely turn.

"How would you like to join me for dinner at Le Chez?" he asked Lidia over the phone.

"Ooh, that fancy place in Providence?"

"The very one. Shall I pick you up Saturday night?"

"Why don't I meet you there? I'll be in town shopping."

"Splendid."

Owen never used words like "splendid" but he'd never met a woman like Lidia, either. She was virgin territory in the most delightfully unvirginal way. When she met him at Le Chez on Saturday night, he was careful not to register alarm on his face when she showed up with her friends Irene and Rita. Not even when she suggested they join them for dinner. Perhaps that's what popular girls did! Dated with an *entourage*. The very word was so cosmopolitan Owen felt a stirring downtown. He didn't even squawk about paying for all four of them. And that Rita was no stranger to Cabernet.

Later that very evening, when Lidia completely jumped the gun and called Owen her "boyfriend" in front of her friends, he didn't question her. That would have been humiliating. Certainly he was feeling all fuzzy with love, but they had never formalized definitions. Perhaps definitions were passé? Engineers were notoriously behind on trends.

The following week they chatted several times over the phone. Owen considered growing his hair out and using gel. He called Lidia "Liddy" once in a gush of otherness. Feeling utterly brazen he wore his Members Only jacket to work. Sexually, Owen waited for Lidia to take the lead. It was only proper. He wouldn't dream of pressuring his new girlfriend to meet him behind Cogswell Tower or anywhere else so he could perform his boyfriendly duties. But Lidia seemed content to conduct their fledgling relationship over the phone. Their sexy picnic lunches appeared to have dropped off Dexter's Ledge. Ever the optimist, Owen chalked it up to holiday stress. But after Thanksgiving, when Lidia treated him more like a table centerpiece than the strutting Tom Turkey he envisioned himself to be, he wondered if something might be amiss. He was quite certain boyfriends were not frozen out *entirely*.

"Hmmm," he said to himself. "Hmmm."

Methodically, Owen dissected each moment of their two erotic encounters to pinpoint where he may have gone astray. True, they were quite, um, *speedy*. And the frosty air did nothing to highlight his manhood. He was eager to display himself indoors, perhaps after the plumping steam of a shower? Surely the woman couldn't blame him for the vagaries of Mother Nature! Not when he had clearly stated that he lived in his own apartment.

The only possible blunder Owen could think of was a hulking one. His stomach flopped over just thinking of it. Had he misinterpreted Lidia's whispered declaration of *readiness*? Instead of a sexual green light, was it something else entirely? Perhaps a statement of desperation from an aging woman who's the last of her friends to marry and have children? Had she been asking for a ring instead of a fling?

Lord have mercy. Owen felt ill. But he said nothing. While a gentleman may *think* these thoughts, he certainly never utters them.

"I need to see you."

Lidia called Owen at work just as he was neatening his desk for the weekend. Alarmed by her leaden tone, he didn't dare suggest they meet at the back of Cogswell Tower, not even with a down sleeping bag.

"That would be lovely," he replied, trying to sound chipper for both of them. "Shall we grab a bite to eat? Bring the entourage!"

"Why don't I swing by your place?"

Owen exhaled. His shoulders relaxed. The sexy whisper was back in Lidia's voice. He could hear the twinkle in her eye. Finally, things were looking up. "Give me twenty minutes to change the sheets."

Lidia laughed and Owen's heart soared. On the way out of the office, he practically skipped. Conrad shouted, "You turkey leftovers this weekend or the main course, O-Man?"

"Why, I believe I'm dessert!"

Chapter 9

THE BUS STOP across Riverside Drive was empty, but Muriel knew the M5 would arrive soon . . . or in half an hour. You never knew with that line. The posted bus schedule was merely pole decoration. Something to read while you waited. In the early afternoon sunlight, the two sisters were on their way to lunch.

"Pick someplace fabulous," Pia had said, "and wear your new scarf. And that white shirtdress I bought you for your birthday."

Hearing the desperation in her own voice, Muriel had replied, "I bought heirloom tomatoes. I'm quite sure I can make something lunchy out of them."

"Nonsense. I'm taking you out. I insist."

Fearless teenage boys skidded their clacking skateboards down the stone steps of the monument in Riverside Park. Puggles tugged at their leashes, toddlers skittered after pigeons who walked from side to side in exactly the way they did. On teak benches in the shadow of young elms, Jamaican nannies and their charges met to gossip and dole out gluten-free pretzels. "Joshua, share with Aidan now." For a brief moment, Muriel understood why people liked the outdoors. Then she felt the weight of her hair on her head and wished she was back in her apartment.

For the second time that day, Muriel's body had melted into the shape of a wine bottle. A dress had meant shaving her legs. A white dress meant she couldn't wear her black Spanx. And the scarf, well, that meant she'd feel more choked than she already did.

"Fabulous it is," she had said, surrendering, knowing exactly where her perfectly perfect sister would want to go.

OWEN USHERED LIDIA into his tidy apartment with a sweep of his arm even as he ached to sweep her *into* his arms and ravenously take her on the freshly Hoovered carpet.

"Milady," he said, opting for a more gallant approach.

Lidia smiled, but it was the type of smile that had more darkness in it than light.

"What's wrong?" Owen asked.

"I have news," she said.

Owen swallowed. "News?"

"We should sit."

Right then and there he knew his life was over. Not in the *dead* sort of way, but in the *never again the same* way. No one delivers good news sitting down. Happy news inspires leaping, hugging, back slapping. All upright activities. Only dire news causes knees to buckle. At that moment Owen wished Lidia would quietly back out of his apartment the way she'd come in.

Rewind herself. Really, they didn't know each other well enough to share life's disappointments.

They sat.

"Tea?" Owen offered.

"Thank you, no." Lidia was suddenly as prim as a head-mistress.

"All righty then. Your announcement." Owen held his breath.

As the news washed over him, Owen struggled to maintain his dignity. Though he *had* recently vacuumed, it would have linted his wool slacks to do what he wanted to do: crumple to the carpet in a heap. The worst possible outcome of their brief outdoor encounters had occurred.

"I'm an honorable man," he said, clearing his throat to cam-ouflage his hyperventilation. "Whatever the cost to take care of this, I'll pay. Plus a ride, of course. And absolute secrecy." With his trembling right hand pressed onto his thudding heart he promised, "I will tell no one. I swear."

"No," said Lidia.

"No what?"

"No, thank you."

Owen blinked. When Lidia repeated her refusal to even *con-sider* termination—announcing she was a devout Catholic—he reminded her that he was Catholic, too. God, he happened to know, was a world-renowned forgiver. His flock was entitled to a "Get out of hell free" card at least once in their lives. It was practi-cally in the Bible.

"No," she said flatly.

"*No?*"

"No."

Ever the gentleman, Owen didn't say, "Screw you, then." That would have been uncouth. Instead, he promised to compile a list of respected adoption agencies. "Imagine the number of suitable families looking for Caucasian children. There must be hundreds. Maybe *thousands*. God will praise your selflessness. Think of the joy you'll bring to an infertile couple!"

"No," said Lidia again, this time punctuating it with a petulant stamp of her foot.

Owen gaped at her. What the hell did she want? Good lord, they'd only done it twice. They were practically strangers. Well, not *practically*. They were strangers! He'd wanted to see *Death Wish II* the night they met, for God's sake. They didn't even have the same taste in movies.

"You can't possibly think we should marry?" he asked, his mouth hanging slack.

"I don't. But God does."

Owen almost laughed. It was the *eighties*. Had the woman never heard of the sexual revolution? Women's lib? The pill? Had God never spoken to her about the twentieth century?

Lidia abruptly stood up. She took Owen's hand and placed it flat on her slightly rounded abdomen. "There's a human life growing inside of me."

God forgive him, Owen wanted to jerk his hand away. But Lidia took Owen's other hand and pressed both of them hard against her body.

"*Our* creation, my darling," she whispered, bending down so she was right up to his ear. There, she inhaled his earlobe into her mouth and nibbled on it as if it were a tiny cob of corn. Letting her feathery blond hair spill all over his face, she kissed him. First his eyelids, then the tip of his nose, then his bottom lip, then both lips. Her tongue found the roof of his mouth and danced there. Sliding her skirt up over her thighs, she straddled him. With his hands still on her torso, Owen was as tiny limbed as a T. rex. He fell backward on the couch, helpless, moaning as she unzipped his wool slacks. He muttered, "Oh God," as she somehow maneuvered his manhood through the maze of fabric that separated them. With his girlfriend on top of him, moving in the most exquisite undulating manner, Owen decided it might not be so very terrible to make her his fiancée after all.

Chapter 10

PAPA CZERWINSKI MADE a call or two. He knew people. His tentacles spread far beyond the tiny state of Rhode Island. There were men he'd grown up with in the old country, other bakery owners on the East Coast, restaurateurs, loans he'd made, favors offered and accepted. He was a man with options. His daughter needn't be a topic for tut-tutting over afternoon tea and *pączki*. "Such a big baby for a preemie. So soon after the wedding. You'd think a couple who barely knew each other might want to wait one Christmas, at least."

Above all else, Papa Czerwinski was a businessman. Already he could hear the way his customers would grumble: "The Irishman will be making the babka now? What, *tradition* has become a dirty word?" Best to get the new husband and the large baby with the Celtic last name out of town before the rabble had a chance to be roused. He picked up the phone. He made a call or two. While Pia was still a baby bump, Papa arranged for his new son-in-law to accept a position at an engineering firm in midtown Manhattan.

"Oh! Manhattan is fabulous!" Lidia's dark eyes were alight. "At last I'll see the world." To the baby still in her belly she said, "See how much you've given me already?"

Owen's parents saw the entire situation differently.

"'A lack of willingness on either side can void the marital contract and annul divine sanction,'" Owen's father read from a pamphlet his parish priest had given him. "It says it right here, son, a *lack of willingness*. You can still get out of this thing."

"How can I be unwilling to claim my own child?" Owen asked. "Give him or her a legitimate last name?"

That shut him up. A child, of course, complicated everything.

"I'm afraid it's a done deal, Dad."

What else could anyone say?

The reality was, Owen felt like a cartoon character hit by a two-by-four. Everything happened so fast, his cranium was still metronoming back and forth; his ears rang so loudly he could barely hear anything else. One moment he was marveling at the divine geometry of a woman who could swivel her hips on top of him in both a circle and a square, the next he was watching that same woman walk down the aisle toward him wearing an empire-waisted wedding gown at Our Lady of Perpetual Sorrow.

While Lidia happily lost the last vestiges of her elfin waist at her parents' bakery, Owen drove four hours down Interstate 95 to find his soon-to-be family a suitable home in their new state. On the way, in the blessed quiet of the car, he had time to think. Lidia, he decided, was being foolish. *Manhattan* was out of the question. Raising a child in an apartment with no yard? No school down the block he or she could walk to? No street to play kickball in? It was absurd. If she had a fever in the middle of the night, what, they were going to wait for an *elevator*—perhaps stopping along the way for one of their drunken neighbors— then stand in the rain for a cab? It was virtually child abuse! Plus, Manhattan was so noisy. Who could hear themselves think with all those groaning buses and their screeching brakes? He had a better idea.

"*Queens?*" Lidia had said, aghast, when Owen called to tell her he'd found them a nice house across the river. "What are you talking about? When I told you I wanted to live on the east side, I meant the Upper East Side of *Manhattan.*"

"Four bedrooms, two and a half baths, a yard big enough for a swing set, eat-in kitchen."

"Or maybe Sutton Place. I'm sure I was quite clear."

"An entire house instead of an apartment, Lidia."

"Were you not listening? I specifically ordered a doorman building."

"Ordered?" Owen got quiet.

"You know what I'm saying. I'm not the Queens type."

Inhaling slowly, Owen replied, "The town is called Middle Village. It's a family neighborhood—a *village*—and only a subway ride to the city."

"Queens isn't me, Owen. It's not *us*, I mean."

"You haven't even seen the house. It's lovely. And light. And very much me. I mean, *us*. You'll like it there, Lidia. We all will. I promise."

"Isn't Queens *Italian*?"

Owen's grip tightened on the phone. "What on earth does that mean?"

"I'm just saying, at the very least, if push came to shove, we should live in Greenpoint, Brooklyn. There are five Polish bakeries on the main avenue alone."

"How do you know that?"

"Papa has connections."

"We don't need your father's connections. I have a good job in the city. A straight shot on the subway from our house in Queens. I can *walk* to the train station."

"Without my father's connections, you would have such a nice job in midtown Manhattan?"

Owen stiffened his jaw. Lidia said, "I'm just saying."

It was useless reminding his new wife that her old-school father had set up his job to protect her from their lip-flapping neighbors. That he'd loved his firm in Central Falls and hated to leave it, hated to leave Rhode Island, period. Even more useless was putting words to the thoughts he couldn't push out of his mind: *I told you I'd run down the hill for protection. I offered money and a ride and absolute secrecy.* Lidia made life-changing choices without one whiff of concern for him. How dare she?! Most frustrating of all was her habit of pushing all culpability right out of her mind, as if it never had been the truth from the start.

Manhattan is fabulous! he'd heard her say. Owen pressed his molars together. He had always despised people who used the word "fabulous" and now he was married to one.

"You see my point, don't you?" Lidia asked, softly.

"Yes. I know exactly what you're saying."

"It's settled then." Relief flooded her voice. "You'll do the right thing, *mój piezczoch.*"

Owen answered, "I already have. Our deposit on the row house in Queens is nonrefundable."

After slamming down the phone, Lidia had refused her husband's calls the whole time he was in New York setting up their new life. Which, Owen discovered, wasn't so terribly awful after all.

PIA JULA SULLIVANT was born on a hazy summer afternoon in a Queens hospital not far from the row house in Middle Village where Owen and Lidia lived in polite cohabitation. In the delivery room Owen couldn't help but notice that his blushing bride had morphed into Satan. Several times she growled at him like a rabid dog. Once, Lidia barked, "Get out of my face, you prick!"

"*Hee hee whoo whoo.* Breathe, darling."

"Cram your own damn breath down your throat and die!"

Owen's equilibrium was shot. His tidy life was a shambles. He could barely feel his limbs. Still, he persevered at his new wife's bedside, even as her eyeballs bulged out of her head and he waited for her head to spin in full circles on her neck. She smelled like a hungover bum. Ungrateful, she frequently ordered him out of the room (even screamed for a priest!). Still, he persisted. It was the gentlemanly thing to do as much as it—physically—pained him. Lidia pierced the skin of his palm with her long fingernails more than once. In the grip of a contraction, she squeezed his hand so hard he feared for his metacarpals! Literally adding insult to injury, she turned her mottled face toward him and spewed profanity. Already stunned by the physical disgustingness of childbirth—Good lord, had she *shat*?—Owen was shocked by her bad manners. In spite of her pain. Sure, he understood lashing out when your insides felt as though they were being ripped out through your private parts. Still, he'd been nothing but kind and accommodating. Calling him a "dickwad" was uncalled for.

Though Owen desperately wanted to back away from the birthing bed, slip into the restroom and wriggle sideways out a window, he stayed. He never let go of Lidia's claw nor suggested someone spray air freshener. The brutality of childbirth unnerved him. And the very randomness of nature—the way a single sperm can derail an entire life—upset him deeply. One wiggling haploid invades an egg. A diploid is formed. Cells divide. The zygote fuses onto the uterine wall, leeching nutrients from its host. Expanding like a rising cinnamon bun, a heart begins to flutter; limbs, spine, nervous system take shape; weblike veins spread tiny lines of red throughout the organism. The host body changes, rounds out, seeks a nest, demands security. Choice evaporates like a droplet of rain in a cracked lake bed. The child must be born into a stable union. God has His rules. The parents have their say. The legal system intervenes with a contract that, really, was only established so males could ensure paternity. As if a marriage license could keep a woman faithful. Preposterous! The whole machine completely ignores the very real disruption of a baby. With barely enough time to adjust to the absolute *presence* of marriage—the required conversations across every dinner table, the sound of breathing in your bed all night in spite of those lusciously curved lips, the almost instantaneous ceasing of sexuality, the crossed wires that continuously spark, the inability to come home from work and silently retreat to the basement to fiddle with the water-purification unit you were creating out of river rocks and riparian soil, the wrenching loss of silence itself—a needy mammal is wiggling like an upended cockroach, utterly helpless, dependent upon you for its very life? How could nature allow such carelessness?

Yet Owen never uttered a word about it. He was not that kind of man.

"Breathe, Lidia, breathe. *Hee, hee, whoo.*"

"Cram it, you bastard!"

Owen Sullivant was many things. A bastard he was not.

Chapter 11

ADMITTEDLY, THEY SHOULD have taken a cab. But Muriel preferred the bus. Cabs so often smelled like the driver's hair pomade. Plus, did they *ever* disinfect those vinyl backseats? Even so, waiting for the Riverside Drive bus on a Sunday was maddening. Three separate flashes of white were false alarms. One was a FedEx truck, another the Access-A-Ride minivan. The third was a FreshDirect delivery. Muriel knew from experience that the bus never came when you scanned the horizon for it. You had to look away and pretend you had all day to wait.

"So . . . ," she said to Pia, turning her back on the flow of downtown traffic, "how's Emma?"

Attempting to appear nonchalant, Muriel jutted one foot forward at a sporty angle, then immediately retracted it when she noticed that her big toe stuck out of her peep-toe pumps like an unpedicured bratwurst. In the banana-colored sunlight, wearing the white shirtdress for the first time, its buttons tugging open in tiny diamond shapes down her front, she felt like a hulking transvestite. Suddenly, she couldn't figure out how to arrange her arms in a feminine way. Pia's pouffy handbag swung carelessly in the crook of her arm. "Lovely as ever," she said serenely.

"And Will?"

"Working around the clock."

"Mom and Dad? Heard from them lately?"

"I met Mama for lunch last week. Dad is Dad."

Muriel nodded.

"You're well?"

Pia nodded. That about summed up what they had in common and Muriel didn't need to turn around to know that the bus wasn't even out of Harlem yet. With her older sister, there was always more unsaid than said. And asking about their brother, Logan, was a waste of time. An artist living in New Mexico, he'd divorced the family years ago.

Silence expanded between the two sisters like a darkening oil spill. A razor nick on Muriel's bare shin stung from the hasty grooming. And though she hadn't dared look, she was fairly certain her panty lines were not only visible through the white fabric, they were unevenly situated on her ass, as well. One higher than the other, both causing unsightly butt bulge.

"Things good at work?" Pia again fussed with Muriel's frothy scarf.

Please, God, Muriel silently prayed, *send the bus with the next green light.*

"Full of spit, as usual." Muriel burped up a laugh. Then she watched as Pia exhaled in the same judgmental way she exhaled when she glanced around Muriel's recycled apartment.

Flying saliva, it was true, was a hazard of Muriel's profession. Even though *profession* was stretching her job description to its outer limit. Muriel was a casting assistant. A job that sounded more glamorous than it was. In reality, she printed scripts from PDFs and alphabetized head shots and downloaded audition scenes onto Joanie's computer. When actors came into the office to audition for a part, she retrieved them from the waiting room, did her best to calm their nerves (which never worked), and stood off camera to read the other roles. Flooded with stress-induced spit, many actors couldn't help but emote their DNA all over Muriel's face, particularly when Joanie was casting a drama with an *accent*, which she had been all week.

"Ever since I *vas* a boy in Prague, *ach*, I've been roaming the globe searching for some*ting*, some*vun*. You are my last *c*hope."

The projectile usually landed squarely on her cheek, though Muriel never flinched. To wipe spit off during an audition was unprofessional, upsetting to an actor. Her job was to relax everyone, Joanie included.

"I'm here, Vaclav. You can rest now." Muriel calmly read her lines.

"*Ach*, at last, my *dahlink*."

More than enduring salivary bullets, Muriel's biggest struggle was not rolling her eyes. Lately, so many actors were *models*—pretty boys whose spray tans were too orange, teeth were too white, and hairlines began in the middle of their foreheads. Their character interpretations were cartoonish. *Chopeless,* one might say. Patiently, Muriel read her lines and waited for the audition scene to end.

"Lovely," Joanie would say, hoisting her heft up from behind the camera and holding out her fleshy hand. "Thank you for coming in."

"I wasn't fully feeling the Russian accent. I could work on it."

"Good idea. And Prague is in the Czech Republic."

Softly, Muriel would take the actor's arm and lead him out, whispering, "You were great," before returning to wipe his bad acting off her face. In her bottom desk drawer, she kept a Costco-size canister of antibacterial wipes.

"Getting spit on is an *insult,* not a life," Lidia once told her youngest daughter, forgetting it was *she* who first ignited Muriel's interest in theater. How very like Lidia to overlook her role in shaping her daughter's life. Lidia had introduced Muriel to red velvet curtains that swept open with a muted *swoosh,* swelling music that pressed against her sternum, satin dresses that rippled across a stage like cake icing, love songs so heartbreakingly rendered tears would stream down her face. Lidia had opened the door to a theatrical world of passion and perfection, inviting her youngest daughter to step through before so cruelly snapping it shut.

"Feel that?"

At the bus stop, Pia faced the Hudson River. A half smile on her lips, she appeared to be mesmerized by the cursive peaks of gray-blue water in the wake of the Circle Line ferry. Muriel pointed her face toward the river and tried to feel.

"The breeze is splendid," said Pia.

"Ah."

"Sailboats fill me with such longing. It's as if everyone on the water knows the answer and we don't even know the question."

Muriel stared at the lone dinghy on the river and blinked.

Turning back toward her sister, Pia said, "Every good and perfect gift is from the father of the heavenly lights."

"Even sunburn?"

Pia didn't laugh. As she often did when she was with her, Muriel wondered how it was possible they were sisters at all. Though, God knows, she had *tried* to be a Sullivant woman worthy of her sister's and her mother's respect. Which primarily meant, of course, *married*.

COLLEGE BEGAN MURIEL's years of actively looking for a mate. In class, in the library, in the dorm, in the quad. Guys were everywhere, just nowhere near interested in her. And when she *was* able to secure a date, she was usually too distracted by her critical inner voice to hear the particulars of a regular conversation. Like the night she invited a guy named Paul from her sociology class to watch a movie with her in the dorm's media room. The film starred Julianne Moore. Paul remarked, "Freckles are cute," but at that exact moment, Muriel had been looking down at her bare forearms wondering, *What's the cutoff point between a freckle and a mole?* Was there some sort of medical measurement? It would be centimeters, of course, or millimeters. Something a regular person couldn't decipher. Maybe a freckle was flat and a mole was raised? As she stroked her arms in the mottled splatter of TV light, she noted that they felt like a pilled sweater. Her heart sank. Of course her freckles were moles. She'd been foolish to think otherwise. If not, would they contain so many errant hairs? A mole was probably a follicle incubator, like dung-fertilized earth for a sprouting seed.

"Don't you think?" Paul had asked.

"Yes. Moles *are* a hideous blight. Sorry. I'll wear long sleeves."

He shot her a look that struck Muriel as belittling. If Paul thought she was going to wear turtlenecks, too, well he'd better think again.

Somehow, Muriel had never learned the basics of chitchat. Her vision of relationships was defined on the Broadway stage when she was a young girl accompanied by her mother. Grown, whenever she was with a boy she liked, she felt compelled to burst out in a show tune. Most guys found that insurmountably odd.

After college, when the pool of possibles evaporated considerably, Muriel reworked her strategy. She trolled opening-night theater parties and closing-night theater parties and holiday parties and every invitation she could wrangle from Joanie in search of a suitable mate. She listed herself online and only shaved ten pounds off her real weight so as not to shock a potential suitor when he met her in the ample flesh. After work, she nibbled on happy hour buffets and drank vodkas with club soda and lime because she'd read in a woman's magazine that they were "low in calories and high in class." Still, most of the single straight men she met seemed like frat brothers, as if a date might begin in a rented limo and end with a food fight through the open moon roof. They drank beer from tipped-up bottles and blatantly evaluated her cleavage with furrowed brows.

"For Pete's sake," Pia had said, "of course you're going to meet drunken idiots in a bar."

She had a point. So Muriel sat on benches in Riverside Park reading *National Geographic*. She took an investment class at the 92nd Street Y and a guided medicinal herb tour in Chinatown. She even gave church a go. Sunday mornings were no longer slated for reading every word of the *Times*. Muriel paid homage to the heavenly father by singing hymns and smiling beatifically at St. Patrick's Cathedral instead of eating Zabar's crumb cake in bed on her frayed towel. She thumbed through the Bible for divine direction and swallowed the obvious hypocrisy when it rose like bile in her throat. *Judge not lest ye be judged*? Who on God's green earth was more judgmental than a Christian? *Live and let live*? What about gay marriage? Or atheism?

Muriel even bought two Grace Kellyish sweater sets—one butter yellow, the other Easter pink—and spent an ungodly amount of money and time in a midtown salon stripping the brown out of her hair and looking like Big Bird until they recolored it chilled chardonnay blond. Dark roots instantly spread like Ebola. Mirrors startled her. Her face looked as round as Charlie Brown's without its brunette boundary. She couldn't wait to save enough money to color it back.

This foray into holy towheadedness had not been entirely fruitless. The previous year, she'd met a man named Kent at a singles event in an overlit Unitarian church basement near her apartment. He'd made her laugh by introducing himself as "Bond. Kent Bond." A line he'd probably used a thousand times.

"Sullivant. Muriel Sullivant," she'd replied, tucking a strand of chilled chardonnay behind her ear, hoping her dark root line didn't look too skid markish.

"Muriel?"

"Clearly, my parents were on drugs."

"Mine never grew up. My middle name is Clark."

Muriel overlaughed and Kent ate it up. He had a pleasant enough face and a squishy body that felt comforting to hug. He liked the same things Muriel did: Netflix, flavored popcorn, free theater tickets, and Ollie's takeout. He asked her out. She said yes. Over dinner, they shared stories about a twentysomething's life in Manhattan.

"I have three roommates!" said Kent.

"I can cook, wash my dishes, and grab a gallon of ice cream out of my freezer without moving one inch," Muriel volleyed back.

Kent and Muriel dated, hit it off, then created two butt-shaped divots in her bed in front of the TV. Their sex life was silent and painless, rarely lasting longer than a commercial break.

"You good?" Kent would ask, breathless and flat on his back after six pumps and a grunt.

"Sure. Good. Great."

Great? Muriel berated herself for lying. Wasn't forthrightness the hallmark of a mature relationship? Hadn't Dr. Phil once said that very thing? Or perhaps she'd read it in the same magazine that advised low-cal, classy vodka. If she was truly forthright, "good" was in another universe when it came to Kent's sexual skills. Even "adequate" was skirting earth's outer atmosphere. But Muriel was emerging from a prolonged sexual drought and wasn't up on the current protocol. If your boyfriend was bad in bed, was it bad form to tell him? And how, exactly, did one go about that?

"You good?"

"Define 'good.'"

"You know, satisfied. Spent."

"Spent? Um, no."

"Sheesh. I had a great time."

"Yes, I see that."

"You didn't?"

"Define 'didn't.'"

Clearly, there were pitfalls galore. If a boyfriend wasn't particularly curious about—or interested in—his girlfriend's nether regions how did said girlfriend negotiate a better deal? "I'll climb on top if you'll meander downtown?" Muriel had always been awful in business.

After a few months, Muriel decided that sex with Kent was like pizza. Even the worst slice was better than starvation. Bond, Kent Bond, was a good nuzzler and loved to fry bacon on a whim in the middle of the night.

High flying, adored. So famous, so easily.

Nothing can thrill you. No one fulfill you.

Together, they sang lyrics from *Evita*. Muriel would probably still be with him had their relationship not taken a uniquely New York City turn.

"So, Muriel, by *law*, your lease passes on to a spouse?"

"Feel like ordering in tonight?"

"And 'spouse' is defined as marriage alone?"

"I'm thinking Thai."

"Can it be a civil union? Or, say, common-law?"

"*Mee grob* eaten off my bare belly. Grrr."

"If you think about it, possession is nine-tenths of the law. Why do we have to do anything as boringly legal as *marriage*? Can't we change the locks? I have a little money saved up for court costs if it comes to that."

"What are you saying?"

Kent got down on one knee. "I want to take our relationship to the next level."

"Are you asking—?"

"Yes. Will you add me to your lease?"

Shortly after Muriel changed the locks on *Kent*, she fell back into herself the way an animal-shaped rubber band returns to its original contour. She restored her brown hair and funereal wardrobe and explained to God that St. Patrick's Cathedral was all the way across town. The *Times* crossword puzzle *alone* took up an entire Sunday. What, He wanted her to get Alzheimer's?

At the bus stop with her angelic sister, Muriel tugged at the scarf knot around her neck and felt anger rising in her chest. A *scarf*? And a white dress? Had Pia not noticed her uncovered clavicle all these years, the turtleneck gifts that went unworn even in New York's iciest winters? How could she insist Muriel wear a pink and orange scarf over transparent white cotton? Had the woman never noticed her crow-colored wardrobe? Had her sister never even seen her at all?

Cursing the MTA for its obvious indifference to paying passengers, Muriel decided that as soon as they were comfortably seated on the bus, she would act like the woman she was instead of the little girl she felt like around Pia and make her move. Untying the scarf with purpose, she would say, "This is really more you than me." Period. She would give it back. Then she would take a deep breath and confidently address the elephant between them.

"Why exactly are you here?" she would ask. "What exactly do you want from me?"

Yes, that's exactly what she'd do.

Chapter 12

NOT THE SLIGHTEST bit apologetic for being late, the bus driver grinned and said, "Hello, ladies." Muriel dipped her MetroCard twice, paying for her Connecticut sister, but refused to return the driver's smile even as Pia chirped about the glorious day and let her fingers lightly touch his arm.

"Here." Once they were seated Muriel handed Pia an antibacterial wipe. "How many germy New Yorkers touched that driver's very same arm?"

Pia responded with a condescending pat on Muriel's bare knee. A touch that Muriel promptly sterilized as well. "I have another wipe in my purse if you need it," she said. Pia simply smiled that faraway smile she used to signal the end of a conversation.

Sitting side by side, gently bumping shoulders at every red light, the sisters watched the Upper West Side pass in a slide show of urban/suburban splendor. Riverside Drive—one of the prettiest streets in the city—was a well-kept homage to the beauty of old New York. The air smelled as soft as meringue. Sunshine reflected pink off the brownstone windows. Hexagonal pavers on the park side created a Parisian-style promenade with teak-and-wrought-iron benches placed beneath mature London plane trees whose trunks looked like elephant legs. Beyond the green strip of park, the Hudson River flickered in the afternoon sunlight like a new box of tinsel. If not for the ugly huddle of Trump monstrosities south of Seventy-second Street, the western edge of the upper island would be a postcard.

Muriel pressed her lips together in a determined way and reached up to loosen the damn scarf. "Really, Pia," she said, inhaling, "this is much more yo—what's wrong?"

Pia's eyes were wet with tears. For a moment, she couldn't speak. Muriel stared at the quiver of her throat as she swallowed, her hands like seal fins, ill-defined flaps of skin jutting out from her wrists. Should she *hug* her sister? Comfort her in some way?

"I'm glad we didn't take a cab," Pia said, swiping her lower lashes with the ring finger of her right hand. "I'd forgotten how pretty your neighborhood is." Reaching an arm around Muriel's shoulders, she pulled her close and held her tightly. A startled Muriel let her body crumple over as Pia kissed the top of her head. She stared down at the strained buttons of her white dress. The scarf stayed put.

"Are you okay?" she finally asked.

"Fine."

"Sure?"

"I'm sure."

Of course she believed her. Pia was always sure.

St. John's Cemetery—the multiacre sprawl of headstones and weeping statuary along Metropolitan Avenue, where mobster John Gotti is buried—was the liveliest part of Middle Village, Queens. According to Lidia Sullivant, that is. She never tired of reminding her husband and the rest of her family how much she'd rather be on the other side of the East River.

"Where the *living* live," she often said.

One winter Saturday in their Middle Village row house, young Muriel heard her mother's precise footfalls down the hardwood stairs. It was her favorite day. No school. No church. Her homework was already done. But the clipped sound of Lidia's spiked heels coming toward the kitchen quickened her pulse. Even though it was lunchtime, she considered tossing her peanut butter sandwich in the trash.

"How soon can you get dressed up?"

"Me?"

Owen was sudsing a paintbrush at the sink. His back tensed at the sound of his wife's voice. Through the kitchen window Muriel spotted her teenage brother, Logan, fussing with wires and sparks on the back porch. She thought, *Pia must be out somewhere with her friends.*

"Yes you, silly. Would you like to see a real Broadway show?"

As if waiting for the punch line, Muriel stared up at her mother and blinked. She took a big swig of milk and felt the painful descent of a wedged wad of peanut butter and bread. Wearing a steel-gray wool pantsuit and matching shoes with pointy toes and heels, Lidia stood with a fur-lined Burberry trench draped over her arm. "Well?" she said, impatiently. "Want to go or not?"

"Do I!"

Grabbing the remains of her sandwich, Muriel scrabbled up the stairs. Silently, Lidia took the newspaper off the kitchen table and waited for her daughter in the front room.

It was a cold December day. Mother and daughter hurried to the subway stop a few blocks away, red cheeked and chilly. Lidia carried her fancy shoes in a fancy tote. They took the M train to Wyckoff Avenue, then transferred to the L line, which rumbled aboveground through Queens before descending into the tunnel below the East River. Owen had been mistaken. It *wasn't* a straight shot from Middle Village to midtown Manhattan. There were transfers and gum-splotted station platforms. The air belowground reeked of scummy water and human decay. Had driving through Times Square not been so atrocious and parking not so absurdly expensive, Lidia wouldn't have dreamed of setting foot on a subway train. Why, one time the linoleum floor on the train was so filthy she was loath to step on it! More often than not a homeless man, smelling of death itself, lay slumped in a corner. Plus there were all those welfare queens with their litter of children. Clearly they spent their government handouts on fried food and drugs. Why else would they look so bloated and so frequently forget to use birth control?

Of course, if Lidia was with Owen, she would insist he drive her into the city, drop her off at the curb in front of wherever they were going, and park nearby no matter what the cost. It was only right, after all. He did force her to live in Queens. With Muriel, however, the trains were good enough. The last thing she needed was to worry about tipping every open palm in a Manhattan parking lot and finding the garage again when there were so many identical garages hidden in the bowels of every high-rise.

For Muriel, that frosty Saturday afternoon with her mother was the best day of her life. She couldn't stop smiling. She loved everything about subways and trains—the way their rhythmic growl pummeled her chest, the side-to-side shimmy, the salty taste of grit in the underground air. All those interesting people with their braided hair and puffy jackets. To her, trains sounded determined, as if tracks were a mere suggestion of where a train might choose to go on its own. A subway car might loosen its own third rail and take off one day, not caring in the slightest who was onboard. Trains were the sound of freedom, of escape.

Beneath her best coat, Muriel wore a green velvet dress with satin trim. A gift from her grandmother Piacek Jula—Pia's name-sake. The dress was too young for her, the kind of overfussy dress a flower girl wears to a wedding, then never again, but Muriel wore it anyway because she knew it would please her mother. She also knew the next time she saw her *babcia*, her grandmother would ask, "How did it fit? Was it too tight?" Family members were always asking Muriel if her clothes were too tight. As if they didn't have eyes in their very own heads.

Sitting on the hard plastic seat, with her shoulder touching her mother's, Muriel felt utterly grown up in spite of her snug little-girl dress. They faced the window, rocking in tandem with the *ba dum ba dum* sound of the tracks below. Muriel wanted everyone on the train to see that she was with her mother on the way into New York City. Just the two of them on an outing to see a real live Broadway show—without Pia to hoard her mother's hand and affection, without Owen to silently hover or Logan to darken the day with his sulking.

Though cold out, it was warm and thick aired inside the train. Queens flickered past like a flip-book. Puffy graffiti tags defaced the metal underpasses, paint flaked off the brick faces of dirty walk-ups. The apartments along the elevated tracks were so close you could see life inside: flickering TV sets, kettles billowing steam. Scanning the gauzy curtains for faces, Muriel saw an old lady with pink curlers in her hair and a man in an undershirt with an ashy cigarette dangling from his lips. *Their windows must rattle when the train passes*, she thought. Did they feel the same rumble in their chests, the same longing to get out?

"How do they sleep, Mama, with the noise of the train?"

"Keep your voice down, Muriel."

In the tunnel beneath the East River, the rail joints echoed loudly off the greasy tiled walls. Muriel twisted herself around to look out the window for orange sprays of sparks, the flare of a used Kleenex tossed carelessly onto the track. She felt a rush of exhilaration with the metallic scraping of the train's brakes. What if it didn't stop? *Couldn't* stop? And how did they get heat into a string of subway cars a block long? Did trains ever crash into each other? Hit head-on? Did a maid come through in the middle of the night and scrub the scuffed-up floors? Did she work all night and sleep all day and never see her children when they came home from school? Did her kids feel like they had no one at all?

"Do orphans have no *mother*, or no parents period?"

"Sit up straight, Muriel. Your dress is getting crushed."

By the time Lidia and Muriel arrived at the Times Square station, it was about twenty minutes before curtain. The underground air smelled vaguely of vomit. Muriel covered her nose with one mittened hand, gripped her mother's open palm with the other. Most of the travelers around them were in a rush to catch a train, make a connection, or exit up the stairs into the cold. Like a giant polka, people automatically sidestepped one another, except for the leaners who rested against riveted support beams with their hands out and their eyes glazed over, or the man in the corner with white crust around his mouth and a droopy coat hanging off one shoulder, its lining loose.

"Don't stare," Lidia said, though she really meant, "Don't look." Lidia believed you could make bad things disappear by looking the other way.

Outside, the afternoon air was the color of lead. Muriel's cheeks stung instantly. The theater was only three blocks from the subway stop, but they were swarming with humanity. The sidewalk was crunchy with tiny salt rocks after the previous day's snow. Hardened ice mountains along the curb were black topped with soot and backfire. Yet there was a distinctive kindness in the air. Bonded by the 9/11 attacks three months earlier, New York City had suddenly become a small town.

"Let me help you with that."

"No, after *you*."

"Lovely day, isn't it?"

Everywhere were previously unfamiliar conversations. Nowhere was the city's new Mayberry veneer more apparent than in Times Square. Once filled with neon signs promising GIRLS! GIRLS! GIRLS! and faded posters featuring topless women with black bars covering the nipples on their watermelon breasts, Times Square had morphed into Disneyland's Broadway. The billboard sky drew Muriel's eyes upward even as Lidia bulldozed through the crowds pulling her daughter behind her. They passed tourists with cameras pressed to their faces, caricaturists, a manly looking girl shivering in hot pants, someone in a giant red Elmo suit, and several sidewalk vendors with hunched shoulders who shifted left and right on their duct-taped sneakers. Young Muriel had never seen so many different people in such a small space. It was beyond thrilling. She wouldn't have been surprised to see a procession of elephants galumphing down the center of the street. Only when the throng spontaneously erupted in applause as two New York City firefighters were spotted on the street did Lidia stop and become part of the people around her.

"I see why you want to live here, Mama," Muriel said, adoringly. But her mother didn't reply. She only smiled in a sad sort of way.

When they finally got to the theater, it was close to curtain. Through the golden doors, in the warm interior, Muriel gasped when she saw the green and orange swirls in the painted ceiling, the gilded molding, the glowing chandelier, the braided gold fringe at the bottom of the red velvet curtain. She burrowed into the soft worn chenille upholstery on her seat and put her hand on her chest to feel the thudding of her heart. It felt like she was sitting inside a jewelry box, as if she, herself, were a pearl. Inside that theater, the outside world disappeared. No longer was she a lonely and chubby kid.

With her *Playbill* sitting pristinely on her knees, Muriel softly folded her hands on her lap and beamed at her beautiful mother. At last Lidia genuinely smiled back and Muriel felt a rush of warmth wash over her. What a lucky girl. That magical Saturday belonged to *them* and no one else. It was a mother-daughter special day that was all hers. So there.

At that moment the lights in the theater blinked. Stragglers were escorted to their seats. Muriel felt the shift in the crowd as everyone settled in. Purses were snapped shut, throats were cleared. Cellophane crinkled as hard candies were unwrapped. Facing front, she listened to the mess of notes as the orchestra tuned up.

That's when it happened. It was less than an instant, really, though it felt as long as life itself. The houselights faded to black. A complete eclipse of light. The curtain swept open sideways. *Swoosh.* The silence was so thick it was audible. In that solitary moment of absolute stillness between the last sputter of light and the first chord of music, Muriel felt the most exhilarating sensation. She was completely *aligned*. Amid a collectively held breath, in the middle of a sea of tilted heads, she felt a pure sense of containment, an utter oneness with the world. Her brain didn't buzz with unanswered questions, her waist didn't strain against her clothing, her feet didn't feel too big for her ankles, and her nose wasn't too large for the allotted space on her face. In that single moment of weighted anticipation—like the last second before sleep, before waking up in a dream—Muriel's heart ceased to beat with the longing to be someone else. To be Pia, her perfect sister. For the first time in her young life, she felt present and accounted for.

Though she didn't know it then, Muriel would fall into her fate that Saturday afternoon. Or fate would fall on her. By the time the cast twirled onto the stage she would be hooked for life.

With a gut-lurching jolt, the orchestra flared. The stage lights blazed yellow. Transfixed, Muriel was so immersed in the colorful wonder unfolding before her eyes, she barely noticed when her mother leaned over and whispered, "Be right back," and didn't return until intermission.

Chapter 13

THE M5 BUS rumbled down upper Broadway, past the green glass walls of Julliard and the illuminated grand stair in front of Lincoln Center. Through the window Muriel watched her city pass by: a Duane Reade drugstore, salad bar deli, nail spa, dry cleaners, bank, another bank, and, of course, a Starbucks. The same pattern repeated all over the island.

Pia said, "So much to do." Then she sighed.

Muriel agreed. New York was great that way. It was a comfort knowing the whole world was outside her door—well, down four flights and east two blocks—if she ever felt like entering it.

Uncharacteristically reaching down to squeeze her hand (what was with all this *touching*?), Pia softly smiled and stared out the window. Muriel recrossed her ankles and fastened a casual look on her face. Now that her sister's tears had dried up, she prepared herself to say, "Let's get this over with, sis. Why are you here?" Though of course she'd never use the word "sis" and had no idea why she'd even thought of it. Next she'd call something "fabulous."

They hit traffic near Columbus Circle, but the driver skillfully knit through crisscrossing cabs to pass the vertical mall and loop around the elliptical plaza. Fountains were spurting skinny arcs of water; purple spires of *Liriope* and persimmon-colored buds of *Cotoneaster* decorated the bases of honey locust trees. After they turned right on Central Park South, Muriel both saw and smelled the line of hansom cabs waiting for tourists, their hairy-footed horses scraping the asphalt with crusty yellowed hooves.

"So, what brings you to our fair land?" she blurted out, instantly biting the inner flesh of her lip and cursing her idiocy. "I mean, to what do I owe the honor?" Turning her head away, Muriel wanted to leap out the window and throw herself under the bus tire. Why all semblance of human personality deserted her around her older sister she hadn't a clue. In the same way she could never comprehend why she gobbled up free samples of mini bagel bites at Costco even though gluten immediately gave her a stomachache. Some things were just mysteries of life.

Subtly sliding her hand out from beneath Pia's, she released a nervous spew of conversational buckshot. "Of course it's always great to see you. Especially on such a beautiful day. It really is so very lovely outside, don't you thi—?"

Pia reached up and stroked Muriel's cheek with the backs of her first two fingers. It shut her up instantly. Not sure what else to do, Muriel let her face hang there like a bolt of sateen. *Was Pia checking for exfoliation?* Good God, would the nightmarish day never end? Smiling softly again, Pia covered her mouth and coughed, resettling her hand in her lap. Then she returned her million-mile gaze through the bus window. After a lifetime of memorizing her sister, Muriel knew it was useless pushing Pia to talk before she was ready. It was the frustrating trait of a person who'd never known the loneliness of not being listened to.

"I can't wait to see the grand spot you've chosen for lunch," Pia said, at last. By then, the bus was almost at Fifth Avenue. Lurching into traffic, they turned the corner and stopped across the street from FAO Schwartz. Muriel stood up. "This is us."

Pia looked out the window. "Bergdorf's?"

"Follow me."

Tugging the white shirtdress over her hips and adjusting the suffocating scarf, Muriel led her sister down the bus steps and back up Fifth Avenue a few yards before turning to walk across a cobblestone square past the Pulitzer Fountain of the naked goddess Pomona.

"Ah, Muriel," Pia said, stopping. "It's perfect."

Muriel beamed. It felt good to please someone who was so hard to please. Thank God she'd read the *New York Times* review.

"You can't smell the horses inside."

Together the two sisters walked toward the regal red carpet leading to the fabulous entrance of the Plaza Hotel.

IT WAS IMPOSSIBLE not to feel grand or magnificent or glorious or splendid at the pitch-perfect blending of old and new known to all New Yorkers as "The Plaza." The front steps are so alluring they practically suck you through the shiny brass revolving door. Overhead, a black lacquered molding is filigreed in gold. It probably isn't real gold, but it might as well be.

"Ladies." As if welcoming Cinderella to the ball, a gloved doorman bowed his head slightly when Pia flitted up the red-carpeted stairs. Not far behind, Muriel attempted her own light-footed flit. In his top hat with its gold-braided trim, the doorman looked like an actor onstage. The "Be My Guest" scene in *Beauty and the Beast*, or, more accurately, *Grand Hotel*. Muriel felt the same fluttery anticipation she felt right before the curtain rose on Broadway. For a moment she forgot about the tugging buttons of her dress.

"Glorious day," she said to the doorman, sounding not one bit ridiculous. Gallantly, he swept his arm across his chest and replied, "Indeed."

The Sullivant sisters leaned into the heavy rotating door and pushed themselves through time. In the central lobby, Pia stopped cold and gasped. Muriel nearly toppled into her.

"Oh, my," Pia said. "I haven't been here in ages."

Overhead, a crystal chandelier as large and shiny as a new car sent snowflakes of pearly light dancing about the square lobby. Milky bellflowers in a huge center vase infused the air with the aroma of harvested hay. Their soft petals were an explosion of violet. Pia's heels sank into the thick floral rug. Tourists and guests entered through the revolving door and sidestepped her. The rubber strip along the edge of the circulating entrance *flap*, *flapped* with each revolution.

"It's this way," Muriel said, but her sister didn't budge. As if standing alone, Pia dropped her shoulders and tilted her head back to see the ornate white ceiling. Her handbag dropped down to her fingertips; her lips went slack. The dappled light powdered the length of her satiny neck. She let her eyelids fall shut as if imagining a *Downton Abbey* sort of world where women wore silk shoes and teardrop earrings and diamond-studded hair clips to dinner. Their men retired to the study after dining to smoke cigars and sip cognacs and furrow their foreheads over the sorry state of England.

Next to her sister, Muriel studied the mosaic tiles along the edge of the lobby's red floral rug. "I never did stay here," Pia finally said in a whisper.

"You still can. Only part of it was made into condos."

"Yes. Well." Pia opened her eyes.

Together, the sisters made their way to the rear of the hotel, past a jaw-dropping side lobby, its marble floor so polished you could apply lipstick in its reflection. They circled around the famous Palm Court with its sky-high stained-glass ceiling curved upward like a colossal bejeweled brooch. It cast an ethereal yellow light onto the white-linened tables. Pia ran her fingers along the carbonite stone wall in the long hallway and said, "Isn't God amazing? Creating man with the ability to imagine this?"

"Conrad Hilton, one of the owners years ago, destroyed the original stained-glass ceiling to install air-conditioning. God created him, too."

Pia didn't respond.

A brass-edged escalator carried the sisters down to the basement level, where they were going to have lunch. Like a secret city, it was a Gatsbyesque expanse of shops and gourmet food, an unearthed treasure of chocolate, pizza, elaborate millinery, custom perfumes, sushi, charcuterie, oysters, artisanal cheese, coffee, and cupcakes. Anything anyone with style could ever want to eat or buy.

"Two for lunch?"

A hostess greeted them at the Food Hall—a huge open room dotted with high communal tables and curving Carerra marble counters. Each counter faced a food station, though as the hostess explained, "You can order anything you want at any station."

Before Muriel could request a quiet corner away from the noise, Pia said, "Seat us in the middle of the action." Shrugging, Muriel followed the hostess to two bar chairs in front of a large sizzling grill. One of the grill chefs clacked his tongs in greeting. Two older men in suits that cost more than Muriel's monthly rent looked up when the sisters sat down.

"Ladies," they said in unison.

"Gentlemen," Pia replied in a Marilyn Monroe sort of way. Muriel blushed even as the men ignored her. Many times she'd witnessed the way a man's gaze lingered on her sister. At thirty-one—precariously close to New York's expiration date—Pia was still asked for her phone number. Muriel, eight years younger, was asked for directions. Never had Pia been a woman unseen. Men wanted her in their limo, on their arm, in their bed.

"Any chance we can buy you ladies lunch?"

Muriel quietly fluffed her scarf, allowing her sister to let the men down easy. The man nearest Pia—with his tan hands and spangly watch—looked at Pia alone. While attractive *enough*,

Muriel was the sort of woman men looked *through*. They saw their iPhone messages clearly, or the swivel of young hips in tight pencil skirts, but men rarely noticed Muriel unless they were standing opposite her in Joanie's office trying to land a part. Even then Muriel was convinced most male actors gazed deeply into her eyes merely in the hope of spotting their own tiny reflections.

"Why not?" Pia said, causing Muriel's mouth to fall open like an unlatched basement window. "Unless you're Hindu," she added gaily, "you only live once."

Both men erupted in laughter and the tanned one flagged down the waiter. "I'm Richard, and this is my business partner, Edward," he said, reaching out to shake Pia's hand.

"I'm Sonny, and this is my sister, Cher."

They laughed again. Muriel laughed, too. How could you not? When she wanted to, Pia could wring charm out of the air itself. As could their mother. When she wanted to.

 # Chapter 14

"C'MON, SLOWPOKE!"

Pulling her mother's arm behind her, Muriel expertly weaved through the weekend crowds in Times Square.

"I'm on your tail, cowgirl!"

Saturday matinees had become a tradition. A *tradition*. Muriel was beside herself with joy. They caught the L train into the city, interlocking fingers on the subway. Together, Lidia and her younger daughter dashed up Broadway through the winter's cutting air, the breezy warmth of spring, the perfect limbo of fall. On those Saturdays Muriel felt positively carbonated, as if she'd once been an orphan and was now an only child.

"Giddy up, Mama. We don't want to miss curtain."

"Yeehaw!" On rare occasions, Lidia even *skipped*.

With her chin lifted, Muriel felt superior to the unfortunate people without loving mothers like hers. She felt sorry for her siblings, too. Their mother had chosen *her*—not her tongue-clucking sister, not her brother Logan who rammed headlong into people on the sidewalk because he never looked up from his feet. Not even Owen, who never kissed her mother on the lips. Clearly, he didn't cherish his wife the way a husband ought to. The way it was onstage. Lidia wanted Muriel—and only Muriel—to escort her into the city on their special Saturdays.

Instantly Muriel forgave her mother for treating her so off-handedly all her life. They dressed in fancy outfits. Lidia, elegant in her double-strand pearl choker; Muriel, all grown up in a pashmina shawl. They were two girlfriends on the town, together at last. It didn't matter that Lidia had once blatantly preferred Pia. Those days were over. It was now Muriel's turn. Her sense of living on the outskirts of her family was gone for good. At last, *she* was the special one.

"I love you, Mama."

"You, too, *moje kochanie*."

Muriel knew well what love looked like; she'd seen it from the orchestra section—the way the Phantom gazed at Christine through his mask while she sang in her soft pink spotlight, how Curly and Laurey followed their hearts despite the turmoil in the entire state of Oklahoma! That was *love*. Even con man Harold Hill changed his whole life for Marian the librarian in *The Music Man*. They didn't know what love *was* till there was them.

True love was selfless and forever, lit with cool blue gels and accompanied by violins and sometimes cellos. Love was passionate and heartfelt and sung full out up to your lover's face, touching noses almost. Genuine love was harmony. No fear of a cracking voice or hitting the wrong note. No self-consciousness. And as the music swelled, love was expressed in an urgent kiss that melded two faces, lips pressed on lips, transcending all conflict. Nothing like the listless pecks her father deposited on her mother's cheek before he left for work. The same type of kiss with which Muriel grazed Babcia Jula's papery skin, her nose wrinkled and her lips pinched because she hated the smell of mothballs and lilac perfume. Real love was nowhere near anything she'd witnessed or experienced at home.

Even as a girl, Muriel saw that her parents' marriage was a lie from its first two words: "I do." Neither willingly did anything the other wanted to do. Lidia wanted to move into the city or back to Rhode Island, Owen dreamed of living on an isolated ranch in Montana. Lidia loved shopping, Owen loved playing chess. Lidia wouldn't even consider buying her husband's slacks at Sears.

"What's *wrong* with wearing silk?" she once asked Owen, who simply stared at her in disbelief.

"Do you actually think I'm the silk-wearing sort?"

From the start, the Sullivant marriage was a series of silent fulminations. Basement doors were slammed, cold dinners were dumped in the trash, hardwood stairs were pounded upon, grudges were locked in eyebrows. Owen Sullivant had been flailing from year one. Fatherhood struck him so abruptly he felt the pull of his previous life the way an amputee feels an itch on a phantom limb. One day a petite blonde is on top of you—on top!—the next day you cease to exist.

"Hand me that diaper, will you?"

"The one with the bear on it?"

"Ach. I'll get it myself."

Always able to fix what was broken, Owen was completely at sea.

"A man needs a son," said Father Camilo, the Pawtucket parish priest to whom Lidia confessed, "My husband is distant and silent."

Through the confessional lattice, he said, "A marriage built with mortar requires cement." Father Camilo's wisdom brought Lidia back to her home church in Rhode Island every month or two.

"Go home and be his wife," he said.

"I don't love him," she whispered.

"Holy matrimony is God's covenant for life."

She leaned close. "How do I endure?"

Father Camilo paused only slightly before advising, "Give him a son. A man needs a son."

So Lidia got busy. She bought a digital thermometer and a small notebook. Beginning with the first day of her menstrual cycle, she noted her body temperature when she first woke up. Before her feet touched the floor. Religiously she kept a chart. She hid Owen's condoms in the bottom of her jewelry box.

"What the deuce?" he said, rifling through the drawer in his bedside table. In the first years of their marriage, they made love Saturday afternoons, like clockwork. Lidia charted that, too. Her reward for accepting her husband inside her was ordering dinner delivery from Uvarara, their favorite Italian restaurant on Metropolitan Avenue. On sex day she didn't have to cook.

"We don't need that silly thing," Lidia said in the kittenish way Owen hadn't heard since before Pia was born. She shut the drawer next to his side of the bed and rolled over onto her back. "It's time we were proper Catholics."

"But—" Owen was weak. He'd felt so lonely in his fledgling family he saw a life raft when Lidia whispered, "A son will change everything. I promise."

When Lidia didn't conceive right away, she turned to her mother for help. "Will you spend the weekend with Pia?"

"*Oczywiście.*" Of course.

Lidia organized a surprise trip to Cape May on the Jersey shore when her chart told her she was most fertile. The rhythmic insistence of the waves would get them both in the mood.

That night in the hotel bathroom, Lidia bathed and powdered herself and teased her hair at the crown and took a deep breath knowing her husband waited on the other side of the door with a bottle of sherry and two crystal glasses borrowed from the lobby bar.

"Ready for me?" she asked through the door.

Owen laughed nervously when he stated, "I believe I will be once we get going."

Though he tried to stifle it, he sighed. Before they were married, sex had never seemed like so much work. God forgive him, but the thought flew through Owen's mind that he'd rather be on the shore watching birds. A month later when Lidia announced, "I've missed my days," he felt faint. But eight months after that, Lidia turned out to be right. Everything did change. Owen had his first glimpse of effortless love. Logan Ennis Sullivant silently entered the world.

"Not a peep, this little peanut," Lidia had said, cradling her tiny infant son. Weighing only six pounds full term, Logan exited his mother's womb with his eyes wide open and one hand curled beneath his chin like Rodin's statue *The Thinker*. From the start he seemed to quietly evaluate his surroundings as if preparing for a pop quiz. He never wailed when his nose and mouth were suctioned, slept soundlessly in the hospital incubator. Once home, he stared at his parents with a penetrating expression.

"How can it be that a baby doesn't cry for his mother?" Lidia asked, unsure how to rear a child who didn't seem to need or want her. Lifting Logan out of her arms, Owen held him aloft and gazed into his baby's curious eyes. "He's my son."

That was that. Father Camilo had been right. Lidia had Pia and Owen had Logan. Muriel, conceived years later after a holiday party and too many flutes of champagne, belonged to no one. Even her cobwebbed name was carelessly chosen. "Who names a child Muriel? I mean, God, Mom."

"Don't use the Lord's name in vain, Muriel."

"An innocent baby. What did I ever do?"

"Muriel was your sister's choice," her mother told her.

"You let a *child* pick my name?"

"She saw it in a book I was reading. Very famous."

"The fat old lady in *Courage the Cowardly Dog*?"

"That's a cartoon, Muriel. I was reading *Animal Farm*."

"I'm named after an *animal*?"

Lidia looked bored and shrugged. "*To jest to, co to jest.*"

It is what it is.

Muriel's mother named her after a goat and raised her as an afterthought. Until their special Saturdays changed everything.

Chapter 15

IN A MATTER of minutes, Pia had consumed a full glass of Rioja, half a prime rib slider on brioche, a side of raw oysters with mustard aioli, and several Parmesan cheese fries.

"Oh my," Muriel said for the second time that day. Her sister had always been a frisée and grilled skinless chicken kind of girl. Dressing on the side. Club soda with lime.

"You only go around once," Pia said, licking her fingers.

Richard and Edward, the two men seated next to them, were enchanted. Muriel couldn't help but roll her eyes when metrosexual Richard, with his professionally buffed fingernails and man-scaped brows, said, "I love a woman who eats like a truck driver but looks like a socialite." It was such a bullshit male fantasy—effortless beauty. Muriel wanted to inform the two drooling men that Pia's looks were nothing *but* effort. She practically lived in a salon. She normally ate like a starved rabbit. If Pia had a job or no housekeeper or no rich husband to provide a limitless ATM card, she could never afford the time and money it took to look so effortless. Private Pilates classes, weekly manis and pedis, microdermabrasion, Botox, Restylane injections, full-body waxing, a trim and highlights every six weeks. And she *did* have a husband, by the way. In spite of the way she was acting. That's what Muriel wanted to say. Instead, to test her theory that some women were born with the ability to blind men, Muriel quietly smeared a little salad dressing on the tip of her thumb, then delicately licked it off. Both men turned away in disgust.

"Another round, please," Pia said, leaning back and draping her beautiful hand suggestively on the passing waiter's arm.

Having barely started on her first glass of wine, Muriel sucked in her stomach, curled her ragged fingernails into her palm, and muttered, "Not for me, thanks. I'm fine for now."

"Oh, Cher. Don't be such a stick."

Muriel willed her face not to register shock at Pia's bizarre new personality. As her sister frothed her flirtation, Richard and Edward laughed with their heads flung back and their Adam's apples bobbing up and down. They regarded Muriel in an infuriating *"Must you wear that?"* kind of way. She'd seen that look on her mother's face a million times. Dry mouthed, Muriel adjusted the linen napkin in her lap and took another forkful of the baby arugula salad with lemon vinaigrette she'd ordered in an attempt to appear petite.

"When you're not being a stick, what do you do for a living?" Edward asked, dutifully wedging her into the conversation he really wanted to have with her sister. Before Muriel could formulate an answer Pia said, "What does anybody really *do* for a living? Most of us just pass through."

"Duly noted," Richard said, revealing his job as a lawyer.

Personal injury, Muriel thought, duly noting Richard's tacky gold pinky ring. Edward never pressed the livelihood question, which bothered Muriel since most people were impressed by her job. At the very least they asked for Broadway recommendations. Of course, few knew that a casting assistant was really a glorified NERF ball. The soft frame off which bounced nerves and words. (Hard angles would never do in casting, not when there were so many hard feelings.) By the time the second round of wineglasses was delivered, she was again invisible.

Pia drowned another slider with hearty swigs of wine. A flap of prime rib dangled briefly between her white teeth before she sucked it into her mouth with a Hannibal Lecterish *thup thup* sort of sound. Muriel could hardly believe her eyes. She'd never seen her sister so crass before. It was unnerving. She seemed unhinged. Casually leaning close to her ear she whispered, "You okay?" Pia loudly replied, "Seriously, Muriel, you really do need to live a little."

"Muriel?" Richard raised both brows.

"Seriously, Muriel," Edward echoed, "why not live a little?"

She wanted to slap all three of them in their good-looking faces.

"My little sis is a fossil, I'm afraid," Pia said.

Muriel smiled fakely. "Just call me Maiasaura." When they all stared blankly, she was agog. Had they never seen *Jurassic Park* or *Dinosaur Week* on the Discovery Channel? Regrouping, Muriel flicked her lank brown hair in what she hoped was a lighthearted manner and said, "Living has always been Sonny's specialty."

A FUDGE-FILLED CHOCOLATE cake with hot fudge drizzle. That's what Muriel was thinking about one matinee Saturday while she sat alone in the theater during intermission watching the audience stand and stretch. Her mother disliked overdone chocolate, but Muriel thought it impossible.

"It's *chocolate*, Mama," she would say in the Times Square Applebee's. "The only thing better is more chocolate!" Lidia would smile patiently, her face flushed and joyful. Coffee and dessert after matinee Saturdays was the sole time Lidia didn't frown when Muriel was herself. Even though she drank black coffee while Muriel devoured her favorite triple chocolate meltdown, she never once asked her fleshy daughter, "You sure you want to eat that whole thing?" Dessert at Applebee's was almost as delicious as the Broadway shows themselves. It was their secret time together. Neither mother nor daughter needed to verbalize the fact that they didn't want to go home. Not just yet.

That particular Saturday intermission was the perfect day to be indoors, engulfed in the chilled cloud of a blasting air conditioner. The humid summer heat felt like sweatpants after a long jog. Lidia hadn't wanted to take the subway into the city earlier. "We'll look like wet rats," she said. That morning she'd washed and set her hair.

"C'mon, Mama," Muriel had whined.

Taking the car wasn't nearly as fun as the train. She couldn't sit shoulder to shoulder with her mother, breathing in her jasmine scent, snaking her fingers around her cool palm. In the car was a radio, a windshield, side mirrors to consult. Cars didn't travel under the East River in a tunnel that smelled like adventure itself.

Muriel had an idea.

"I'll go down to the platform first. The second I hear the train coming, I'll yell and you can run down."

It was the thick steamy air underground that made the subway unbearable. Lidia wore a blue silk dress that was so thin it looked like a ripple of water. Already it was hanging limply.

"Okay." Lidia stayed up top while Muriel swiped her brand-new MetroCard and positioned herself near the bottom of the stairs. Her mother had been right. The subway air did feel like a suffocating wet wool blanket. Instantly, her hair stuck to her head. The soles of her bare feet felt sticky in her sandals. Her purse, precisely big enough to hold a *Playbill*, was floppy in her hands. Minutes passed like ketchup from a narrow-necked bottle. Suddenly, her chest felt the familiar rumble of an oncoming train.

"Mama!"

Lidia scurried through the turnstile and down the stairs on her classic pumps in time to hear the train's doors *bing bong* open. Inside, the air-conditioning was blessed relief. "Ah," they both said at exactly the same time, as if they were exactly alike. Muriel scrambled to a seat with enough room to make sure they were close, but not so close her mother would pull away.

In Times Square that Saturday the gutters stank of dead water; the sky was the color of faded jeans. By now, Muriel knew the area better than her own neighborhood. Circumventing the weekend crowds, she led her mother in a roundabout way beneath the overhang of the Booth Theatre, through Shubert Alley, past the mounted show posters. Lidia's rakelike fingers felt warm in her daughter's hand, damp with summer trapped between their grip.

A throng milled about in front of the theater as always—men sucking on a final cigarette while their wives waited inside in the bathroom line, friends meeting with a cheek kiss, out-of-town theater parties disembarking from their chartered buses. Muriel marched right through the open doors. Behind her, Lidia handed the usher their tickets and followed her daughter into the frosty lobby. Programs in hand, they padded down the carpeted path to their seats—always on the aisle near the back of the middle orchestra section, exactly the way Lidia wanted it.

As if she'd arrived home after a long trip, Muriel melted into her seat and inhaled the familiar scent. Coffee, cologne, and that indefinable theater smell. Upholstery cleaner, maybe, or stage makeup? Burned dust from hot footlights? All she knew for certain was that she could be blindfolded and still know the moment she walked through the lobby doors of a Broadway house. Perhaps, she thought, it was the collective aroma of anticipation, a glandular preparation for the fact that *anything* could happen on a live stage.

"Know what that is, Mama?"

Muriel pointed up at a flickering light along the inner rim of the ornate oval ceiling.

Narrowing her eyes, Lidia said, "A fire hazard?"

"A ghost." Muriel had read all about theater ghosts in the library, how they haunted Broadway in the middle of the night. Long after the stagehands locked the props away and mopped the footprints off the stage, apparitions wandered the wings, some endlessly awaiting their entrance cues, strutting and fretting their hour upon the stage as in *Macbeth*. Others preferred to communicate directly with fresh audiences by "winking" with the houselights as they settled in their seats.

"It's going to be a good show," Muriel said, excited.

Nestling into the velvety cushion of her seat, she quietly waited for the lights to dim and the pure moment of transport to take her away. She never opened her program; reading it only wrinkled the pages. Instead, she unsnapped her handbag, pulled out a small manila envelope, and slid the program safely inside it. At home, she would insert the pristine program into a protective plasticine sheet and add it to her notebook—a chronicle of the best moments of her life. Where she *learned* about life, really. The way God meant the world to be, with love bursting straight from the heart, draped in colorful dresses that twirled like pinwheels. Kisses with such utter surrender the woman's neck bent all the way back, the very artery of her life exposed.

At last, the lights began to dim. The crowd went silent. In the fading houselights, Muriel let her eyelids droop, pressing them tight with the final flicker until she felt it. *It*. That singular moment of perfection in the collective silence, the promise of all that's possible. It was her favorite moment, the suspended nanosecond between the end of one reality and the beginning of another. In a weighted *whoosh* the curtain swept open, the orchestra struck its first chord, and Muriel opened her eyes to magic.

Lidia was already gone.

The first time Muriel noticed that her mother vanished as soon as the lights went out inside the theater, she had asked, naturally, "Where'd you go?" at intermission. Flushed and breathless, Lidia looked sheepish when she said, "Dawdle in the restroom and they won't let you back to your seat."

Another matinee day, when one of the dancers onstage did a backflip from a standing position, Muriel wanted to excitedly elbow her mother but the seat next to her was still empty. "You okay?" she asked when she found Lidia rushing in through the theater's front doors toward the end of the fifteen-minute break.

"Never better, *misiaczku*. I needed fresh air is all."

A few weeks later Lidia didn't take her seat at all before the show started. "My knee is bothering me," she had said in the lobby. "I'm going to stand in the back awhile." Muriel sat alone for the whole two hours because she never did spot her mother's silhouette. Perhaps she was in the bathroom again? The line *was* always long and that particular intermission did seem shorter than intermissions usually were.

"Did you take aspirin?" she asked her mother when they found each other after the show.

"Aspirin?"

"For your knee."

"Ah. Yes. Yes, I did." Quickly, Lidia added, "Ready to satisfy your sweet tooth?"

By the time *Mamma Mia!* opened, Lidia was leaving Muriel

alone in theaters as a matter of course. *What better babysitter?* she told herself. Muriel would never leave a show until the actors had bowed, dispersed to the wings, returned for an encore bow, and, if she was lucky, returned once more with their hands over their hearts, their lips folded over their teeth in feigned emotion, folding their torsos over their thighs then rising to blow kisses to the crowd roaring overhead in the mezzanine.

Eventually, Muriel grew accustomed to sitting alone in the dark. She stopped asking questions even though she'd seen lots of people follow the usher's tiny flashlight to their seats after a show began. Once she searched the restroom during intermission and examined the feet under every door. Ushers talked quietly to each other and looked at her with worry ridges in their foreheads. "Where are your parents, honey?"

"My mom has bad knees," Muriel would say, pointing to a random female figure in the back of the theater. As Muriel had discovered, whenever she waved, *someone* near the bar always waved back.

Afraid her special Saturdays would end if she made a fuss, she kept quiet. She made excuses for her mother. Probably, she had trouble sitting still. Maybe the view was better from . . . wherever she was.

Muriel told no one how hurt she felt. Why didn't her mother want to sit with her? She was grown up, honestly she was, never squirming or kicking the seat in front of her. Not once did she unwrap a candy after the show started or slyly open the program to try and read an actor's credits in the dark. When she didn't understand something that was said or sung onstage she kept it to herself until *after* the final curtain call when the whole audience was allowed to talk. Wasn't that the adult thing to do? Why did her mother prefer to be elsewhere, away from her, faded into the dark?

That Saturday's show, *Into the Woods*, was long, but Muriel could have sat there, transfixed, another hour or two. As the final curtain fell, she leaped to her feet along with everyone else, careful not to smash her handbag with its pristine *Playbill*. One by one, the actors bowed. Muriel stepped into the aisle to see them better. Cinderella, Florinda, Lucinda, Little Red Riding Hood. Who would smile? Who stayed in character? Which actor crumpled forward like a rag doll, who barely nodded his or her head? It was her favorite part of any show—when the actors became themselves again. In their final bow, she could catch a glimpse of who they really were.

As soon as the ushers opened the side doors, sunlight flooded the theater. It was still daylight outside. Like slowly rolling marbles, the crowd found the nearest exit and spilled onto the street. Flushed with pleasure, Muriel shuffled to the back of the theater, searching for the customary flutter of her mother's hand. "Yoo-hoo!" Usually, it was easy to spot her—the lone static presence in a sea of moving heads. That day, though, everyone was moving. Perhaps Muriel was blinded by the sudden light?

At the back of the theater, Muriel stepped out of the human current leading to the outside. Digging at a hangnail with her teeth, she waited beneath the mezzanine staircase.

Stay put. That's what Lidia had said when Muriel wandered off at Six Flags a few years earlier on a family trip. Her mother was angry that day, had grabbed Muriel's upper arm and shaken it so hard it hurt all day. "You'll *never* be found if you move."

So she didn't move. She stayed put and watched people file past her. They chattered words like "magnificent" and sang songs from the show.

"Careful the thing you say, children will listen . . ."

Everyone was more alive than they had been when they came in. Which was why Muriel adored the theater. In the dark, you could be reborn. Your imperfect life could be exchanged for a brand-new model.

"You okay?" An usher appeared as the crowd thinned out. She wore black slacks and a black shirt. Removing her fingernail from her mouth, Muriel flashed a thumbs-up. "Never better."

"Where are your parents, honey?"

"My mom's, uh, in the bathroom."

Insecurity had sneaked into her voice. It surprised her. Not until she spoke it out loud was she sure it was a lie. At that instant, Muriel knew her mother wasn't in the theater at all. She cleared her throat. "She'll be out any minute."

"Wait here." The usher descended the stairs to the ladies' room, a stack of programs still clutched to her chest.

At that point the lobby was nearly empty. Muriel's cheeks flushed. More than anything, she didn't want the usher to know that Lidia had left her alone. As if she didn't want to be seen with her. As if sitting next to her younger daughter for two hours was an unbearable chore. She felt ashamed. How could she explain to a stranger that their Saturdays were *special*? They had their own rules. It wasn't like her mother had squeezed herself through the bathroom window and dropped to the alley below, the only remnant of her a torn piece of fabric caught on the windowsill's bent nail. Muriel *knew* her mother wasn't there. She hadn't run out on her, for God's sake.

"Do you have a cell phone?" the usher asked, returning all sad faced.

"No."

"Does your Mom have one?"

"Yes."

"Do you know her number?"

"Of course." She was eleven, not five.

As the usher dug through her pockets for a pen, the blood in Muriel's red cheeks betrayed her. Gripping her purse with both hands, she said, "I just remembered. Mama asked me to wait for her outside."

"Hold on, dear, let me—"

Without waiting for a discussion, Muriel pivoted toward the heavy brass exit, her sandals catching on the plush theater carpet as she scurried out. If they called her mother, she'd be in trouble for sure. And she so wanted to see *Hairspray* when it opened.

Afraid the usher might follow her, Muriel rushed out the doors and ran up to Seventh Avenue half a block away. There, she pressed herself against a concrete wall behind a curve in the building, her heart thudding. Not sure what else to do, she stood there breathing hard. *You'll never be found if you move.* Lidia's voice ran on a loop inside her head. *Stay put.*

She stayed put.

It was still warm out, though not as oppressive as it had been before the show. The late-afternoon sun was quickly fading to orange. Beneath her skirt, Muriel felt the flesh of her bare thighs press together. The rubber soles of her sandals stuck slightly to the gum-speckled sidewalk. In the corner where she stood, a faint smell of urine made her pull away from the wall. Leaning forward, Muriel peeked back at the theater. Thankfully, no one had followed her. But her heart sank when she saw that, soon, no one was there at all. The ushers stepped out and kicked up the stops that held the doors open. The theater folded into itself. As suddenly as the throngs of people had gathered before the show, all had disappeared now. Pedestrians passed by freely, no longer stepping into traffic to loop around the crowd. No one smoked a final cigarette nor kiss-kissed a friend's cheek. It was empty. In a matter of minutes, the beautiful theater became a building. Nothing more. *Poof!* The magic was gone. Muriel felt tears sting her cheeks. All of a sudden, loneliness swept over her. Her heart hurt.

"Watch?"

Muriel whipped her head around. A man selling watches from a briefcase suddenly stood next to her. The whites of his eyes were yellowish and he smelled like wet laundry.

"No, thank you," she said, gently tugging her skirt lower over her bare knees.

"Disney? Mickey Mouse? Rolex?"

"No, thank you."

"Swatch?"

"I don't have any money."

He snapped the briefcase shut and moved on though his

smell remained. Muriel gripped her purse with both hands and stared back at the front of the theater as if the intensity of her gaze could materialize a mother. She scanned each shape on the sidewalk for the familiar one she knew. She prayed, "Dear God, please bring my mama back soon." Without a clue about what else to do, she waited, staying put, sucking the flesh of her bottom lip, determined not to cry. Only babies cried. Isn't that what Pia always said? Grown-ups lifted their chins and focused on the next hurdle.

"It's called *composure*, Muriel. Look it up. Live it."

Tucked into the concrete corner, not touching the urine-stained wall, Muriel practiced composure. She acted like Pia. She stood diving-board straight, swallowed her tears and her fear, and waited for her mother in five-minute increments. *Is that her? That's her, isn't it? Hey, there's a blue dress. Is that Mama's blue dress?*

With each passing minute, the sidewalk grew grayer and the air thickened with the oncoming night. Mosquitoes buzzed by her ears. Muriel swatted them away with her purse, careful not to flap it too hard and bend the *Playbill*.

"You lost, little lady?" a vendor called out from behind his table full of sunglasses across the street.

"I'm waiting for my mom." Muriel coughed into her hand, hoping to erase the quiver in her voice.

"You been waiting there an awful long time."

"She told me not to move."

"Want me to call the police for you?"

"She'll be here any minute. She said to wait here."

"The cop station is right around that corner. About a block away. Smack-dab in the middle of the street. Can't miss it. Young girl like you shouldn't be out alone after dark."

Muriel nodded and promised to run to the police station if her mother didn't show up soon. Which, of course, was a lie. Never would she go to the police. Heavens, no. Muriel wasn't a baby; she knew how these things went.

"When did you last see your mother?"

"*Before* the show started?"

"How often does she leave you sitting alone?"

An outsider wouldn't understand their special Saturday matinees, how Lidia had bad knees and whatnot. It would be impossible to explain how mature she was, how she never talked *at all* during a show. Besides, didn't the police make you swear to tell the truth and nothing but? She would have to confess where she lived and recite phone numbers and they would call her parents and her dad would be mad at her mom and her mother would be mad at her and their special Saturdays would end for good.

Muriel peered around the edge of the building again and begged God to send her. *Probably,* she thought, *she's lost in Times Square.* Certainly it could feel like a maze at times. All those neon lights. People shoving fliers for comedy shows into your hands at every turn. Maybe somebody stole her mother's purse. Or she'd tripped off a curb and fallen into the gutter. Who could stand to wear the same clothes after that? The smell was disgusting even when the dead water was still on the street! She probably had to go shopping for a new dress. It couldn't be easy finding something nice to wear around there, not when the stores only sold tourist T-shirts with I ❤ NY on them. Probably, she'd taken a cab to Macy's and was stuck in traffic on the way back to pick her up that very minute.

Is that her? That's her, isn't it? Her dress was blue, wasn't it?

Was she waiting for her at Applebee's? Expecting her to go ahead and order her favorite triple chocolate meltdown? *It's chocolate, Mama. The only thing better is mo—*

Suddenly, at the far end of the block, across the street, Muriel saw a shape that was as familiar to her as the back of her own hand. A blue silk dress moved like a deep ocean swell. Uncombed blond hair bobbed up and down with each quick step. The woman seemed distressed, her eyes darted left and right. She walked in a near run. Behind her was a man. Holding her elbow, he steered her through the growing dinner crowd on the sidewalk. He, too, looked around, even behind. At that moment, the man tightened his grip on her mother's arm and pulled her into a doorway covered by a small green awning. She drew back, but he held firm. His free hand reached up and cupped the back of her neck, beneath her blond hair. He pressed his body against hers; she didn't resist. It looked as though she *melted* into him. Right up close to her face he said something. She nodded, looked away, then sprang back to him. With breathless proximity—the way Muriel had seen it a million times onstage—Lidia surrendered to the man's embrace with a Broadway kiss, her neck bent all the way back, the very artery of her life exposed.

Quickly, Muriel left the corner and ran back to the theater, her sandals slapping on the sidewalk, hoping her mother wouldn't turn in her direction and see her. With her chest heaving, she stood beneath the brightly lit marquis and faced in the other direction. Away from the doorway where her mother was pressed against a man who wasn't her dad. Hopefully she could make it true—bad things could disappear if you looked the other way.

"There you are!" Lidia said, running up behind her, winded. "I've been worried sick."

"Hello, Mama!" Muriel said, too brightly, her chest on fire with the attempt to conceal her panting.

"Was it a short show? I mean, shorter than normal? It *must* have been shorter than normal. I know shows are never *this* long, but, see, I had a horrible bout of claustrophobia. You know what that is, right? The whole world feels like it's closing in. Really, there's no cure other than fresh air and space. So, what could I do? I had to get out of there. I walked around the block, then around again. I completely lost track of time. Then I came back to pick you up and I couldn't see you anywhere. Were you in the restroom, *kochanie*? Maybe you went to Applebee's for ice cream cake?"

Muriel stood blank faced. She'd never heard her mother so talkative, never seen her hands flapping so birdlike in front of her face. As she spoke, she was out of breath, as if she was still running from the doorway. When she said, "I'm so, so sorry," she didn't *look* sorry at all. Her eyebrows weren't pressed together, her head wasn't bowed. Instead, she had the same look a dog has when you flip on the kitchen light and catch him digging through the trash.

"I never get ice cream cake at Applebee's," Muriel said.

"No? Okay then. Pie, pudding. You can have whatever you want."

Her heart slid downward in her chest. Tears rose in her eyes. In all the times they'd been together, had her mother never really seen her at all?

"I want to go home." Muriel opened and closed the snap on her purse. Her toes felt cold. She wanted to get on the train, get off at Metropolitan Avenue, walk to her house, climb the stairs to her room, shut the door behind her, and slide her feet into fuzzy slippers.

"Probably for the best," Lidia said, her voice up an octave. "Your father will be waiting."

They walked up to Broadway in silence. Instead of their usual extended route through Times Square in the colorful glow of neon, Lidia led her daughter to the smaller subway station on Fiftieth. "We'll transfer," she said in a clipped kind of way. The metal turnstile revolved with a definitive *thwunk*. Underground, the air was muggy and the overflowing trash can smelled like rotting bananas. For once, though, the train came fast. The doors opened and the two Sullivants stepped into the air-conditioning, taking the first two seats near the door. Muriel tried to make herself small so her shoulder wouldn't bump against her mother's when the train took off.

Before the M train screeched against the rail on its way below the East River, Lidia encircled her daughter's shoulder with her cool bare arm and pressed her lips to the top of her head. Muriel wished she could retract her neck like a turtle. Softly, into Muriel's hair, Lidia said, "There are things you need to know, sweetie, and things you don't."

Sweetie? She'd never called her "sweetie" before. Muriel stared at graffiti etched into the window on the other side of the subway car, imagining the boy who did that. In the middle of the night, with only his friends in the car to egg him on, he pulled a giant paper clip out of the small change pocket in his 501 jeans. Opening it like a penknife, he furiously scratched back and forth while his friends stood sentry at either end of the car. She could almost hear them laughing in that supercharged teen way.

The train tossed Muriel and her mother together like socks in a dryer. Lidia said, "Look at me," but Muriel stared straight ahead. Gently pinching her daughter's chin between her two fingers, Lidia tried to turn Muriel's head. Her fingernails were filed in a perfect U shape; her polish was the exact color of her skin. Bloodless and white. Muriel resisted until she felt her mother's nails dig into her flesh.

"You're almost grown up now, aren't you?" Lidia asked.

Muriel didn't answer. Head up, facing her mother, she noticed her lipstick was smeared beyond the borders of her lips. She wanted to say, "You'd better fix that before Dad sees it." But she didn't. She said nothing, kept staring at Lidia's lips, watching them move as she said, "Grown-ups can tell the truth without telling every detail of it."

Being a grown-up wasn't so hot, Muriel decided then and there. It meant absolute silence from curtain up to curtain down even when there was no one in the theater to talk to. Grown-ups smiled with their lips, not their eyes, pretending nothing was wrong when there absolutely was. Muriel wanted her mother to let go of her face. With her head tilted up like that, she couldn't avoid seeing the lines around her tense, messy-lipsticked mouth.

"I need you to understand what I'm telling you, Muriel."

Tugging her chin away, Muriel said, "I understand." Then she flattened her back against the subway seat. Lidia leaned forward and bent over to make sure they were eye to eye. "I'd hate to end our special Saturdays because I lost track of time. That would be awful, wouldn't it?"

Like a sudden stop on the M train, Muriel felt her world dislodge in one jerking motion. She struggled for composure, tried to halt the tremble in her lips.

"Sweetie?"

Silently, Muriel nodded.

"Okay then. Let's make a deal right here and now. Whatever happens on our Saturdays is between *us*. You and me. Nobody else's business. We can see any show we want, eat any dessert we want. Daddy doesn't have to know a thing. No one does. I'll be really careful never to lose track of time again. I promise. Okay? What do you say? Can I continue to have my special matinee days with my very special girl?"

Muriel lifted her head and stared her mother straight in the eyes to ask the one question that had been haunting her since she'd seen her in the fading daylight, standing beneath an awning across the street, her neck bent back, her hair tumbling past her shoulders, tucked into a doorway where she thought no one could see her, having a Broadway kiss.

"Wasn't that Father Camilo?"

Chapter 16

THE ENTIRE LUNCH was surreal, as if they'd descended on the brass-edged escalator of the Plaza Hotel and into a parallel universe. Muriel had never seen her sister act so strangely. She seemed intoxicated on two glasses of wine. And when Pia abruptly announced, "Time to go," leaving Richard and Edward pouting like schoolboys, she left the waiter a hundred-dollar tip and hurried into the bathroom to throw up.

"What can I do?" Muriel asked, helpless, from the next stall.

Between heaves, Pia said, "I've always been a cheap drunk."

Outside, in the horsey air of Central Park South, Muriel hailed a cab.

"Let's walk," Pia said.

"Walk? You just threw your guts up."

"I'm fine now," she said, as serenely as ever. "Walk with me."

To be truthful, Muriel wanted to put her sister in a cab and send the driver straight to the train station. She'd eaten so petitely at lunch she was already feeling a rumble in her stomach. Across the street, she could catch the M5 and be home in twenty minutes. Her day could pick up where it left off, before she was so rudely interrupted. There was still time to put the old towel back on the bed, crawl under the comforter, and pop open the metal lid on the Garrett's tin. She could still snuggle into her Sunday.

"Could we ask for a lovelier day?" Pia lifted her face to the sun.

Muriel stared, agog. "You just roarked at the Plaza!" Then she stopped on the sidewalk and waited for Pia to notice and stop, too. When Pia turned around, Muriel said, "You never did tell me why you're here. Why, exactly, are you here?" She reached up to untie the scarf.

Pia being Pia didn't respond. She simply gazed at the ridiculously expensive knickknacks in the store windows along Central Park South and said, "Isn't that emerald turtle divine?" Like a teenager, Muriel theatrically rolled her eyes. In the hundreds of times she'd taken the bus past these very same stores, she'd never once seen a soul enter or exit. They appeared to be fronts of some sort, as if the real business was conducted behind a two-way mirror in the back-office door. Or worse, they were tourist traps for wealthy foreigners who didn't want to stray too far from their luxury hotels to buy a memento of their trip to a New York City luxury hotel.

They walked. Muriel fumed. She yanked the scarf off her neck and made a one-act play out of dramatically jamming it in her purse. Pia was holding her hostage. It wasn't fair. Enough was enough. And never would she call a bejeweled turtle—or any-thing else—*divine*.

In silence, they continued west toward Columbus Circle where Muriel had every intention of kissing her sister good-bye.

RISING UP LIKE two giant flasks, Time Warner Center on the western curve of Columbus Circle is a vertical mall. Whole Foods fills the basement, a twenty-five-million-dollar penthouse kisses the sky. In between are chic, expensive retail shops into which Muriel Sullivant would never set foot.

"Window-shop with me," Pia said as they neared the inter-section between shopping and the bus home.

"I already have a window." Muriel leaned in to kiss-kiss Pia's cheeks and ask, "You know how to get to Grand Central, right?"

"Don't make me go home just yet." Pia's purging had com-pletely sobered her up. In the bright sunlight, however, Muriel did notice that her beautiful sister was pale in a yellowish sort of way. Her eyes seemed more deeply set into their sockets. Shop-ping was the last thing she needed and the very last thing Muriel wanted. Now or ever.

"Not today, Pia. I have, um, stuff to do."

"Ten minutes, *max*. Please."

Muriel stopped and looked at her full on. "What is *with* you?"

Pia sighed. "I was hoping you would be. My little sis. Whom I see so seldomly." With the confidence of a woman who is never denied, Pia marched straight for the entrance to the vertical mall before Muriel had a chance to process the *Brady Bunch* way in which her sister was now frequently using the word "sis." Yes, the day had been odd, indeed.

"You could use a new pair of shoes, Muriel," Pia tossed over her shoulder. "If you can call those things on your feet *shoes*."

And her original sister was back.

Of course Muriel followed. As she always did. She plodded along in her cheap peep-toe shoes, which, she suddenly noticed, really belonged on an elderly woman's feet.

Inside the mall Muriel balanced herself on the escalator by resting her wrists on the handrail. Germs didn't care if you were in an upscale mall or not. She asked Pia, "Looking for something in particular?" Then she inhaled the sickening sweetness of the overly perfumed air. Pia smiled her angelic smile and meandered, floor by floor, standing in front of one softly lit window display after another. Right foot jutted out, left hand on her chin, tilting her head this way and that, she seemed intent on evaluating every damn mannequin in the mall. Sis Big Foot stood loyally behind her.

"What do you think?" Pia asked, finally. "Like it?" She pointed to a placid-faced mannequin wearing an elegant gray satin sleeveless dress.

"It's you," Muriel said, honestly.

"I think so, too."

Muriel was stunned. Together, they walked into the store.

"Can I help you ladies find anything?" A toothy twentysomething approached them the moment they set foot through the door. Muriel said, "Could you please show me your size sixteens?"

"She's pulling your leg," Pia said to the salesgirl's befuddled expression, flashing the most genuine smile Muriel had seen all day. In its glow, Muriel felt radiant. "I'll be over in accessories," she said, beaming.

While Muriel sauntered away, Pia said, "That gray satin in the window. Do you have it in a size four?"

The salesgirl nodded and left to fetch the dress. "The dressing rooms are at the back of the store," she said. "Go on in. I'll bring the dress to you."

Overhearing, Muriel thought, *Toto, we're definitely not in T.J.Maxx.*

"Muriel?"

Muriel looked up. "Yes, sis?"

"Come with me?"

"You're done already?"

"To the dressing room."

"The dressing room?"

"I need you."

Muriel scoffed. "Since when do you need my help buying clothes?"

"Today. I need you today."

Briefly wishing she'd drunk that second glass of wine after all, Muriel sighed and followed her sister to the back of the store.

Unlike the shower-stall versions she was used to, with their muslin pull curtains that never quite reached the end of the rod, this dressing room felt like a walk-in closet. Plenty of room for two. There was even a slatted wood bench. Still, there was no way to avoid the accusing three-way mirror and interrogation lighting. Muriel felt compelled to confess she was premenstrual.

"Nature makes you *fatter* when you're fertile? Like it isn't hard enough getting a date?"

Rustling up a courteous laugh, Pia gently touched Muriel's hair. Involuntarily, Muriel pulled away. Then, feeling ashamed, she returned her head to the palm of her sister's hand and left it there, hoping the dress would arrive to save her. Instead, Pia removed her hand and turned to examine her face in the mirror. A grim expression stiffened her lips. Muriel sucked in her stomach. When she crossed her legs, she was horrified to notice she'd missed a spot while hastily shaving earlier. In the water balloon bulge of her white calf, tiny black dashes looked like an asphalt scrape.

"Here you go." Politely, the salesgirl *tap, tapped* on the dressing room door. "I also brought you a size two. They run a little large."

Muriel uncrossed her legs and tucked her Yeti feet beneath the bench. To give Pia privacy while she slipped out of her clothes and into the dress, she memorized the contours of her lap, wondering if they made Spanx in white.

"Zip me?"

When Muriel looked up, she was startled to see the bony spine in Pia's back. As she zipped up the dress, she noted that it was the size two.

"Well?" Pia asked, turning around. She smoothed the front, angled to the right, then left. Form fitting, the sleeveless, slate-colored satin dress fit her well. A bit gaping in the armholes, but perfectly suited to her slim frame.

"I like it," said Muriel.

"Me, too. Wow, that was easier than I thought." Pia exhaled hard and ran her hands down the front of the dress again.

"What's it for? Does Will have some work thing or something?" Noting that her lip gloss could use refreshing, Muriel sat back down and poked around in the bottom of her purse. "You taking a cruise or something?"

Pia stood absolutely still, her gaze lingering on the scalpel-straight part of her hair. Muriel said, "Aha!" and brandished the lip gloss like a trophy.

"Muriel—," Pia started. Then she stopped.

"Too shiny?" Muriel tilted her puckered, freshly glossed lips up at her sister. "Too pale?"

Said Pia, solemnly, "We need to talk."

Letting her head fall forward, Muriel blew air through her sticky lips. "Here we go," she said. Finally. Lecture time. Pia had waited until they were trapped in a dressing room beneath the incriminating overhead light to launch her dissertation. Wasn't that just like her! *Don't you think it's time you grew up? Seriously, Muriel, don't you? The Bible clearly states you must be fruitful. Multiply. Fertility declines dramatically after thirt—*

Alarmed by a strange guttural sound, Muriel's head popped up. Pia was facing her. Her right hand rested on the left side of her chest as if she was about to say the Pledge of Allegiance. "Ah, Muriel," she said, "I've been dreading telling you this."

"It's not like I haven't heard it before."

Pia took a deep breath but said nothing. She sat on the bench next to her sister and rested her free hand on Muriel's knuckles. Tears rose in her eyes. All of a sudden Muriel felt a surge of blood rush to her cheeks.

"What is it?"

Pia's mouth opened and closed like a carp.

"What? Is it Mom? Will? *Emma?*"

Muriel could feel her heart hit her sternum. Her cheeks burned. Tears had spilled over Pia's lower lashes and were slowly rolling down her cheeks. One heavy drop landed on the lap of her satin dress and quickly spread in a dark circle. The overhead light baked the top of Muriel's head.

"You're scaring me, Pia. What's wrong?"

"I'm sick," she said so quietly Muriel thought she'd misheard. Noting Pia's hand still on her chest, Muriel asked, "Your heart?"

Pia slowly shook her head no and let her hand fall away. Her lips hung loosely on her face. Without meaning to, Muriel stood up and grabbed Pia's clothes from the hook on the wall. She held them out to her. Insanely, she wanted Pia to put her own clothes back on. If they moved quickly, they could run back to the Plaza. Richard and Edward might still be there. The chef would clack his tongs again. They could order dessert. Another round of drinks.

"I don't want Will to pick out my dress," Pia said softly. "Or Mom. I want it to be perfect, and I've lost so much weight lately."

Still holding Pia's clothes, Muriel flicked her head as if a gnat buzzed past her ear. Pia stood and gently took her clothes out of her sister's grip and set them on the bench behind her. Then she lifted both hands and placed them on either side of Muriel's warm, magenta-colored cheeks. Her hands felt cool, like their mother's. Her touch was so soft it was almost not there at all.

"It's God's will," she said. "There's nothing we can do."

Speechless, Muriel gaped at her sister. The bones on top of her arms were round knobs, the hollows on either side of her neck were so deep they could hold water. Her shoulders were hunched and their blades were as curved and sharp as a boat's propeller in dry dock. Actually, her skin was more green than yellow. Greenish gray. How had she missed that outside? And Pia's eyes were recessed so far into her skull they cast a shadow. With her lipstick faded, her lips were nearly white. She'd vomited at the hotel, coughed on the bus and in her apartment. Plus, those were *ribs* on either side of that skeletal spine. My God, was it possible she'd been looking at her sister all day and not seen her at all?

"I don't understand." Muriel's voice sounded like it was coming from down the street.

"My breast. Now lungs and liver. Some bones. I didn't know until it was too late."

Dizzy, Muriel's brain crashed. She missed the meaning of her sister's words. Something about her bones? Had she broken one? Too late for what?

"I need your help," Pia whispered, suddenly looking so fragile it was as if *Muriel* was the strong one. "Can you help me?"

Unable to trust her mouth to release a coherent word, Muriel nodded.

"I'm going to buy this dress and give it to you to hold for me. This is the dress I want to wear. Period." Pia looked down at the dark teardrop stain. "That should disappear without leaving a mark. If it doesn't, can you have it dry-cleaned?"

Muriel blinked and swallowed as Pia went on. "Natural polish and natural lips, none of that thick makeup they trowel on you. Will has to deal with Emma. He won't know how to handle these things. He won't care about them. But I do. I *care*. Do you understand? I need to make sure I can count on you to make it happen."

"What are you telling me, Pia?" Muriel felt the heaviness of the very air around her. With no preliminary welling of tears, she simply started to cry.

"It's going to be okay." Pia's arms encircled her younger sister. Softly she cooed, "I need you to be strong for Emma. Can you do that for me?"

Again Muriel nodded, though she was nowhere near telling the truth. Pia was the strong one in the Sullivant family. And Lidia. Muriel was the afterthought.

Pulling back, Pia stroked her sister's hair and said matter-of-factly, "Don't let them restyle my wig. I have it done every week and it's exactly the way I want it."

Wig? Muriel looked at her sister's shiny blond hair, the way it brushed against her shoulders so evenly, so flawlessly. Even after being bent over a toilet bowl, after clothes mussed it up. Her hair fell perfectly back in place. Shame bowed Muriel's head. It was true: she'd been so full of herself she hadn't seen her sister at all.

"One last thing." Lifting Muriel's chin with her cool, bony hand, Pia gazed deeply into her younger sister's wet eyes. "This is the most important thing I've ever asked of anyone. I trust you, Muriel. Will you grant me one last wish?"

She sniffed hard, nodded, steeled herself as Pia inhaled the whole world into her chest.

"Don't tell Mama."

"Wait. What? *No.*"

"You know it will kill Mama to lose me. And it will kill me sooner to watch that happen. I can't bear it. I'm asking the impossible, I know. But, please, Muriel, can you keep my secret?"

With the fullness of her body and soul, Muriel wanted to flatly refuse. She wanted to shake her head and sheepishly confess she was one of those people who blurted out the truth no matter what. Honesty occupied every fold of her heart. That's what she longed to say. It pumped through her veins, formed the sinew that bonded her muscles to her bones. "Sorry, Pia," she wished she could utter, "I'm not your girl." No way could she be counted on to keep a confidence. Not her. Pathetic, but true. No chance it could be done. But of course that was a lie. Keeping secrets was Muriel's specialty.

Part II

None So Blind

Chapter 17

IT WAS ABSURD the way it happened. If the scene had played out in a movie or a book, Pia would have groaned and thought it contrived. Funny the way life can shake your beliefs down to their skeletons, make you realize you don't know anything at all.

On the very morning of her thirtieth birthday, when Emma was eight and her love for her mother still glowed around the edges like a tourist painting of Jesus, Will Winston handed his wife a plain white envelope.

"A flat diamond?" she asked, playfully.

"Open it."

Inside, neatly clipped together, were two first-class plane tickets and a spa brochure. Pia sucked in a mouthful of air. "You didn't."

"We leave tomorrow morning."

She kissed her husband softly on the lips. "You'll love it. I promise."

Will smiled. It felt good to please a woman who was so hard to please.

It had been an ongoing issue in their marriage, the way Pia so often felt like a single parent. Even with Blanca there every day vacuuming, dusting, emptying the dishwasher, refilling it, making Emma's lunches, marinating dinner in the fridge for Pia to sear on the grill pan when Will got home late, she felt alone in her beautiful home. Sometimes, when her husband sat across from her at the kitchen table, she felt most alone of all. It was the jiggle in his knee. The way he vacantly smiled at her and nodded when she hadn't even asked him a question.

"It's so obvious you'd rather be elsewhere," she said, more often than she wanted to.

"I'm here, aren't I?"

"I want you to *want* to be with me. With us. Even when you're home, your mind is at the office."

Will said, "The mortgage will pay itself?"

"You wanted this huge house, not me."

"And yet I notice how quickly you and Emma settled in."

The bite in their voices alarmed her. Not so long ago, they'd kissed each other in doorways.

Before sunrise most mornings, Will was up, eating toast in three bites and scrambling to catch the early train into the city. Foreign currency exchange markets were active twenty-four hours a day; a missed few hours could cost millions. Particularly with the euro in such flux. If he wasn't on top of it, a younger, smarter trader would be. The firm's investors were fickle. Long term, to them, meant a full day. Panic set in overnight. The fact that he'd already made them wealthy, well, that was to be expected. What had he done for them *lately*? The pressure never let up.

Honestly, Will *loved* it. The feeling of skirting the very edge of a fault scarp, fractured rock chipping beneath his feet, losing his footing, jerking backward, rebalancing and righting himself—it was exhilarating. He was a high roller in the VIP room at a casino, a heli-skier outrunning an avalanche. Though he'd never admit it to his wife, Will would be happy in a bachelor's studio eating Chinese out of the carton every night. Hell, he'd be fine on the couch in his office with fresh shirts delivered each morning. They'd bought the Connecticut house because Pia wanted it. The way her eyes lit up in the circular marble foyer, her open-armed whirling in the master bath like Julie Andrews in the Austrian Alps. Will had only pretended to want that monstrosity. Before they were even done with the walk-through, Pia was mentally remodeling the kitchen!

Though he'd never admit it out loud, Pia and Emma were his life, but making money was his passion. His addiction, really, as devouring as heroin or meth.

"Let's do a spa vacation," Pia had suggested months earlier. "Just the two of us."

"A spa?"

"You golf while I get a massage. I play tennis while you have a steam. We meet back at the suite for predinner sex."

Will had joked, "Can't you come by the office for a nooner?"

At best, vacations, to Will, were the equivalent of eating lobster. They sounded better than they actually were. If not done *perfectly*, lobster was a mouthful of rubber. Really, no more than an excuse to eat melted butter. The ideal vacation to Will was absolutely *not* a spa. If he was going to go away at all, he wanted a resort with Wi-Fi. He wanted *excess*: overeating pancakes at breakfast, overdrinking wine at lunch, overspending at four-star restaurants after the sun went down. Lobster done so exquisitely it melted in your mouth. Even on family vacations, when Emma was hanging on his arm and soaking up his example, the last thing Will wanted to think about on a vacation was his health. A spa? No way. Pia was into all that healthy stuff, not him. She could eat salads daily without losing the will to live. She could do yoga without feeling dizzy and leave her iPad at home without feeling sick to her stomach.

"Someday," he had said every time his wife suggested a spa, though they both knew he didn't mean it.

Until one day, he did.

"Why now?" Pia asked, teary eyed, the morning of her birthday.

Will shrugged. "Why not?"

It was as good an answer as any. Much better than the truth—that he'd forgotten her birthday entirely until Blanca reminded him the day before. Panicked, he instructed his secretary to set everything up, spare no expense.

"You don't have to lift a finger, my love," Will said to his wife. "I've taken care of every detail."

Lidia was going to stay at the Connecticut house with Emma. A limousine would pick them up in the morning, drive them to the airport. Another limo would be waiting in West Virginia at the other end to deliver them to the elegant Greenbriar Spa. All Pia had to do was pack a bag, kiss her daughter and mother good-bye, and meet her husband at the front door.

"I ordered you a special sushi entrée for the plane," Will said, beaming. Truly, he had the best executive assistant in New York.

Pia flung her arms around her husband's neck and said, "I've died and gone to heaven."

THE GREENBRIAR WAS a polished gem rising up from the foothills of the Allegheny Mountains. Like Pia herself, it was a graceful beauty—all class and propriety. Though thoroughly modern with its multiple golf courses and restaurants—a steakhouse, even!—entering the Greenbriar was like walking into a Jane Austen novel where horseback riders were called "equestrians" and pheasants were hunted via wing shot.

"Oh, darling. It's perfect," Pia said the moment she walked through the grand front door. Beaming, Will couldn't agree more.

That night, after a very unspalike meal of Wagyu rib-eye steak and bananas Foster, on top of the white Egyptian cotton comforter on their king-size bed in the stunning Heritage suite, with the air conditioner blasting and the Bose playing her favorite CD (Will's secretary really did think of everything), Will hungrily grabbed his wife, expertly unhooked her Simone Perele bra with his left hand and kneaded her breast with his right. Abruptly he stopped.

"What's this?"

"Has it been that long, my sweet?"

"Seriously, Pia, have you felt this?"

He rolled off her and she sat up. Lifting her arm overhead, she put her hand on her breast, felt what he felt. It was a hard pebble, an M&M beneath her skin. Instantly, Pia felt the blood in her body drain down to her feet; she felt faint, as if the wine she'd had with dinner had suddenly taken effect. In that moment, less than a second of human time, she sensed the ground shift beneath her. A faint deviation in the earth's rotation, a speed bump, a celestial hiccup. Just like that, Pia Winston knew her old life was over for good. Literally, she felt her heart break.

"Oh that," she said, dismissive. "It's nothing. A cyst. Where were we?"

Grabbing her husband, she pulled him back to her, holding him so close he couldn't see the tears welling in her eyes. That night, as wildly as they had before Emma was born, they made love. Pia pressed her body flat against Will's, wanting to meld with him, wanting to disappear. Afterward, he fell back on the sheets, winded, saying, "Why didn't you tell me spas were so sexy?"

The next morning, Pia took a hot shower before her Detox Kur and warm stone massage; the day after she booked a cellular repair facial with collagen mask.

"You want décolletage, too, Mrs. Winston?"

"*Pourquoi pas?*"

Will played golf every day and answered e-mails on his iPad by the infinity pool. Together, they hiked the nature trails behind the stately hotel. In the evenings, after dinner, they played roulette in the casino and Pia kissed Will's dice for luck at the craps table. Across the dinner table, they held hands and toasted their charmed lives with glasses of Château Monbousquet Bordeaux.

"You were right," Will said. "This place is perfect."

"Yes. Perfect." Again, Pia's eyes filled up.

In the same corporeal way Pia had felt the first cells of Emma dividing inside her on the night she was conceived, she knew malignant cells from the gravelly lump in her breast had already infested her body. Not sure why, she just *knew*. Like waking up one second before the alarm goes off, you don't want to believe it's morning already. Didn't you just fall asleep? If you close your eyes again, let sleep retake you, perhaps time will run backward? In the darkness behind your eyelids, doesn't the world disappear?

For the rest of the week, Pia decided to close her eyes. She thought of nothing but pleasing her husband, enjoying herself, and celebrating their love. A few more days of being herself couldn't hurt. Soon enough she'd become someone else—a patient, a survivor, a statistic. One of those women with a head scarf and a pink ribbon. Why ruin their trip?

As each day passed, it became easier to forget what she knew. Stunningly so. By degrees, her brain dismantled all frightening thoughts. The talent of the cherished child. Ugliness needn't be dwelled upon, not when her existence was filled with such beauty. By week's end, Pia had nearly shut out the whole messy business entirely. On the way home, her consciousness shifted back to Connecticut: Emma's ballet shoes were hurting her feet, Root Beer was due for a lepto booster. Lidia would greet them with *pyzy,* her favorite Polish dumplings. Pia would have to double up on Pilates for the next few weeks to repair the damage of all the rich food she'd been eating. She sighed happily. Manageable problems were her favorite. They made her feel worthwhile. By the time the limo pulled into their circular drive, the only thought of her health was a shallow one: Emma was at that awkward age when kids were so easily embarrassed. A mother without hair would spoil her entire year.

Chapter 18

PIA WAS QUITE certain the PTA hadn't consumed her mother's life. Nor myriad school activities. But times had changed. There was the monthly PTA newsletter to compose and publish and the nutrition committee minutes that seemed to have a life of their own. Plus, she had to organize the Audubon Trail field trip for the entire third grade, and raise money for the kids' overnight museum tour in Manhattan. Chairing the landmarks committee had always been more exhausting than she'd anticipated. With all those clashing personalities, it was like running a day-care center. Both pairs of Will's dress oxfords needed new soles and he seemed to use the front of his silk ties as a napkin. Pia practically lived at the dry cleaners when she wasn't returning books to the library or filling the tank with gas. Always, *always* there were errands to run. Endless. Emma was struggling with multiples and arrays and had to be dropped off and picked up at the tutor three times a week. Plus, she'd stubbornly decided to go vegan, of all things. Grocery shopping took twice as long with all that label reading. And her earnest and impressionable daughter had refused to sleep under a down comforter or even wear wool. Keeping her warm through a Connecticut winter was a challenge all its own.

Beside her bed, a stack of flagged magazine articles nagged at her—not to mention the relentless book club chapters! What had possessed her to join a book club? As if she didn't already have enough to do. And Blanca, their longtime housekeeper, needed a lawyer for her eldest son who had been arrested in a bar fight in Bridgeport. Blanca was practically family. Pia couldn't send her to just *anyone*. Their own attorney recommended several less pricey lawyers who had to be interviewed and evaluated. Blanca barely spoke English. What, she could talk to lawyers on her own? Certainly not in her vulnerable state with her son at risk. Not to mention the very real fact that Pia's regular lunches in the city with Lidia ate up entire *days*.

Who had time to see a doctor?

"Emma, where's your backpack?"

"Not that shirt with those pants, Will. It's the wrong shade of blue. And don't forget to meet me at Emma's school at four. Do *not* call me to cancel. You are her parent, too."

"Less bleach on the sheets please, Blanca. I can smell it in my sleep."

Truly, without her constant oversight, Blanca would watch Spanish soap operas all day and feed Emma nothing but those fattening tamales. Lidia would die of boredom in Queens and

Will and Emma would wander pointlessly around their back-yard bouncing off each other like zombies in the night. Pia was the heartbeat who made everyone's life worth living.

Not that she ignored her own needs. Far from it. Pia ate color-ful vegetables and whole grains; she awoke a half hour earlier to fit in morning yoga and took Pilates twice a week. Having read a *New York Times* article about the scientifically proven value of friendship, she made a conscious effort to schedule "shop-ping dates" in the village with at least one friend per week. In the car—and she was *always* in the car—Pia vowed to schedule a checkup at the gynecologist as soon as possible.

Each morning in the shower she quickly passed her soapy hand over the solid lump on the side of her left breast. Even as Will insisted she see a doctor every time he felt the same spot, unchanged, she assured him she would, then silenced him by asking, "Aren't *you* overdue for a physical?"

By the time Pia lay flat on her gynecologist's examining table, her feet in the stirrups, her right hand on her left breast, casually asking, "Is this anything?" more than a year had gone by.

"Hmmm," the doctor said, palpating her breast.

"Hmmm good or hmmm bad?"

"Let's schedule a mammogram."

"I'm thirty-one," she stated, as if that might convince him to change his mind.

"Let me call Dr. Rushkin. He's the best. Can you see him to-morrow?"

"Tomorrow? Impossible. I'm having lunch with my mother."

"Cancel it."

At home that night, Pia said nothing. Why worry Will? Instead, at dinner she said, "Emma, my darling, there's nothing wrong with yogurt."

"It's *dairy*, Mom."

"Plenty of vegans eat dairy."

"Not me."

"Your bones are growing. You need calcium."

"Not if it comes from an animal with a face."

The following morning, up early and at the Pilates studio before her instructor even arrived, Pia pressed her spine into the floor mat and stretched her arms straight up. A ray of morning sunlight caught a facet in her wedding ring. "I'll get a manicure after my mammogram," she thought, noting the tiny chip in the top coat. "I'm sure Tara can squeeze me in."

As soon as Pilates class was over, she dressed and kiss-kissed her instructor and got into the car and looked at herself in the rearview mirror. Her eyelids hung more heavily than usual, her skin was the color of cheap paper. How had Will overlooked the change in her? The way her shoulders seemed crimped. Did her husband not really look at her at all?

Pia put on her dark glasses and backed out of the parking spot. On her way to the radiologist's office, she swung by the dry cleaners to pick up Will's favorite suit and drop off several tomato-stained ties. Obviously, he'd been eating a lot of pizza lately. She emitted an exasperated puff of air. If not for her, Will would live the same way he had in college.

"Glorious day, isn't it?" Pia said, flashing her easy grin at a Westport woman who looked exactly like her. Same honey blond hair color. Same pressed white shirt tucked into skinny jeans. Both drove hybrid SUVs. Cypress pearl paint, the most exquisite greenish-gray. The car needed gas, but she'd fill up after. More than anything, Pia hated to be late.

Dr. Rushkin's waiting room was nicer than most. Upholstered sofas lined the walls, classical music softened the air. *Architectural Digest* and *People* magazines were the current issues. A tall clear vase held real flowers and fresh water. Pia filled out the clipboarded form the receptionist handed her.

6.   Date of last breast exam? *Never.*
7.   Lumps? Tenderness? Nipple discharge? *Possible.*
8.   Family history of breast cancer? *No. No one. Not anyone.*

"Mrs. Winston?"

Pia looked up.

"I'm ready for you." A technician in blue scrubs stood smiling at the doorway, her hands gently clasped in front of her. Pia handed over the clipboard and followed her into a small room with a huge machine that resembled a telescope on steroids.

"You're right on time," Pia said, making polite conversation.

"Dr. Rushkin doesn't like to make his patients wait."

The technician's life revealed itself in her no-nonsense movements, her wash-and-wear haircut and dimpled hands. She was a mother, no doubt. One who stopped off at Wendy's drive-through on her way home, too tired to make dinner. Her husband had a favorite chair. Remote in hand, he melted into it while his wife unpacked the white bags and smoothed the burger wrappings into plates. When asked how their school day went, her kids glumly said, "Fine," and ate their meals in six bites.

"Everything off from the waist up, Mrs. Winston," the cheerful technician said. "Open at the front." She handed Pia a blue fabric gown wrapped in cellophane and said, "I'll be right back."

After neatly hanging up her bra and shirt on the door hook, Pia pulled open the cellophane and shook the gown open. She put her arms through the gown sleeves and tied a bow at the top. The room was standard-issue medical: scuffed eggshell walls, gray linoleum floor, a rolling stool, and a monstrous beige machine of unyielding metal. Softly knocking, the technician said, "Ready?"

"Ready."

Pia inhaled hard. She wasn't ready. Not at all. Nausea gripped her stomach. She wanted to push past the technician and run through the waiting room and exit the hospital and fling open the car door and race home, not caring one whit who saw her nakedness in the flapping blue gown.

"Put your arm right here."

With the skill and speed of someone who had seen every size, shape, and condition of a woman's breast, the technician chatted about her bum knee as she peeled back one corner of Pia's gown and ladled her breast onto the cold glass plate of the X-ray machine. "It's never been the same since I played soccer with my seven-year-old," she said. "Hold still, please." Retreating behind a glass partition, she pushed a button that lowered the top half of the glass plate down to flatten Pia's breast. "Deep breath in. Hold."

"Owww," groaned Pia.

"Sorry. Hang in."

Silence, pain, intense tugging on the skin of her chest, buzzing, then release. The glass plate lifted up.

"First time?" the technician asked sympathetically.

"I'm thirty-one."

"Ah." Taking the plate out, replacing it with another, the technician repositioned Pia's breast and repeated the whole process. "I try to be gentle with the virgins." She laughed. "Deep breath in. Hold."

The awkward, painful process was over in fifteen minutes and Pia was escorted into an examining room down the hall.

"Dr. Rushkin will be right in," the technician said before quietly shutting the door behind her. Pia nodded, mulling over the protocol. When a woman manhandles your breasts, should you at least ask her name? Bond as mothers? *How does your seven-year-old like school?*

While waiting for the radiologist to come in, Pia stared at the blank light board and cradled her sore breasts as if they were two small children who'd had their first vaccinations. She wanted to place them safely back into her bra. Soon, there was another soft knock on the door.

"Come in."

"Good morning, Mrs. Winston." The doctor entered and tossed her breast X-rays onto the light box. "Let's see what we have here."

Bearded and soft bodied, resembling a rabbi more than a radiologist, the doctor stroked his chin hair as he looked at the spidery blobs on the screen. Pia heard him breathe in, then out. Then in again.

"See anything?" she asked, knowing, of course, that he had.

"Could you please lie down and lift your left arm over your head?"

Down she went onto the crinkly paper covering the exam table, watching the deliberately placid expression on the doctor's face as he pressed his fingertips around her left breast in a circle, focusing on the one area she knew he would. She wondered why her whole chest hurt until she realized she wasn't breathing.

"I'd like to do a biopsy," Dr. Rushkin said matter-of-factly. "There's an area of concern." *Area of concern*, Pia repeated in her head. Like Chernobyl or Fukushima. A poison zone. "Right now?" she asked.

"Yes. You have time?"

Without waiting for an answer the doctor picked up a plastic bottle of gel and squirted a quarter-size amount onto a sonogram wand. "It won't take long. Lie still, please." Pressing the wand to the side of Pia's left breast, he watched the image on a monitor. Pia subtly twisted her neck to see. It was similar to Emma's ultrasound. Then a darker thought intruded: *Emma's image was the beginning of life; this is the outline of death.*

"I'm numbing the area now. You'll feel a small pinch."

With the spot marked on the sonogram screen, he injected her breast with an anesthetic. As he continued, he narrated his actions.

"Tiny incision. Locating the tissue. Hold still. There."

Pia heard a snapping sound. She felt pressure, like a painless hole punch. When he said, "The bleeding will stop soon," she wondered if she would have time for that manicure after all.

"Keep the gauze and bandage on overnight."

Dr. Rushkin showed her the maggot-size piece of pink tissue he'd removed and inserted in a glass tube. She looked at it, then looked away. A piece of her body was outside herself, beyond her control. Soon, she would belong to medicine. No longer a person, but a patient. There could be no more denying. No further lying. Though the incision stung a little, it was no worse than a nick from cuticle scissors. Which reminded her: she should call Tara at the nail salon to see if she could take her first thing tomorrow morning, after she dropped Emma off at school.

THE PHONE WOKE her. Will's side of the bed was empty. He was already downstairs. The aroma of morning—coffee, buttered toast—eased her abrupt awakening. When Will didn't answer on the third ring, she picked up.

"Hello," she said, heavily, sleep still trapped in her throat.

"Mrs. Winston."

Those two words knocked the wind out of her. Dr. Rushkin's distinctive voice, a throaty monotone, sounded whisperish even when he spoke normally. She could picture his thumb and index finger stroking the beard on his chin. In her mind she could see his sad eyes.

"Good morning," she said, steeling herself. A radiologist, she knew, wouldn't call first thing in the morning with good news. Doctors sent good news through the mail in a form letter with their signature scribbled at the bottom. With a difficult notification they divested their desks of it early in the day, before patients arrived and bedside manners were required. Even so, when Dr. Rushkin's low voice announced, "The biopsy came back positive," Pia paused, not sure if *positive* meant good or bad.

"Are you saying I have cancer?" she asked.

"Yes," he said. "You have cancer. The lab just faxed me the results."

Suddenly, Will appeared at his wife's side holding two mugs of steaming coffee. "What did you say?"

Cupping the phone, Pia whispered, "Thanks for the coffee, sweetie," in a dismissive way. Will sat on the bed and set the mugs on her bedside table.

"Coasters," she mouthed. Into the phone Pia said, "Can I call you back?"

There was a pause before Dr. Rushkin said, "This can't wait, Mrs. Winston. Do you have a pen?"

"Yes. Yes, I do. One moment." She reached past Will into the bedside drawer for a pen and a Post-it note. Then she said, "Go ahead," and wrote down the name and phone number Dr. Rushkin gave her. He said, "I'll tell him to expect your call this morning."

"Will do!" Pia chirped before hanging up.

"Who was that?"

"The coffee smells divine, my love." Pia reached for the warm mug and encircled it with both hands, trying to still the shaking.

"Pia."

Pasting a fearless expression on her face she said, "It appears as though God is testing us today."

Chapter 19

"Everything off from the waist up."

Those six words replaced the only other words Pia had regularly heard in a doctor's office: "Don't forget sunscreen." Dr. Rushkin had been referred by her gynecologist, the best in Connecticut. Rushkin, in turn, referred her to the best oncologist in the state, Marc Payton. Joked Pia, "If our doctors were the *worst* this could all be a mistake."

Will hadn't laughed. He hadn't said much of anything since he heard the awful news. Not once did he say, "I felt that lump more than a *year* ago. You assured me it was nothing." He didn't glare at his wife with a set jaw. Never did he angrily turn to her and scream, "How could you be so goddamned careless with your life?"

His feelings of fury, he told himself, were probably fear. Losing Pia, the linchpin of the Winstons' life, was unthinkable. Why, she made his very life possible. Without her . . . there *was*

no without her. Period. And there was no use flinging accusa-
tions or demanding an explanation. As much as he wanted to
know, *needed* to know how she could do this to him—how she
could be so goddamned careless with *his* life—what good would
it do? It was too late. They could never turn the clock back to
that night at the Greenbriar when Pia could have caught her
cancer early. Christ, they were at a health spa! Doctors were on
staff. They could have X-rayed her chest the very next morning
and seen that the hard pebble was self-contained—a misshapen
wart that could be scooped out with a surgical melon baller. Instead of a fucking facial, why didn't she go to the clinic? It was
right there at the resort! At the very least, they would have told
her to see an oncologist the moment she got home. Pia let him
play golf while her cancer was morphing into a jellyfish, its tentacles spreading and eating away her life? How could she be so
goddamned selfish?

Will said nothing. He felt his chest burn as he held her hand
and bit his tongue and sat next to his wife in Dr. Marc Payton's
office—the best oncologist in the state of Connecticut—while his
entire world exploded in front of his face.

"There's no way to sugarcoat this," Dr. Payton said. Head of
oncology at Connecticut General, he had the ideal sprinkling
of gray in his inky black hair. Enough to trust him, but not so
much that you mistrusted his ability to keep up with the cutting
edge. His office was distinctly Swedish in decor. Finely grained
light wood, clean lines, no frills. On his wall was the obligatory
framed diploma, on his desk photos of his athletic son, lovely
daughter, and fit blond wife.

"Spell it out." Will gripped Pia's fingers so hard she could no longer feel her hand.

Dr. Payton looked down at the manila folder on his desk. "The PET scan has revealed some distressing news. The cancer in your left breast has metastasized, Mrs. Winston. Meaning, it's spread."

"We know what the word means, Doctor," Will said. "How far?"

"Far, I'm afraid. The scan shows evidence of cancer in your lungs, rib cage, and liver. I'm sorry."

Dr. Payton spoke directly to Pia even as Will asked the questions. Pia extricated her hand from Will's painful grip as Dr. Payton said to her, "Had we caught it earlier, we would have more treatment options."

"How could I possibly discover breast cancer?" Pia asked, indignant. "I'm thirty-one. Isn't a baseline mammogram at forty?"

Will shot her a sharp look as Dr. Payton quickly said, "I didn't mean to imply in any way that this is your fault. An aggressive tumor like this is rare at your age. And not at all fair, Mrs. Winst—"

"Call me Pia."

"Of course. Pia."

"There must be a mistake. I feel absolutely fine."

That was a lie. For the past several months, Pia felt almost crippled by exhaustion. Her body ran out of gas by noon. She'd never been like other women who dragged their asses through life. Always, Pia had energy to spare. Will had married a domestic CEO, she often told him, who ran Winston Corp. with ease and confidence. Until lately, she had been great at her job. Never once needing an afternoon nap or a fortifying cappuccino. Balls were never dropped. For the past few months, however, she'd felt energy drain right out of her body the moment she pulled herself out of bed. And she never told a soul that she'd once parked in a far corner of the lot behind Ann Taylor to sleep in her car one afternoon because she feared driving home. The mere energy it took to concentrate on the road seemed beyond her. Is that what cancer felt like? A punctured fuel tank? A deflated balloon?

"There's no mistake," Dr. Payton said. "Cancer affects everyone differently. Clearly, you have a high tolerance for discomfort."

Pia straightened herself in the soft chair.

"What's the plan?" Will said, leaning forward.

As she watched Dr. Payton's lips move, Pia heard only buzzing in her ears. How many times, she wondered, had he delivered this same bad news? Surely, it was the worst part of his job. Patients probably slumped over in their chairs, sobbing. Did they scream, "No, no, no!" Did black mascara run down their faces in two long tread marks? She noticed a teak tissue box on the patient side of Dr. Payton's tidy desk. In her mind she pictured the scene: An interior designer dressed in a Chanel suit sat in this very chair and reached her hand forward. "The box should go *here*," she said. "Within reach." Fumbling for a tissue would never do, not at a moment like this. And she would advise against leather upholstery. ("Too impersonal.") Though she would urge regular cleaning of the wool fabric. Smelling a previous patient's desperation would be insensitive, at best.

". . . aggressive round of chemotherapy. Commencing immediately."

Pia glanced about the room noting the soothing wood tones, taupe carpeting, filtered overhead lighting. Had it all been on the designer's blueprint? Decor to soften death's blow?

"Mrs. Winston?"

She turned her head. "Pia, please."

"There is no easy way to deal with news like this, Pia. Breast cancer research is well funded and moving forward daily. There have been remissions at your advanced stage. All we can hope is—"

Remission, she thought. The very word itself hinted at impending doom. As if cancer were merely on the run and would eventually turn itself in.

"What about surgery?" Will asked.

"Surgery is not a viable option."

"We want a second opinion."

"Will." Pia looked apologetically at Dr. Payton. Death was no excuse for bad manners.

"It's okay," Dr. Payton said, to which Will replied, "*Nothing* is okay about this." There was no time to be polite. That morning, as they sat in Marc Payton's waiting room, Will had been shocked to see so many sick patients. Eyebrowless ladies in turbans, sallow-skinned men with portable oxygen tanks, caregivers wearing surgical face masks, lamppost-thin women hugging themselves into layers of thick cabled sweaters. If Payton was the best, why did his waiting room look like death's foyer?

"A second opinion is entirely understandable." Dr. Payton lightly pressed his fingertips together. "I would advise you to schedule a consult immediately, however. These cancers spread at an alarming rate. I'll messenger the scan results to whomever you choose. But, please, Mrs. Winston—Pia—get treatment as soon as you can. If this were me, or my wife"—for the first time he spoke directly to Will—"I'd start today."

Pia lifted her perfectly pointed chin. "That's not possible. Emma has a soccer game."

THE SECOND OPINION was *worse* than the first.

"Quality of life is a consideration here," they were told. "Some of my patients choose palliative care at this point."

"*Palliative?*" Will tensed up, as though he was about to punch the doctor in the face. Pia rolled the word around and around in her head like sheets in a dryer, until her thoughts were a giant knotted ball.

"Thank you," she said politely, holding her purse with both hands to steady the shaking. She then stood up and walked out of the room without looking at a soul. After finishing the consult on his own, Will found his wife sitting in the car, staring blindly out the windshield.

"Sweetheart—"

"Take me home."

"We'll go to Sloan-Kettering in New York."

"Please, Will. I want to go home."

In silence, Will drove his wife to their beautiful Connecticut house, its four dormer windows embedded in the pitched slate roof. A fieldstone facade extended all the way to the three-car garage. Glossy white shutters trimmed each French window, and, of course, a gently sloping emerald-colored lawn rolled down to

the street. Anyone driving by that home would think the inhab-
itants had it made. Not a care in the world. *How stupid people are*,
Pia thought. *Utterly clueless.*

Inside, Blanca was drying her hands on a kitchen towel, her
thick eyebrows pressed together. "Okay, Miss Pia?"

"Fine," said Pia with a sad smile. "Would you please put the
water on for tea?"

Alone, Will climbed the staircase to their master suite. Blanca
had already made the bed, opened the drapes covering the
gleaming glass doors leading to the sundeck. He peeled back the
comforter on Pia's side of the bed, arranged it in a neat triangle,
fluffed her down pillows, and smoothed the soft linen sheets with
both hands. Then he walked into the huge closet on his side of
the dressing room, shut the door behind him, and wept.

Chapter 20

IMMEDIATELY, PIA WAS sucked into the cancer vortex. Her body ceased to belong to her; it was now the property of Connecticut General's shiny new cancer wing. What Pia needed to do, the white coats told her, was *fight*. The very cells that gave her life had become enemy invaders crouching in dark corners, reloading ammo. Battling them on their own turf was her only means of self-defense. But they were wrong. For the first time in her life, Pia Winston understood that *surrender* was her only option. If she stood a chance at all, it would be because she released herself to the ugly machinery of cancer—hard plastic scanners with doughnut-hole entrances; robotic arms shooting burning, disfiguring radiation; thick IV needles attached to cloudy tubing; saggy bags of hideous pink fluid.

"Everything off from the waist up."

Without question or comment, Pia had to do what she was

told. Surrender to a team of strangers. Giving *in* was the only way not to give up.

But surrender had never been her style.

"This way, honey." Will gently cupped Pia's elbow as he guided her to the hospital's elevator. He spoke in a reverent whisper. She wanted to elbow him in the sternum.

"I'm not an invalid," she said icily.

Looking like a lost child, Will shifted his hand to his wife's back. Pia felt the warmth of his flat palm. It took all her strength not to whip around and glare at that hand until Will returned it to his own damn body.

"We'll need to sit down with Emma," she said. As soon as the elevator doors opened, she stepped inside and nestled in the far corner. Will stood woodenly beside her.

"Level C, please," he said to the woman in scrubs nearest the buttons. She nodded and darted a sympathetic glance in Pia's direction.

In that slowly descending elevator, Pia's heart beat so hard it hurt. She wanted to jam the red emergency button, kick open the doors. What good was all that Pilates if she didn't have the strength to pull herself out of an elevator stuck midfloor? If she kicked off her shoes she could probably outrun Will, what with all that pizza he ate at the office. Outside she would hide, then call a taxi. She'd have the driver drop her off at the Sound. Will would never think to look for her by the water.

Over and over since Dr. Payton had looked up from that sickening manila folder, Pia replayed different scenarios in her mind. What if she'd never answered the phone when Dr. Rush-kin called with the bad news? If she'd been away with Will, or at her parents' house in Queens, she would be perfectly fine now, absolutely alive instead of on an elevator to death. If Will had bypassed her breasts that night at the Greenbriar when they made love, and every other time since, she'd be at the organic dry cleaners right now. Easily, she could have ignored the lump she felt in the shower. Easily, she had! It's not like she'd felt *that* sick. A nap in the car? What's the big deal? Fatigue is a national mal-aise. She'd heard it on the evening news. All she had to do was alter her lifestyle somewhat. Blanca could pick up Emma from school while she napped. They could have the windows tinted on the SUV so none of her gossipy neighbors could ever see her curled up on the backseat. If no one had told her she had cancer, perhaps her body would forget it, too. Didn't she once hear about a woman who outlived her husband because he never told her that the doctor told him she had only months to live? How could one early morning phone call destroy a whole life?

"The new wing is nice." Will watched the numbers descend into letters on the digital display over the elevator doors.

Pia nodded, but she didn't agree. The very name was wrong. *Wing.* It was absurd. Wings were uplifting. They gave you flight, took you elsewhere, not down to the basement level where human beings were irradiated and injected with poison. That wing, with its mini Starbucks and laptop stations in the lobby, was a farce. Who were they trying to fool? Coffee aroma only slightly masked the fact that they were in a hospital that smelled the way all hos-pitals do: disinfectant, Betadine, latex gloves, and rotting flowers for people who never did get well. Plus, the infusion unit—the final hope for the sickest of the sick—was closer to hell than heaven. Of course her treatment was in a basement. There would be no means of escape.

When the elevator went *bing* and the doors opened, Will sounded pitiful with his overcheerful, "Here we are!" Pia followed him off, but turned to leap back into the elevator when she saw a gray-faced man and a Vermeer woman: white lipped and lashless. Quickly, Will grabbed her arm.

"This is us."

Suddenly weak in the knees, Pia gripped her husband's strong shoulder. Why had she answered that damn phone?

"Everything off from the waist up."

Each morning was the same routine. Will and Pia dropped Emma off at school together, then Will left his wife at the hospital entrance, a few yards from the elevator leading to the infusion unit.

"I can stay," Will offered each day, even as they both knew he didn't mean it. Like Pia, he'd rather be anywhere else.

"I'm fine," she said. "Go be a master of the universe."

They kissed good-bye. A bittersweet connection. Each morning's kiss was numbered in their minds, though neither would dare utter such an unthinkable thought. Pia was careful to walk fully upright and wave cheerfully as Will drove off. As if chemo was college and Will was a proud parent.

At first, it was true. She *was* fine. This isn't so bad, she thought. The wide pink leatherette recliner was comfortable enough. The

IV needle only hurt a little as it punctured the bouncy vein on the back of her hand. It felt like any other shot or the sharp prick of donated blood. With her iPod buds in her ears, she closed her eyes and let her head fall back against the soft chair, listening to the party favorites Will had downloaded for her. It was the music they played when they made love—all pulsing beat and memory of dancing drenched in sweat and abandon. The sound of freedom.

"All done."

That's what the nurse said after the first full dose, her hand gently shaking Pia's shoulder.

"That's it?"

"That's it."

Pia sat up, took a deep breath expecting a wave of nausea. She reached up to stroke her hair, bracing herself to feel a clump let loose in her hand. But there was nothing. She felt fine. When Blanca picked her up, she didn't go to bed when she got home. Instead, she called the salon to see if Tara had time for a full-leg wax and a paraffin manicure. Her nails were a mess. She drove herself to the appointment and made it home without the slightest desire to park beneath the tree at the far corner of Ann Taylor's back lot.

On day two she felt fine, as well. That whole first week, in fact, made her question chemotherapy's frightening reputation. Perhaps other patients were less strong? Less fit?

"I'll take my own car, darling," she told Will.

"You sure?"

"I'm meeting Mama in the city for lunch."

Hiding her illness from Lidia would be easy, she thought, relieved. Why had Dr. Payton been so glum? Was it his healing strategy? Prepare his patients for the worst so he would seem like a miracle worker? *Payton over at CG is the* best. Was his dire diagnosis merely a means of enhancing his reputation? Surprising herself, Pia felt hopeful. She brought homemade antioxidant muffins for the nursing staff.

"Blueberry, pomegranate, and flax seed," she chirped. "Try this one with chia seeds."

"You're the best," they replied, which of course Pia believed. God had selected her for extraordinary things, given her phenomenal strength. Her mother had taught her as much from the very beginning. Why, look at Emma. How many women could produce such perfection? Clearly, God had decided her time wasn't up. Her very life would be testament to the fact that prayers were not only heard, they were answered, too.

"Love the hat, Jareesha."

Pia waved to her "bosom buddy" in the neighboring recliner, the ashy woman at the end of the row who wore a baseball cap with fake Pippi Longstocking braids springing out comically from the sides. At least it wasn't a turban, Pia thought. No one looked good in a turban, not even Greta Garbo or Lana Turner, no matter what the movie magazines said. Nestling into the recliner, Pia inserted her iPod earbuds and turned the music up loud.

Then it hit.

When the nurse tapped her shoulder that day, Pia's hand moved slowly to pull the buds out of her ears, to turn the music off. Suddenly, she felt as if the recliner had been dipped in quicksand.

"Let me help you up." The nurse took her arm.

"I must have fallen asleep," Pia replied, confused. A knowing look on her face, the nurse slipped her strong arm around Pia's back and said, "Lean on me, honey."

Uncomfortable leaning on anyone, Pia swung her leaden legs to the side as a wave of nausea overtook her. She slapped her hand over her mouth. In one expert move the nurse grabbed a vomit tray with her free hand and placed it under Pia's chin just in time.

"I'm sorry," Pia sputtered, mortified.

"Rest here a minute or two." The nurse tucked Pia back into the recliner. "I'll be right back with some water," she said, replacing the full vomit tray with an empty one. Before she returned, Pia had thrown up again.

That day—really, she could pinpoint the exact minute—cancer abducted her. The pink poison running through her veins held her life hostage. She was powerless to stop it. Though she tried not to, she pictured the shifting color of her organs in her mind. They darkened around the edges, the way hamburger meat turns purplish if left out on the counter too long. She imagined pus-filled lesions bursting open in soft tissue, frayed strings of muscles that were no longer able to stick to bone. She could almost smell the rotting of her own flesh. In one awful moment, Pia became a cancer patient. No longer God's blessed messenger,

Pia Winston would soon be one of those women in a scarf, the type people looked at, then looked through.

While she waited for Blanca to pick her up that day, Pia glanced around the infusion unit and thought, *Thank God the hospital had the sense not to paint the new cancer wing* pink. Her disease was *black*, not the color of newborn girls.

Chapter 21

Dazed, Muriel descended the escalator in the vertical mall with her sister close behind her. Head down, she gripped the rubber rails with both hands and watched the metal teeth flatten and mesh together at the bottom before sliding beneath the ground. As the first floor approached, she barely had the energy to step up one inch to avoid getting sucked under.

On the way down, Pia rested her chin on Muriel's shoulder the way she had in her apartment. Again, Muriel inhaled her sister's scent—pressed linen, botanical shampoo, expensive elegance. It was a fragrance she'd smelled all her life. Muriel wanted to reach back, encircle her sister's head in the crook of her arm, and announce, "I love you," but the escalator hit bottom and they broke apart. Besides, saying those three words now would only highlight the fact that she'd never uttered them out loud before.

"I'll go with you to the train station," Muriel said instead, awkwardly taking Pia's arm.

"Just because I'm dying doesn't mean I'm an invalid."

Pia laughed and Muriel tried to. Then Pia stopped and said, "Before I got sick, I never thought about that word: 'invalid.' Pronounce it differently and it becomes in*val*id. As if being ill means you're no longer legitimate. You're void. There's some truth to that."

Muriel wanted to tell her sister that she was the most valid person she'd ever known. That feeling invalid had zero to do with being sick. But it felt wrong to say anything even close to that, so she said nothing at all.

A line of cabs idled in the shaded curve of Columbus Circle. Pia walked toward the front of the line and handed her sister the shopping bag with the gray satin dress in it. Her look said it all: *I'm counting on you.*

"I won't let you down," Muriel said. "I promise."

"Mama already senses something is up. I've avoided her for weeks. You have to be strong for me, Muriel. I'm begging you not to tell her."

"I won't. I swear."

Knocking on the cab window Pia said, "Grand Central," to the driver. He nodded. She opened the cab door and gracefully folded herself in. Muriel stood there with her shoulders slumped, the shopping bag dangling from her fingertips.

"What else do you need?" she asked, helpless. "What can I do?"

Pia shut the door and rolled down the window as the driver inched into traffic. "There is one thing," she called out to her younger sister.

"Tell me. *Anything.*"

"Forgive me."

With that, the cab lurched into an opening in the lane and took off. Muriel stood like a block of wood and watched Pia roll the window back up. Through the rear window she saw her wave good-bye over her shoulder, then pull the seat belt across her chest and snap it in place. Muriel noted how the outline of Pia's perfect hair grew smaller as the cab disappeared around the corner. She wanted to shout, "Of course!" Had she known it would be the last time she saw her sister with any semblance of life, she surely would have. She would have chased after the cab, caught it at a red light, slapped her palm against the window until Pia rolled it down again. Ignoring the grime ridge it would create on her white dress, she would have reached both arms into the hot car to hug her.

"It doesn't matter," she would have said. "Siblings are cruel sometimes." Even as the driver grew impatient and angry honking blared around her, she wouldn't let her sister go. "I forgave you years ago."

Earlier, in her apartment, she would have returned Pia's kiss in the kitchen, hugged her even, used the tight space between them to inhale her, to memorize her face and the way her collarbone created two deep hollows at the base of her neck. In front of the mirror, she would have pressed their cheeks together and compared features, freckle by freckle. "My nose is wider," she would have said, "and your jawline is more defined." She would have searched for their parents' genetic contribution.

"You got Mom's hips; I got Dad's height."

Lifting her sister's hand, she would have placed its flat palm against hers, measuring the width of each finger, counting the folds in each knuckle. She would have traced the life line on the fleshy inside to see how long they had together. Then, she would have held that same hand up to her beating heart and told Pia how much she meant to her, how she'd wanted to be exactly like her for as long as she could remember, from the very beginning of her consciousness, the first moment she discovered she wasn't enough the way she was.

"I'm sorry I never was the sister you wanted," she would have whispered, letting that sentence hang aloft so Pia could feel its sincerity, the breaking of her heart. When Pia scoffed, she would have admitted, "I tried. Honestly, I did." Then she would have asked, "Can we start over? Right here? Right now?"

Yes, that's what she would have said and done. If only she had known or been another type of person entirely.

Chapter 22

EACH MORNING, FOR the briefest second between the fading of her Ambien and the dawning of her day, Pia felt normal. In bed, for one blip of time, she forgot her fate. Nausea, her constant companion, was still asleep. Time, her enemy, was suspended. The feeling was as luscious—and fleeting—as the final moment before anesthesia knocks you out. That ecstasy, the lifting of burden. You try to grasp it even as you long to melt into it. It's a glimpse of heaven, a preview of the way you'll feel when God finally greets you.

"At last, my child, we meet."

He will wipe away every tear from their eyes, and death shall be no more, neither shall there be mourning, nor crying, nor pain anymore for the former things have passed away.

Pia lived for that solitary moment between unconsciousness and waking, beneath the cool cotton sheets of her bed, where her satin slippers waited on the floor below like seraphim. God's breath was a soft caress on her cheek. *What no eye has seen, nor ear heard, nor the heart of man imagined, is what God has prepared for those who love him.*

Memorized Scripture comforted her like waves gently rolling onto sand. A meditative loop. In that split second, her existence was still the holiness of ordinary life: errands and motherhood and chitchat with her facialist, manicurist, the pharmacist, and the new guy at the wine shop.

"Good morning, lovely. How are you feeling?"

Poof. With the crash of a storm swell hitting the shore, it was gone. In its place was Will's face. The love in his eyes was permanently shaded by fear. Propped up on one elbow, robust in his silk T-shirt, with his round cheeks and white teeth and Russian trapper hat of hair, Will gazed down at his wife and asked, "Need anything?"

Slowly, Pia reached her pale hand up to cup her husband's stubbled chin. She left it there a moment, feeling the warm prickle of his flesh. *What can I say,* she thought. *The truth?* That she wanted him to stop asking that question every morning. Both questions, really. The answers were always the same: she felt like crap and she needed a miracle. The hope in his eyes made her feel hopeless. She wanted things back the way they were. The careless way he assumed she would always be there, his selfishness. If she could, she would have rubbed the desperation out of his eyes.

Is today our last day? Tomorrow?

Pia wanted Will and Emma to stop tiptoeing around her.

Leave her alone with a box of saltines and Vicodin. Not forever, only long enough to muster the strength to bear the most painful part of cancer: its *reflection*—in Emma's young face when her mother missed yet another track meet, in Will's panicked expression each time she started coughing and couldn't stop. It was the way her hairdresser's eyes went white when a clump of Pia's hair came out in his hands. After that, they stopped gossiping about the latest celebrity Botox blunder. The newest Hollywood marriage to fall apart. "Can't *anyone* stay married in that town?"

Pia ceased being a person and became a disease. Hair appointments felt like wakes. Silence descended in the salon when she walked in.

"How are you holding up?" the stylist would ask so solemnly Pia wanted to slap him.

"I'm still in here," she wanted to scream. "My body is dying, not me."

God give me strength. People forget that you're alive until the very moment you're not.

"Fine," she said, instead. The word intended to shut everyone up. And out. To erase those pitiful sighs. Not that it did any of those things. Soon Pia stopped seeing her hairdresser at all. There wasn't much hair to do anyway after her second chemo cycle.

What did she need? *Honesty.* The uncensored facts about cancer's collateral damage. How friends would lunge forward at the beginning bearing fruit baskets and stories about so-and-so's sister-in-law who had such-and-such cancer. "She's still alive!"

they'd say, encouragingly, not realizing how that very sentence highlighted the improbability of it.

"Have you tried acai berries?"

"Meditation?"

"Acupuncture?"

"Organic grass-fed beef?"

She needed a friend who had the courage to say, "Christ, Pia, you look like shit." One who would show up without makeup or with a chipped manicure on her worst hair day so Pia wouldn't feel so ugly. She wanted to see someone else's dark circles, needed a friend who had the confidence to listen more than worry about what to say.

"You don't know what to say to me?" Pia wanted to shout. "Too bad. I didn't invite you here. I'm going to die and so are you. Deal with it."

How was she feeling? That's what Will wanted to know?

Pissed.

Cancer, she now knew, was like a recurring spousal argument.

"You think I *want* to nag you?"

"Apparently."

"What I *want* is for you to take care of things without me having to ask you to."

"You don't feel taken care of? This house? Those shoes? Your life?"

"That's not what I mean and you know it."

"What I know is that you don't have to be on my case every minute."

"If I don't say something, it doesn't get done."

"Try me."

"Deal."

Briefly, things get better. Until the inevitable relapse.

"You can't *smell* that garbage?"

Cancer doesn't listen. It doesn't give a damn.

Let it go, you tell yourself. *It's beyond your control.* Tuck your anger beneath the blessings in your life. Pray. *Be strong and courageous. For the Lord, your God, goes with you. He will not leave you or forsake you.*

It's only garbage. Is it so awful that it reeks? Turn the other cheek. Walk away. And when you see the dirty socks on the floor, the wet towel draped over the edge of the tub, the pile of junk mail scattered on the kitchen table, the coffee mug making a ring on the bedside table with the coaster right *next* to it, turn away again. *Let it go.* Breathe. Focus on the positive.

Cancer doesn't listen. It doesn't give a *shit*. It's a petulant, disrespectful man-child leaving bits of blackened tissue all over your body. Forcing you to clean up its mess. A *bout* with cancer? Who initiated that idiotic phrase? Cancer is a siege, a war, a massacre, not a spell. Jesus.

Will, God bless him, was suffocating. All that hovering. As if *he* could make Pia better by following her from room to room. Why had he never had time for her when she was well? Now, when she needed solitude to wallow, bald headed, behind her closed bedroom door, curled in a ball beneath the covers with her face buried deep in the pillow, screaming, *now* he was available to take her emotional temperature every minute?

"Feeling scared, honey? Sad? Frustrated? Upset?"

All of the above. Satisfied? Now leave me alone.

And why didn't anyone warn her that her husband *would* leave her alone? He'd stop reaching for her in the middle of the night and she'd stop wanting him to well before that? That she'd cease to feel like a woman entirely?

The therapist who made the rounds each week in the chemo basement had a way of softly stroking Pia's hand that drove her mad. She said, "It's okay to admit you're scared."

Scared? Bull*shit*. Pia was exhausted. Bucking up wore her out. Pretending she wasn't dying because nobody could handle it, well, that sucked the life out of her more than the rampaging cells now eating away at her lungs. Fury seemed to be the only thing able to fight its way through her collapsed veins.

"Want to help me? Explain why I got breast cancer at thirty-one? Not even old enough for a baseline mammogram! Explain to me how I was expected to believe that a mass in my breast was cancer? Women my age have cysts, not cancer."

"I hear that you're upset."

"You're damn right I'm upset. I'm not the cancer type."

"What type would that be?" The therapist's supercilious tone made Pia want to douse her in chemo juice.

"You know exactly what I mean—women who are unable to express their feelings. Doormats. That's not me at all. How many times had I told Will that his twelve-hour workdays made me feel like a single parent? And when Emma's school was considering adding more vending machines, I wrote a furious letter. Why, a couple of weeks ago, I asked Blanca to stop wearing that flowery perfume when she came to work. It was giving me a headache. Does a woman who can't communicate say *that*?"

The damn therapist didn't answer, merely nodded and stroked Pia's hand as if it were a puppy's paw.

Therapy was crap. All those platitudes: *Put yourself first. Don't be afraid to ask for help.* The only help she wanted was a machete to hack through the manure. Someone to tell her how ashamed she'd feel. Embarrassed by her body's weakness. Why didn't the therapist tell her that everyone who saw her would Rolodex through their own lives to make sure they hadn't done whatever she'd done to cause her cancer.

And what, exactly, *had* she done? Gone braless too often? Had overly spirited sex? Too many bong hits in college? Warm baguettes slathered in butter? Truth be told, she really *had* put Will's needs ahead of hers. He gave her a great life, a perfect child. So many other women had to work, feel their lives press down on their shoulders like a rucksack full of books. Not her. Pia was blessed. God smiled upon her again and again. Had that fact been secretly eating away at her? Had *guilt* turned her pink cells black? Did she have Emma too late? Sex too early? Too many years on the pill? What the hell did she *do*?

Answers. That's what she wanted. Not an insipid therapist with liver spots on her bony hands. Why had her body betrayed her? Been unfaithful, cheated on her while she was at the gym. Had she not treated it lovingly? Given it everything it needed? Vitamin water, yoga, Pilates. Was she not good *enough*? If she'd been paying more attention, this never would have happened.

Why didn't a therapist tell her that cancer would feel like the other woman?

It's your fault. All your fault.

The murky shadow of guilt hung over Pia's waning life. It followed her to the parent/teacher conference at Emma's school that was cut short when she started coughing, into her walk-in closet as she tried to dress for the cocktail party Will's firm was hosting—the one she swore she was well enough to attend.

"Wear that shimmery white dress," he'd requested, both eyebrows pumping up and down.

"You got it," she'd said, sexily, grinning through her nausea.

In the closet's full-length mirror, the sight of her naked body was shocking. How had she ever carried Emma in that concave belly? Her kneecaps were the only part of her spindly legs that touched at all and her shoulders were two doorknobs. When she zipped up the white sequined minidress Will had bought her at the Greenbriar, the one she'd worn to dinner on their last night there, the dress he'd nearly ripped off her when they got back to the room, it swam on her. The armholes gaped. Her collarbone jutted out like a shelf bracket. The dress draped so pathetically on her skeletal frame she was ashamed to show herself to her husband.

Frantically, Pia flipped through her clothes for something else to wear, trying on every cocktail dress she owned. But the outcome was the same. She looked awful. Like Dachau. Like death. She couldn't go. If she went to the party with Will, his office would be abuzz with whispers the next day.

"Did you *see* her?"

"She's anorexic."

"Poor Will. It must be hard living with someone mentally ill. Do you suppose he's having an affair?"

"I wonder if they're headed for a divorce. If so, I get first dibs."

What she *needed* was permission to drop out of her marriage, miss family dinners, be a bad mom, sleep through breakfast. She needed Will's assurance that he wouldn't fall in love with someone else, that he meant it when he vowed, "In sickness and in health." No matter how forcefully she pushed him away, she needed to know he'd stay put. Mostly, she needed him to help her bear the faraway look in their daughter's eyes.

"Emma will pull away from you. She needs to protect herself right now and you have to let her. You'll feel a crushing desire to grab your daughter and hold on so tightly she'll melt into your ailing flesh. It will tear you up, but I'll be here to hold you together."

That's what a good therapist would have said, instead of letting her see it—and feel it—for herself. Day by day, Pia witnessed her own disappearance through her daughter's eyes. She became a hologram, nearly faded into thin air. Emma looked right through her. To Emma, her mother's body seemed to have no blood in it at all; her loose gray skin looked like a dirty towel hanging in the bathroom. Seeing her constantly flat out on the couch or in bed was a pain. Always cold when it was a hundred degrees out. Too tired to do anything. And why didn't she wear her wig all the time at home? That stuff sprouting from her head didn't look like hair at all. It wasn't blond anymore and it was completely gone in patches; the rest was see-through and as wiry as old sweater threads. A pointy ridge on top of her skull made her look like an iguana. It's a total myth that heads are round; her mother's head looked like a football, even in a scarf. Really, her mom didn't look like her mom at all anymore and it made Emma not want to look at her because each time she did, she forgot what her real mother looked like a little bit more.

The *truth*. That's what Pia needed. The bald truth that hope would slip away so subtly you wouldn't notice until it was already gone. Life would become a counting of days. Minutes. You would look backward through photo albums instead of forward to anything. Why did no one tell her *that*?

"Next week, *rybka*, let's treat ourselves to high tea at that darling new cafe in the Village."

"Sounds fun, Mama."

"It's been so long since I've seen you, my *kochanie*."

"I know. I miss you."

"It's a date then? We'll meet Friday afternoon in the city?"

"Perfect. Oh, wait. *This* Friday?"

"Would Thursday be better?"

"No, Mama. I'm so sorry. I forgot all about Emma's school thing."

"What thing?"

"The parents have to volunteer at the school all week."

"What kind of nonsense is this?"

"I know. Can you believe it? The principal is young and modern."

"Ha. Old and old-fashioned worked fine for you, thank you very much."

"How 'bout the Friday after, Mama?"

"Or this Thursday?"

"The Friday after is better for me."

"Okay, *rybka*. We'll meet then and treat ourselves to high tea."

"Sounds fun. Can't wait."

Why didn't anyone mention how good she'd get at lying? At keeping people at bay? It was the only skill that had sharpened since her body went south. Had someone told her she'd get *good* at something—even dishonesty—she might not have felt so useless.

Late nights were the worst. In the particled darkness when Pia's sleep meds failed, with Will's measured breathing the only sound in the room, the house, the entire universe, Pia's demons effervesced. It was impossible to force them down. In those hours, fear literally paralyzed her. Curled in on herself, she was helpless to stop the sharp terror of death from stabbing her in the chest. *My God, why have you forsaken me?*

Unable to move, she confronted the relentless pain in her bones, the way they seemed to splinter against one another. She cursed her damned body for its hoggishness. A whole family depended on her. Her lovely Emma—the sparks of womanhood were beginning to flare. In her young face, you could see the faint outline of the woman she would become. Her stubbornness would flower into independence; those gangly limbs would grow into a body every woman would envy. Already, she carried herself with elegance beyond her years. Emma needed a mother to help her accept her extraordinariness without arrogance. As Pia knew well, beauty had to be managed skillfully. The line between self-assurance and snobbery was razor sharp. Will couldn't do it with that damn iPad affixed to his hand. Stock reports ran silently on every television. He could raise a daughter on his own? Never. Not *her* daughter.

In the blackness of those endless nights, Pia tumbled into a pit of loneliness so deep she couldn't see so much as a pinpoint of light. In despair, she envisioned a future without her. Emma would walk down the aisle with Will and his new wife. Another woman would clutch her daughter's hand in the delivery room repeating, "Breathe, sweetheart. *Hee hee hee. Whooo.* You can do it." Those tiny yellow socks, the kind that every woman holds aloft sighing, "Awww," would be wrestled onto kicking, toe-splayed feet by someone else. There would be no birthday cupcakes to decorate with smiley faces, no chilly Halloween nights standing on the sidewalk watching little animals pad up to a front door carrying plastic pumpkins and chirping, "Trick or treat!" Will would never encircle his tan, muscular forearms around her waist while she cooked her mother's hunter's stew, pressing his front into her back while whispering, "I am one lucky son of a bitch."

On those nights, too, in the deepest crater of her pain, Pia gave herself permission to fantasize about letting go. It would be so simple, so peaceful. The ecstasy of nothingness, the glorious end of expectations, the utter calm of passing. Cheating death was no way to live. Fighting was beyond exhausting. An extra Vicodin or two was all she needed to ease the fear and clear her way. Not suicide, but surrender. God would understand. Surely he never meant for his children to suffer when they could let go of this world and join Him in the next so easily. Life, she now understood, was a gift that could be returned. A heartbeat was a *choice*. She had the power to emancipate her body and free herself into the void. Knowing that was a comfort, a shred of control.

"I can go whenever I want to," she whispered to Will one evening when even morphine failed to bring relief. Worn out, he nodded, honestly unsure of which option he wanted her to choose.

No one told Pia that she might *want* to let go.

The truth. That's what she needed. In all its ugliness. The goddamned unretouched *truth*.

At her most defenseless, when Pia lay coiled on the bathroom rug, hollowed out from the constant retching, when the angry red radiation burn on her chest tugged at the scarred skin from her armpit to her sternum, when the swelling in her arm from the poisoned lymph nodes and the purple-black bruises where her plump veins were before they collapsed made her wince with every movement, when the central line in her chest infected her blood and all she wanted to do was lie down and give up, Pia needed someone to help her sit upright, fling open the bathroom window and knock out the screen so she could lift her chin to the sky and shout, "Fuck you, God, you prick. You goddamned fucking motherfucker."

Had a therapist genuinely wanted to help her, she would have told her that death blackens your soul. It makes you hate everything, even God. She would have stopped petting her fucking hand and yelled at God with her.

That's how she was feeling. *That's* what she needed. Not that she could tell Will or anyone else. Who wanted to hear it?

"I don't need a thing, sweetheart," she said each morning as her husband propped himself up on his elbow and stared down at her with his shadowed eyes, as her queasy stomach announced itself and the day already felt like a sandbag on her chest. "I'm fine. How are you?"

Chapter 23

THAT DAY AT Columbus Circle, Muriel had watched her sister depart in a cab the way it would be filmed in a movie or staged on Broadway. The forlorn wave in the rear window, her lingering look of good-bye. On-screen there would be misty rain, a hosed-down street to make the asphalt reflective; onstage a yellow spill from an old lamppost would encircle the actress in a lonely spot. The scene would be underscored with chords from a single violin.

Long after Pia's cab merged into the belching miasma of midtown traffic, Muriel stood on the sidewalk staring at the site where Pia had been, sensing the imprint of her kiss on her check. Smelling her clean scent. Feeling the corded handle of the dress bag resting in the nest of her curled fingers. She left Columbus Circle in a daze, crossing diagonally against all lights, wondering why drivers kept honking at her. At the bus stop, she had intended to wait for the M5, but climbed aboard the M104 instead, not even aware of it until the bus continued straight at

Seventy-second Street instead of turning left. "Hey," she shouted. "He missed the turn."

As if speaking to a mental patient off her meds, an elderly passenger asked, "Where are you trying to go, dear?"

For days afterward, Muriel felt befuddled. Twice, at the Vaclav casting session, Joanie had to prod her.

"Miss Sullivant? Care to join us?"

With her script hanging limply in her hands, Muriel would jerk her head up and blush. The actor standing on his mark across from her would look all put out.

The strangest sensation settled into either side of her forehead. Static, almost, as if her brain was between channels. By the end of the week, however, she felt tuned in. Muriel became convinced that she'd *misheard* what Pia had told her. It wouldn't be the first time her nerves interfered with her hearing. On her first date with Kent Bond, she thought he said, "I went to Northwestern," but he was really talking about his desire to visit Seattle.

In the hundreds of times Muriel had rerun the scene in the dressing room she was certain that "cancer" was never uttered. When you have cancer doesn't the actual *word* come up? It's not like there were synonyms for it. (Organistic erosion? Cellular chaos?) Besides, who died of breast cancer anymore? Why, the science section of the *Times* recently labeled it a "chronic disease"! Soon those pink-ribbon walks would fade in the same silent manner as the rainbow-hued AIDS walks had. On to the next trendy disease. Asperger's, perhaps? What color would its ribbon be?

Yes, that whole messy business with Pia was a huge misunderstanding. Perhaps Pia had really been confessing her plan to get *implants*. Maybe Will had said something hurtful to her regarding her boyish frame. Which wouldn't surprise Muriel in the least. On the class ladder, Will had always been a rung below his wife.

On her lunch break, in the dappled sunlight beneath a Siberian elm in Union Square Park, Muriel sat on a bench and called her sister. Together, they could laugh about how silly and self-absorbed she'd been. "Now that I can see beyond my own belly button," she'd say, "tell me again why you want me to hang on to that gray dress?"

Pia's cell went straight to voice mail so Muriel hung up without leaving a message and called the Connecticut house. The phone rang three times before Will picked up.

"Muriel."

His voice was black. He said nothing for a long moment. Then he inhaled a breath that seemed to swirl up from his toes, gather in his throat, and tumble out past his teeth. In that audible breath, Muriel, too, lost her air. Her body sank onto the bench like a sack of rice. All of a sudden, she felt so tired she imagined sitting there, immobilized, as the sun darkened to orange and the park lights flickered on. Pigeons would land on her shoulders and shit down her back. In Will's exhalation, Muriel's denial dissolved like castor sugar in boiling tea.

"Is Pia, um, home?" she asked, stupidly, sounding like a teenage girl.

Really, Muriel wanted to hang up. Her impulse was to pop

the smart card out of her cell and fling it down the nearest storm drain. She wanted to clamp her hands over her ears like a child and pretend she'd never heard Will say her name. In her mind she would continue to picture him at work, surrounded by computer screens. Pia would be at the spa in the village, the latest exfoliating concoction bubbling on her skin. Emma—lovely Emma—would be consumed by the boy who stared at her in ecology class. Should she stare back? Ignore him?

"Aunt Muriel, why are boys so weird?"

Had Muriel not heard the moan at the end of Will's breath, she could still entertain the fantasy that Pia had gone Hollywood with a boob job. She could plot a way to leak it to Lidia in a petty manner that would make her sister look shallow.

"I never thought she was the type to alter what God gave her," she would say, tossing her hair. "Funny, she's always seemed so confident."

Had Will not exhaled the truth, Muriel could look the other way.

"She's asleep," he said, sighing once more.

"Oh." Muriel felt the weight of the phone in her hand.

"It's fairly bleak around here, I'm afraid."

"I'm so sorry."

"We all are. What can you do?"

"Is Emma okay?"

"What do you think?"

"I didn't mean . . . I mean—"

"Forgive me. This whole situation is fucked."

A bloated silence expanded between them like pizza dough. Muriel's brain went blank. She tried to recall what Marvin sang to Whizzer in the soundtrack from *Falsettos* but all she could remember was Whizzer's song "You Gotta Die Sometime."

"If you need anything . . ." Muriel's voice trailed off.

"I do. Keep Lidia occupied. She's been sniffing around and Pia refuses to see her. I can't keep her away forever."

Ah, yes. Muriel swallowed. She pressed her eyes closed. "Of course," she said, wishing, of course, he'd asked for anything else. Let Emma move in. Spend weekends running errands around Connecticut. Donate half of her liver. "I'm on it, Will. You can count on me."

The moment she hung up, Muriel called her mother.

"Why?"

That's what Lidia said when Muriel suggested they meet in the city for lunch.

"It'll be fun, Mama. Just us girls." She winced. Even when Muriel was a girl she'd never been one of the girls.

"What's going on with your sister? She won't see me."

"Nothing," Muriel said quickly, overopening her eyes while she talked on her cell, hoping that an expression of innocence might lighten her voice. "Why do you ask?"

"Aren't you listening? I said she won't see me."

"There's a fabulous food court at the Plaza." Again, she winced. Words like "fabulous" sounded absurd in her mouth, as if her tongue was playing dress-up.

"Is she okay?"

"Who?"

"You know very well who!"

"Why do you ask?"

"Aren't you *listening*, Muriel?"

The difference between lying for someone and lying *to* them was vast, Muriel suddenly noticed. Lidia Sullivant was as easily redirected as a hurricane headed for a trailer park. There was no nudging her off course. In desperation, Muriel heard herself promising to invite Pia to join them. "It'll be fun! Just us girls!"

The following week, when Lidia came bustling through the door of the downtown sushi restaurant Muriel had picked (based on a *Times* rave review), her first question was, "Where's your sister?"

"Sake?"

"I called her this morning and Will said she was asleep."

"It's made with highly polished rice."

"She's not ill, is she?"

"Waiter!"

Muriel's eyebrows felt sweaty. After her mother sat down and eyed her sharply, her mouth fell open and she began to blather. "Funny story, Mama. Pia was, um, riding Emma's bike. You know, the new one they got her for Christmas? The one with all those, um, gears? And, well, she'd accidentally taken NyQuil during the day, the *green* liquidy one that zonks you out . . ."

Breaking the first rule of successful lying, Muriel overexplained Pia's absence. She knew better. Endless hours of crime stories on TV had taught her that the best liars stuck as closely to the truth as possible. *Yes, I've been in that house. I was invited in for a glass of water. Naturally I might have touched all* sorts *of things.* Still, she couldn't help herself.

"You know how steep their driveway is. Wasn't it recently re-graveled?"

Groaning impatiently, Lidia reached into her purse for her cell. Before Muriel could stop her, she called Pia on speed dial. Muriel noticed that her sister was number *one.* Was she even on her mother's contacts list?

"Darling!"

Astoundingly, Pia picked up. Muriel's heart fell into her stomach. Where the hell was that waiter?

"I'm here with your sister," Lidia said. "Are you okay, *ko-chanie?*"

"The bike didn't crash, per se," Muriel said loudly, leaning across the table. "It sort of *skidded.* You know, that thing that happens with a motorcycle on a sharp curve? Only not that bad, of course."

Covering the mouthpiece on her cell, Lidia said, "Shhh."

Mercifully, the waiter arrived.

"Two sakes, please. Large."

Lidia listened and nodded as Pia said something or other. In a motherly way, she cooed sympathetically and muttered, "Aw." With pursed lips, she shook her head. *Tut, tut.* When the waiter returned with a ceramic flask of steaming sake and poured two cups, Muriel singed her throat by downing hers like a vodka shot.

"Heavens, Muriel," Lidia said after she hung up. "You're so dramatic."

"Dramatic?" she croaked, pouring herself another cupful.

"Pia is *fine*. She didn't say a word about any cycling accident. Will needed her at the last minute, is all. You know how demanding he can be."

It had never even occurred to Muriel to blame it on the man.

"The eel roll is supposed to be fabulous, Mama. Shall we order two?"

THE WEEK AFTER, Muriel met her mother at an Italian restaurant in Queens.

"I read that the calamari here is to die for," she said, smoothing the napkin flat on her lap.

Lidia replied, "Black isn't as slimming as everyone says it is." Then she added, "That white napkin will leave lint all over your pants."

"Yes. Well. Hmmm." Muriel scanned the menu from top to bottom. "I think I'll have a salad."

"Caesar salad is as fattening as a Big Mac."

"Okay, then, uh, the Italian Cobb looks fab."

Lidia groaned, "Did you not see *salami* as one of the ingredients? Not to mention Parmesan cheese."

By dessert—which she didn't dare order—Muriel decided it was best to avoid edibles with her mother. They were in New York! There were plenty of other things to do.

"Hey! The Barney's warehouse sale starts Monday, Mama. Want to meet me after work? The deals are delish!"

Really, she *had* to stop talking like a Real Housewife.

For her sister, Muriel plodded along with her mother to Barney's ("Emma would look darling in this!"), the Museum of Modern Art ("De Kooning's brushstrokes feel so, I don't know, *violent*."), Lidia's nail salon in Queens ("Perhaps a natural shade to elongate my fingers?"). Each time Muriel saw Lidia, she was subjected to a full-body scan.

"Coupon?"

"*Coupon?*"

"For that drugstore hair color?"

"Why yes, actually. Buy one, get one half off."

"Foundation, too?"

"No, that was full price."

"Same drugstore, though, I'm guessing. Thank goodness they don't sell clothes. Or do they? I must say, Muriel, your T-shirts look very mass market."

On Saturdays, from time to time, Muriel took the M train to her parents' home for a visit.

"What's new in showbiz?" Owen would ask, sitting in his favorite easy chair at one end of a highly polished coffee table. His wife, straight-backed, sat in the matching chair across the room.

"Muriel is *hardly* in show business."

Ignoring her, Owen would say, "Aren't you still in casting?"

"Since when is reading lines on a page *casting*? Let's not live in a fantasy world, Muriel. You're more of a secretary, am I right?"

"Do secretaries even exist anymore? *I* don't even have a secretary. Besides, I believe the correct term is 'executive assistant.'"

"Since when is an engineer an *executive*?"

"Our daughter lives in the greatest city in the world, Lidia. How many young people can say that?"

"Sure, she's young now, but with no man on the horizon her fertility is aging by the minute."

From her familiar perch on the outskirts of the household—as if Muriel had always lived in the suburbs of her family—she watched her parents spar like Foreman and Ali, eventually asking, "Any leftover *golabki*?"

For her sister, Muriel lived with a stomach tied in all manner of knots.

Chapter 24

MORE THAN ANYTHING, keeping Pia's secret weighed heavily on Muriel's eyelids. On the way to work, she fell asleep against the bus window. Twice, she'd dropped off in the middle of *Jeopardy!* with an open carton of Ollie's takeout toppled over on the frayed towel on her bed. Sitting through a Broadway show was nearly impossible. She'd missed a whole chunk of the second act of *The Book of Mormon*, waking up perplexed when Cunningham was in charge.

Late August didn't help matters any. During New York's muggiest month, Muriel slogged through the suffocating air, her damp forehead spiked with Julius Caesar bangs. The moment she arrived at the office, she turned on the air conditioner full blast and leaned in close, pulling open the neckline of her mass-market T-shirt so the cool air could dry the sweat that had soaked through to the underwire in her bra.

"Good morning, sunshine."

Joanie shuffled in midmorning. Unlike most large people, she didn't sweat. She grunted and puffed and groaned when she lifted her heft off a chair. Yet in the years Muriel had known and worked for her, she'd never seen as much as a glisten on her boss's forehead or upper lip. "I do all my sweating on the inside," Joanie explained, whatever that meant.

That particular summer day was a quiet one. A Friday sort of feeling was in the air though it was midweek. At last, Vaclav had been cast and that project was wrapped up. Joanie was now searching for an actress to star in a new independent feature. The film's financing was secured (such as it was), the script was polished, locations were scouted, and a male lead was cast. The female lead, as usual, was more challenging. Producers were hunting for a beautiful, slender, young (of course, of course, of course) actress, able to convincingly portray a temporarily homeless single mother hiding an addiction to meth. One whose face and physique were attractive enough to desire, yet not surgically altered in any obvious way.

"No Botox addicts," the cocky postpubescent producer told Joanie, "though a boob job would be okay. Unless it's a double D or something."

"Got it."

"Nothing pornish."

"Good to know."

"Think Halle Berry in *Monster's Ball*."

"Terrific." After Joanie hung up the phone, she said out loud, "Kill me now. Doesn't he know Halle has the only natural breasts left in Hollywood?"

With her cheeks still pink from the commute into work, Muriel was slumped in her desk chair thumbing through a stack of color head shots and pulling out promising résumés.

"Another SEP," Joanie announced, dispirited, from across the room. With a sympathetic shake of her head, Muriel swiveled her chair slightly away so Joanie couldn't see how sleepy she was already becoming. A Halle Berry, they both knew, was hard to find at any price. A temp-size salary with an inexperienced leading actor and an unknown director? Well, no question it was an SEP: a "Sow's Ear Project." A one-in-a-million shot at turning nothing into something special. Casting was everything.

Joanie was on the phone all morning. Always, there was a slim chance that a known actress would want to redirect her career with an indie. Particularly a beauty who could excite critics by forgoing flattering lights and makeup. A "Charlize" Joanie dubbed it after Charlize Theron's bloated turn as a serial killer in *Monster*. Apparently, any movie with a stunning woman gone ugly—and the word "monster" in the title—will kindle the all-important buzz needed to propel a star into Oscar contention. With a "name" everything else was negotiable.

"Crap," Joanie said after hanging up the phone. She reached for a Hershey's Kiss from the bowl on her desk and unfurled the silver wrapping. The word she hated most in the English language was "unavailable."

Muriel's job that August morning was to ferret out an unknown talent, help her boss find a needle in Hollywood's haystack of young women who were told by their high school drama teachers, "You know, you're pretty enough to be an actress."

Someone with the charisma and talent to carry a small film to Sundance. Her eyelids began to droop right away. The bland faces in the head-shot stack blurred into a single beauty ad that had been retouched to boring porelessness. Muriel tried to focus on the same dimpled tip at the end of each surgically restructured nose, same envelope of a forehead, same chevron eyebrows locked in mock surprise over the same soupy Bambi eyes. But it all felt so meaningless. What did a nose have to do with anything? Really, *what*?

"Well?"

From her desk across the room, Joanie unsheathed another Hershey's Kiss. A silver foothill of discarded wrappers rose up from the ashtray, their tiny flag tags sticking out in every direction.

"Nobody promising yet," Muriel said.

"That's not what I asked you."

Muriel lifted her lashes. "What did you ask me?"

Popping the chocolate into her mouth Joanie rolled it around before saying, "I asked if you'd turned to stone. I've been talking to Mount Murielmore for the past fifteen minutes."

"Sorry. I'm a little off today."

"Today?"

"Lately."

"A little? Do you also think Osama bin Laden is a little bit dead?"

Muriel hiccupped a laugh, then refocused on the head-shot pile on her desk. Juicy, smacking sounds were audible from across the room as the chocolate settled into Joanie's molars. Once the

Kiss was gone, she followed it with a nicotine chaser, lighting her cigarette the way a man would, cupped in both hands to protect the flame from an imaginary wind. From its perch in the corner of her mouth, the cigarette tip glowed orange as Joanie drew in a lungful. "Out with it," she said in a billow of smoke.

Muriel looked up. Then she looked away.

"I can't read a script without glasses," Joanie said, "but I'm not blind. Something has been eating at you for weeks. I've been giving you space, but time's up."

Sucking on the inner flesh of her bottom lip, Muriel glanced down at the freckles on her hands. What was the difference between a hand freckle and a liver spot anyway? Would anyone make an effort to distinguish between the two? At twenty-three, would onlookers assume she had early liver spots or late freckles? Combined with the moles on her arms, she might as well cover herself in tenting.

"Time's *up*, Sullivant."

Muriel pinched the corners of the head-shot stack into perfect alignment. She refused to look her best friend in the eye. Each time she did she was startled by Joanie's measuring stare. The way she cocked her head and sat as still as a cheetah lying in wait. It was impossible to hide from that woman. So far, Muriel had only been able to evade. She *wanted* to tell her what was going on. Honestly, she did. Every cell in her body longed to open its membranes and release the secrets that had been putrefying like a body part buried in the backyard. With her best friend, she ached to dissect each moment in the dressing room with Pia, the way that single teardrop spread like a pond ripple on the gray satin fabric. (It dried without a stain; she checked.) Muriel's muscles twitched with the desire to *confess*. She'd spent an entire day with her dying sister and only seen herself. And since that afternoon at the Plaza, she'd spoken to Pia only twice. Twice! Conversations that had been little more than lurching starts and stops. A teenager learning to drive a stick shift.

"How are you doing?"

"Fine."

"Fine? I mean, is ther—"

"Well, tired, of course."

"Of course. I meant, what ca—"

"What's up with you?"

"Me?"

"Anything good on Broadway?"

"Uh. Let's see, um."

"How's work?"

"Work? Good, I guess."

"Good. Good."

"Pia, I jus—"

"I know."

"It's just that I wanted to tell yo—"

"You don't have to say anything."

"I feel so, I don't know, *awful*. Is there anythi—"

"I'm fine. Really. Fine."

When she wasn't belching up half sentences or overlaughing at something innocuous Pia said or listening to the vast static of silence as her brain shorted out and she could think of not one single thing to say to a sister she'd known all her life, Muriel felt like a donkey braying into the wind. How could she tell Joanie how often she'd stared at the phone in her apartment and been unable to reach over with her mule hooves and dial? What kind of uncaring person did (didn't do) that?

"Still waiting," Joanie said, her steady gaze piercing straight through the smoke. Muriel made a face.

In the unbraiding of her emotions, strands of truth shamed her. Muriel was also *pissed*. Why had Pia not said something sooner? What kind of sister says nothing until it's time to buy the dress she'll wear for eternity? She'd seen her a couple of times before their lunch at the Plaza—once at the family house in Queens for Sunday supper, another time at a ballet performance of Emma's. Both times Pia looked tired. But she said nothing! Had Pia been *testing* Muriel, waiting for her to grab her sister's bony arms and insist, "I *know* something is wrong. I see it, I feel it in my gut. I'm not leaving until you tell me what's going on." Was Pia punishing her for failing at sisterhood yet again, the one time it mattered most?

Worse, Muriel suspected that she'd been so insignificant in her sister's life, so very nonexistent, the mere thought of telling her about her diagnosis never entered her head. Not until she needed someone to be the guardian of her final look and keep their mother at bay.

"Waiting, still." Joanie's stare bore a hole in Muriel's temple.

"I have to pee."

Standing, Muriel circled around her desk and loped into the restroom, aware that Joanie's wildcat eyes were watching her every footfall. A paper flag from a Kiss wrapper in Joanie's ashtray flared from an ember in her flicked cigarette. Taking another deep drag, Joanie seemed only to crouch lower in the brush.

In the quiet of the closet-size bathroom, Muriel held her wrists under the cold water stream. She rolled her neck in a circle, hoping to lure blood up to her brain. Letting her eyelids fall shut, she inhaled the bleachy smell of the automatic toilet cleaner, the lavender aroma of the hand soap. Her mind drifted back to one sunny afternoon with her sister, years before, when Lidia had deliberately left them home alone. When Pia's cruelty was sport.

Forgive me.

It wasn't your fault. Siblings are mean sometimes.

IT WAS A Saturday. Muriel's favorite day before her mother's infidelity abruptly scalpeled matinees out of her life. After she saw Lidia's Broadway kiss with Father Camilo, they never went into Manhattan together again. They never spoke of it, never checked the weekend newspaper for the latest show to come to town. Matinee Saturdays simply *stopped*. Curtain down.

Before long, it felt as though the theater had been a fantasy. The sequins, the feathers, the swelling violins, the high-kicking legs. All of it had been a dream and Muriel was now awake. Guilt was now her weekend companion. Why had she told her mother she saw them? Oh *why* didn't she make sure Lidia believed her when she agreed never ever to tell?

Saturdays, for Muriel, were now ordinary days when she hung around the house without much to do. Her one friend from school spent weekends with her father upstate. Logan was preparing to leave for art school in the fall. He didn't mind when his little sister followed him into the basement or out in the yard to watch him work on a bent metal sculpture or a collage made of colored glass. But with his hair spilling over his face, Logan's focus was so intense it was like staring at a sculpture itself.

"At art college," Muriel asked him, "do they ever make you take actual tests? Like with a pen?"

Without looking up, Logan replied, "Not sure."

Like his father, Logan prized silence. Words, they both believed, were best served as appetizers, never a main course. The truth was, Muriel barely knew either one of them. By the time she came along, Logan and Owen lived in a muted testosterone world, with Lidia and Pia chattering around them. Circling bodies in the asteroid belt. Collisions occurred, though infrequently. Muriel—a product of one such celestial accident—rotated in her own orbit, tumbling through her family in a slapdash sort of way.

After Muriel saw her mother kiss Father Camilo she felt confused and scared and sorry for her dad. Then it faded away because during those years Owen didn't seem as if he felt anything at all.

On that do-nothing day, Muriel pressed her nose against the jamb of the swinging dining room door, peering through the crack, watching a flushed Lidia dart around the entryway stuffing things into her purse. Keys jangled and tissues flashed white. In the wall mirror, she flattened her eyelids to check her shadow, rubbed her index finger over her front teeth. Just because Muriel didn't go into the city with her anymore didn't mean Lidia didn't go on her own. She probably drove her car over the bridge and skipped Times Square altogether now that she didn't have to drop her daughter off at a show. Maybe she met Father Camilo in a dim downtown alley that smelled like wet dirt and beer. Smoking a cigarette, he would be waiting in the shade of a Dumpster. Or they flat out met in a hotel and immediately hung the DO NOT DISTURB sign on the doorknob. Together, they would end each visit by crafting an alibi.

"MoMA's new exhibit is so fabulous I could have stayed all night."

Lidia often picked a fight with her husband on Saturday mornings. Not every Saturday, just the days when she'd stomp upstairs afterward and change into a flowing dress and spray her hair all stiff and puffy at the top and carefully apply eyeliner and leave the house in a huff.

"Just because you make me *live* in Queens, Owen, doesn't mean I have to spend my life here. I'm not in prison; it only *feels* like it!"

Even as a twelve-year-old, Muriel saw right through her. Owen merely looked away.

Honestly, Muriel wondered why her mother said anything at all. It didn't appear as though Owen cared. His lips were usually pressed into a horizontal line. His eyes looked out of focus. He, too, had begun disappearing on Saturdays. Sometimes Sundays, too. Work, he said. A cooling project using solar power, he said.

"But isn't the sun super *hot*?" Muriel had asked him. Slightly curving his lips, Owen pinched his daughter's chin on his way out the back door.

Grown-ups, Muriel had come to believe, were two faced. They insisted their kids tell the truth when they themselves rarely did. More often, they said the *opposite* of what they really meant.

"That's a lovely thing to say," Muriel once overheard her mother growl at her father.

"I tell you what you want to hear."

"What I *want* is to hear what's really on your mind."

"You're truly interested?"

"Of course I am. You're my husband."

Owen sucked in a deep breath. "Okay, then. At the moment, I'm mulling over a possible *vertical* loop of geothermal circulation. I've been developing one at work. It's for a new plant that manufactures candles and other wax-based products. As you might imagine, they have particular challenges with calefaction. That's *heating*, of course." He stopped. "You sure you're interested in this?"

Lidia said, "*That's* been on your mind?"

"Well, not every minute. I've also been considering the base blueprint. If a beta test holds up, we could produce a viable prototype by the next ICMSE convention."

From her hidden perch on the stairs, Muriel could see her mother's lips stiffen into a twig. Her eyes stared so far into nothingness she appeared blind. When Owen paused to take a breath, she leaped in with, "Fascinating!" then felt for dried spit at the outer edges of her mouth.

Weddings vows should be changed from "I do" to "I'll *say* I will but I won't." That's what was on Muriel's mind.

On that warm Saturday Muriel watched through the crack in the door as Lidia readied herself to leave the house. Pia leaned against the foyer wall and stared at her mother through sexily overgrown bangs. She retracted her foot just enough to let her mother pass. Lidia curved around her sulking daughter's slouch with the slightest sway of her hip. Together, as always, they moved as fluidly as seahorses in the ocean.

"God, Mama, what am I supposed to do with her all day?"

"Don't use the Lord's name in vain, Pia. How many times have I told you that?"

"Too many," Pia said, petulantly, shifting her weight to the other foot. Lidia shot her a reprimanding look before adding, "It's too hot to play outside."

"What, I'm supposed to stay *in* with her?"

A ravishing twenty-year-old still living at home, Pia would rather be anywhere but in Middle Village, Queens, with a twelve-year-old gnat named Muriel. Barefoot, Muriel watched through the crack in the door. She felt the grit of the hardwood floor on the soles of her feet. Her shorts pinched at the waist. The tank top she wore felt snug. Babcia Jula called her soft flesh "baby fat" even as Lidia and Pia rolled their eyes. Could you still be called a "baby" if you were very nearly a teen? Certainly not if you were such a grown-up secret keeper. With her sliver of sight, Muriel coveted her sister's long, straight legs. Even with one crossed over the other, Pia's cargo shorts didn't bunch up in the crotch. Her wispy haircut—striped with white blond highlights—framed her tanned face. The hot pink polo shirt and matching Crocs were so stylish she could step right into *Seventeen* magazine. Merely looking at Pia made Muriel feel like a slug.

"This once," said Lidia, "let Muriel play dress-up with my clothes."

Pia moaned as Muriel's heart lurched. Had she heard correctly? Dress up in her mother's clothes? Though she was too old to officially play dress-up, pretending to be someone else was Muriel's favorite thing to do. Especially in her mother's sparkly dresses. On the rare occasions when she was home alone, she would sneak into Lidia's forbidden wonderland. Long and narrow, Lidia's closet was organized by color and style. Probing its depths was like entering a kaleidoscope—so many exciting combinations, all hung on padded pink hangers. Each dress in the formal section was shrouded in its own garment bag with a peekaboo plasticine window. Ever so silently Muriel would slide the zipper down, lift the heavy dress off its padded perch, step into it, then prance about her mother's bedroom as if onstage— where life was lit to blur flaws and music rose joyfully out of the ground and goodness always, always won in the end.

In the entryway, as Lidia rushed to leave, Pia whined, "Why me?"

"She's your sister. Let her have a little fun. You can watch a DVD in my room. I bought *Legally Blonde* for you. Reese Witherspoon is supposed to be darling. Only don't let Muriel eat a *thing* while she's wearing my clothes. And make sure she puts everything back exactly where she found it. I don't want to find reds mixed in with blacks and whites. Understand?"

"When will you be home?"

Lidia dug for something at the bottom of her purse. "Hopefully before your father gets home."

"Do I *have* to?" Pia whined.

"Yes. You have to. Watch the movie. I left it in front of the TV."

If Pia had had her way, they never would have spent that afternoon together in the first place. Pia would have called a friend or a boy and met at the mall or taken the train into the city. Muriel would have sprawled on her bed, reading. Or sneaked into her mother's closet on her own. Really, she couldn't possibly blame her sister for what happened that day. Not when Pia never wanted to be anywhere near her from the start.

"Do this for me." That's what Lidia had said.

It wasn't your fault.

Leaving only the faintest scent of perfume behind, Lidia scurried out the front door. Muriel waited for her mother to yell, "Good-bye, Muriel!" but she said not a word, as if they'd never taken the train beneath the East River on matinee Saturdays, never smelled the dank air together, never read graffiti tags or dashed through Times Square holding hands, never watched love unfold upon a stage. As if Lidia had never needed Muriel at all.

"I'm trying on the beaded dresses first." Muriel pushed through the swinging door.

"God, Muriel," Pia sneered. "You're such a spy."

"Don't use the Lord's name in vain."

Pia shot her little sister a disdainful look. Had Muriel not witnessed the dress-up offer, she was quite sure Pia never would have honored it. Even in college she acted like she was the most popular girl in high school. God.

With her bare feet slapping the hardwood, Muriel skipped up the stairs into her mother's bedroom. The air conditioner was running full blast. The room smelled like freezer frost. Lidia's blue satin bedspread was like Lidia herself: icy, smooth, perfect. On top of her dresser was an oval mirrored tray, its gold-filigreed edge containing twinkling bottles of amber-colored perfume. Standing sentry in the corner was a wooden valet where Owen neatly hung his jacket every night and deposited his coins. It was the only visible evidence that he shared that bedroom at all.

Skulking in behind her, Pia plopped on her mother's bed, caring not one bit if she dented the satin. She chose a magazine from the stack on Lidia's bedside table and lazily flipped through it. Dashing into the magical closet Muriel chirped, "Remember that dress with the shiny beads that Mom wore to that Christmas party? Remember?"

Pia, being Pia, didn't answer. Not that Muriel expected her to.

Inside Lidia's closet, Muriel inhaled her mother. She closed her eyes and breathed in every exciting place Lidia had been. Manhattan, mostly, though Italy once when her parents went on a vacation that took them away for an entire week. Pressing her face into the row of hanging fabric, she grabbed as many clothes as she could, hugging them to her body. Her heart felt full. Muriel knew what Pia didn't know. *This* was her mother's way of apologizing. Lidia regretted all those times she'd left her alone in a theater. She was sorry to end their special Saturdays. She trusted her youngest child never to tell a soul what she'd seen. And Muriel would never let her mother down. She would pray that Lidia's sin would be forgiven. Though she didn't fully understand what she'd seen that day, Lidia's reaction let her know that God would be upset. If not, why not continue matinee Saturdays as they were?

Unhurriedly, Muriel ventured into the depths of her mother's closet. She ran her right hand lightly along the sleeves. Some clothes were soft, some woolly, some stiff with top-stitching. "I forgive you, Mama," she whispered. "And God will forgive you, too."

Muriel knew exactly which dress she was looking for. From Lidia's bedroom, she heard Pia turn on the TV.

One day when I'm grown up, Muriel imagined, *I will have a row of fancy dresses*. Matching shoes and handbags, as well. In her mind she could picture holding her hair up with both hands as her husband zipped up the back. He would nuzzle her neck the way she'd seen so many times onstage. "That's *my* wife," he'd say to everyone who admired her. Muriel's heart thrummed with the very notion of belonging to someone. She's mine. I'm his. We're *one*.

Eyes alight, Muriel found what she was looking for. She hoisted the heavy bag off its hanger and set it flat on the floor. No need to sneak today. On her knees next to the garment bag she lowered the zipper, careful not to snag any of the beads. Lovingly, she ran one hand down the front of the dress. Black satin, with spiky clear beads that dangled like icicles. Letting her eyes fall closed, she remembered the night her mother first wore it.

"How do I look?" Lidia had asked, twirling at the foot of the stairs.

"Stunning," Pia said, honestly.

Clasping both hands over her heart, Muriel had gasped, "Oh, Mama, you look like a movie star." Logan had nodded in his silent way, while Owen, in a black suit with a stiff bow tie had said, "Lovely." Then he went outside to warm up the car.

Even then, Muriel vowed that when she grew up and wore a dress like that her husband would be unable to turn away.

The bespangled dress made a noise like pennies in a change purse when Muriel lifted it out of the garment bag. Unzipping the back, she lowered the dress to the ground so she could step into it. She pulled the straps up over her tank top and shorts, felt the fringe at the bottom tickle her shins. It was heavy, like a shimmering suit of armor. Inside that dress, Muriel felt completely protected. Like a princess in her very own tower.

"Pia," she called out, "zip me up?"

Posing in the full-length mirror at the far end of the closet, Muriel turned this way and that. Then she scanned the Polaroid photos attached to the boxes overhead to find a suitable pair of shoes. Music floated in from the TV.

"Pia."

No answer.

"Pia!"

"What?"

"I can't reach the shoe box."

"So what."

"Give me a boost."

As always, Pia took her own sweet time. While she waited, Muriel held the shoulder straps in place. She imagined how she would look when she was old enough to highlight her hair.

"Pi-*a!*"

Suddenly, Pia stood in the doorway of the closet, smirking, holding a book in her hands. "Lookie what I found," she said in a singsongy way.

"Those." Muriel pointed up to one of the shoe boxes on the shelf. "And zip me up please?"

"Don't you want to see what I have in my hand?" Pia asked.

"Mama would let me try on her shoes, too."

"Are you *sure* you don't want to see it?"

An impatient Muriel said, "Pia. Zip me up."

"Not until you see what I have in my hands."

Muriel clucked her tongue. "You are such a pill."

"Shut up, Muriel."

"You shut up."

"It's Mama's *diary*. And I don't think I'll show you after all."

A wave of electricity shot through Muriel's body. Her arms got hot. "Don't read that," she said, wheeling around to face her sister. "It's private."

"I already read plenty. Plen-*tee*."

Fear flushed Muriel's cheeks. Her heart pounded.

There are things you need to know, sweetie, and things you don't.

"Gimme that," she said, holding out her hand. The strap on

the heavy dress fell off her shoulders. She lifted it back on, but it fell off again. Pia stood there grinning. Muriel said, "Mama is going to be mad."

"Not if she never knows."

"You won't be able to keep her secrets!"

"Oh, I think I can."

Pia blocked the exit to the closet.

What Muriel knew well was that Lidia would be mad at *her*. If her mother's sinful secrets took flight, like a cloud of angry bats swooping forth from a cave, she would grab her youngest daughter and shake her by the arm and freeze her with that icy stare. "Why didn't you stop her, Muriel? Why!?" If Owen came home first, and Pia told him before Lidia had the chance to make her *swear* that she wouldn't, she would be enraged. It would be all Muriel's fault. Instead of looking away, Lidia would never look at her at all.

"Hand it over," Muriel said, rushing her sister.

Pia laughed out loud. "Why should I?" Easily, she held the journal high enough over her head to be well beyond Muriel's reach. The sparkly dress suddenly felt unbearably heavy. Muriel wanted to surrender to its weight and crumple to the ground in a billow of shiny fabric. She wanted to hide beneath it and sleep with the bats in her own secret cave, nestled safely in their shared darkness.

"There are some things you need to know and some things you don't," she said to her sister.

Scoffing, Pia replied, "Muriel, you are as odd as odd can be."

Surprising herself, Muriel coughed up a laugh. Suddenly, she saw the pointlessness of it all. There she was, standing in her mother's dress, in her mother's closet, protecting her mother from the sin she'd committed. What did she care if Lidia's secrets took flight? She didn't let them loose!

"Go ahead and read Mama's diary. See if I give a whoop."

Muriel jutted her chin forward. She turned and walked to the back of Lidia's closet to return the heavy dress to its plastic shroud. Honestly, if Pia knew the truth, it would be a *relief*. She wouldn't feel so alone. A shared secret was a bond instead of a burden. A *connection* with her sister. Pia would sneak into her room after dinner, shut the door without a sound, flop down on her bed, and whisper, "I still can't believe it. A priest? Can you believe it?"

"I know!" Muriel would say, and Pia would press her index finger up to her sister's lips. "Keep your voice down. Mama can't know that we both know." Bellies down, knees bent, feet crisscrossing in midair, Muriel would bump shoulders with Pia. Even though she didn't fully understand what she'd seen that day, she would pretend that she did. She'd sidle up to her older sister and whisper the one question she'd been dying to ask *someone* since that late afternoon on Broadway: *when Mama kissed Father Camilo like that, did it mean they were* both *going to hell?*

"I *can* keep a secret, you know," Muriel proudly called out from the depths of the closet. "Remember the day you buried me at the beach?"

Pia ignored her and opened their mother's journal. Muriel

hung up the black beaded dress. "Besides," she said, "I already know what's in Mama's diary and I've never told a single solitary soul."

Pia read: "'My darling first daughter is as perfect a child as a mother could want.'"

"That's not what it says."

"'From the moment I saw her face, I knew God gave me a miracle.'" Holding up the diary, she showed her sister the very paragraph.

"*That's* what it says?" Muriel rolled her eyes. In a bossy tone, Pia continued, "'As a young woman, my Pia is smart, beautiful, slender, athletic, and independent. In life, she will achieve anything she wants.'"

Groaning, Muriel flipped through Lidia's other gowns to choose her next selection. Pia droned on, but Muriel ignored her. What a stupid thing to write! How utterly perfect Pia was? Like anyone needed to document *that*. Like the whole world didn't witness it every day of their lives. Muriel rifled through the rack to find another shimmering dress to try on. Maybe something silver?

"'Logan has the temperament of an artist. Years ago, I ceased trying to understand him.'"

"Blah, blah, blah," said Muriel.

"Then I guess you're not interested in this *long* paragraph about you."

Muriel's eyebrows shot up. In her shorts and tank top, she trotted to the Pia end of their mother's closet. "She wrote about me?"

"'Muriel,'" Pia began primly, as if reading the heading in an encyclopedia. "'My second daughter is a huge disappointment.'"

"It doesn't say that."

Pia held up her mother's journal. Her finger tapped the first sentence four times. "Dis-ap-point-ment."

Standing motionless, Muriel felt the soft carpet beneath her bare feet. She commanded her face to look blank as Pia continued reading. "'Muriel is everything Pia is not. Clumsy, chubby, loud. Her teeth will need braces.'"

Muriel closed her mouth.

"'Often I wonder how she could be a part of me.'"

The sting of tears hurt Muriel's whole face. In an effort to keep them from escaping, she clamped down her crooked teeth. "I don't want to hear any more."

"Too chicken? *Bak, bak, bak.*"

"Too mature. Unlike you, who still lives at home." Muriel spun around and marched back into the depths of Lidia's closet, running her tongue along her gums to keep the tears at bay.

"'My biggest concern,'" read Pia loudly, "'is Muriel's habit of lying. It's sad to say a child can't be trusted, but Muriel cannot. I suspect something serious. Pathological? Will have her tested before high school.'"

Muriel's mouth fell open. "No way does it say that."

Pia brandished the diary entry. "Right here in black and white."

Though Pia kept reading, Muriel only heard snippets. A strange buzzing sound filled her ears.

"'. . . disturbing fantasy life . . . antisocial . . .'"

Pia stood between her and the narrow closet exit. Muriel's chest burned, as if the oxygen inside that closet had turned to carbon monoxide. Could clothes soak up air itself? Was she now breathing in her own exhalations? Muriel made a move for the door, but Pia stepped forward to block her. "'I have caught Muriel lying so often I must concede that she is *unable* to tell the truth.'" Pia looked up. 'Concede' means it's true whether you like it or not."

"I know what 'concede' means," Muriel lied, sniffing back tears. Whether she liked it or not, tears ran down her cheeks in two thick lines. She quickly wiped them away with the edge of her tank top.

"Why are you so mean?" she asked, her chin quivering.

"It's not mean if it's the truth," Pia replied with the haughtiness of a girl who had always gotten what she wanted. One whose place in the world was as solid as a slurry wall. Muriel shoved past her. Pia spun around and followed her out of the closet. "You don't have to *cry* about it, baby Muriel." Snapping the diary shut, she announced, "Dress up is over. I have to study."

"Fine," said Muriel, glaring. Then Pia returned Lidia's diary to exactly where she'd found it: sandwiched neatly between the remote control and the new DVD cover of *Legally Blonde*. Directly in front of the television set. Where Pia couldn't help but find it, open it, and read it.

Pia, being Pia, would have been unable to keep it to herself.

"Do this for me," Lidia had said.

Muriel's mouth fell open. Pia said, "You tell, you die," before striding out like a supermodel, leaving Muriel alone in her mother's room.

Never had young Muriel felt so awfully, horribly, terribly grown up. As if she'd been both stretched to her limit and weighted down at the same time. She stepped toward Lidia's diary slowly. Before lifting the remote control off the top of it, she memorized its position. She left nothing to chance. Ever so gently she set the remote aside. She reached for the journal, though, of course, she knew exactly what she was about to see inside it. Opening its stiff, new binding, she inhaled the doughy scent of fresh paper. Inside, she saw the writing just as her sister had read it.

. . . Pia is smart, beautiful, slender . . .

Logan has the temperament of an artist . . .

. . . Muriel . . . unable to tell the truth . . .

Then she turned the page to confirm what she suspected. Lidia had made *one* entry at the beginning of the book. Period. One entry that marked her three children for life: Pia was perfect in every way, Logan was a troubled artist, and Muriel was a liar. There, in black ink on white paper, was precisely what Lidia wanted her—and Pia—to see. Lidia's insurance policy.

It's sad to say a child cannot be trusted, but Muriel cannot.

Her mother had set the whole thing up. Now, it wouldn't matter what Muriel said. If she ever told anyone about that day beneath the awning when Father Camilo bent Lidia's head back in a Broadway kiss—baring the very artery of her life—no one would believe her anyway. Lidia had documented Muriel's fantasy life. Her inability to tell the truth. Pia, her responsible eldest daughter, would now back her up. She was safe. Who would believe the word of a prepubescent child?

At that exact moment, Muriel felt the very last bits of her childhood slither away. She didn't try to stop them, corral them somehow. It would have been useless. How could she remain a child when she knew so many ugly truths about adults? About her own mother? Lidia would lie to keep her child from telling the truth. Instead of shielding her daughter, she protected herself. Never had Muriel felt so very alone in her very own family.

You tell, you die.

Didn't Pia know by now what Lidia should have known as well? Muriel would never *ever* tell. Keeping secrets was her specialty!

Muriel returned Lidia's diary to its original position on top of the DVD, as if it had never been read at all. She put the remote back, too, and made sure her mother's bedspread was perfectly smooth before she left the room. Down the hall, she heard music blaring from behind Pia's closed bedroom door. She heard her sister singing. Still barefoot, she tiptoed to her own room where she shut the door behind her and dragged her desk chair over to the open closet. There she climbed up to reach the top shelf where her *Playbill* collection was stored in its special notebook. The notebook was heavy, each pristine *Playbill* protected in its own plasticine cover—like Lidia's fancy dresses. Hugging the notebook to her chest, Muriel climbed off the desk chair and sat on her bed. Page by page she slowly looked through her treasures. Merely gazing at the covers made her remember how happy she'd once been. On matinee Saturdays. Before everything went awry.

Chapter 25

HAD THERE BEEN a window in that tiny office restroom Muriel might have attempted to squeeze through it. Outside she would have sidled along the sills, tuning out the city traffic below, calming the thudding of her heart, until she reached the corner where she'd shimmy to the ground like a monkey. For one more day, she would have forgotten.

Instead, she dried her face and hands and returned to the inner office where Joanie sat smoking a fresh cigarette.

"It's my sister," she blurted out.

"What about Barbie?"

Without warning, Muriel opened her mouth and let loose an ungodly noise that shocked both of them. Her shoulders curled forward and her arms dangled like wet towels on a bathroom hook. Water spilled over her bottom eyelids like from a forgotten bathtub.

"Good Christ," Joanie said. Grunting in her fussy way, she

stood and smashed her cigarette into the overflowing ashtray with a screwdriverish twist. She made her way to Muriel and enveloped her in folds of fabric. "No good can come from holding that shit inside," she said quietly into the top of Muriel's head.

After a few moments of silence, she added, "Let it all go, baby girl. I'm here to catch it."

Not at all meaning to, that's exactly what Muriel did. She released the energy it took to keep her head up and let her forehead burrow into Joanie's cushioned shoulder. She made no effort to stop the waterlogged story from sluicing forth in a flood of words and weeping. The warmth of Joanie's round body was as comforting as a chenille robe. Her smoky smell, along with a powdery sweetness, stirred something deep within her friend. The gentle pat of Joanie's fleshy hand on her back made Muriel miss the mother she'd never had. A mother who would light up when she walked into a room, feel an ache when she left. One who would sneak up behind her as she stood at the mirror, hug her with her whole body, then nestle her chin into the divot of her collarbone, press her face against her cheek and say, "My nose is wider than yours. Your jawline is more defined." She would compare features, freckle by freckle, searching for her contribution, delighting each time she found a genetic link. "I gave you that cleft in your chin." A mother who would use the tight space between them to recall how they were once one person. "Feel my heart beating? That used to be your heart, too, *moje kochanie*."

A mother like Pia had.

In gulps of air Muriel opened the spillway and let the secrets surge. Some of them, anyway. About Pia's illness. The gray satin dress. The way she found out how her mother really felt about her. The crushing hurt of it all.

It's not your fault. Siblings are mean.

"Jesus Christ," Joanie said, embracing her more tightly.

"I feel so helpless about my sister. I don't know what I'm supposed to do. What do I do?"

Without hesitation, Joanie stepped back and wiped the wetness off her friend's damp cheeks. First one, then the other as the air conditioner blew back the curls in her wild hair.

"You go back into that bathroom and splash more water on your face. Swish around a little mouthwash while you're at it . . . just saying. Then you grab your purse, wait for the elevator, and take a cab to Grand Central. Get the hell out of here, Muriel, and catch the next train to Connecticut."

THE VERY NAME of the state made Muriel feel inadequate. Connecticut's summers didn't feel as miserable as the sweaty mangle of humanity in Manhattan did; its winters inspired poetry. Somehow, the state seemed immune to mess and crankiness. At least the parts of it Muriel had seen, which were the sections of Connecticut that housed Pia and her family. To Muriel, the nutmeg state felt like a Broadway set. Vignettes of white-steepled churches; lime green trees; stone retaining walls stacked like craggy puzzles; mansions set back from the street atop manicured knolls; children in Converse sneakers riding bicycles along quiet country roads, their reflective helmets strapped tightly beneath their chins. Even the lone time she'd taken the east side bus with Joanie to the Connecticut casinos, it felt as if they were on the yellow brick road from *The Wiz* the moment they left the interstate.

On the train north, Muriel came close to throwing up. She'd never had motion sickness before, but that morning her glands flooded with saliva, her stomach felt roped into a knot. Using a sanitizing wipe to open the latch to the lavatory, she stood over the stainless steel toilet bowl with the chugging train jostling her violently from side to side. Vainly, she tried not to inhale the stale urine smell. Did male commuters even *try* to hit the bowl? Bracing her legs in a wide stance so as not to touch the wall or sink or, God forbid, the toilet itself, she hung her head and spit into the bowl. How had she let Joanie talk her into this? Pia had made it clear she didn't want to see her. She'd left explicit instructions. *Natural polish and lips. Don't let them restyle my wig.*

Barging in unannounced and uninvited, well, it wasn't something a Sullivant would ever do. Not a Muriel Sullivant, anyway. Pia's housekeeper, Blanca, would probably turn her away at the door. "Miss Pia is out," she'd say in a practiced way that left no room for discussion. Only Muriel would know why the car was in the driveway. She'd look up to see the sheer curtain fall closed on Pia's bedroom window.

"Family doesn't need an invitation," Joanie had said to her before she left New York. "Not at times like this. Now go."

In her vulnerable state, with her puffy red eyes and mottled neck, she'd believed her. "What do I say when I get there?" Muriel had asked, sniffing. "What do I do?"

Joanie was clear. "Empty the dishwasher if it's full, scrub the toilets if they're dirty, pick Emma up at school, buy groceries if the fridge is empty, recycle junk mail piled on the kitchen counter, make tea, flip through *People* magazine with Pia, hold her hand. Be her *sister*."

Muriel burped up a laugh.

"If she wants to be left alone," Joanie added, softly, "leave her alone. But don't let your sister pass without her knowing you were there. That you cared enough to show up. Even if it means squeezing her hand and saying nothing. If you don't, you'll never forgive yourself."

Of course she was right. Of course.

While Muriel struggled to maintain her balance over the train's toilet bowl, she shook her head at the very notion that she would need *instructions* on how to care. Wasn't that something families learned naturally?

Not her family. Not from the very beginning.

"You should spend Christmas with your family," Babcia Jula had said to her only daughter, Lidia, the first holiday after Pia was born. They had already moved to Queens. Lidia hadn't bothered to buy a Christmas tree.

"We are, Mama. We're coming home the Saturday before."

"Your *new* family."

Lidia was taken aback. "What are you saying?"

"*Nic, nic.* I'm just saying."

"You don't want to see your granddaughter?"

"Of course I want to see your little *niemowlę*. It's not me. You know how open minded I am."

"Papa?"

"That man is as stubborn as a hedgehog."

Lidia felt a flush rise in her cheeks. "He's going to have to accept my husband sometime."

"Hedgehogs don't always agree."

"So I can never come home? Is that what you want?"

"Not what I want, *kochanie*, but the way it is. You made your bed with an Irishman, now you must sleep in it. I only tell the truth because I care."

"*Care?* How can you say you care when you refuse to see your only grandchild?"

"Don't be dramatic, Lidia. I'll see little Pia one day in New York."

"One day? It's her first Christmas!"

"You'll understand when your baby grows up. Your father cares so much about you he can't bear to see a Sullivant in your arms. And me, I care too much about you and little Pia to allow such an upset on Christ's birthday. If we didn't care, you could bring *anyone* home. Have a premature child with any man. But we care too much to witness the ruin of your life."

Care. In her family it had always been a four-letter word.

Over the loudspeaker the conductor announced, "Westport. Next stop. Westport." Muriel spit into the bowl once more, then used a fresh Sani-Cloth to unlock the lavatory door and let herself out moments before the train lurched to a stop at the platform. Once outside, the fresh air made her feel slightly better. At least her stomach stopped its cartwheels.

Westport, Connecticut, seemed to be zoned for escalating elegance. In the two-mile stretch from the station to Pia's home, the houses closest to the petite station were humble and overgrown with untended shrubbery. Up a hill, the brown facades lightened to pale yellow. The hedges were flattened into a military crew cut. Around a bend, the houses became homes; farther up, the homes became mansions. By the time she entered her sister's neighborhood, the *estates* were erected in stone, their shutters painted French blue or white linen. Balletic weeping willows stretched over the wide avenues in drippy arches. Save for the loud buzz of leaf blowers, the streets were silent. At this hour of the morning in this part of Connecticut, it seemed the only living souls were gardeners.

"It's going to be okay," Muriel whispered to herself in the backseat of a cab so clean she didn't even use the bottom of her shirt to open the door. Still, she fretted over what she might see. Would Pia be bald? Skeletal? Would the veins in her beautiful hands rise up like green tributaries? Would she be too weak to lift her head off the pillow?

At the foot of her sister's circular driveway, Muriel's hands shook slightly as she paid the fare. Her stomach made its presence known again. She pulled herself up and stood there, rubbing her hand gently across her belly. "Deep breaths. One in, one out."

"The right address?" asked the cabdriver, staring at her. Only then did she notice she'd neglected to shut the back door.

"Oh, yes. Sorry." Muriel quickly closed the door and watched the driver accelerate, his tailpipe belching a puff of white smoke.

Be a sister, she told herself. *This is what sisters do.*

The Winston estate was a regal stone goddess with white shutters and tiny dormer windows inserted into the gray-shingled roof. In the clear Connecticut sunlight it glowed like a retouched photo. Pristine. Manicured. Flawless. Like Pia herself. (*Was she still?*) Feeling hopelessly mass market, Muriel climbed the steep driveway. The rough pavers felt warm beneath her feet. Her heart pounded against her sternum. By the time she reached the shiny red front door, she was chuffing for air. For a moment she stilled herself. *It's called* composure, *Muriel. Look it up. Live it.*

Before she had a chance to *tap, tap* and turn the knob, she heard Root Beer barking and footsteps on the interior marble. The heavy wooden door swung open and the Winstons' house-keeper, Blanca, stood there, drying her hands on a dish towel. Muriel opened her mouth to speak, but it took a moment for her lips to wrap around the right words. In the interim, Blanca stunned her by throwing both arms around her.

"Miss Muriel! You've come on the perfect day."

THAT VERY MORNING, with the early sun still lemony, Pia awoke confused. *Am I in heaven?* she wondered. Her bones didn't scream at her, her lungs didn't clutch with each breath. When she turned her head to see God, she saw her husband, Will, asleep. His familiar breathing sounds—soft in, hard out—filled the air. His muddy smell clung to the sheets. For the first time in months, she inhaled him without choking. Slowly, Pia sat up in bed and stretched her arms overhead, gingerly at first, waiting for the stab of pain to curl her in on herself. Instead, she felt the elastic comfort of elongated muscle. Her neck, though stiff, didn't sound like crushed tortilla chips when she swiveled it back and forth. When she lifted her rib cage, the bones felt supported by cartilage for the first time in months. The shooting pain was gone. The queasiness was replaced by hunger. It felt as if a high school buddy had suddenly appeared in her bedroom. They hadn't spoken in years, but the moment they saw each other, their running conversation resumed. Fresh and limber, they fretted over inconvenient pimples and oafish boys and the unfairness of having to try out for cheerleading squad in a premenstrual bloat. Like it would *kill* them to wait five days? Magically, Pia felt herself return.

I thank my God through Jesus Christ, Pia silently prayed. "Will?" she whispered.

"What's wrong?" He awoke instantly.

As she had so many times before she became ill, Pia slid into the warmth on Will's side of the bed and kissed his furry chest. She pressed her bone-thin body flat against his.

"God answered our prayers, my love. I'm back. It's me."

Chapter 26

EVERYTHING IN PIA's home was shiny. The milk-white marble floor in the entryway was buffed to a glassy finish, the chandelier overhead sparkled like a Tiffany display case. Floor-to-ceiling windows reflected a bluish shimmer. It resembled a model home. Or, Muriel realized for the first time, the lobby of the Plaza Hotel. Too elegant to live in. Unless you were Pia Winston.

"The Lord has given us a miracle," Blanca said. "Come, come."

"What's happened?"

Blanca made the sign of the cross over her chest and hurried into the kitchen where a teakettle was whistling. Muriel scuttled behind. In Pia's airplane hangar of a kitchen, a giant island sat in the center like a square spaceship. Its black granite top mirrored the huge silver fruit bowl that sat upon it; creamy white cabinetry and stainless-steel appliances around the perimeter of the space didn't have a single smudge. Muriel had to laugh at Joanie's advice. The mere thought of cleaning a dirty toilet was unthinkable. Her sister never had to ready her home for guests. The limes in the countertop bowl were always plump and juicy. She had a machine that made club soda on the spot. A dirty dish in the sink? Yeah, right.

"The worst is over," Blanca said, lifting the steaming kettle off the stove. She poured boiling water over several tea bags in a thick glass pitcher. "Our Pia is better today."

"Better?"

"She's back from the very edge."

Every vein, artery, and capillary in Muriel's body seemed to widen its borders. She felt a physical surge of relief. Her skin pinked; her eyes drew water. Until that very moment she hadn't understood how scared she really was or how shallowly she'd been breathing for weeks. After a lifetime of yearning to be like her sister, how could she navigate life without her? However could she possibly know whom she was supposed to become without Pia's example in the world?

Muriel exhaled a moan of deliverance. She'd always assumed there would be time to fix what was broken between them. Now there was. Her eyelids briefly fell shut. *Thank you, God,* she silently prayed. Was this one of His mysterious ways? Never would she have comprehended the urgency without this close call. Again, she blew a deep breath out. From now on, she would stop being such a baby and be a *sister.* Whatever that meant, she would figure it out.

Blanca flicked her black hair toward the back of the house. "Miss Pia is on the sunporch. You know the way? I'm making iced tea."

Feeling effervescent, Muriel left her purse on the island chair and set out for the far side of the gangling house. She passed a powder room tiled in clear mosaics and a guest room with a moss-colored gingham paint treatment. Root Beer scampered ahead to settle on his microfiber bed in the media room, circling around and around it until he sensed the ideal moment to plop down. Wide footed in her black loafers, Muriel felt light. Brick by brick, the burden of keeping her sister's secret from their mother was knocked off her shoulders. She skipped down a long hall adorned with photographs of the picturesque Winston clan. There was Emma, tanned and chopstick legged, romping through waves; Will in a sports car with the top down, his hair as thick as mink. Stunning Pia peered at the camera from beneath the rim of a beach hat. In a totem-pole pose, all three Winstons grinned with their ample lips and straight teeth. The last time she'd seen those photos she'd scoffed. *How clichéd,* she'd thought. As if they were the photogenic people you'd find in a store-bought frame before you inserted yourself.

"Petty," Muriel muttered, ashamed that she'd ever been so judgmental.

Continuing down the hall, she walked by Will's leathered man cave and Emma's ballet pink bedroom suite that was larger than her whole apartment. It was messy in a rich girl's way—carelessly strewn with shoes and electronics and designer bedding.

At that moment, an odd sensation descended upon Muriel. It felt as though she had imagined Pia's illness entirely. Never had it been real. Instead, it was the product of a night sweat and the fitful dreaming that followed a winter's awakening in an old brownstone with an unpredictable boiler. Without warning it turned on late at night and blasted steam into the radiators. Sleepers awoke in the headachy discomfort of a steam room and fell back into a restless hothouse sleep, cooled only by frosted air swirling in from a window they rose to crack open. Come morning, the temperature had righted itself but the sleep cycle was nonetheless askew.

Women like Pia didn't die and leave women like her behind. Muriel was now quite sure of it. The universe wouldn't allow such folly. It would rebalance before things spun too dangerously out of control. With each footfall deeper into her sister's home, she felt the planets realign, once again orbiting the sun in an orderly fashion.

At the farthest end of the house—their "West Wing" as Will called it—Muriel turned toward the backyard and saw two white-paned French doors. They were both open wide. Above them were the accordion pleats of custom silk Roman shades.

"Pia?"

More of a question than a greeting, Muriel thought it unlikely that the child-size head cresting the back of a slatted wood chaise belonged to her larger-than-life sister. Stiffly, a neck swiveled. A silk scarf, white with a gold-chain pattern, was tied in a knot at the nape of the neck. Two skinny legs clad in black pencil jeans swung onto the floor. Hunched shoulders draped in a cashmere shawl faced her and Muriel saw her sister for the first time since their shopping trip at the vertical mall.

"Muriel!" Pia's hollow eyes opened wide. "What a delightful surprise!"

Speechless, Muriel quickly swallowed her shock. She had never seen skin so ashen, eyes so deeply sunk into a person's head. Pia's lips were two strips of flesh the color of old panty hose, the hollows in her cheeks could house a stack of tea bags. When her sister reached her hands out, Muriel saw every vein, every tendon, every striated ligament.

"You look beautiful," she lied.

"This scarf makes me look like a cancer patient, I know. If I'd known you were coming, I would have worn my wig."

"No, you look great. Really. The scarf looks great. Really." Muriel exhaled a nervous laugh. Her sister was a skeleton. A world of lonely peered out from her eyes. Muriel could barely look at her without bursting into tears. "I meant to bring cake," she said lamely, having briefly considered swinging by the village bakery so as not to arrive empty-handed.

Pia laughed gaily. "Cake? We should have *champagne*. You've come on the best day of my life. My cancer is gone. What shall I return to the Lord for all His goodness to me? Those horrid treatments finally worked."

Letting the shawl slide off her shoulders, Pia raised both ropey arms over her head and said, "Ah, Muriel. I'm back."

Muriel wanted to ask, "You mean you've been worse than this?"

"Jesus spared me," said Pia, beaming and looking heavenward. "'He that believeth in me, though he were dead, yet shall he live.'"

Awkwardly shifting her balance from her right foot to her left, Muriel lost the ability to control her tears. In heavy droplets they fell to her cheeks. "I've wanted to call you. I . . . I didn't know what to say."

"Shhh, shhh. It's okay now."

"I never said a word to Mama. I swear. I kept your secret."

Rising with difficulty, Pia retrieved a clean tissue from her jeans' pocket and handed it to Muriel, who pressed it to her eyes.

"I've been such a jerk. So selfish."

Pia cooed, "It's okay. Truly."

As Joanie had done, as a loving mother would do, Pia wrapped her spindly arms around her sister and held her close. Muriel shut her eyes and let her soft body melt into her sister's frail frame. For the first time, she let the baggage go. In Pia's embrace, she released the tension she'd always felt around her. Was her hair combed? Her breath sweet? Her muffin top contained? Her thighs smooth beneath their Spanx? Was she good *enough*? In the warmth of Pia's arms Muriel let the remaining words go unsaid, confessions unconfessed. To say anything else would ruin it. Pia was going to be okay. That was all that mattered.

Pia pulled back first. She smiled as she ran her hands down Muriel's unruly mane. "Soon," she said, "my hair will be as thick as yours."

THEY SAT ON the sunporch all afternoon in the cool current of the overhead fan. Emma was at ballet day camp, Will was at work. Blanca carried in a pitcher of iced tea, two glasses, mini red velvet cupcakes, and a big bowl of blueberries.

"I eat them like popcorn," said Pia. "Nature's cancer killer."

Muriel couldn't even *imagine* eating blueberries as if they were popcorn. Yet nestled into the chaise next to Pia, overlooking the spectacular expanse of their professionally mowed New England backyard, tossing blueberries into her mouth, sipping iced green tea, and chatting as if they were bona fide friends—real sisters—never had she felt so very nearly normal.

"Will's firm is hosting a black-tie New Year's Eve cruise on the Hudson," Pia said.

"Ooh."

"Midnight. Right past the Statue of Liberty."

"Ah."

"He was all nervous telling me because, you know, he *has* to go and schmooze with his clients."

Imitating Lidia's voice, Muriel said, "Stop talking Jewish, you're a Catholic, for God's sake!" Pia laughed out loud and ate a mini cupcake in two bites. With her mouth full, she continued, "This morning I said to him, 'Honey, I need something from you.' His eyes got all serious."

"Aw."

"He says, 'You don't have to go. I understand.' So I say, 'No, you *don't* understand,' and he goes all hangdog. Like I'm going to tell him how hellish chemo is, like he doesn't already know. That's when I move in for the kill."

Giggling in a girlish way Muriel had never seen before, Pia leaned close to her and said in a low voice, "I put my lips right up to his ear and whispered, 'I'll need your credit card. Mine doesn't have enough limit to buy the sexy dress I'm going to wear for you.'"

Feeling free and funny, Muriel tilted her head back and sang from the Broadway show, " 'We're your Dreamgirls, Dreamgirls will never leave you.' "

Grinning, Pia said, "Will lifted me off the ground and practically broke every bone in my body."

Muriel beamed.

"Aside from Emma's birth, it was the happiest moment of our lives. Thanks be to God who giveth us the victory through our Lord Jesus Christ."

Muriel took a sip of iced tea.

Truth be told, Pia's recent evangelical leanings had unnerved Muriel. Burrowing so deeply into the Bible seemed inconsistent with a woman who bought new Louboutins each season at the flagship store. And Pia had never taken religion too seriously in the first place. One Easter, years ago, when the entire family watched *The Greatest Story Ever Told* on TV, Pia fliply said, "John the Baptist would have had *way* more converts if he'd added shampoo."

After a breath's silence, the family erupted in laughter.

Owen (*Owen!*) quipped, "But then he would be known as John the *Bathist*." Lidia roared.

Even silent Logan had a contribution: "The Jordan River Spa?"

Muriel never forgot that night, the way they were like a real family. Sitting in one room together, undivided by twos, laughing, united, normal. The utter simplicity of it! Too soon, however, that feeling was drowned out by others in which so much was left unsaid.

But now she understood. Seeing how close Pia had come to the end of her life, it made sense that she would wrap herself in

Scripture. Leach strength from the teachings of those who had been through so much pain. If the word of God couldn't soothe you when your earthly body was breaking down and heaven's light was in sight, what was it all for?

On that porch in Connecticut, as the sunlight darkened into late afternoon, Muriel kicked off her loafers and tucked her feet beneath her. She felt the fan's breeze on her face and silently thanked *whomever* was out there for this second chance with her sister. No longer could she see Pia's shocking appearance. It blended into the image she had in her heart. As ever, she was her perfect sibling, the one who romped on beaches and slow-danced with boys on stair landings and successfully wore white and looped scarves around her neck with French flair. She was Pia, the "it" girl, teen, woman, *person* Muriel had longed to be all her life.

"I never meant to hurt you," Pia suddenly said, out of the blue.

Taken aback, Muriel didn't respond.

"Well, I suppose I did back then," Pia said. "God forgive me. But honestly, Muriel, I can't believe I was so vicious."

"You were only the messenger."

"Still."

The waning sun turned the backyard grass the color of spinach. Pia poured both of them a refill of the iced tea Blanca had made. Her hand wobbled with the weight of the pitcher. In a clacking rush, ice cubes tumbled into the glasses. "Emma will be home soon."

"Oh! Do you need me to pick her up? I'd be happy to—"

"Blanca gets her. It's not far. Wait till you see her, Muriel.

She's—" Pia put the pitcher down. Her head rested against the wooden chaise. "Well, she's *everything*, that's all. She's my heart. The absolute best thing I ever did, ever could do. One day, when you're a mother yourself, you'll know."

"If I ever become a mother."

"Oh, Muriel." Pia leaned forward and took her sister's hand, squeezing it hard. "Of course you will. You *must*. Having a child is the closest you'll come to seeing God on earth. It's the truest love imaginable because it literally grows within you. From the moment you feel the flutter of that tiny heart, or a foot poking you from the inside—can you imagine it? A *live* foot the size of a peanut kicking inside you! It's unlike any feeling in the world. You can't help but marvel at the miracle of it. The process of falling in love begins at that moment. There is nothing you wouldn't do for that child. And by the time your baby is born, oh my lord, those tiny fingers around your finger will flood you with such intense love you'll drown in it. Blissfully! You won't know how you ever took a single breath without it."

Muriel looked away. Not all mothers, she knew well, felt such bliss.

"Sometimes I look at Emma and I can't believe God could be so good to me." A sigh traveled through Pia's body. "That's why, after all these years, I can't understand how Mama could do that to you."

Muriel curled her fingernails into her palms.

"Why did she write those awful things about you? A child. Why would she call her *child* a liar?"

The one biblical verse Muriel knew by heart swirled around

her head. *You will know the truth, and the truth will set you free.*
That, she also knew, was a lie.

"I never told Mama I read her diary," Pia said. "I know it didn't
seem like it at the time, but I felt ashamed of what I'd done. Both
to her and to you. That's why I've never said anything all these
years. I'm so sorry, Muriel. Can you ever forgive me?"

"Of course. Yes. I forgave you ages ago."

Again squeezing Muriel's hand, Pia said, "Thanks be to the
Lord." Then she asked, "Why would Mama do such a thing?
Why, in God's name?"

The sweet Connecticut air filled Muriel's lungs. She thought
about her mother and Father Camilo. About sin. The affair she
witnessed was so long ago, it seemed like someone else's life. As
if she had imagined it after all. At the time, Muriel hadn't been
mature enough to truly process what she'd seen; now that it was
so far in the past, she was quite sure God had forgiven them both.
Still, hiding somebody's secrets takes its toll, she'd come to believe. Sometimes it feels as if you've been gripping something so
tightly for so long you forget how to let go at all.

"I have no idea why Mama wrote those silly things," Muriel
said. "I was just a kid."

Never would she tell. She'd made a promise and that was that.
Besides, it was a beautiful day in Connecticut. Why darken it?

As orange striations of sunset stretched across the sky, Emma
bounded onto the sunporch wearing a white cotton shift over her
ballet pinks. She squealed when she saw Muriel, kissed her aunt
and her mother, and pirouetted for them twice. Her cheeks were
reddish from exercise, wisps of blond hair spiked out from her

ballet bun. She snatched two mini cupcakes and scampered off to her room. Emma was so stunning, so innocent, Muriel couldn't bear to imagine her motherless. Instantly, she shook her head to jostle the thought out through her ears.

"Stay for dinner?" Pia asked.

Muriel stretched and stood up. "I should get back to the city," she said. It had been a perfect afternoon. Flush with familial love, she had an idea of how to make it a perfect evening, too.

"We'll talk soon," she said, her eyes filling up. "Thank God my beautiful sister is back."

ON THE NEW HAVEN line west, with Long Island Sound through the window the color of a flickering fireplace, Muriel made a phone call.

"Mama?"

"Has something happened?"

Muriel laughed. "I was hoping you'd be free for dinner."

"Your father is working late. I hadn't planned anything special."

"Perfect. Let me treat you to Uvarara in the village."

Lidia was silent. Muriel could hear her mother's brain working. Finally, she asked, "What's happened, Muriel? Is it Pia? Have you seen her?"

Again Muriel laughed. "I've seen her. She's fine. As perfect as ever. Now I want to see you."

"Why?"

The train was overcooled, as it always was in the summer. Muriel rubbed the goose bumps on her bare arms. Through the smudged window she watched pristine Connecticut blink past. Redbrick houses were reflected in the glassine water. Slatted docks jutted into the Sound. Sailboats zigzagged in the water, leaving elongated V-shaped wakes. Her mind flashed on something Pia had said that day in New York while the two sisters waited for the bus to take them to the Plaza Hotel.

Sailboats fill me with such longing. It's as if everyone on the water knows the answer and we don't even know the question.

Now, for the first time, she got it.

"Because you're my mother and I miss you." Life needn't be more complicated than that.

Lidia said nothing for several breaths. Muriel gently wobbled left and right with the shimmy of the train. She heard the *ba-dum ba-dum* of the tracks, felt the anticipation of a journey tingle her fingertips. For a brief moment she let her eyelids fall shut as she envisioned herself on the M train to Wyckoff Avenue, not quite a straight shot into Manhattan, wearing a snug green velvet dress with satin trim, too young for a girl her age.

"The *polpettine* are fabulous there," Lidia said, softly.

Muriel grinned. "I was thinking the *fazzoletti*."

"Maybe we could split the two?"

"Perfect."

Perhaps in her universe the planets took a bit longer to realign. Feeling as if she'd just that moment fully grown up, Muriel said, "I'm on my way, Mama. See you as soon as I get there."

Chapter 27

THE PHONE STARTLED Muriel awake. She thought it was the downstairs buzzer. UPS. FedEx. But the light in her apartment was hazy. The sun was barely up, its silvery rays poking softly through the curtain sheers. The phone rang again.

"Hullo," she said, sounding like a man.

"Muriel."

The way Will said her name, with a period instead of a question mark, said it all. His voice was so tired she could almost see it crumpled in the back of his throat.

"But I just saw her a week ago," she said, losing her air.

"We lost her last night."

"But her treatments had worked. That's what she told me. She said she was going to be fine."

"It happens that way sometimes," he said, sadly. "One last rally."

Muriel's left hand covered her mouth in disbelief, then it slid down to her chest as if she needed to help her lungs expand and contract.

"But it's *Pia*," she said, almost to herself, a flood of images racing through her mind: her sister's long blond ponytail swaying like a hula dancer when she walked, the way she ate a single tortilla chip in ten tiny bites, the impossible narrowness of her hips, the perfect ridge of her wrist bone, the smooth tan of her arms and the flatness of her toes, the way everybody smiled when she did. As if she was right there with her, she saw the confident jut of her sister's chin. How could an entire *life* vanish in the middle of the night?

"Emma and I were with her," said Will quietly. "She wasn't alone."

"Emma. Oh, God." Muriel pictured her niece bounding onto the sunporch all praying-mantis limbs and satiny skin. Her blue eyes would now be red. Muriel's heart broke.

"Pia went to bed early last night," Will said so softly Muriel strained to hear. "Right after dinner. Emma and I knew something was wrong. That day you'd seen her, well, she was so happy for a few days afterward. Her old self. But things got bad again. It was like a punch in the gut. Last night was worse than usual. Blanca made her soup, but she only pressed the cup to her closed lips. She only pretended to eat. Her eyes were glassy. I knew the painkillers were kicking in. So I helped her to bed.

"You saw how she was. So tiny, she barely weighed anything. I put her in bed and I could see her fighting sleep. I think she knew the end was near. Her jaw hung open. She was so weak, Muriel, she couldn't keep her mouth closed. She kept mumbling,

'I'm sorry. I'm sorry.' When I kissed her forehead, it was cold. Like she had no blood left at all. So I called Emma in. The three of us lay there on the bed, Pia between us. We held her hands and whispered in her ears. We told her how much we loved her, how she was the light of our lives. Even Root Beer was there at the foot of the bed. He, too, knew the end was coming."

His voice raspy, Will said, "We stayed like that much of the night. All of us together on our bed. Pia faded in and out but she knew we were there because she squeezed my hand from time to time. Emma, God bless her, fell asleep even as she fought it with her whole being. I promised I'd wake her if it was time. I was afraid I'd fall asleep myself, but Blanca stayed the night and brought in hot espressos and cold compresses for my eyes and somehow I managed to stay awake. Then, my God, it was the strangest thing."

Will stopped. In silence, Muriel waited, unaware she was holding her breath until air involuntarily rushed into her lungs.

"It was about three in the morning. I remember looking at the clock and thanking God he gave us one more day with her. All of a sudden, a *whoosh* swept into the room. I don't know, some kind of . . . energy. That's the only way I can describe it. It felt like someone opened the back door and a blast of fresh air came rushing through. Pia's eyes shot open. Emma woke up at that same instant. 'Mommy,' she said. She hasn't said 'Mommy' in years. Pia smiled at her. We both saw the love in her eyes. It was absolutely clear, unclouded by pain or meds. Pure *love*. And it was her. Our Pia. She was back. Emma and I both burst into tears, it was so damned beautiful and unexpected. We circled our arms around her, held on to her. Then she sighed this utterly contented sigh and let go. Just like that. She released herself. We literally felt her soul leave the earth. It was the most profound experience I've ever had. My daughter and I felt Pia enter heaven."

"Oh, Will."

"It was truly amazing. I feel blessed to have experienced it."

Muriel took another noisy breath. Tears streamed down her cheeks. The image of heaven as a joyful destination made her feel hopeful, as if time really didn't run out. Repairs could always be made somewhere.

"What do you need?" she asked, helpless. "Tell me what to do."

A long silence followed in which Muriel could hear Will's breathing. A labored inhalation followed by air forcibly pushed through his nostrils, as if he was ordering his lungs to fill themselves, then commanding them to expel the oxygen they had trapped within their bronchial tubes. As if breathing was no longer automatic. She knew his answer. *Nothing*. What could anyone do? No one could bring her back, reshape her diseased cells into plump organisms, erase the speckled blackness beneath her eyes, ease the angry pain in her bones. No one could restore the soft touch of her hair or return the hungry look she used to give her husband when they awoke on languid Sunday mornings and decided to stay in bed. No one could do a goddamn thing.

"Tell Lidia."

"What? No." Muriel surprised herself with the force of her answer.

"I can't do it," Will whispered.

"No," Muriel repeated. "No."

The last time she'd seen her mother was a *first*. It was actually fun. She saw her the same day she'd last seen Pia. They had dinner at Uvarara—Lidia's favorite restaurant in Middle Village. Happy from her Connecticut visit with Pia, Muriel was relaxed and confident.

"*Na zdrowie!*" She toasted her mother with a glass of Chianti.

"Dating anyone special?" Lidia asked. "Anyone at all?"

"No. You?"

Lidia laughed. Throughout their dinner, her jabs were only flesh wounds. Habit, really. Across the candlelit table, Muriel saw her mother in a new light: an aging woman who was beginning to feel the weight of the mistakes she'd made. Confessed Lidia after a second glass of wine, "Had I been a happier wife, I would have been a better mother."

That night, Muriel felt hope that a new relationship could be found in the wreckage of the old, the way seeds sometimes take root and sprout at the very bottom of a dump.

"Please . . . " Will's heavy voice trailed off. Muriel shut her eyes and felt her heart sag. Her brother-in-law was asking the impossible. Without even knowing Pia had been sick, news of her death would kill their mother. Never would she forgive Muriel for shattering her life out of the clear blue.

She said nothing.

Will said nothing.

In his leaden exhalations, Muriel heard the weight of the past few months. Or had it been years? How long had Pia kept the secret of her terminal illness? Had she been sick last Christmas? At Lidia's annual birthday dinner? How many months had the slim figure she'd so envied been the emaciation of disease? The perfection of her haircut and color, had it been an expensive wig for more than a *year*? Shame overtook her. The truth had been right in front of her eyes, yet she hadn't seen a thing. Apparently, she was more like her mother than she thought. Choosing to believe that bad things disappeared if you redirected your gaze.

Why, Muriel suddenly wondered, *had Pia not called* her *to say good-bye at the very end? Had they not begun again?* Why, Muriel questioned over and over, had her sister not given *her* one more chance to ask for forgiveness?

"I tried to be who you wanted me to be," she would have said. "Honestly I did. I'm so sorry I never measured up."

Forgive me.

In the long silence over the phone, Muriel heard the toll Pia's illness had taken on her husband's life, too. When Pia passed, his light went dark. Slowly, he'd watched the sexy woman he loved and desired fade before his eyes. Her tanned and toned arms became bruised and slack. Her smooth hair went wiry; her body skeletal. When your spouse has cancer, can you ever complain of sore muscles? A tension headache? Can you golf while she's in the chemo chair? Watch a television ad for shampoo and guiltlessly wish you could comb your fingers through thick hair? After work, over a quick beer with the guys, can you commiserate about wives who spend a fortune at Neiman Marcus, then complain that you're never home? Like money rains down from the sky! *Women.* Can't live with them or without them. As your wife disappears before your eyes, can you ever afford to look the other way? Can you stop loving someone who's nothing like the woman you fell for in the first place?

"I'll tell her," Muriel said, abruptly. Which, of course, Will knew she would. Then she remembered the gray satin dress in the back of her closet, neatly folded, still in its shopping bag with the tag on it. *Natural polish, natural lips. None of that thick makeup they slather on you.* Pia was counting on her. *Will won't care, Muriel. But I do. I care.*

"I'll be out later this morning. After I talk to Mama."

Will thanked her and hung up. Muriel felt like throwing up. On wobbly legs, she walked into the bathroom and splashed water on her face. Braced against the bathroom sink, she looked in the mirror and saw the reflection of Lidia's daughter. The only daughter she had left.

"You can do this, Muriel," she said out loud. Hadn't they recently had a lovely dinner at Uvarara? Sure, her mother fell back into herself and talked about Pia the entire time, but change didn't happen overnight. Seeds of closeness had to be planted, watered, fertilized, given air and warmth before they blossomed into even the tiniest fragile buds. They had time. Didn't they?

"You *can* do this," Muriel repeated, forcefully, swallowing the emotion that stung her whole face.

Even though she repeated it over and over, she didn't believe herself one bit.

Chapter 28

THE NINETY-SIXTH STREET subway station arched into the gray sky like a *Star Wars* storm-trooper helmet. Muriel knew the route by heart. She swiped her MetroCard at the turnstile and descended the stairs to the downtown express, getting off at Fourteenth Street. There, she transferred to the L, followed the herd down the stairs and around the corner to the M. She knew everything there was to know about this transital umbilical cord attaching Manhattan to Queens, from the way the train felt like a clothes dryer on the west side of the river, a washing machine on the east, to the acrid smell of the *New York Times* versus the inky aroma of the *Post*. On cold rainy days, the city trains smelled like wet wool. Borough trains smelled of dripping leather. Even the seats were different. Manhattan's orange row of seating was shaped into the curves of individual asses, a single overspilling passenger disrupted the whole row. Across the river, the long side seating was gray-blue and smooth, always warm from a recent exit.

With Pia's shopping bag in her hand, Muriel sat on the train in stupefied silence, her lips parted, as if a stranger had walked up and yanked her hair. The neural connection between knowing Pia was gone and actually *feeling* it was clogged with a to-do list: get to Queens, tell Lidia, get back on the train to Grand Central, take the Metro-North to Connecticut, deliver Pia's gray satin dress. Without resistance, she let the train jostle her from side to side, flopping far over at each stop. The bag made crinkle sounds as it swayed in the grip of her closed fist. It was still early—more people on their way into the city than out—so the eastbound M was nearly deserted. By the time she reached the end of the line, Metropolitan Avenue, the only other person on her subway car was a scruffy post-teen in an oversize sweatshirt, asleep, soon to be on his way back west.

"You can do this," Muriel muttered to herself for the hundredth time that morning. Her stomach was a tight knot. Her ears buzzed from deep within. It took muscle memory to exit the train and climb the stairs to the street. How, exactly, do you tell a mother that her favorite daughter has died in the night? Do you suggest sitting down first? Have a tissue ready? Would Lidia faint? Bury her weeping face in Muriel's shoulder? Was it *her* job to be brave?

Muriel's breath hitched as she walked along the avenue. In the suddenly cooling pre-fall air, some of the leaves in the cemetery to her right were already the color of blood oranges.

The sidewalk felt hard beneath Muriel's thin-soled shoes. Lidia didn't know she was on her way. She hadn't called ahead. There were some things you had to do face-to-face, before other walls went up.

Putting one foot in front of the other, Muriel crossed Metropolitan Avenue at the light and made her way to her parents' row house two blocks away. Lidia would be starting her busy day. Dressed, no doubt, in slacks with a DRY CLEAN ONLY tag. Owen would already be gone, his coffee cup rinsed in the sink.

"Mama?"

The front door was unlocked, a carryover from their Rhode Island neighborhood days. Muriel stepped into the silent foyer. In a rush of feelings, her youth surged forward: the ache of not belonging, of being the fifth in a family of four. The third child to parents who wanted only two. She shut her eyes for a moment and pictured herself coming home from school, praying no one would be home so she could slide across the marble tile in her socks, eat peanut butter with a spoon, unsuck her stomach, turn on the TV as loud as she wanted, and watch daytime dramas that were more intense than her own. She could hide in plain sight.

Strong coffee scented the air. Muriel set the shopping bag down beside the door. At the back of the house, Lidia appeared in the arched passageway to the kitchen, drying her hands on a dish towel.

"What are you doing here?" she asked.

"I—" Muriel stopped. Stunningly, she hadn't planned this far ahead. It had taken all the energy she could amass to get her body this far. Her brain went completely blank. "I've come for a visit."

Lidia said, "Didn't I just see you?"

"Yes! And wasn't it fun?" Muriel clamped down her back teeth in embarrassment. Lidia groaned. "You know I hate surprises," she said flatly.

Following her mother into the family kitchen—a room so familiar she could draw every inch of it with her eyes closed— Muriel noted the white Roman shade covering the window, the stainless-steel side-by-side refrigerator, the glass-topped table, the gleaming KitchenAid mixer in metallic pearl. Lidia had just cleaned up the breakfast dishes; the countertop was still wet from her sponge. Her pressed cream-colored slacks brushed lightly against the tips of her insignia-embossed velvet loafers.

"Is Dad home?" Muriel asked.

"If you've come to see him, you wasted a trip. He's already at work."

"I came to see you."

Lidia's impatient look was unmistakable. "Have a cup of coffee then."

Sipping her coffee, Muriel sat and stared at her mother as she busied herself shining her kitchen. She sprayed Windex on the glass-fronted cabinets, used her fingernail to scrape a fleck of food off the chrome toaster, then buffed the residue fingerprint with her damp paper towel. "Well?" she said, finally. "Are you going to make me beg you?"

Though it had only been a week earlier, their dinner at Uvarara seemed ages ago. Lidia's hard edges were back. With her heart thrumming, Muriel set her mug down on the table. She rested her hands flat on her lap and softly said, "I'm afraid I have bad news."

"You've lost your job."

Lidia's response was so swift it startled Muriel into asking, "Why would you say that?"

"I knew it was only a matter of time. That's no job for a maturing woman. Your lesbian boss was sure to hire someone more age appropriate eventually. A teenage intern, perhaps."

Muriel stared at her mother and blinked.

"No, I haven't lost my job."

"You will. Mark my words. Matter of time."

Lidia leaned her back against the kitchen counter, one hand on her slim hip. "What is it then?" she asked, begrudgingly, as if Muriel's bad news was an annoying waste of her time. As if she'd be required to muster motherly empathy for which she was in no mood. Not today when she had so many other things to do. Their mother/daughter night out had been a nice change of pace, but that was then. Today, she would have to reschedule her manicure if Muriel didn't speed things up and get back on the train. The laundry wasn't going to wash itself.

"I don't know how to say it, Mama."

Lidia sighed. "Just say it, Muriel."

"It's . . . it's . . . it's *Pia*."

"What about Pia?" Lidia now stood erect. Muriel's tongue seemed to swell like a waterlogged loaf of bread. She opened her mouth, but words couldn't make their way around the squishy mass of flesh and taste buds.

"Tell me." Lidia's face had turned to stone. "This instant."

She took a step forward. Muriel's lips felt slimy. "Will called me this morning," she sputtered. "Pia has been sick for a while, Mama. She didn't want anyone to know. She made me promise. I noticed how pale she was, and thin, when I saw her. But I didn't really *see* it. Know what I mean? I didn't understand how bad it was."

Tight lipped, Lidia said, "You told me she was fine. I asked you if you'd seen her."

"I did see her in Connecticut the same day I saw you. She said her treatments had worked. She was sure the worst was over. Will said it happens that way sometimes. One final rally. But last night, in her slee—"

Without warning, Lidia reached her hand back, swung it around, and slapped Muriel hard across the face. "Liar!" she shouted. A shocked Muriel held her burning cheek.

"How dare you." Lidia's voice was a carving knife.

"I know you're upset."

"This is low even for you."

"Mama, did you hear what I said? Pia passed away last night."

"Shut up! You've always been jealous of your sister. Did you think I didn't see that? What, you thought I was blind?"

Her mouth hanging open, Muriel didn't know what to say. Her cheek was hot, her chest burned. Hatred flared red in her mother's eyes. Lidia declared, "I might have expected something like this from you. You've always been a liar."

Muriel sucked in a breath. She closed her mouth, lowered her hand to her lap. "I'm not lying."

"Even as a child you couldn't be trusted. Lies. Always lies. Trying to make me believe you saw things that you didn't see. Trying to ruin my life with your lies. Who do you think you are? Special? You're no one special, believe me. *Pia* is special. You're as common as dirt. Look at you. Your fingernails, your hair. Or, I have a better idea. Look at your*self* in a mirror, Muriel. Know what you'll see? A *liar*."

Stone faced, Muriel said, "You think I *want* to be telling you this?"

Lidia turned her back. The air in the kitchen was again misted with Windex as she furiously resprayed all the shiny surfaces around her. She ripped paper towels off the vertical roll on the counter and wiped so hard they balled into a damp wad of pulp. Muriel could still feel the imprint of her mother's hand on her cheek, the sting of the slap. With the taste of ammonia on her tongue, she said slowly and carefully, "I never was a liar and you know it."

"That in itself is a lie."

Muriel stood up. The chair scraped across the floor. "Turn around, Mother."

In ever-larger circles, Lidia polished the countertops.

"I said, 'Turn around.'"

Defiantly, Lidia spun around. Chin lifted, she said, "What are you going to do? Hit me?"

Muriel wanted to. She longed to feel the tug in her rotator cuff as she reached back, then swung around and smacked that smug look off her mother's face. She hungered to see Lidia's neat hair spill over her eyes, feel the residue of wrinkle cream on the palm of her hand. The thrill of watching Lidia bite down on her lower lip, leaving a mauve rim of lipstick on the edge of her upper teeth, excited her. She pictured a handful of paper towels falling to the spotless floor as she waited, still as a stone, for a red welt to blossom on her mother's cheek. She would watch it flower, bit by bit, like an opening rose. Yes, that's what she wanted to do. *Itched* to do. But she didn't. Controlling every syllable out of her mouth, Muriel said, "I saw you. You know I saw you. And you also know I never told *anyone* about you and Father Camilo."

"Shut up, Muriel."

"I won't shut up. I'm sick of shutting up. I'm *done* shutting up. I won't lie for you anymore. I don't care if everyone knows the truth: Dad, Will, Emma, the church."

Lidia's cheeks flushed hotter. "Damn you to hell."

"Damn me?" Muriel laughed. "That's a joke, right? It wasn't *me* having sex with a priest."

Lidia reached back to slap her daughter again, but this time, Muriel was ready. She caught her mother's wrist with her hand and squeezed it, both women shaking from head to toe.

"No one will believe you," Lidia said viciously. "I documented your past as a liar. It's all written down."

"Ah, yes. Your journal." She tossed her mother's wrist back at her. "Very clever, Mama. The way you left that out for Pia to find. It kept me quiet for a long time. *Hurt* me for a long time. But not anymore. You know what? I don't *care* if anyone believes me. Let them question me, hook me up to a lie detector test. I have nothing to hide. You want to take a lie detector test with me, Mama? Do you? A family outing! We'll get our nails done first!

"My days of keeping everybody's secrets are *over*. The bats are out of the cave! Pia had cancer. You had an affair with Father Camilo. Dad was—is?—probably seeing someone, too. Your whole marriage is a joke. There's never been any *real* love there. Did Logan find out? Is that why he escaped from our family the moment he could, and never came back? I don't even *know* my own brother! Our family is nothing but lies. But not me. Not anymore. Hallelujah, Lord! The truth has set me free."

Sucking in a lungful of air, Muriel blew it out hard. "Ahhh," she said, "I feel lighter already. Imagine that, Mama. Me. Feeling *light*." With that, Muriel wheeled around and stomped out of the spotless kitchen to the front door, grabbing the shopping bag with Pia's burial dress. She'd made a promise to her sister. A promise she was going to keep.

Chapter 29

DEATH IS A part of life. What a bullshit platitude. Death is so permanently entrenched in its own nonbeingness, the word "life" shouldn't be uttered anywhere near it. It isn't even the *end* of life. It's the beginning of forever being gone. A journey for the deceased . . . maybe. Desertion for the living? Absolutely. Death is an abandoned child at the mall—in Times Square—all she can do is clutch at her shirt to contain her heartbeats while she scans each silhouette, waiting, until darkness comes.

That's what Muriel was thinking as her sister's funeral unfolded around her. *Death*, she thought, *needs its own vocabulary.*

"You're the sister?"

One by one, Pia's friends and neighbors filed into the white clapboard church with the shiny red door, so quaint it was a country cliché.

"I'm sorry for your loss."

The pointed steeple rose into the blue Connecticut sky; the

grass was so green it looked painted. Pia had selected this story-book church for her service, not their regular beige brick behe-moth of a parish (that was down the street). A final nod to her impeccable style and taste.

"I'm so sorry for your loss."

On the landing of the stone steps, Muriel stood to the right of Will and Emma. Will looked tired. Emma, as her mother always had, looked strikingly serene. Dressed in a navy blue skirt and crème-colored shirt, she looked fully grown. As if she'd become a woman overnight. Father and daughter held hands and greeted mourners with nods and sad smiles and the language of bereave-ment: *Thank you for coming.* Watching them, Muriel instantly understood their past several months. They had gone through Pia's illness *together.* The only two people in on the secret from the start.

"I'm sorry for your loss."

"Pia will be missed."

Thank you for coming.

To Will's left, Lidia was dramatically draped in a black veil. She leaned heavily against a stoic Owen, sobbing quietly into a handkerchief. A flutter of white caught Muriel's eye each time Lidia lowered the linen kerchief away from her teary eyes. That's all she saw beneath that black veil. Not once did Lidia look in her daughter's direction. In fact, Lidia hadn't spoken a single word to Muriel since that morning in her kitchen in Queens.

"What's going on?" Owen had asked.

"Ask her" was Muriel's curt reply.

"Grief," he'd said, sadly. And he left it at that. Her father, like the whole family, was an expert at selective blindness, blurring the ugly reality in front of his face the way a cameraman softens the wrinkles of an aging actress. No one mentioned the fact that Pia's brother, Logan, wasn't there at all. Had he even been called? Inside the church, Papa Czerwinski and Babcia Jula—Pia's grandparents who had once refused to let her inside their home—both kneeled and prayed with their heads burrowed in their hands. Over the years, they had come to accept the blond child with the Irish last name. Then the second, then the third. How could they not? Lidia's offspring were their only hope of grandchildren. Time softened their rigidness. Especially since Lidia fled to Rhode Island often to escape the prison of Queens.

On the day of the funeral, it was easy enough for Muriel to steer clear of her mother. Death's aftermath, she noticed, was crowded. Hovering relatives with Pyrex dishes and friends with containers from Whole Foods had filled the Winston house the night before. The small church was packed to the rafters. Muriel's one true family member—Joanie Frankel—was waiting for her inside the church. She'd come by herself on the train and made her way to the service even, as she'd once told Muriel, "Churches give me hives." In spite of the spectacle—all those skinny women in their oddly angled hats—she resisted the urge to lean close to her friend's ear and snidely compare Pia's funeral to a royal wedding. She didn't have to. Muriel saw it for herself. One friend of Pia's showed up in a mink stole and spiked black heels. She air-kissed everyone and pasted a pouty expression on her cherry-red lips. Another wore white from head to toe—complete with wrist gloves—as if receiving first communion. *This looks like a funeral scene more than a funeral,* Muriel thought. So many well-cast extras.

Extra. That's what she'd been in her sister's life. Immaterial to the central plot. Background. She glanced down at her shabby black shoes and wished she'd bought new ones that day with Pia, when she'd had the chance.

"I'm sorry for your loss."

"We were so shocked."

"She never said a word. I sensed something was wrong, but I never dreamed . . ."

"I'm going to miss her smile."

"You're the sister?"

"I'm so sorry for your loss."

"Thank you for coming."

Perhaps death did have its own vocabulary after all.

EARLY THAT MORNING, with the sun barely a promise, Muriel had taken the train alone into Westport. As before, the rails jostled her left and right. Her stomach felt more settled, though. Her entire being seemed to be elsewhere. Through the train window she absentmindedly watched the cities along the Sound pass in a blur of bobbing white boats. New Rochelle, Greenwich, Darien, South Norwalk, East Norwalk. At the Westport station, she stepped off the train into the warm air and found the same driver she'd had several days before sitting in his same cab. Parked in the shade of a white pine, the car's hood was covered in fallen spiky needles. "Remember me?" Muriel said, stupidly, tapping on the passenger-side window. The driver stared blankly over his newspaper. He said, "Of course." But, of course, he was lying.

The viewing at the funeral home wasn't scheduled to start for more than an hour. Still, Muriel gave the driver the mortuary address. With a furrowed brow he glanced sympathetically at her in his rearview mirror. Muriel looked out the side window. She didn't want him to say a word. If he did, she'd have to comfort *him*, let him know she was okay when she didn't feel okay the slightest bit.

Truth was, along with sadness, Muriel was awash in *guilt*. If she'd been a better sister—more loving, more open, less awkward—Pia would have been unable to let her life slip away without saying good-bye. In her final week, nothing could have kept her away from a phone.

Remember that Christmas morning when we awoke to the whole city blanketed in snow?

Muriel wouldn't remember, but she would say she did. "We thought it was magic," she would say, and Pia would whisper, "It was."

She would know why her sister was calling, but she wouldn't say. They would exchange "I love yous" and silences that were so filled with emotions words were not yet invented to adequately convey them.

"I'm not sure what's going to happen next," Pia would finally utter, "but I couldn't bear it if I left this world without acknowledging how important you've always been to me." Coughing, she would laugh. "Even though I displayed it in the worst possible way. I was truly awful to you, Muriel, wasn't I?"

"Hideous."

Together, they would laugh harder than they could have as one.

"I hope you're sticking around to torture me more," Muriel would say.

"Me, too."

In Pia's final silence Muriel would hear Pia's promise to see her in heaven. She knew Muriel would resist if she said it out loud. So Pia would let her heart whisper the vow: "One day—without pain, or judgment or fear—you'll feel a surge of love so strong it will nearly knock you over. Like nothing even close to an experience on earth, an intense sensation of love will overtake you. And there I will be. Waiting for you. So we can be reunited into the loving arms of a God so vast he can encircle the universe."

The mere thought of seeing her sister again soothed some of the aching in Muriel's chest. Death felt so damned permanent. Still, she couldn't shake the hurt and self-recrimination. How had she let herself fade so far from her own sister's life that she was little more than a Connecticut extra?

The parking lot at the funeral home was empty. Muriel paid the cabdriver and waited for him to drive off before she climbed the front steps and nervously turned the handle on the front door. Her heart was pounding. She'd never been in a funeral home before. Would it smell like putrid flesh? Formaldehyde?

"Hello?" she called out, quietly stepping into the empty entrance room. It looked like an elegant home. And smelled like one, too. Muriel exhaled, relieved. A carved butler's desk stood tall against one wall, sage green velvet chairs were circled around a brown leather ottoman. The wallpaper was muted fleur-de-lis. *Pia would like this room*, Muriel thought. Then it occurred to her that Pia had probably chosen it. A woman who buys her own final dress would never leave the funeral home up to chance.

"May I help you?" A man buttoning his suit jacket appeared from the hallway.

"I know the Pia Winston viewing doesn't start for a while," Muriel said. "I've come from New York."

The director opened his mouth to say no. "I'm the sister," Muriel quickly added. "I've taken the train. Five minutes alone with her? Please?"

He seemed to sense that she wasn't going to leave. Perhaps he'd seen the cab drive off from one of the upstairs windows? Tugging at the white cuffs peering out from his dark jacket, he said, "Wait here a moment, will you?"

Muriel waited. She stood in the center of the pretty room and noticed the beautifully camouflaged tissue boxes on every surface. She pictured Will and Emma sitting in the two armchairs, both reaching for a tissue at the exact moment they felt the vast aloneness of life without the woman who made their lives so livable.

"She happens to be ready," the funeral director said, returning. "Because you're family . . ." His voice faded into padded footsteps down a wide hallway. Muriel followed him. The same muted wallpaper lined the hall. Table lamps, instead of overhead lighting, added to the homey feel. More tissue boxes were discreetly placed on half-moon tables. The director stopped at the open door of Pia's viewing room and said, kindly, "Take all the time you need."

With a respectful step back, and a pious head bow, he turned and left Muriel alone in the hallway. She was startled. Shouldn't he . . . *escort* her in? Make sure she didn't scream or faint? What if she took one look at Pia's dead body and vomited on their pristine carpet? It took a moment for Muriel to realize he'd given her exactly what she'd asked for: a few minutes alone with her sister.

All of a sudden it became clear that walking required a complex set of coordinated movements. There was leg lifting and balancing on one foot and kicking the knee forward and leaning the torso in just so. All for one step! How did people do it so effortlessly? Muriel wasn't sure she could manage. Her legs felt like tree trunks, rooted to the carpeting below her feet. Perhaps the cabdriver was nearby reading the *Post*? Surely he didn't just drive around wasting gas on the odd chance someone needed a ride? This was *Connecticut*, after all, the land of the hybrid SUV.

If she hadn't worried about annoying the funeral director—almost certainly he'd donned his jacket for the express purpose of dealing with her early arrival—she might have turned her head and called out, "Sir? Excuse me. I seem to have changed my mind." Instead, Muriel lifted one wooden leg and flung it out in front of her. Then the other.

The smell of roses struck her first. They strongly perfumed the air in a heavy greenish scent. Gold drapery lined the walls.

White chairs were organized in neat rows. A wooden podium held an open guest book. Muriel hung back with her head down. Never before had she seen a dead body, certainly not one so previously full of life. She was scared. Would Pia look skeletal? Would she remember her sister forever as flat and still? Not bounding down the front steps of their house or gliding down the aisle like an angel in her wedding gown. The whole church had gasped at her beauty that day. Would Muriel now gasp again?

Sucking in a fortifying breath, she forced herself to step closer. Then she looked up and, yes, she gasped. Pia was—as Muriel should have assumed she would be—*gorgeous*. Surrounded by giant bouquets of bursting yellow roses, Pia was laid out in a gunmetal casket in her gray satin dress. The effect was stunning—a sunburst surrounding a storm cloud. Dramatic and magnificent. So very *her*. Muriel pressed both hands to her chest. Even in death, her sister took her breath away.

"My God," she said, kneeling on the cushioned rail positioned in front of the casket. Pia's wig was styled perfectly, the tiniest flip at her collarbone. Primrose pink lipstick softly colored her lips. The slightest hint of blush and foundation warmed her pale cheeks. Her face looked relaxed and unlined. Pain free. Somehow, she looked healthier than she had when Muriel had last seen her. As if cancer no longer enslaved her body. She was free. French-manicured nails tipped her fingers, not too long, not too square, exactly as Pia would have wanted. Her hands were folded into a dove on her torso. A pearl rosary was entwined in her slim fingers. The gray satin dress was ironed and smoothed. Muriel had feared she would burst into tears. Instead, she beamed. "Oh, Pia. You would be so happy. You look *perfect.*"

For a long time, Muriel knelt in place and silently stared. She marveled at the way Pia's eyebrows arched into a sharp inverted V. The bridge of her nose was narrow and smooth, its tip a martini olive. Both cheekbones surfaced just under her eyes, as high as they could go, really, and her lips were fuller on the bottom than the top, ever so slightly tipped up at the corners. In close-up, the face she'd seen a thousand times looked entirely different. More human, somehow. Oddly, more alive.

Muriel reached her hand out to touch Pia's face, but she stopped in midair, afraid that her sister's skin might feel hard or cold. Would it be a mannequin's cheek? That, she didn't want to know. Forever she would rather remember Pia's touch on the sunporch, her urgent grasp when she described having a child as seeing God on earth. Pulling her hand back, Muriel rested it on the soft railing of the kneeling pew. Then she continued to stare, struck by the privilege of time to memorize her sister's face. No one was there to say, "God, Muriel. Take a picture, why don't you?" No one could break the spell by pulling her away. For once, for the first time, Pia was all hers.

"It's me," she whispered, finally. "Muriel."

Quickly, Muriel glanced behind her to make sure they were alone.

"I wanted to talk to you for a minute, Pia. Just us. One last time."

Muriel tucked a strand of hair behind her ear as tears threatened. Her voice wobbly, she said, "We never got a chance to talk at the very end. I know things went south fast, but I was hoping to say one more thing. It's been on my mind for a while. There never seemed to be the right moment. But now, it's just you and me. So here goes."

Again, Muriel looked over her shoulder to make sure no one else had come into the room. "You asked me to forgive you, Pia, and I did years ago. But I've always been too afraid to ask you for the same thing. From the moment I was born, I knew I never was the sister you wanted me to be. Somebody *you* could be proud of. I tried. Truly, I did."

Unable to hold them back, tears wet Muriel's face. "You must have been shocked to see me grow up. So unlike you and Mama. Such a foreign being. Who is this round thing? I felt your disapproval always. Your disdain." Muriel looked down. "Still—"

She closed her eyes and sniffed. The thickly scented air entered and exited her lungs. Saliva pooled behind her lips. She swallowed hard. Opening her eyes, she folded her hands in prayer.

"Can you manage this one last thing—wherever you are—wherever your soul is? *Release* me. Please, Pia. Forgive me for not being somebody you could love. Forgive me my trespasses so I can forgive myself. Set me free. Don't make me live in your shadow anymore. Help me find my own light."

As she took a breath to confess how many times she'd rerun the past weeks and months, recasting the sister role, rehearsing her part until she got it exactly right—*doing* instead of wondering what to do, knowing how to comfort, how to be there naturally because that's what real sisters just *knew*—the funeral director appeared in the door frame with his solemn expression and dark suit and softly said, "Miss Winston?"

Muriel turned her head. "I'm a Sullivant," she said, wiping the tears from her cheeks with both hands.

"Excuse me for interrupting you, Miss Sullivant. Other family members are here. May I send them in?"

"Of course." Muriel's lips bent in a closed-mouth smile. She made the sign of the cross, not sure if it was proper protocol or not, then stood and quietly left the funeral home out a side door. *Let Lidia have time alone with her favorite child*, Muriel thought. *It's only fair.*

INSIDE THE SMALL church, jewel-colored stained-glass windows lined both upper walls. Celestial rays of blue and orange filtered down onto the white pews. Pia's closed casket—covered in the yellow roses from the mortuary—sat at the front, below the linen-covered altar. A large stunning photograph of her reminded everyone of what they had lost.

Before the funeral mass began, the family solemnly walked to the front pew and seated themselves. Owen's parents were there, too. Lidia arranged her veil in precise folds across her face. Will and Emma stared straight ahead. Muriel sat upright and willed herself not to cry. Above the altar, a giant Jesus gazed mournfully down from his crucifix. Muriel stared at the black-red teardrop of blood that was painted next to the open wound in his crossed veined feet.

"Many of those who sleep in the dust of the earth shall awake;

some shall live forever . . ." Beside her, in a whisper, Owen practiced his reading from the prophet Daniel.

From somewhere above, a harpist filled the air with trills of angelic notes. The musky scent of incense clouded the air. Not too much. Just enough. En masse, the congregation turned to watch pairs of scrubbed altar boys, dressed in their red cassocks, carrying gold-filigreed processional candles soberly up the center aisle. They circled around Pia's silver casket and settled themselves to the right and left of the altar. As if on cue, the crowd leaned back in the pews and waited. With kids fidgeting in their stiff Sunday shoes and relatives coughing and Connecticut women slyly reapplying lipstick while their husbands glanced at their Rolex watches, the side door to the sacristy opened with an eerie creak. Muriel tilted her head to face the noise and gasped audibly. There, Father Camilo emerged—palms pressed together and head bowed piously—to say her sister's funeral mass.

Part III

Gone Today, Here Tomorrow

Chapter 30

AMERICA, AS FAR as Muriel could tell, was a monotonous repetition of Targets, Walmarts, Home Depots, Costcos, and mall after mall after mall. There were also Burger Kings and Cinnabons and Starbucks and Pizza Huts and rest stops that usually had an assortment of all four. Joanie Frankel, seated next to Muriel in the rental car, was a camel. Each time she snuffled awake, Muriel asked, "Need a potty break?"

"Not yet." She'd then nuzzle back up to the headrest and fall soundly asleep again. Muriel had never seen anyone sleep so much. Or use the restroom so little. Was there a colostomy bag beneath those folds of fabric? Had she developed narcolepsy on the George Washington Bridge?

It was a sixty-hour road trip. Which they planned to do in a week, sharing the driving load. Three days out, one day there, three days back. Of course, flying would have been much faster, but Joanie Frankel didn't fly, and Muriel didn't want to admit it, but she couldn't go alone. Not with her grief so prickling. So she endured the road. The gray blur of asphalt reminded her of Pia's final satin dress; the rhythmic rocking of the car brought her back to that magical afternoon on the sunporch when she'd been so lovingly embraced by the sister who had once been so cruel to her.

Months had passed since the Connecticut funeral. Pia's absence left more of a hole in Muriel's heart than her nonpresence in Muriel's life ever had. She felt cheated. She wanted answers. Her confusion and sorrow had become a fermented burbling brew, brown edged and smelling of rot.

Snorting, Joanie jolted awake.

"Rest stop?" Muriel asked.

"No need." Yawning dramatically, she added, "You may have noticed I have a bladder the size of a Prada bag."

AFTER ELEVEN HOURS on the road, the two women dragged their rolling suitcases into a Holiday Inn Express near the interstate on the outskirts of Cincinnati. Both devoured messy barbecued pork ribs out of Styrofoam containers and fell into a comatose sleep. In the morning, after American cheese omelets that looked like neatly folded napkins, they showered and dressed and were ready to continue their journey.

"Wanna drive?" Muriel asked her best friend.

"Not just yet, if you don't mind."

"I don't mind, if you're up for a small detour."

"Canada?"

Muriel laughed. "A bit less out of our way. All you need to do is relax and open your mind."

Brandishing a thumbs-up, Joanie landed on the passenger seat in a fabricky puff and opened the window, breaking every rental rule by lighting a cigarette. "I blow it out the side!" she said, indignant, when Muriel shot her a reprimanding look.

"And it blows right back in."

"That's my fault?"

They drove about half an hour or so. At exit 11, the asphalt mellowed into Kentucky farmland. It was gorgeous countryside. Fields of prairie bluegrass were, indeed, *blue*. And the cloudless sky was the color of corydalis flowers. Heaven and earth blended into one stunning azure horizon. Even Joanie managed to stay awake. The swaying fields seemed to calm her. Aside from an espresso brown horse here and there, lazily flicking its tail, it felt as if the two women were the last humans left on the planet. Not another soul was to be seen for miles. It was startling, therefore, to veer around a bend and spot a modern glass-and-brick building rising out of the flat earth. Yet there it was, low and wide, suddenly crowded with families in gigantic square shorts, clunky white sneakers, and thick sweatshirts with loud logos.

"Walmart rehab?" Joanie asked. Muriel laughed and parked in the large lot beneath a poplar tree. Cutting the engine, she stepped out of the car and stretched her arms overhead. The air smelled faintly of fertilizer. Muriel wore black sunglasses, black jeans, black loafers, a black T-shirt, and a black pullover sweater. "Wiccan chic," Joanie had chided her that morning. As usual, her own outfit was a layered amorphous gauzy print. When Joanie moved, her clothes sashayed all around her.

Together the two women walked up a landscaped path to the entrance where a sign read PREPARE TO BELIEVE.

Joanie stopped dead. "Dear God."

"We were so close to it. How could we *not* check it out? Especially since Pia was so into it. I need to understand what she was thinking."

Joanie thought for a moment, then she nodded. Lifting her head, she set her jaw and cocked one eyebrow. "I'm prepared. Bring it on."

In they walked into another world. The world according to God: the Creation Museum. *Prepare to believe.* Instantly, Joanie draped her arm around Muriel's shoulder.

"Let's see if they are prepared to believe what their own Bible says: love thy neighbor."

"Please don't make a scene," Muriel whispered through smiling teeth.

There was a line to buy tickets. Joanie pasted an angelic expression on her face and took Muriel's hand in hers as they inched forward. Muriel attempted to pull her palm free, but Joanie held fast. At the cashier's, Joanie asked, "Do you have a married couple's discount?"

The befuddled older woman behind the counter said, "Um, no." In her gentle Kentucky drawl, she added, "But if you purchase museum and planetarium tickets together it's the best deal."

"Just the museum, please," Muriel said, overgrinning. "We only have half an hour."

Turning to Muriel, Joanie said, "Can you pay, sweetheart? I've left my chain wallet in the pocket of my flannel shirt."

Quickly, Muriel jerked her hand free from Joanie's grip and gave the cashier her credit card. Beside her, Joanie lovingly stroked her hair.

"You really are a pain," Muriel said as they left the counter with their tickets in hand.

"Did you see those ticket prices? It's less to enter the Met! What about their commandment not to steal? Aren't the *poor* blessed in their book? Don't they get into heaven first? Apparently, they can't get into this museum at all. Not to mention the planetarium. Their 'deal' is a family's food budget! And did you notice that they're open on Sunday? *God's* day. I seem to remember a commandment in the original ten that forbids working on the Sabbath."

"Are you done?"

Joanie fluffed up her curly hair. "For now," she said haughtily.

"Good. Put your New York away and open your mind."

Raising both hands in surrender, Joanie pressed her lips together and made a zipping motion with two fingers. Silently, she followed Muriel to the opening exhibit: *Genesis.* Of course.

Laid out like a biblical Ikea, the Creation Museum is a walking tour through the Bible, billed as a place where the *true* origins of the earth can finally be told. Complete with animatronic dinosaurs and an actual ark, it winds a path through the seven Cs of the fundamental Christian take on history: creation, corruption, catastrophe, confusion, Christ, cross, and consummation. First stop: the cavelike opening to the beginning of life on our planet. Over the loudspeaker, a godly voice asks, "Ever wonder how the Grand Canyon was *really* created?"

"No," said Joanie out loud. Muriel shot her another look. In they went. *Prepare to believe.*

Instantly and proudly, science was slammed. Since the Bible states that God made the earth and the universe in six days—and both, according to the holy book, are only about six thousand years old—the Grand Canyon couldn't possibly have been formed by millions of years of erosion the way secular science would have you believe. The *truth*, they said in the first stop on the creation tour, was that the Grand Canyon was made by a massive worldwide flood. And it was fast. God's deluge gushed forth, scrubbing the earth clean of everything sinful and dirty. When the water receded, *poof*! There was a huge crack in Arizona that would come to be known as the Grand Canyon. Thankfully, several fortunate creatures were able to ride out the storm by cramming themselves onto Noah's ark, two by two. Dinosaurs among them.

"Are you kidding me?" Joanie said, agog.

Admittedly, it was a lot to swallow. *Pia believed this?* Muriel thought. Behind them a father with a low side part in his hair and ironed slacks said to his young son, "Makes sense to me. If it was *erosion*, where did all that dirt go?"

Joanie dug her fingernails into Muriel's sweatered forearm. As they walked deeper into the Bible, she periodically stopped and blinked, silenced for perhaps the first time in her life. God's master plan emerged before their eyes and ears. Seems He created dinosaurs on day six, the same day Adam and Eve came into being. Clearly a full day on God's calendar. Scientists who used carbon dating to determine the age of a fossil were only wasting their time, a voice-over said. Why bother? If a dinosaur wasn't small enough to wedge itself onto Noah's ark, it was killed in the massive flood about four thousand years ago. Therefore even the very oldest dinosaurs were the same age as the oldest humans. They romped through the Garden of Eden with Adam and Eve—their big slobbery pets. Should you wonder why human bones were never found with dinosaur fossils, the voice-over loop had an explanation: "It simply means they weren't buried together. In the same way humans aren't now buried with crocodiles."

"Oh my God," Muriel said out loud, flabbergasted to see that this version of creation was stated as *fact*. Not "Prepare to hear our theory or a fairy tale" but "Prepare to *believe*." She thought back to the one word Pia used to explain it all: faith.

"Never let anyone tell you that you came from an ape," the man with the hatchet hair part said to his impressionable son. "You came from *God*."

"I've got to get out of here," Muriel said, tugging Joanie's sleeve.

"Right behind you, sister."

On fast-forward, they snaked through the biblical maze—past a replica of Noah's ark, past more animatronic dinosaurs (who themselves couldn't fit into the ark), past Corruption Valley and a display of a porn-obsessed teen who obviously let the evils of secular society into his hormone-ravaged life—and emerged just as the planetarium show was scheduled to start. A brief one, apparently, since the entire universe was formed the instant God decreed, "Let there be light." Furious, Muriel sputtered, "Do they simply *ignore* the fact that God gave humanity a brain and common sense? Does no one care that our teens rank among the lowest in math and science?"

They couldn't leave the Creation Museum fast enough. In the car, Muriel set the GPS for the quickest route back to the sanity of the interstate. On the way, through the idyllic landscape of northern Kentucky, all she could think about was her mother and her sister and their God and Father Camilo and sin and lying and secrets and the depressing truth that there were none so blind as those who would not, under any circumstances, allow themselves to *see*.

Chapter 31

MEERS, OKLAHOMA, WAS the town where they spent night two. Well, *near* it anyway. Meers itself was in the middle of nowhere. Muriel had selected it because she'd seen an *America's Best* episode on the Food Network about a restaurant there that served one of the best burgers in the country. Seven inches around, no frills like onions or relish, made from cattle grazing a few feet out the back window. How could they resist? They didn't.

"Seriously off the hook!" Muriel said, biting into the best burger she'd ever eaten. The only thing better was the homemade peach cobbler they had for dessert.

On the way to the car, stuffed and drowsy, Muriel tossed Joanie the keys. "You're up," she said, so tired she was nearly asleep on her feet. Joanie gripped the keys in her cushioned palm and said, "I guess this is as good a time as any to mention that I don't have a driver's license."

Muriel blinked. "You *lost* it?"

"By definition, to lose something, you need to have something."

A quote mark formed on Muriel's forehead. The sun was setting on the vast field of vegetation on either side of the dusty country road. She still felt the bumpy tire suspension in her arms. "You never *had* a driver's license?"

"Who needs to drive in New York?"

Her mouth hanging open, Muriel slowly asked, "You know how to drive a car, right?"

Joanie replied, "I hear it's like riding a bike."

Muriel couldn't believe her ears. "It's nothing like riding a bike!" Then she stopped. "Wait a minute. I've never once seen you ride a bike."

"I hear it's like driving a car."

After a muted moment, both women burst into laughter. "Why didn't you tell me you couldn't drive before we left on our *road* trip?"

"I knew you wouldn't want to drive the whole way by yourself."

"Well, *yeah*."

"And if you knew I couldn't drive, you wouldn't want me to come. You would have flown. Which would have meant changing planes and standing in your socks in those interminable security lines and feeling as graceful as a caught lover sneaking out the bathroom window.

"In the waiting area—like you were a *magnet*—a harried young mom with her crusty-nosed kid and his phlegmy cough would sit next to you and ask, 'Could you please watch little

Johnny for *one second* while I run into the restroom?' Before you had a chance to say no—not that you ever would—Johnny would sneeze in that all-out, open-your-face sort of way that kids do and you would want to barf because you'd be quite sure his snot should be quarantined by the EPA."

Muriel laughed out loud. In a gentle voice Joanie said, "I know you so well, baby girl. You'd suck it up and wipe the toxic waste off that kid's face even if it meant using all the Sani-Cloths in your carry-on bag. The wipes you had slated for the headrest on the plane and the latch releasing the food tray. You would have to sit upright the whole flight, certain that the previous passenger had head lice. A migraine would develop toward the end of the flight when the only air in that sealed metal tube was recirculated farts and exhalations from strangers. Several of whom you smelled firsthand when nachos were unwrapped on the tarmac. The only blessed relief you might—*might*—possibly have is if you missed your connecting flight and had time to run to the snack store to buy more Sani-Cloths for twenty dollars a pack."

Circling around the front of the rental car, Joanie put the keys back in Muriel's hand, then squeezed them lovingly.

"You're welcome," she said, kissing her best friend's cheek. "Besides, we're practically there, right? Just a quick drive tomorrow through Texas."

TEXAS MIGHT AS well have been the entire United States. It felt so endless, they gave up seeing a border sign halfway through the state. And they were driving across the thin part! For miles, they saw not an animal, not a tree, not a house, not a country store.

Simply flat brown nothingness interrupted by an occasional rusty ranch gate leading nowhere. Both women were stunned into silence. Instantly and permanently, they understood that Texas was like no other place on earth. The *moon*, perhaps, but nothing remotely resembling the blue planet on which they lived.

"That explains it," Joanie said, finally, shaking her head. Muriel knew what she meant. A politician from Texas *had* to view the world differently. How could he or she not? For one thing, the state is so huge it would be impossible not to feel like the biggest badass on the block. And with so much open space, how could Texans develop any real sense that they shared the country—the world—with others?

"There *are* cities somewhere in this state," Muriel offered. "Beautiful cities like Austin and Dallas."

Joanie scoffed. "Every member of Congress—from Texas to Alaska—should be required to live at least one year in a small Lower East Side co-op conversion. If you can amicably deal with a neighbor who leaves wet laundry sitting in the only washing machine all day, another who stinks up the building with cigarette smoke (*moi*), one who freaks out if you change your doormat, another who considers a bake sale a viable way to raise money for tax increases, and still another who lets her dog bark incessantly day and night—not to mention a prissy spinster who wants to fine everyone for every little infraction—well, you can pass any bill and broker any peace."

Muriel snuffled up a laugh as Joanie lit her third cigarette of the day. She inhaled luxuriantly and blew the smoke sideways out the open window, where, of course, it immediately blew back in. Into the billow she said, "That bitch sends me one more fine notice and she can smoke my *ass.*"

As it had in the first long stretch through Pennsylvania, the second through Ohio, and the third from Kentucky to southern Oklahoma, a road trance overtook Muriel. Not sleepy, she nonetheless felt a deep calm descend on her, like hot fudge over warm pound cake. As soon as Joanie settled into sleep, she stared out the windshield and watched the gray asphalt disappear beneath the wheels of the rental car. The lines in the highway passed her peripheral vision in flashes of white. As always, her mind wandered to Pia and the surreal fact that she would never grow any older. One day Muriel would out-age her. Never would Pia meet the man who would take Emma's breath away or the child who would become her child's heart.

Tears rose in Muriel's eyes as they always did when she thought about the ordinary life her sister would miss: Christmas dinners, Will's New Year's Eve cruise around the Statue of Liberty, the scent of the lawn as the mower passed below her bedroom window, Emma's next birthday and all the birthdays to follow. The simplicity of connection. Was is possible therein lay the meaning of life?

THEY ARRIVED IN the midst of a thunderstorm unlike anything Muriel had ever seen. The heavens exploded in a deafening kitchen fight. Pots banging, dishes crashing to the floor, glasses hurled against a wall. The two women ran into the lobby of the hotel, but Muriel stood just inside the door and watched the sky, mesmerized. Lightning cracked the gray-black darkness and shook the air. It looked like Dr. Frankenstein's lab. The rain fell so hard, the lightning illuminated shiny cellophane sheets. Thunder rattled the windows and rumbled through her entire body. It was terrifyingly beautiful. Muriel couldn't turn away even if she'd wanted to.

As abruptly as it had begun, the tyrannical storm stopped. Spent, its tantrum subsided. Calm descended into a silence so complete it felt as though Muriel's ears were filled with cotton. "Sign from God," she said quietly to herself. They had come a long way, but they were exactly where they were meant to be. She smiled. "Tomorrow, the sun will shine."

Chapter 32

SANTA FE, NEW MEXICO, sparkled like a prom queen. In the distance, jagged mountain peaks encircled the town in a snow-topped tiara. The Sangre de Cristo Mountains—blood of Christ—were an aptly named reminder of the city's violent past. Each evening at sunset, they flared a fiery red.

Muriel awoke early, though it looked like midnight in the hotel room. Before she'd dozed off the night before, Joanie had shut the blackout drapes. In the dim light of the bedside lamp, Muriel could see her friend's hazy outline in the next bed. She had the face of a pixie. The covers pulled tightly under her chin, she smiled in her sleep, looking impish, as if she was dreaming about romping through a forest full of chocolate trees.

Soundlessly, Muriel lowered her bare feet to the nubby carpet and crept into the bathroom. Her reflection in the mirror was the first jolt of the day. Three days of road food and cigarette smoke had taken its toll. Her skin was pasty, her stomach pushed

against the fabric of her pajama T-shirt. Since the first day's barbecued ribs hadn't yet fully left her system, she could feel them
clinging to the insides of her arteries in quivering custardy blobs.
The Meers cobbler, she could tell, was already nestled into the
soft pockets of flesh at the top of both thighs.

Turning away from the mirror, Muriel turned on the shower.
This was no time to judge herself harshly. Not when she needed
all the confidence she could muster for the day ahead.

LIKE EVERY OTHER town in America—probably on earth—Santa
Fe had its center, its outskirts, and its outlying neighborhoods.
Unlike other towns, Santa Fe appeared to be made of gingerbread. The entire city was constructed of the same reddish brown
adobe. Or so it seemed to Muriel as she set out from her outskirts hotel. Even the Walmart was shoe-box shaped and mud
colored. Driving past it felt like she was at Disneyland, on the
New Mexico ride.

Old Town was altogether different. The central plaza—from
which the rest of the city radiated—was the real deal. Its Spanish
architecture and authentic pueblo style had a sprinkling of Vic-
toriana, reflecting its history as the oldest European city west of
the Mississippi. The previous night's rain had washed the pueblo
dust from the sidewalks; the midmorning air was as sharp as
ultra high def.

Alone, Muriel drove through Old Town where Native American artists spread their handcrafted wares on colorful blankets,
chili peppers dried in the sun, and artists painted in the shade

of old porticos. It was a beautiful combination of old and new. Living history on display. Before she left the hotel that morning, she'd gathered supplies from the lobby breakfast room and left them upstairs for Joanie. Mini muffins, a banana, a hard-boiled egg, orange juice. When she awoke, Joanie could get her own coffee. Muriel also left a note: "Wish me luck." They both knew she had to make this leg of the journey alone. No more secrets. No more hiding.

Armed only with an address and a GPS, Muriel wasn't at all certain she would succeed. In fact, now that she was near, it felt ridiculous to be there at all. Certainly there were easier ways. Like *calling*, for one. But every instinct told her it had to be a face-to-face meeting. If not, as she well knew, it would be too easy to look the other way.

"*Nike* it," Joanie had advised her. "Just do it."

The plan in motion, Muriel gripped the steering wheel and circled around Old Town Square, the museum of art with its Georgia O'Keeffe collection, the Palace of the Governors—all of which seemed to rise out of the orange dirt itself. Yellow sunlight fell unimpeded to the still-damp earth. The cloudless sky was a stunning baby blanket blue. It was the kind of day that inspired people to tilt their heads back, close their eyes, and joyously stretch their arms into the sky. Muriel would have done just that if she was the type of person to do such a thing. As it was, she drove to the highway outside of town with her teeth pressed together.

"You can do this," she muttered, even as she questioned those four little words. Had she merely heard them on a stage once? A line of pure fantasy? Surely there were people who *couldn't* do things, right? Failures, despite pep talks and best efforts?

"Please drive to highlighted route." The GPS led the way. Swallowing her doubt, Muriel made a left onto the Old Santa Fe Trail, then a right onto the Old Pecos Trail, then another right onto Route 285, the straightaway out of town. Ready or not, she was on her way.

The Mars comparison outside of Santa Fe was impossible to overstate. The main highway ran flat through a vast expanse of orange nothingness. Muriel saw not one other car. Her only companions were cabbage-head bobbles of gray-green desert scrub. Sitting upright in the driver's seat, she was alert for jackrabbits and aliens.

Soon enough, however, the barren landscape calmed her. She settled into the cushion of her seat and watched the speedometer rise. In her mind she imagined taking flight—the long highway a runway. First, the front tires would lift off, then the back. With a *whump* they would tuck themselves into the undercarriage of her car. She would feel the earth's gravitational pull on her chest, marvel as she always did at air's power to lift metal. A momentary wobble would cause her to catch her breath. But as the car straightened itself into the atmosphere, she'd hunger to open the window and taste a cloud. Metallic, certainly, in the same way an old ice cube, shrunken and forgotten in the back of the freezer, had the faint tang of copper.

"In point three miles, turn right."

The GPS voice brought Muriel back to earth. Reducing her

speed, she prepared herself to turn right a few yards beyond a hand-painted sign that welcomed her to a town called Galisteo.

"Toto, we're not in Kansas anymore," she said out loud.

In Galisteo, the entire landscape changed. More terrestrial than *extra*terrestrial, less eerie. Instantly, there were signs of life. Cacti reached their spiked arms up to the turquoise sky. Speckled horses flicked their tails in hay-filled paddocks. A weatherbeaten home was set back from the road, its split-rail fence gray from sun and snow. The main artery into town was covered in swirling pinwheels of rust-colored dust. If it had rained there the night before, all evidence of it was gone. Car tires had orange veneers. In town, though the traditional adobe style was evident, Galisteo had a scrappy artist's vibe that Muriel loved at once. It was a genuine desert beauty, the kind that needed no makeup.

"Ahead, turn right."

Following the GPS instructions, Muriel took a right and drove up a hill on a gravelly dirt road. An orange cloud billowed up to the windows. The car's suspension vibrated in her hands. She continued past a row of multicolored mailboxes—one painted in polka dots—that sat atop their weathered posts like unsold hammers in an old hardware store. On her left, an old church graveyard was dotted with headstones that bent every which way, their epitaphs long since blurred by wind. Beneath her tires, the unpaved earth sounded like sizzling bacon. Though the windshield was dirty, she could see small square clay houses—real adobe instead of colored cement—on either side of the road. They were randomly spaced, like brown dice dropped from heaven. The concentration needed to drive through the thick dust eclipsed

Muriel's nerves. By the time her GPS announced, "Arriving at destination," she was calm enough to face whatever might come her way.

On the crest of a hill overlooking miles of desert, Muriel pulled over and cut the engine. The dust cloud settled around her. Set back from the road, she saw a small house made from adobe that was more pink than orange. It reminded her of one of Pia's birthday cakes. Lidia had colored both the cake and the icing pink. Even as a toddler Muriel had marveled at the perfectly square slice she'd been given. Almost too pretty to eat.

Opening the car door, Muriel stepped out and stretched her rib cage in the unfiltered sunlight. Then she reached back into the car for her sun hat. Her foray into America had shown her how very bright open spaces could be. There was no such thing as a shady side of the street.

Outside was absolute silence. Not a dog barking or a television tuned to *The Price Is Right*. No Connecticut leaf blowers. At an angle from the pink house was a rectangular outbuilding of the same color. A stone path forked off to both front doors. Gray agave bushes and greenish tufts of Indian grass sprouted from the bases of several smooth boulders edging the raised porch of the house. Magenta succulents had been planted on top of both flat roofs.

"Cool," Muriel said quietly. Alive insulation.

In her thin-soled loafers, she felt the gravel crunch beneath her feet as she walked up the driveway to the path. The hems of her blue jeans were quickly coated in dust. A lizard darted in front of her, freezing in place briefly, before wriggling into the agave shade. The closer Muriel got to the front door, the more nervous she felt. Honestly, she hadn't planned further than this, certain that some sort of master plan would materialize on the spot. At the moment, however, her heartbeat drowned out all intelligent thought. The best she could muster was a zippy knock on the door, one that casually said, "Yoo-hoo! You have a visitor!"

No one answered. Muriel knocked again. *Tap, tap, tap. Yoo-hoo-hoo.*

Still, no one. Pushing her wide-brimmed hat to the back of her head, she pressed her ear to the door. She heard not a sound. Fully aware she'd hate it if someone did the same to her, she nonetheless walked over to the uncurtained window and peered through. Inside was spare and bright with white furniture set almost randomly on the dark hardwood floor. A kiva fireplace in the corner had faint soot marks above the arched opening. In front of it was a small rectangle of red Navajo rug. Muriel was surprised by the ordinariness of the room. She'd expected something less, well, Santa Fe.

"Don't move."

Muriel froze. The male voice behind her had the rasp of a smoker. She felt the blood drain out of her face. "I'm, uh—"

"*Quiet.*"

She swallowed her words. Slowly, the man said, "Never turn your back on a snake."

Snake? Muriel whipped her head around. Standing at the bottom of the porch steps, holding a long metal pole with a claw at the end of it, was her brother, Logan. As she opened her mouth to speak he said, "Shhh."

Brown skinned and creased around the eyes, the sandy hair Muriel remembered was now slightly gray, surprisingly thick given Owen's flyaway fluff. Logan pointed to a pile of firewood a few feet away from his sister. He said, "Don't give him a reason to attack you."

"It's me, Logan. Your sister," she whispered, shakily.

"I know who you are."

The knees of her older brother's Levi's were chalky with plaster dust. His hands were callused and veined. Within his man's face, Muriel saw the boy she'd once known. Barely known, really. He left home after high school. The few times she saw him after that were little more than dinners with a sullen stranger. Grunting answers to their mother's counterfeit concern.

In one swift motion, Logan climbed the stairs and lunged his pole into the woodpile. Up came a wiggling brown snake frantically flicking its pink tongue. "Only a bull snake," he said calmly. "Nothing to worry about."

With that, Logan Sullivant turned on the heels of his paint-splattered work boots and ambled into the brush.

Chapter 33

Logan Sullivant had always been a riddle to his little sister. Seven years older, he treated her much the same way Pia did: a gnat, always buzzing about his head, returning to circle around him no matter how many times he swatted her away. Like their father, Logan rarely said much. From the beginning, conversations with him were shadowed in subtext.

"What's that?" Muriel would ask, sitting on the basement steps (hiding from Lidia, usually) as she watched her brother fashion something out of white tubing.

"What do you want it to be?"

"How should I know?"

"Precisely the point."

She never understood him. Like a lucid dreamer Logan lived within his own head, conjuring images no one else saw. "Flamingos," he once said to a pile of discarded wire hangers in the recycling bin.

No one was surprised when Logan grew up to become an artist. From the start, he saw beauty in trash. A broken pencil was painted white to become a picket in a tiny fence for a school project, a crumpled newspaper was shaped into a wilted rose. On a sketch pad at the dinner table he'd silently draw the tilt of a fork against a plate or the way his milk coated the side of the glass. The walls of his room were one big collage of magazine photos, curlicued scraps of metal, scribbled poetry, ticket stubs—floor-to-ceiling canvases that offered the clearest view into his original mind.

Muriel was in awe. Mostly because her brother's creativity was encouraged. "Be anything," Lidia said to him. "But be something."

To her she said, "Are you *sure* you want to eat that?"

Clearly Owen's genetic offspring, Logan had scruffy dust-colored hair that stuck up more on one side than the other, exactly the way his dad's did. It grew in a similar pinwheel at the crown. Both men's bodies were Popsicle sticks. From the back, their outlines were identical. Together they explored the dunes in Narragansett and Long Island, bending over at the same moment to pick up the same shard of sand glass. They watched birds nesting through shared binoculars, dismantled engines and old radios and discarded kitchen appliances down in the basement to see how they worked. In the same way Pia was a miniature Lidia, Logan was a pint-size Owen. Perhaps that's why Muriel always felt so lost. When you're number five in a family of four, who's *your* mirror image?

But Logan never saw his sister Muriel grow up. He left home

a few months after his high school graduation and rarely came back. Like so many other things in the Sullivant family, his absence was unspoken.

"Where's Logan?" young Muriel asked one Christmas during the traditional *wigilia* on Christmas Eve. The family sat in the living room, on the good furniture, awaiting the arrival of Christ.

"Don't tear the *pająki*, Muriel, with your flapping clumsy hands."

After sunset, as Muriel was sent to the window to watch for the first star, she asked, "Will Logan be here by dinnertime?"

"Light the star supper candles, Pia," Lidia had replied behind her.

Once the *opłatek* wafer was broken and passed around to all, Lidia placed a jagged piece of it on an empty plate. "Is that Logan's *opłatek*?" Muriel asked, but Lidia said nothing and Owen turned away. The next morning, when Muriel noticed there were no presents under the tree for her brother she quietly asked Pia, "Has Logan run away?"

Pia said, "Pass me that big shiny box, will you? The one with the silver bow?"

On New Year's Eve, when Pia was at a friend's house and her parents were at a cocktail party and Muriel was left with an elderly babysitter who slept on the couch with her mouth hanging open and her bent, panty-hose-covered toes smelling like sweat and old shoe, Muriel thought she saw a shadow pass beneath the light in the entryway and slither up the stairs.

"Logan?" she called out. But no one answered. Too scared to investigate, she huddled near the babysitter and watched an old black-and-white movie with her heart pumping wildly, praying that the sitter would be able to wake up if an ax murderer was on his way into the den to split open their skulls like cantaloupes.

The next morning, when the aroma in their home turned into roasted turkey and Lidia wore her apron over her crème-colored slacks, Muriel sat at the kitchen table and asked her mother, "Will Logan be here for supper tonight?" Turning her back, Lidia said, testily, "Those sweet potatoes aren't going to peel themselves."

Eventually Muriel stopped asking. One thing she knew for sure about her mother: if she didn't want to discuss something, it didn't get discussed. Pia barely spoke to her pesky little sister about *anything*. And after Logan left, her father bundled himself more tightly into his silence. Often it felt like he was a visitor, as if it was only polite to keep himself and his possessions contained. Don't make a fuss. Logan was gone. That was that.

AFTER DEPOSITING THE bull snake beneath a boulder behind his house, Logan flicked his head at his sister and said, "I'm in here." Then he silently walked into the adobe building next to his house. Muriel followed. Inside, she looked left and right and up and down and said, "Wow."

Logan's art studio was a wonderland of color and light. The exact opposite of the dank Queens basement in which Muriel had always seen him. Her memory of her brother was a film noir movie, nighttime coloring even when the sun was out. Mystery around every dingy corner. In Galisteo, he was in plain view. Within the thick adobe walls, creamy sunlight streamed in from the huge windows. A smooth gray cement floor felt cool beneath the soles of Muriel's shoes.

In the far corner of the studio, an autopsy-style sink with a handheld sprayer and long stainless-steel ledge was scrubbed and shiny. Along the far wall was a row of narrow cubbies, each holding upright its own mounted canvas. Bins of things were organized by color and content: green shards of desert glass, multicolored bottle caps, newspaper inserts, sun-bleached animal bones, bits of foil and crinkled cellophane, dried plants, smooth stones. A pristine recycling center. Her arms at her sides, Muriel looked around in awe.

"Sorry to hear about Pia," Logan said abruptly. He positioned himself behind a large marble-topped island in the center of the room, tools hanging from the sides like boat fenders off a bow.

"So you know?"

"Yes, I know."

"How did you find out?"

"Dad."

Muriel nodded. Logan picked up a mini blowtorch, the kind Muriel had seen TV chefs use to caramelize a crème brûlée. Bent over a painted blue canvas he went back to work. He ignited the torch and burned small round holes at the edges of the frame. Clumped together, they looked like black balloons.

"So," Muriel sputtered, her mind suddenly full of tumbleweeds. Logan didn't look up. As he always had, he went about his work as if Muriel wasn't there. As she always had, Muriel silently watched him. Her hanging arms soon felt like wads of chewed gum, stretched, seeming to grow longer and thinner by the minute. Her feet also felt pliant and sticky. No longer foot shaped. If she looked down, she was afraid she'd discover they'd turned webbed and orange. All she could think was, *Now that I'm here, what the hell am I doing here?* Two thousand miles and she was speechless?

Muriel let her head dangle forward. Her memory cast back to one particular Sunday morning in Queens when she sat on the top basement step watching her father and brother at the work-bench below, necks bent in quiet concentration, a caged lightbulb gently swaying from a wire in the rafters. She was hiding from her mother. It was after their matinee Saturdays had abruptly stopped, before Pia had found and read Lidia's diary.

Overhead, Muriel heard high heels scrape angrily across the linoleum kitchen floor. "Muriel? Are you *deliberately* trying to make us late?"

In a superior way, Pia said, "I'll wait in the car, Mama."

Barely daring to breathe, Muriel said nothing. The dirty base-ment step left patches of gray dust on her pink Sunday dress. A dress too young for her, too tight. In the musty darkness, she hugged the two-by-four baluster and stared at the backs of her brother and father as they stood shoulder to shoulder in front of the worktable.

"Hand me that copper tubing, will you, son?"

"Whole coil?"

"We'll cut as need be."

That Sunday, Logan was home from art school for a rare weekend. He spent most of it right where he was—in the basement beside his dad. In case she never saw him again, Muriel memorized the way his hair curlicued into the divot at the base of his neck, the easy way his shoulder bumped his father's shoulder, not unlike the way hers used to bump Lidia's when they rode the subway into the city together on matinee Saturdays. Sitting there, Muriel watched her brother and father as if they were animals in a zoo. A rare species of family in which communication was cellular. Words weren't necessary. When they were spoken, they weren't misunderstood. Their conversations weren't two semis passing on a midnight highway.

Without warning, the basement door swung open, blowing dust onto Muriel's Sunday dress. "For heaven's sake, Muriel, get off that filthy stair."

Head tilted up, young Muriel looked at her perfectly coiffed mother in her flesh-toned pumps and tasteful wool dress the color of mashed potatoes. "I'm not going to church today," she said. "Logan doesn't have to go. Dad doesn't have to go. Why do I?"

"Muriel, get up."

"Do I have to go, Dad? Do I?"

Owen said nothing. He pretended he didn't hear even as Muriel knew perfectly well he did.

"Get up off that floor this instant," Lidia said.

"No."

"Now."

"*No.*"

Lidia's nostrils flared like an angry bull's. Muriel set her jaw. In a flash of white, Lidia reached her hand back to slap Muriel's face.

"Will Father Camilo be at church?" Muriel asked, defiantly.

Lidia stopped. Her breath hitched. Quivering, her hand hovered in midair. Like a rubber band in a slingshot, her gaze bulleted down the stairs to her husband's hunched shoulders, then shot back up to her daughter. Aside from her trembling, Muriel remained still. She clung to the stair post with white knuckles. Steely eyed, she didn't back down, only fixated on the jet plume of red smeared across her mother's lips and the bloodshot bulging of her eyeballs. For the first time, she saw hatred in those eyes. Where before she'd seen indifference, impatience, even disgust, she now recognized the unmistakable blackness of a contempt so deep it had probably been there all along. Muriel wished she'd quietly stood up and gone to church. Once you see darkness like that in a mother's eyes, it's hard to ever again find light.

"Fine," Lidia spat at her. "Go to hell if that's what you want."

In another swirl of dust, Lidia slammed the basement door and stomped overhead. Muriel's heart pounded in her ears. She felt the air suck out of the house when the front door opened, then heard silence after it *whomped* shut. At that moment, the house felt so vacant it was as if no one had ever lived there at all. Soundlessly, Logan handed his father a length of copper coil. Owen snipped a section off with a bolt cutter. The excess fell to the cement floor in a tinny bounce. Thin voiced, Muriel asked, "Whatcha making down there?"

"Stuff," Logan replied, his back still to his sister, his focus on the job at hand. Exactly the way his father was and would always be.

"Like what?" Muriel asked, trying not to cry. No one answered her. Not that she expected them to.

ON THAT FRESHLY scrubbed day in New Mexico, Muriel lifted her head to watch her brother work, as she had so many years ago. Only this time she witnessed it from the front. He arranged bits of colored paper around the black holes he'd burned on the canvas. He rummaged through one of his recycling bins for God knows what. When she finally asked, "Whatcha making?" he answered, "Stuff," precisely as she knew he would.

"I drove here from New York," she said, eventually. "I don't know if you know, but I live in the city now."

"I know."

"I wanted to see you."

Without looking up he said, "Here I am."

Muriel laughed unnaturally. Her arms still felt rubbery. "Aren't you wondering why I'm here?"

"You'll tell me when you're ready."

Logan picked up the blowtorch again and lit it with a match. A blue and orange flame licked straight into the air. *Why*, Muriel wondered, *isn't he wearing protective goggles?* Couldn't that torch flare and burn his eyes? Some chemical reaction to paint, perhaps? An errant spark that ignites his hair? In the thrashing about, he'd fall into the bin of colored glass, unable to distinguish the sharp ends from the dull. Like a pincushion, he'd be stuck over and over, streams of red dribbling down his arms. She would stand there helpless, hapless, her rubbery limbs flapping.

"I don't know why I'm here," she blurted out.

Logan lifted his head and gazed at her squarely. "Yes, you do." The blowtorch flame now flickered pink. Muriel felt her body soften like a butter sculpture in the last hour of the county fair. "Yes, I do," she confessed, releasing all the air in her body.

Logan didn't nod or shrug or do anything. He stood motionless and regarded her passively. Waiting. The way her father would have.

"I need to tell," she said, at last.

Shutting off the blowtorch and setting it in its metal cradle, Logan circled around the island in his studio and said, "I'll make tea."

Chapter 34

INSIDE LOGAN'S HOME, the bare walls were eggshell, the inoffensive color every landlord paints his rental. The white couch she'd seen through the window was actually grayish and frayed along the edges where passing grubby knees had rubbed against it. Same with the two slipcovered armchairs. All desperately in need of a bleach-laden wash. Muriel was surprised; she'd expected something more . . . *artistic*. The fantastical residence of a creative being instead of the grungy digs of a frat boy. Clearly there was no wife in the picture. No one, it seemed, at all.

Into two mismatched mugs, the kind you'd buy at a garage sale for a quarter, Logan poured boiling water that sent a steamy funnel cloud up to his face. He dunked the same tea bag into both mugs. "Had I known a New Yorker was visiting I would have bought coffee."

Muriel laughed dutifully. "I should have called first." She felt awkward and embarrassed. Primly seated on Logan's couch, with both hands cupping her knees, she looked like a job applicant.

Carrying the mugs into the living room, Logan set them on the dormish coffee table. Stupidly, Muriel glanced around for a coaster. Only then did she notice the leaning pile of old newspapers in the corner, the dirty work shirt draped over the back of the dining room chair, the muddy shoes pulled off at the heel and left where he'd stepped out of them. *How ironic*, she thought, *his pristine studio is full of trash, and his home is such a mess.* It was the type of space a person used for eating and sleeping and showering and little else.

"No wife? No kids?" Muriel asked.

"No and no."

She bent forward to reach her tea. She blew air on the hot surface. Sitting next to her on the couch, Logan turned his body in her direction and leaned on his elbows, fingers entwined, as if to ask, "How may I help you today?" Taking a gulp too large, Muriel singed her tongue and throat. Wincing, she wondered yet again if she had the right to burden her brother with what she knew. Why tell after all these years of silence? Other than freeing her, what good would it do? Certainly none if word got back to Owen and hurt him. He was, after all, still married to their mother.

"You?" Logan broke the silence.

"Me?"

"Wife? Kids? Husband? Dog?"

Muriel chuckled. "No. No. No. No. And certainly not a cat. Mama would go berserk. As it is she thinks I'm destined to become the crazy old spinster on the fourth floor." Looking down, Muriel added, "As it *was*, that is. We haven't spoken in a while."

Smiling sadly, Logan brushed plaster dust off the top of his work boots. He then sipped his own tea and waited. The stillness in his home was striking. Behind the sliding glass door at the rear of the house was endless desert. Dirt the color of oxidation and patches of sun-bleached vegetation. It was so utterly quiet you could probably hear the slithering of the snake Logan relocated so very near his back door. Surely he would clamp his hands over his ears in Times Square. The sound of the express train alone would probably send him running home. Even in Muriel's sleepy uptown neighborhood, the ambient noise of rubber tires on asphalt, helicopter blades *thup, thupping* over the river, dogs yipping at one another, two children racing each other to the corner, would upset someone who lived in such peace. Only when Muriel heard the sound of absolute stillness did she understand why she loved New York City. The noisiness of its very air balanced the cacophony in her head.

"What is it you wanted to tell me, Muriel?"

She looked up. *Ah, yes.* No more stalling. Sucking in a breath, Muriel set her mug down on the table and opened her mouth. In her head, questions flattened up against one another like an interstate pileup, all twisted wreckage and bursts of gassy flames. *Why did you leave and never come back? Did you know Pia was sick? Do you know about Mama and Father Camilo? Does Dad know? What exactly happened to our family anyway? Did we ever even have one?* Tucking a strand of hair behind her ear, she managed to sputter, "You're the only sibling I have left."

"Yes," he said, softly.

"I, um, need to stop all the lying. The hiding. I don't know how much you know."

"Some."

As Muriel contemplated where to begin, Logan startled her by reaching over and taking both of her hands in his. His palms were rough, as expected. But the gentleness of his touch disarmed her. Her hands were like two baby birds in the safety of their mother's nest. He held them so gingerly her defenses melted away. Without warning, tears rose up and spilled over her eyelashes. "I *saw* them," she said in a whispery burst of breath. "Mama and Father Camilo. In a doorway. A Broadway kiss. He wasn't wearing his collar. Her hair was uncombed. I saw them trying to hide. It ended our matinee Saturdays. She was only using me. Mama made me promise not to tell. I never did. Never, *ever*. Not once. Not to anyone. Until now."

Saliva pooled behind her lips. Snot ran from her nose. Logan let go of her hands to stand up and walk into the bathroom. He returned with a roll of toilet paper and held it out to his sister. The gesture derailed her. The fact that it wasn't Kleenex made her dissolve in love for her older brother—this man who lived alone with snakes and cacti and no tissues and square houses that looked like cake. This grown man who was her big brother, a person she barely knew.

Between nose blows, Muriel released the secrets she'd been carting around like a sack of slugs. How Lidia's diary had shamed her for years. How unloved she always felt. She described the cold way their mother looked at her after she saw what she was never meant to see, as if her very existence was an accusation. As if her own mother wanted her to disappear.

"I *wanted* to disappear. I wanted so much to grow up so I could get out. Like you did."

Logan sat still, facing his sister. In a wobbly voice she recounted her lunch with Pia, the vomiting in the bathroom, her skeletal back when she zipped up Pia's gray satin dress.

"I spent a whole day with her and didn't see her at all. How could I have been so blind? So selfish? But I kept Pia's secret, too. I never told Mama. Not until Pia was already gone and Will asked me to. I kept my promise to her. At least I can say that much."

Muriel pressed the damp ball of toilet tissue to her eyes and let her sorrow flow.

"What I don't understand is how a person you love and one who maybe loved you back a little wouldn't *want* to say good-bye? Even a quick one over the phone. Nothing dramatic. One word. *Good-bye*. Flat out, so I could really hear it and understand that it's real. Not waving on her way into a cab or hugging me in a dressing room. Not telling me everything was going to be okay when it wasn't. Why, Logan, when she knew it was close to the end, why didn't she give me one last chance to tell her how sorry I was, that there was never one single day, not one moment, that I didn't wish things were different between us? How I wanted so much to be the kind of sister she could love but I kept messing things up. Honestly, I didn't know *how* to fix it."

With her head hanging, Muriel wept. "I know you don't know me very well, but I was wondering if maybe you could tell me, maybe Mama or Pia told you, or Dad did, or you overheard at some point when I wasn't there. I need to know the honest truth, so I can move on. Do you happen to know why no one loved me?"

The words broke Logan's heart. He gently cupped his sister's chin in his coarse hand and lifted her head. In her damp eyes, he saw the vulnerability of a child. A black hole of hurt. For the first time, he understood the impact of his own choices. "Ah, baby," he said, encircling her in his strong arms. "I loved you. *Love* you. Always have."

Delicately, he kissed the top of Muriel's head. A remembered scent filled her lungs—glue and mud and motor oil—the smell of her big brother. His worn flannel shirt felt like silk against her face. In Logan's embrace, Muriel felt like a girl again, standing behind the swinging dining room door in their Queens row house, staring through the crack, watching her family exist around her. Each on his or her own planet. Muriel, barely a moon.

"Put that burden down now," Logan whispered into her hair. "You've carried it long enough."

With his rough thumb Logan wiped the tears off Muriel's pulpy lips. So softly she could barely hear it, he said, "I should have told you years ago. It's my fault. I didn't consider you at all. I should have. Instead, I got out of there as soon as I could. You were right. I wanted to disappear. But it should have occurred to me that I wasn't just leaving, I was leaving *you* behind."

"Told me what?" Muriel sniffed.

"Father Camilo. Pia was his daughter."

Chapter 35

BUG SPLATS ON a windshield are an art form. Tiny fireworks displays. Reds, of course. But greens and surprising turquoise blues, too. A lavender swath here and there. Veiny flapping wings. Segmented legs. That's what Muriel was thinking as she sat behind the wheel in the Santa Fe Car Wash line.

"How did I see the road this morning through all these guts?"

Joanie shrugged. "Hershey's Kiss?"

She, too, was ready to head home.

Home. Where mosquitoes occasionally interrupted sleep with an ear flyby. Where snakes didn't sneak up on a person while she was peering through her brother's front window.

Joanie knew better than to ask Muriel what had happened at her brother's house. They had a long drive ahead. She would tell her when she was ready. Instead, Joanie had located the nearest power wash and suggested a fresh start. Though she wouldn't be awake much on the road, when she was, she'd rather see more of America, less arthropod anatomy.

The plan was a northerly route starting that very afternoon, if anything could be considered "north" so far south. Mostly, Muriel was determined to escape anything *near* the bloated belly of Texas. So, as soon as the car was cleaned of insect residue, they aimed for Kansas, clipping only the corners of both panhandles in Texas and Oklahoma. Muriel drove for hours in silence, stopping only for gas, food, snacks, restrooms, and—after dark—their hotel for the night. As expected, Joanie dozed most of the way. Which suited Muriel perfectly. She needed the monotony of asphalt to process what Logan had told her. Once again, she couldn't believe how blind she'd been.

"REMEMBER THAT MONTH in Pawtucket?" Logan had asked his sister as she sat on his grimy sofa sipping the still-steaming tea. "When Lidia decided we needed to know our roots?"

Muriel nodded. She remembered it vividly. It was the summer after her matinee Saturdays were guillotined, after Pia had read Lidia's diary and believed her to be a liar. "Do I *have* to go?" she had whined to her father. A summer in bed felt like the most she could muster. Besides, Papa Czerwinski scared her. He was mean. Even as an aging man his arms were as thick as legs. His mustache made him look like a walrus and the fine dusting of flour on his skin gave him a ghostly hue. Plus their grandmother Babcia Jula—despite her rounded edges—clearly preferred her sister. Why leave home to feel left out?

"I *wanted* to go," Logan told Muriel. "It was my first summer out of art school and I didn't want to go back to Middle Village."

"You sound like Mama."

"Couldn't you feel it? When you walked through the front door it felt like you were walking into quicksand. There was so much negative energy. The only time I ever wanted to be home was when no one else was home, or when only Dad was there. I couldn't wait to move out."

The three Sullivant siblings were put on a train to Providence, Rhode Island. Even Pia, who was in community college then, though she still lived at home. To Muriel, it seemed as though their mother wanted them out of the way. Perhaps she was planning to spend a month in the city, hiding in doorways, stealing Broadway kisses?

During the four-hour train ride, Pia flipped through magazines while Muriel read a book. Logan sketched the different hair patterns he noted on the backs of passengers' heads. Once they got under way, Muriel remembered feeling the knot in her stomach slowly unfurl. Perhaps Papa Czerwinski had mellowed in the months since she'd last seen him. She could tell him about Edna Turnblad, who was Tracy Turnblad's mother in one of the funniest shows she had ever seen on Broadway, *Hairspray*. Papa would laugh because Edna Turnblad was really a man in a dress.

Papa and Babcia Jula still lived in Lidia's childhood home, having updated little but the carpeting and the paint. The living room where Lidia first danced with Owen had the same maple end tables with the lamps sprouting out of the center. Babcia's knitting rocker was nestled in the same cluttered corner. Papa still owned the bakery next door. Its cinnamon-butter aroma seeped through the walls. The thick air felt perpetually damp. Over the years, he'd come to accept the children his only daughter bore by that Irishman. (Had Pia not turned out so lovely, he might not have. Quite honestly, the other two he could do without.)

On Sundays when God was nitpicky, Papa would have to confess that the Czerwinskis and Sullivants could not honestly call themselves a "close" family. They lived in different states, after all. But Papa had done his duty. Over the years there were Christmases and Easters and those interminable poorly rehearsed school pageants. Why was one child always facing sideways? They had made sufficient effort. Enough, at least, to stop the meddlesome neighbors from questioning their commitment.

"Grandchildren can be such a blessing. Unless, of course, one is too busy to show love."

An entire month with the grandchildren, Papa knew, would silence the yappy critics he needed to shut up and buy his babka.

"Let me look at you!"

At the Providence station, Muriel's grandparents stood on the platform like a photograph in a history book. Papa, tall and stiff, held his felt hat in his hands. Babcia Jula wore a flowered short-sleeved dress and manly black shoes. She hugged Pia warmly as Papa shook Logan's hand. To Muriel he said, "I knew you'd roll off the train."

Instantly, she wanted to go home. Papa hadn't changed one bit. Other kids went to camp. Why couldn't she?

"Come, come," said Babcia, always flitting around her husband trying to soften the shards of his personality. "We have *pączki* waiting at home."

"This one needs more doughnuts?" Papa flicked his thumb at his youngest grandchild. Muriel crossed her arms over her blossoming chest and stared down at her shoes. Ever confident, Pia scooped up her suitcase and announced, "I, for one, am starving." Then she linked arms with her grandmother and whispered, "How soon can we come back to Providence to go shopping?"

"Is tomorrow too soon?"

With their foreheads pressed together, giggling, Papa's proud bald head erect and front facing, and Muriel's chubby chin on her chest, no one noticed as Logan slipped a train schedule into the back pocket of his sagging blue jeans.

Three people lived in the Czerwinski's Pawtucket, Rhode Island, home: Papa, Babcia Jula, and *God*. A wooden crucifix hung over every door and bed. Pious paintings of Jesus with his bloody palms facing outward adorned the walls. His eyes seemed to follow you wherever you went.

"Ach," Babcia Jula scolded Muriel that first afternoon when she caught her reaching under a cake lid in the kitchen to swipe a fingerful of icing. "Thou shalt not steal." Making the sign of the cross over her chest, she glanced up at the crucifix above the door frame and made an apologetic face for her granddaughter. Then, with her hand firmly on Muriel's shoulder, she steered her to a three-legged wooden stool in the corner of the kitchen and said, "Kneel."

Muriel looked up at her, confused.

"*Kneel.*"

She knelt on the hard stool.

"Pray."

Pressing her palms together, her cheeks on fire, she prayed.

"I can't hear you," Babcia said.

"Dear God, please forgive me for taking a little bit of Babcia's icin—"

"For *stealing* the icing."

"For stealing Babcia's icing. It looked so delicious I couldn't resist."

"Good. I'll be back in a few minutes. God wants you to kneel here and think about what you've done. Don't move until I get back. God is watching."

Muriel didn't move. She faced the wall and bit the flesh on the inside of her lip. Her knees ached. The bare wood pressed a grain pattern into her kneecaps. She felt God's angry eyes burn two holes into the back of her head. Later, after dinner, when the cake was sliced and served to her on a plate, she felt so ashamed she could barely choke it down.

"We are witnessing a miracle, Lord!" Papa boomed at the table. "This one doesn't like cake." When Jula scolded him for his insensitivity, he lifted his keg of a chest and bellowed, "She'd better learn now how to take a joke."

From the first moment of her arrival—to the last—Muriel's time in Pawtucket was torture. God, she learned there, was a spiteful voyeur. He crouched behind sofa backs and hid in drapery folds waiting to catch you in a sin. "Aha! I knew your evil would show itself sooner or later." The Lord clapped with enormous thundering hands. She was certain God kept His teeth in a glass of cloudy water at night the way Papa Czerwinski did.

Each morning in the shower Muriel hid her body in the steam so God couldn't see her nakedness. After Pia called her "bovine" in her superior way, Muriel prayed that her sister would eat something poisonous at the bakery and die. Instantly she regretted it, certain that God was *tut-tutting* above her, His gnarled finger pointed accusingly. At night, she begged God for forgiveness. She pulled a hard chair into the corner of her dark bedroom and knelt on it until her knees hurt so badly she could barely hobble down. In bed she prayed that the month would end quickly so she could return to her own room in Queens with her *Playbill* collection. There, God wasn't judging meanly when she pretended to be Jane Eyre singing, "If I leave this unhappy bliss where will my Eden be?"

God saw it all. He knew she wasn't a liar. Still, He had also seen her mother and Father Camilo. *If one parent goes to hell*, Muriel worried, *do you automatically have to go, too?*

Surely the Lord noticed that Logan disappeared at some point in the middle of the second week. Though no one else did. He stuffed his clothes in his backpack and hitchhiked to the train station in Providence while Muriel and Pia worked in the bakery with their grandparents.

"Why did you leave?" Muriel asked Logan from her perch on his couch in Galisteo.

"Have you ever *thought* something was going to be much better than it actually turned out to be?"

She nearly did a spit take with her tea. Remembering her fantasized mother/daughter Broadway relationship with Lidia, she said, "Why, yes. I believe I have some familiarity with the concept."

"That house in Pawtucket was as oppressive—if not more so—than our parents' house in Queens. All I wanted to do was get back to New York, pack the rest of my things, then quietly go back to school. Of course, that's not quite what happened."

As if reliving that day so many years ago, Logan leaned back on his sofa and stared into nothingness.

"I was so sure Papa was going to come booming up those stairs at the train station and drag me back."

"He thought you were working on an art project in his wood-shed!"

"Yeah. That's what I told him. Still, I don't think I took a full breath until I reached Penn Station."

Once he was back in New York City, Logan took the A train to Fourteenth Street, then the L subway all the way to Wyckoff Avenue before transferring to the M line and riding it to the end. Metropolitan Avenue. A few short blocks from home.

"Owen and Lidia were yelling at each other when I came in. They didn't hear me."

It didn't escape Muriel's notice that her brother called their parents by their first names. Had he always? Had they let him?

"Honestly," Logan said, "I didn't *sneak* in. But I didn't say anything, either. I walked upstairs and tried not to listen to their fight."

But how could he not stop on the top step and turn his head and cock his ear when he heard his mother shout, "What the hell do you care? You have your son."

Owen had curtly replied, "We're a family, Lidia."

"Don't be ridiculous. You're no more interested in me than I am in you. What we have is an arrangement."

"It's a *sin*. The worst kind of sin."

When Logan heard that, how could he *not* freeze in place and listen?

Downstairs, Lidia had marched into the kitchen. Logan heard the familiar suction sound of the refrigerator door opening. He could picture the moist rubber strip, the differential pressure created against the stainless steel. A green Perrier bottle clinked against the row of green bottles and carbonation was released into the air with a distinct *fzzt*. The sparkling water glugged into a glass already on the table. In a controlled voice, Lidia said, "Don't you think we've questioned God's role in all this? Why us? Is He testing us, *chosen* us? I've prayed about it endlessly. We both have. But only one answer keeps coming back to me: in the eyes of God, *love* is transcendent."

"Jesus Christ, Lidia. He's a *priest*."

Logan heard his mother take a gulp of water then set the glass back on the table. "God has forgiven my sin," she said. "He's forgiven both of us. We're consenting adults."

"If the church finds out—"

"You think this has never happened before? Don't be naive. The church has had enough other scandals not to care. Besides, I've made sure no one will tell. Who would? You? Are you prepared to drag your family through the mud?"

The refrigerator door slammed shut with the same tight sound. "Let's be adults, shall we, Owen? For a change." With her efficient gait, Lidia exited the kitchen and marched down the hall toward the entryway. Soundless in his sneakers, Logan tiptoed into his bedroom and slipped behind his open bedroom door. Owen said, "I don't appreciate your condescending tone."

"All right, then. As equals. The pretense stops here. Let's finally face what we've been avoiding for twenty years. Never in a million years would you have married me if I wasn't pregnant with Pia."

"But you were. And I did."

"For that I gave you a son. We both had what we wanted."

Logan's heart pounded. He imagined his father's hurt face. Never had Owen been able to detour Lidia when she was steamrolling his way. "All I'm asking," she said, "is for you to look the other way. As I have. Let's stop pretending, Owen. At long last. We both know a divorce is out of the question. I also know you stopped loving me the moment you found out that Pia wasn't yours. Not that I blame you. But we made a decision—as *parents*—not to tell the children. It was the right decision. Now, between us, can't we quietly live our *own* lives?"

With the stealth of a cat burglar, Logan slid open his closet door. The musty smell of airlessness comforted him. It was the aroma of his childhood. A few old flannel shirts still hung on the rod, his dress shoes lay in a corner, barely worn. Gingerly setting his backpack on the floor, Logan noiselessly folded his lean body into a corner of the closet as he heard both of his parents climb the stairs. Lidia's crisp footfalls were followed by Owen's leaden ascent. They passed Logan's open door on the way to their own room. In his mind Logan imagined his father standing passively in a bedroom with a girly satin bedspread and gilded edgings—a space that had always been Lidia's domain.

"I won't be a divorced man," Logan heard him say. "I told you that from the start."

"Don't you think I know that? Neither one of us can get divorced. That's why I chose you. I don't want a divorce. All I want is for you to *accept* it, Owen. Cam is the man I love. The father of my first child. I won't stop seeing him. I can't. Do you understand that? He's part of me."

Through the strumming of his heartbeats, Logan heard his mother step closer to his father and say, seductively, "In exchange, I'll give you your freedom. Think about it. What's more alluring than a married man?"

At that moment, the phone rang, startling everyone. Owen picked it up and said, "Yes?" uncharacteristically harsh. "Oh, hello, Jula. Forgive me." He cleared his throat. "How are you? The kids okay?"

Logan's eyes shot open. He shrank deeper into the closet and gathered the few hanging shirts about him. For the next few moments, the Queens house was as silent as death itself. He could picture the blood draining from his father's face. After a long, dreadful minute, Owen simply said, "I see."

"What is it?" Lidia demanded to know.

Owen didn't answer her. Instead, he said, "Thank you for alerting us," and hung up the phone. With a panic Logan had never before heard in his father's voice, Owen Sullivant said to his wife, "Check your son's room. I'll check the basement."

Forever, Logan told his sister in Galisteo, he would remember the sound of Lidia's high heels on the hardwood floor. "To this day," he said, "I can close my eyes and hear that awful scraping."

Crouched as low as he could in the back corner of the closet, Logan prayed to disappear. He begged God to help him disintegrate into a pile of dust so he could flatten to the floor and blow away. Feeling like a child, he pressed his eyelids together and willed himself small.

"There was a rush of air as Lidia swept the clothes to one side. I was hunched in a corner, my eyes glued shut. I didn't want to see her face."

Yet, he *heard* her. First, a sharp intake of air. Something between a gasp and the gulp of oxygen a person attempts after a punch in the gut.

"What are you doing here?" she asked accusingly. Logan didn't answer. His knees were pressed up to his forehead, as if his mother might disappear if he refused to look up. Perhaps he could *will* himself back to Pawtucket? Silently, he breathed in the buttery smell of the bakery that still clung to his jeans.

"Get up, Logan."

When he didn't move, Lidia poked her son's knee with the tip of her pointed shoe. "I said, get *up*."

Slowly, Logan lifted his head. He brushed the hair from his eyes and looked full into his mother's face, bracing himself for the furnace blast of her rage. Instead he saw something worse. For the first time, Lidia's face was stripped of all pretense. Her son saw the woman she really was: frightened, weak, *caught*. She had the panicked white-eyed look of an animal with one foot in a snap trap. Logan burrowed his head back into his knees. No longer could he bear to look.

"What did you hear?" Lidia whispered, dry lipped.

Unable to look up, Logan muttered into the denim, "I won't tell anyone, Mama. I swear. No one. Not ever."

Until that day with Muriel, he never ever did.

FORT LEE, NEW JERSEY, was the same tangle of lanes and semi-trucks as it had been when they'd rented the car there a week earlier. The George Washington Bridge had the same gray Erector Set style. Manhattan was a brown skyline in the blue distance. Seated in the cab home, Muriel smelled a familiar scent: cologne-covered body odor. The sweet staleness of eight hours on vinyl. The aroma of *home*.

Reaching across the backseat, Joanie took Muriel's hand in hers and held it silently for a few moments. Then she squeezed. "We rarely get the families we deserve, baby girl. That's what chocolate is for."

It made Muriel laugh. As Joanie always did.

"I guess you're my family now," Muriel said quietly. On the long drive across the country she'd had ample time to ponder the fact that Logan had overheard Lidia say, "I gave you a son. We both had what we wanted."

What we wanted. Muriel was never mentioned once.

"In that case," Joanie said, "I hit the jackpot."

Chapter 36

IT WAS SUNDAY. Muriel's favorite day. The night before, she'd gone with Joanie to see the first preview of an off-Broadway play that was so inventive it restored her faith in the future of theater. Joanie's, too. Perhaps the Disney invasion might be waning after all.

That morning, Muriel nestled into the warmth of her comforter, luxuriating in the perfection of the moment. No one needed her to be anything that day. If she didn't want to, she didn't even have to get up. She could order in, lie around, live in her pajamas. At the other end of the room, the radiator hissed. It was probably chilly out. Maybe she *should* stay in bed after all.

But first, a coffee would be nice. Swinging her bare feet onto the floor, Muriel slid them into her waiting fuzzy slippers and stretched. She rolled her neck in a slow, lazy circle. A cinnamon bagel was cut and waiting in the freezer. She could nearly smell the warmth that would fill her apartment when she toasted it, taste the saltiness of the butter that would melt into the bagel hole, pooling onto her plate. On her way to the bathroom, she stopped by the window and pulled back the sheer curtain.

"Oh!" Muriel drew in a sharp breath. It was snowing. Soft, huge snowflakes lazily zigzagged down from the gray sky. They were as fluffy as cotton balls. *First* snow. The best snow. Obviously, it had stuck during the night. The city was covered in pristine frosting. No way was she going to stay in bed that day. Not when New York City was at its most magical.

Quickly, Muriel peed, splashed water on her face, and donned her long underwear. Breakfast could wait.

IN THE SAME way Maine's fall foliage makes anyone who sees it hunger for a Norman Rockwellian style of life, first snow in New York is so heartbreakingly beautiful it explains why residents pay ridiculous rents for rabbit-hole spaces. First snow alters the city vibe itself. It's so quiet you can *hear* silence. Even the crunching of snow beneath rubber boots and the occasional cab tires is muted. First snow in the city is a communal dose of Ecstasy—everyone is happy, everyone is a neighbor, everyone is a friend. The whole city reflects its light.

With her Sherpa-style hat on, ski pants, lined jacket, and new red mittens from T.J.Maxx, Muriel clomped down the stairs of her building in her snow boots. A shoreline of white had blown through the bottom crack in the exterior door. Obviously, it had been a windy night. But now, the outside air was a blanket of polka dots.

"Hurry up! C'mon!"

Like bits of graphite being sucked onto a magnet, New Yorkers took to the snowy streets on their way into Riverside Park. Kids, puffed up in down, waddled to the sledding hill. Their parents carried cross-country skis on the shoulders of their North Face parkas and dressed their dogs in fido fleece. Others carted garbage can lids to be used as sleds and wore layers of huge hooded sweatshirts. First snow in the city was an equal-opportunity joy. No one was unwelcome.

"Duck, *sucka*!" A snowball fight had erupted across the street.

In front of her building, Muriel tipped her head back and opened her mouth to catch the snowflakes on her tongue. They fell softly onto her face and eyelashes, turning into water the moment they touched the warmth of her skin. The sun was a fuzzy tennis ball; soon it would burn through the clouds, turn the sky a vibrant blue, and melt the top layer of snow into a shiny fondantlike crust. Until then, Muriel wanted to enjoy every moment of the morning. First snow was why she couldn't imagine leaving New York. Without the airless humidity of August, the abrasive sounds of sirens and honking and swearing at slow pedestrians year-round, the stale human smells inside a cab, the rats skittering across the park's promenade at dusk, the gray scummy water in a summer gutter, how could anyone properly appreciate the inclusive silence of a city's first snow?

Muriel wandered into the street.

"Incoming!"

Deftly sidestepping a snowball, she bent down and fashioned a return throw from the perfect packing snow at her feet. In her best imitation of a relief pitcher she reached her arm back and hurled the snowball at the gaggle of shouting boys, hitting one squarely on the chest.

"Uh-oh." Before he could retaliate, Muriel blended into the stream of neighbors on their way into the park, crunching her knee-high rubber boots across Riverside Drive and climbing the snow-carpeted stairs to the open square promontory in front of the Soldiers' and Sailors' Monument.

"Garrett, *come!*"

Ignoring his owner, a puppy, off leash, bounded over to Muriel. A blob of white snow teetered atop his wet black nose. Wriggling with puppy ebullience, he leaped up and planted two snowy paws on her torso, the chestnut hair on top of his head spiked with melted snow. Instantly besotted, Muriel bent down to rub her mittened hands behind his ears.

"Garrett, *down!*" With both arms flailing like a windmill, the owner yelled from across the square, clomping through the crowd in ankle-deep powder with white steam puffing from his mouth. Garrett took one look at his master before taking off, bobbing and weaving like a running back.

"Garrett, *heel!*"

Clearly beyond control, the puppy circled around the square, chasing snowflakes, careening into snowmen, scooping snow clumps into his mouth, burrowing into a snowdrift only to leap back up the moment another dog passed by. He romped with canines, bit their ears, jumped up on children, behaved badly. Nobody cared. They tussled playfully with him, threw snowballs for him to catch and eat. His owner stood by helplessly as Garrett waggled his way back to Muriel, his pink tongue hanging sideways out of his mouth. Hiding behind her, she felt his long skinny tail softly whip the back of her legs.

"Garrett, *sit.*"

As soon as Garrett's owner drew near, his puppy was off and running.

"A highly trained animal," he said, steam shooting out from his mouth. "I'm thinking of showing her at Westminster."

Muriel said, "Garrett is a *girl?*"

"I know. Crazy, right? I named her after my favorite popcorn."

Her jaw dropped. "CaramelCrisp?"

The dog owner looked offended. "Not for the main course. Good heavens, I'm not *that* crazy. Usually I start with a Cheese-Corn appetizer, then enjoy the basic pop with butter and salt. CaramelCrisp—with pecans—is dessert."

Slapping her hand to her chest Muriel said, "Pecans? I didn't dare dream."

Garrett galumphed back, resting the full weight of her panting body against Muriel. "She's grown accustomed to my leg," Muriel sang to the tune of the *My Fair Lady* song. "Like breathing out and breathing in." As she reached down to pet the dog's wet head, Garrett snatched her mitten off her hand and bounded away.

"Oh no! Garrett. Come. *Now!*"

Muriel just laughed. "Let her go. She's having such fun I don't have the heart to stop her."

"If your mitten is ruined in any way, I will buy you a new

one." Then he stopped and added, "What am I saying? Your mitten will be ruined in every way. It'll look like Einstein's hair. You should see my shoes."

When Garrett's owner smiled, his entire face changed. Like Ewan McGregor's. It was impossible not to smile back.

"I'm Muriel," Muriel said, holding out her bare hand.

"I'm mortified." He took off his glove and shook her hand. His bare palm felt warm and soft. Then he slid his steamy glove onto Muriel's cold hand. Like Cinderella inserting her foot into the glass slipper, it felt thrillingly right. The intimacy of the body warmth inside that glove made Muriel blush. She looked down, wondered if she'd remembered to brush her teeth.

"When I'm not mortified, my name is John. And you don't have to rub it in, Muriel, I know my parents had no imagination."

Again Muriel laughed, though she covered her mouth with her hand. John scanned the crowd for his dog. Muriel, trained well by her mother, glanced down to see if his ring finger was bare. It was.

"What kind of dog is Garrett?"

"A mix of Portuguese water dog and Belgian sheepdog."

"Well, there you go. She doesn't speak English."

Now John laughed. "Her English does seem to be limited to 'goodie,' 'park,' and 'din-din.'"

As if on cue, Garrett bounded back. "See?" John bent down and grabbed her, attaching the leash to her collar. Muriel felt a twinge of sadness that they were about to walk away. But they didn't. Instead, the three of them stood in the middle of the square taking in the joyful romping all around them. The snow had stopped its steady fall; flakes were drifting down here and there, blown to the ground by a mild breeze. Rays of sunlight broke through the blanket of clouds. The Hudson River beyond was filled with floating ice. It was gorgeous. The most beautiful day of the year. Muriel was so glad she hadn't stayed in bed.

John's cheeks were as red and round as pomegranates. He wore a navy blue knit Yankees cap. In his puffy jacket, he looked like a gingerbread man. Undefined limbs and a slightly startled expression. Thirtyish, he struck Muriel as more winded than he ought to be chasing a puppy, but running through thick snow could be exhausting. Normally she'd never insert her hand into a stranger's used glove, but it was first snow. The rules were suspended. Feeling the warmth of John's glove radiate through her body, she wondered what he looked like beneath his jacket and hat. Did he have hair? A potbelly? Was he the flannel-shirt type?

Surprising herself, Muriel really wanted to find out.

John asked, "Could you please hold Garrett's leash for a moment?"

"Sure."

Bending over, John scooped up a handful of soft snow and molded it into a ball. "You're about to see why I went to college on a baseball scholarship." Aiming for a crumbling snowman on top of a marble balustrade, he reached both arms overhead, lifted one leg, wound up, pitched, and missed the snowman entirely, only to hit the shoulder of a mother leaning down to button up her child.

"Oh my God," John called out, rushing forward. "I'm *so* sorry. Are you okay? I was a poly sci major. My sport was chess."

The mother was fine, if a bit confused, and Muriel was enchanted. When John returned for his dog, he said, "Using an innocent puppy and an athletic lie to flirt with you? What a cad!"

She couldn't stop grinning, even as her nose ran. Attempting a seductive tone that was made more challenging with her frozen lips, Muriel looked John directly in the eyes and said, "I've always had a thing for cads who play chess." The word "play" came out as "pway" but she didn't relinquish John's gaze. Not even when she reached into the pocket of her jacket to retrieve a wad of tissue and dab at her runny nose.

In an inspired moment, Muriel remembered a scene from the play *Contact*. In it, a mysterious woman in a yellow dress enters and exits the stage and drives the main character mad. Since Muriel seriously needed to blow her nose, she decided to channel the woman in the yellow dress and turn around to sexily walk home across the street, waving over her shoulder. Once in her apartment, she'd quickly blow her nose, brush her teeth, comb her hair, swipe a bit of mascara on her lashes, gloss her lips, then dash back to the park. Hopefully, John and Garrett would still be there.

Handing John his dog's leash, she smiled alluringly before swiveling sexily in her firefighter-size rubber boots. Over her shoulder she waggled her fingers good-bye.

"Muriel!"

Her heart fluttered.

"Yes?" Muriel swung around like a model at the end of a runway, complete with hand seductively on hip.

"My glove."

"Oh."

Of course the hand on her hip was covered in John's warm, huge glove! What an oaf. As she reached across her body to pull John's glove off and return it to him, he said, "No, no, no. Wear it home. I just need to know where I can pick it up later."

"Later?"

"I owe you mittens, too. So, um, after I shop at Mittens R Us."

Muriel laughed. Then sniffed. "I'll give you a pass on the mittens if you happen to have a Kleenex. Unused, preferably."

John reached into the pocket of his puffy coat and retrieved a mini pack. "I was a Boy Scout," he said, sheepishly. "Let me know if you need dry matches or a Swiss Army knife, too."

While Muriel pulled her hands out of his glove and her mitten to blow her nose, John said, "Garrett and I are in the Eighty-seventh Street dog run every morning and night. I know she would love to see you again. I mean, if you bring that mitten with you. And bacon."

For the hundredth time that morning Muriel erupted in laughter. *Why*, she wondered, *had she ever considered spending Sundays indoors?* Fresh air was fabulous. It felt delicious. It made you use words like "fabulous" and "delicious." Somehow, with Pia's passing and Logan's reentry into her atmosphere and the exposure of Lidia's lies and the sense that her life was finally jolted out of its rut, she felt an abundance of freedom. Perhaps she no longer had to plod through life's rainy days with dripping hair. Maybe Muriel could finally successfully wear white and fill her life with sunshine.

As if Pia herself sent it from heaven, two clouds passed each other in the celestial blue sky and a sharp ray of sunlight darted down from between them. It hit the center of the snowy square in front of the monument near the spot where the two sisters had waited for the M5 bus. A lifetime ago.

"Which dog run?" Muriel asked John.

"Down those steps." He pointed. "Follow the barking."

She smiled and nodded and pivoted seductively in her rubber boots. Attempting a sashay, Muriel waved her frozen red fingers over her shoulders as she made her way across Riverside Drive toward home.

Chapter 37

THE WEEKEND *TIMES* was heavy, but Muriel felt lighter than the snowflakes that had melted on her cheeks. Her bare hand was warmed by the venti cappuccino she'd bought at Starbucks on Broadway. The detour made her chilly, but as she made her way home, she envisioned the perfection of the rest of her day: exercising up four flights of stairs, kicking off her damp boots, removing her thick socks, and sliding her bare feet into the slippers that waited beside her bed. Perhaps she would preheat them on top of the radiator? In her sweats and T-shirt, as she read every word of the paper, she would sip her coffee and delight in its robust taste. As it got low, maybe she'd augment it with hot chocolate and tiny floating marshmallows that resembled snowballs. Pausing to turn the page she would think about John's rosy cheeks and Portuguese/Belgian puppies romping in the dog run and popcorn with caramel and pecans.

"Muriel?"

A familiar voice jolted her out of her fantasy. She blinked, unsure if she was really seeing what she thought she saw. Standing in the snowy footprints in front of her building, was Lidia. Her shoulders were pressed together in the cold. She wore army green anklet galoshes over pumps. Her off-white coat was tapered at the waist and she held a leather handbag primly between two hands that were covered in wrist-length sheepskin gloves. Muriel was speechless. Her mother seemed so out of place.

"Is Dad okay?" she stammered.

"He's fine." Lidia looked down, as if she knew she deserved that as a first question.

"What are you doing here?"

Head still bowed, Lidia inhaled the reality that question number two was also warranted. "At the moment, I'm shivering," she said, attempting to sound lighthearted.

Muriel looked at her mother. Of course she had to let her in. Even as she hungered to relive the past ten minutes where she would skip Starbucks altogether and have breakfast at City Diner farther uptown, in the back of the restaurant, away from the front window so no one could see her if they should happen by. Surely her mother would give up waiting after an hour or so of standing in the snow.

"I've come to see you," Lidia said, sounding so vulnerable Muriel's heart softened. "I knew you wouldn't receive me if I called first."

Receive? Muriel half-expected her to produce a calling card. Resigned, she reached into her jacket pocket for her keys. "Come on up," she said, unlocking the vestibule door. Lidia followed her daughter inside the building. In silence they marched up the stairs. Four flights, Muriel discovered, was more than enough time to mentally list every way in which her studio apartment wasn't prepared for a visit from her mother. Her bed was unmade, last night's black tights were inside out where she'd left them, balled up, in front of the open closet door. Dishes were in the sink, a ring was most certainly around the inside of the tub. That damn oily body wash made a ring each time she used it! The toilet seat top was probably up and her winter clothes were down, having not quite completed the seasonal closet transformation. A Costco-size bag of Chex Mix was pinched shut with a paper clip on the dusty table next to the bed.

Muriel felt the leaden knot of dread forming in her gut until—in a rush of clarity—she realized it was beyond time for her mother to see her in her natural habitat. Messy, fleshy, unfashionable, at times unkempt, and altogether nothing like her. Nothing like Pia, either. No more hiding. No more lies. It was time to come out of her disheveled closet.

"You'll be warm inside," she said, unlocking her front door.

"Shall I leave my wet overshoes in the hall?" Lidia asked, breathless from the climb.

"No need." Muriel turned the knob.

They hadn't spoken in months. Not since that horrible day in Queens. Even at Pia's funeral, they barely glanced in each other's direction. Owen had been as silent as ever. Her father's nonpresence in her life—perhaps even in his own life—was a fact Muriel had come to accept. She finally understood that Owen knew how to father a *son*. A mirror image. And by the time Muriel came along, the distance between her parents was too vast for any baby to bridge.

"You raised yourself," Logan had said in Galisteo.

Muriel had agreed. It made her feel awful at first. As lonely as she'd felt growing up. Then a blessed sense of *release* overtook her. If she raised herself, she could continue to do so. No longer was she fated to be her family's disappointment. Or the Secret Keeper. She could raise herself right out of those roles. She could become anybody she wanted to be.

Lidia pulled her wet gloves off finger by finger. She unstrapped her galoshes and lifted her feet out of them, resting the rubber shoes primly against the back of her daughter's front door. In Muriel's tiny kitchen, Lidia set her handbag down on the café chair and unbuttoned her overcoat. "Shall I hang this up in your closet?"

Muriel said, "That depends."

"On what?"

"How long do you plan to stay?"

Standing erect and facing her mother head-on, Muriel willed her eyes not to blink. Lidia looked startled, then crushed. As Muriel watched, astonished, her mother fumbled around in her purse and pulled out a tissue, pressing it to the corner of each eye. "Of course you hate me," she said, softly. "Why wouldn't you?"

"I don't hate you, Mama. Hate gives you too much power."

Again, Lidia looked slapped. "How *do* you feel then?"

Tilting her head slightly, Muriel rifled through her emotions for an honest answer. After a lifetime of hiding and lying for others, the truth took a moment to locate. Once she found it, it almost always surprised her. Without the slightest trace of anger she said, "Absolutely *free*."

With that, Muriel marched over to the window, flung open her curtains, and let the sunlight illuminate every bouncing particle of dust. As she knew it would, the sun had burned away the overcast sky and bore down on the snowy earth, reflecting its bright whiteness. It truly was the most stunning day. Lidia made a space for herself on the love seat at the foot of Muriel's bed.

Muriel asked, "Tea? Coffee? Hot chocolate?"

"I'm fine. Thank you."

Sitting cross-legged on her unmade bed, Muriel stilled herself. She quieted the impulse to rush about her apartment apologizing and tidying up. Instead she faced her mother and breathed, startled to notice how much Lidia resembled Pia. Already she had forgotten the intricacies of their faces, the way both women had cheekbones that rose like boulders beneath their eye sockets. Their slender fingers had the same spidery taper and their lips curled up at the edges. Both blond pageboy hairstyles curled under just so. They were pretty. No doubt. Pia would have been an elegant grandmother, just as Lidia was. Looking at her mother made Muriel miss her sister. More accurately, she missed the relationship she would no longer be able to craft. How she wished Pia had lived long enough to see her become herself! They'd had such a great beginning that day on the sunporch. Perhaps they could have continued on that path? Maybe met halfway?

"I've been wanting to see you for months."

Lidia ventured into conversation the way a skinny-dipper approached a misty morning lake. "Gathering my courage, I guess."

Her right hand gripped her left fist. The tissue from her purse looked like a wad of old gum. Muriel stared at her mother, silent.

"I've made such a mess of things," Lidia said. "I don't deserve it, but I'm here to ask for your forgiveness."

"Ah."

Muriel glanced across the room at an old oak rocker she'd recently found on the Riverside Drive access road the night before garbage day. She'd carted it home from the trash pile and given it a sanitizing alcohol bath. She had yet to restore the wood shine with varnish or Pledge, and several loose spindles needed glue. She was hoping to find the perfect seat cushion, too, at the new Home Goods across from the new Whole Foods.

"An apology," Lidia said softly, "feels woefully inadequate."

Ungenerously, Muriel noted that Lidia wasn't teary anymore. She asked, "I'm curious. What, exactly, would you apologize for?"

"Right. Right." Lidia tucked the used tissue in the pocket of her wool slacks and unfurled her still-beautiful hands, rubbing them together as if it was cold in the warm apartment. "I've made so many poor choices. Where to begin?"

Suspecting that Lidia's worst choice was having her, Muriel braced herself to hear whatever her mother was prepared to reveal. "I was hoping," Lidia sputtered, "you would allow me to explain."

"Explain?"

"Not an excuse. An explanation." When Muriel said nothing, Lidia added curtly, "I am still your mother, whether you like it or not. My history will always be your history. When you have children, they will inherit my past as well as yours."

It was Sunday. Muriel's favorite day. She exhaled and thought about the fat *New York Times* sitting on her kitchen counter. All of her favorite sections were there, waiting: real estate, Sunday styles, book review, the magazine with its pristine crossword puzzle. The thought trotted through Muriel's mind that it was so much harder putting your family behind you when they were right there in front of your face.

"You know I saw Logan and he told me everything, right?" she said.

"Yes, I've been made aware."

"I do have one question, though. Something I didn't ask him. Well, two questions, actually."

Lidia placed both hands flat on her lap. "Yes?"

"Did Pia know? About Father Camilo being her dad, I mean."

Tears sprang to Lidia's eyes with a suddenness that took Muriel aback. "God, no," she said. "Never. It wouldn't have been fair to her. Or your father."

"Fair? To Dad?"

Quietly, Muriel stood and walked into the bathroom. As Logan had, she returned with a roll of toilet paper and handed it to her mother. Lidia stared at it for a moment, then wrapped a section around her index finger and pressed it under both bottom lids. She used a doubled length to daintily blow her nose.

"I deserved that. I've been awful to your father and you. So selfish. I don't expect you to forgive me right away—maybe never—but I want you to know that I never intentionally meant to hurt anyone. One lie got caught in another, then another. Before I knew it, that's all I had. Lies. We were all entangled in them. *I* entangled us. I put you in the middle of it. My own daughter. How could I? I'm so sorry, Muriel. I can never forgive myself for my sins. But God has forgiven me. I'm here to ask the same of you."

For the first time since Lidia arrived, Muriel felt a surge of anger rise in her cheeks. "*God* has forgiven you? How do you know that? Did he send a sign of some sort? A discounted hotel room, perhaps?"

Lidia's face went cold. "I didn't raise a cruel girl."

"No, you didn't, Mama. You raised a liar, remember?"

The pupils in Lidia's eyes seemed to engulf the brown of her irises. Muriel felt her heart pound. She wanted no part of her mother's bullshit God. Her God of convenience. Either the spying "gotcha" God or the kindly old man who would forgive all manner of sin in exchange for an hour on Sunday and a generous donation in the usher's basket. A God who allowed his children to cherry-pick Bible Scripture to suit their narrow-mindedness. One who would allow His followers to love thy neighbor only if thy neighbor was exactly like them. Who accepted *prayer* instead of kindness. A God who would forgive merely for the asking. Pia's God who rewarded her allegiance by plucking her off the earth, leaving only sorrow in her wake. One who praised faith over rational thought, who didn't care if His followers ignored the truth as long as they *believed*. A divine leader who valued dogma over intelligence. A God who let His people be hypocrites. They could kill each other in His name. Over and over and over. Muriel wanted no part of a God who existed purely to forgive humanity's hatred. A shield for sinners to hide behind.

"Did your God happen to ask how you could let Father Camilo say Pia's funeral mass?" Muriel asked through clenched teeth. "Was that a holy kindness to Dad? To me?"

Lidia stared at her lap, the toilet tissue a pulpy mass in her hands. "He couldn't bear to let anyone else do it. He was so devastated when Pia died."

"So he knew she was his?"

"Of course he knew." Lidia forced herself to raise her head and look directly into Muriel's eyes. Taking a deep breath, she composed herself. "Cam and I were together before I met your father."

Cam? Is that what she called Father Camilo? Was that his real name? Struggling to remember her Sunday school classes, Muriel tried to recall if priests changed their name when they married God. Or was it only nuns who married God?

"We met after I graduated from college," Lidia said, her face suddenly weary. "I was living at home in Pawtucket. I'd begun to believe I'd never fall in love. There was no one. And then, there he was."

Muriel imagined her mother at her age. She'd seen photos of how beautiful she was. How tiny. Had Babcia Jula pressured Lidia to marry the same way Lidia pressured her? Had her mother felt stale at twenty-four?

"Cam was fresh out of seminary in Providence and had been questioning his faith. The church sent him to our parish as a retreat. A quiet place to reflect. I saw him one Sunday morning coming out of the sacristy. He saw me, too. We were both . . . struck. That's the only way I can describe it. Before that day, I would have told you there was no such thing as love at first sight. At least not lasting love. But I would have been wrong. Love hit us both like a hurricane. There was no controlling it. We tried. We *prayed*. But there was no stopping it. I've never been more terrified in my life. So completely out of control."

Muriel's buttoned-up mother out of control? She wanted to laugh. Then it abruptly occurred to her that Father Camilo might be the reason Lidia held on so tightly. The one time she let go, all hell did break loose.

"We kept thinking it would blow over. That it was just an affair and Cam would be ordained as planned. But our love only deepened. Then Pia—" Tears dribbled black mascara down her cheeks. She pressed the ball of toilet tissue against her face. Muriel handed her the roll as Lidia said, "This is nothing a daughter should ever have to hear."

"Or see."

With closed eyes, Lidia inhaled to fortify herself. "I'll never forgive myself for that."

The room seemed to shrink as Muriel said nothing. Lidia forced herself to confess. "A hundred times I've asked myself if it was truly love, or some twisted rebellion. The lure of the forbidden. But once I was pregnant with Pia, I knew it was real. We were both *happy*. Even though it was impossible, it's what we wanted."

"So why didn't he skip the priesthood and marry you?"

With fresh layers of tissue pressed up to her perfect nose, Lidia shook her head. "It seems so crazy now, but we were worried about our reputations, our parents. They had strict"—she struggled for the word—"*expectations*. You know Papa. I couldn't bear to destroy him. It would have ruined his life. His business. Cam's parents were old school, too. They would have had to leave their small town. It seems so ridiculous now, but we never once thought we could defy them. It simply wasn't done then. And we were weak, so we tried to figure out another way to have a family."

"By tricking Dad."

Hanging her head, Lidia whispered, "Yes."

"How did he find out? I never told him about you and Father Camilo. I swear. I never told anyone."

For the first time in forever, Muriel saw the softness of love in her mother's eyes. "I know, *rybka*," she said. "I could always trust you. As cruel as it was to make you keep my secret."

Muriel gnawed on her inner lip to brake her emotions. No way would she let her mother off the hook. Not this easily. "So how *did* Dad find out?"

After gently blowing her nose again, Lidia said, "I suspect he knew all along. When Logan was born, he thanked me for giving him a son. He said, 'Pia is part of you and Logan is part of me. We're even.' Right then, I knew that he knew something. Though we both pretended otherwise for years. I know he looked the other way every time I went into the city."

Muriel stared at her feet.

"It's amazing how raising children can manufacture a relationship. Mostly, our family was formed at the dinner table."

As if reading her mind, Lidia added, "And, of course, years later, your father and I tried to create a family with you."

A weighted silence followed in which Muriel wanted to ask the question she'd pondered for years: "Why *did* you have me?" But she knew the truth. Hearing it again wouldn't change things. She'd been a mistake. Plain and simple. No need to go back there, not when she'd been so adept at moving forward lately. It was the same with Pia. She could conjure up a different relationship, one with the two of them lolling on her bed, sharing confidences, interlocking their sock-covered feet. At the end of her life, Pia would call out for the one person who knew her best, her sister. It would be *Muriel's* hand Pia longed to hold, her eyes that would help her sister peer into the frightening abyss. Muriel's heartbeat would be the pulse her sister would want to feel pressed into her flat palm. But none of it was true. Why go there when *there* didn't exist?

"You said you had *two* questions," Lidia said, eventually.

Muriel cleared her throat. "Didn't Pia wonder why Logan never came home? I know I did."

"We told her he wanted to go to art school year-round, which was true. We said he didn't want to come home, that he had a new life he loved, which was also true."

"Pia never questioned it?"

Lidia stood up and circled around to the side of Muriel's bed. She reached her satiny hands up to cup her daughter's cheeks. Muriel was too stunned to pull away.

"Your sister was never you. She didn't want to look at unpleasant things. She didn't need to know every truth. Pia—God rest her soul—was happy living in her protected, beautiful world."

Almost to herself Muriel said, "Like you."

Lidia dropped her arms to her sides. "Yes. Your father and I made it possible for Logan to live elsewhere. We thought it best for everyone. Did he tell you he was unhappy?"

"No," Muriel answered, honestly.

"I'm glad for that. Still—" Lidia curled her lips around her teeth. She whispered, "I did love all wrong," as if she had just that minute noticed it.

For the first time, Muriel saw herself through her mother's eyes. In the midst of her false life, a very real child was born. With each breath, that child was a reminder of concessions made, silences settled into. So unlike her first daughter, Muriel must have perplexed her. Not only had Lidia never wanted her, once she had her, she didn't know what to make of her. *It's* chocolate, *Mama. The only thing better is more chocolate!* As the train jostled them from side to side on matinee Saturdays, Muriel would point to the pathetic faces peering out from behind sooty curtains a few feet from the elevated tracks and exclaim, "How lucky are they that the whole world passes right by their windows!"

With a penetrating stare, perhaps more deeply into herself than into her daughter's eyes, Lidia said, "It's too late for Pia, too late for me and Cam, for me and your dad, probably too late for Logan, too. The only chance I have left is with you, Muriel. My only daughter, my child. I don't deserve you, but I pray that one day you'll consider giving me a second chance."

Muriel had not one clue about what to say. Her thoughts were tangled. *Is it possible you can look at a person your whole life and never see her at all? Can you live with a child who's a stranger? Is a family really a family if they are only connected via DNA?*

"Wait a minute," she said suddenly. "Too late for you and Father Camilo? What happened to him?"

Seeming to crumple in on herself, Lidia said, "We both knew that Pia's death was God's punishment for our sin. Our penance was to separate. After Pia's funeral mass Cam transferred to a parish somewhere in the south. I don't know where. We never spoke again."

"Oh, Mama." Muriel's heart softened. "Whoever God is or isn't, I know He's not hateful. He wouldn't take Pia from you as a punishment. He's forgiving and loving." She stopped, sighed. "As He wants us to be."

Lidia didn't move. Her head dangled forward in sorrow. Sounds of first snow drifted up from the street. Children squealed, dogs yipped at disk sledders being pulled down her block. The rhythmic rasp of snow scrapers across windshields could be heard through the window. Finally, her breath hitching, Lidia said, "I miss her so very much."

"Me, too."

Surprising herself, Muriel stood to wrap her arms around her mother. Even more surprising, Lidia surrendered and hugged her back. Muriel felt their hearts beating in sync. Two hearts that were once one. She inhaled the scent she knew as well as her own. Her chin—with its soft divot—hooked over Lidia's shoulder. Pressing her eyelids closed, Muriel envisioned the way she was once curled inside Lidia's belly, leaching bits of her mother into herself. Growing into the person she would eventually be. Always, no matter what, they would be part of each other. She had the same mother Pia had. Always. No matter what.

"Maybe we can find our way back to each other?" Lidia asked.

"Maybe."

"A tiny crack is the beginning of an open door."

"No more secrets, no more lies?" Muriel whispered.

Stroking her daughter's hair, Lidia squeezed even more tightly as she said, "Today, we are reborn."

Melting into her mother's embrace, Muriel smiled. She didn't feel like squirming away as she usually did, before Lidia felt the roll of fat beneath her bra back, before she smelled the fruity aroma of her drugstore shampoo. Instead, she said, "Can we be reborn tomorrow? Tonight, I have a date."

Lidia pulled back, her face alight. "A date? How wonderful. Who is he? Tell me everything. Where is he taking you?"

Grinning, Muriel said, "I'm meeting him in the dog run."

"*Dog* run?"

A shadow of disapproval briefly clouded Lidia's face. But she flicked her head to shake it off.

"Dress warmly, *moje kochanie*," she said, gently pressing her lips to her daughter's cheek.

About the author

About the book

Insights,
Interviews
& More...

Meet Mary Hogan

Mark Bennington

MARY HOGAN is the author of seven young adult novels, including *The Serious Kiss*, *Perfect Girl*, and *Pretty Face* (HarperCollins). *Two Sisters* is her debut adult novel. Mary lives in New York City with her husband, Bob, and their dog, Lucy.

www.maryhogan.com

Writing Through Grief

I BEGAN THIS NOVEL two weeks after my sister, Diane, passed away. I finished it two weeks after my mother passed. Needless to say, the trash can beside my desk was full of tissues.

Diane's death stunned me . . . even though I knew she was sick with breast cancer. My sister chose to leave earth quietly, telling only a select few that the end was near. Me, she didn't tell. Or did she and I was unable to hear? Her passing left me with a hundred questions about denial (mine), privacy (hers), and sisterhood (ours). I needed to make sense of the senseless, so I wrote about it. By having my older sister "become" Pia for this book, I began to understand her in a way I never could have otherwise. *Two Sisters* was my grieving process.

That said, though I began writing with someone real in mind, Pia—and every other character in this book— quickly took on a life of his or her own. Particularly the character of the mother, Lidia, who is nothing like my own mother. It's a wonderful moment for any novelist when her characters are truly *born*. That is, they cease to be depictions of real people and become themselves.

Through the characters of Pia and Lidia, I was able to explore the destructive power of secrets in a family. I was able to look at God and religion from a different perspective. Owen and Logan—the father and brother characters—taught me about the ▶

3

Writing Through Grief *(continued)*

choices people make and the consequences they live with. And Muriel—the main character—showed me how resilience is the one trait that can trump all others. She also taught me to love Garrett's popcorn while watching Triple D: *Diners, Drive-Ins, and Dives.* ∽

~~~

"Exquisitely written, heartbreakingly honest, *Two Sisters* is the kind of story that will keep you turning pages into the night. A joy to read."

—Jill Smolinski,
author of *Objects of My Affection*

Author Q&A

How much did the book change during the revision process?

I am one of the few authors I know who *loves* the editing process. How great to have a fresh eye on the words you've been staring at for months! Years, sometimes. In my particular case, both my agent, Laura Langlie, and my editor, Carrie Feron, are smarter than I am. Both gave me insights that I never would have had on my own. In particular, Carrie's prodding on some of the religious aspects led me down many interesting roads. Without her intelligent notes, *Two Sisters* would be a far shallower book.

What inspired you to become an author?

Honestly, and without equivocation, I can say that the author Anne Tyler made me want to write books. After finding and picking up *Searching for Caleb* in my college dorm's communal living room, I couldn't put it down. I was agog that someone could infuse the lives of ordinary people with such depth. Her writing was so delicious I wanted to taste every page. Since then, I have bought and read every word Ms. Tyler has published. To this day, I eagerly await her next book. If you should read this, Anne, know that you changed a life. ▶

Author Q&A *(continued)*

Which character is your favorite?

Of course I love Muriel because she loves Guy Fieri and Garrett CaramelCrisp popcorn!

What is your best advice for writers who want to publish a novel?

You know how dieters are always looking for one key to unlock weight loss? For me, it's the same with publishing. There is no magic formula. But one boring thing *does* work: sticking to it is the writer's version of "fewer calories, more exercise." It's not earth-shattering, but it works. The great thing about writing is that you truly do get better the more you do it. Eventually you *will* get published because you're experienced enough to write a marketable book. And while you're at it, you will lose weight if you turn off the TV and stop eating popcorn! Which reminds me . . . it's time to power walk my dog, Lucy. ❧

Reading Group Discussion Questions

1. In what way does belief in God define and motivate the characters?

2. Why is Muriel such a good keeper of secrets?

3. If Muriel and Pia had been closer in age, how might their relationship have been different?

4. Is Lidia's behavior forgivable?

5. Is Joanie a good or bad mother figure for Muriel, and why?

6. Should Owen have insisted on a divorce the moment he learned the truth about Pia?

7. What will happen with Muriel and John (the guy she meets at the end of the book)?

8. Will Lidia and Owen grow old together or will they eventually grow apart?

9. Why did Muriel need to confront her brother, Logan, in person? ༄